HANK GUNN SERIES - BOOK ONE

MANAGED PARANOIA

NEAR-FUTURE SCI-FI THRILLER

Finlay Beach

finlaybeach.com

Managed Paranoia – Book Two
Near-Future Sci-Fi Thriller – Hank Gunn Series

For inquiries or permissions, please contact:
Finlay Beach - Email: fin@openthegift.com

Cover design by Nabin Karna & Finlay Beach

First Edition: February 2023

ISBNs:
Paperback: 979-8-9857705-3-7
eBook: 979-8-9857705-2-0

Dedicated to my grandson, Fin.

Bella

CHAPTER 1

"WE ARE DESCENDING TO sea level to change our flight platform from quadcopter to a wing-in-ground effect configuration, or WIG, which allows for greater efficiency. It will let us speed over a cushion of air at very low altitude, which will preserve battery life and gain hundreds of extra miles. Please standby for docking."

The forward motion slowed and the pod left the reclining position. Her legs dropped downward and they dangled like on an amusement ride. The view of the sea beneath her improved and she made out a raft of boats. They varied in sizes and color, but each had one thing in common, they all looked like bat wings.

Her drone flew a course without hesitation and maneuvered into position over a white wing with a candy-red stripe. She gazed down to see the leading edge of the floating wingtips squash further into the water with the drone's weight. A loud snapping sound reverberated through her and the whine of the props slowed as their housings reoriented. Bella wished she could watch the docking from the outside. The sun sparkling up from the turquoise water seemed to celebrate her arrival and she envisioned the glass and silver pod adding to the light show. But when the docking ended, the pod hanging from the drone reclined slowly and changed her viewpoint to that of a Formula One driver and all she could see before her was the horizon.

The two props behind her moved forward into view and the two which had been on either side tilted forward like an airplane. Each of the four motors increased their whine and water rushed under the wingtips. The newly configured craft increased speed as its wings caressed the surface for a long moment before the water gave up its grasp. There was no more hesitancy in the craft as it took to the air and the altimeter's readout froze at two-point-six meters. The proximity of the water made the speed feel faster than the reading suggested. One hundred fifty knots was not the fastest way to travel, but the customized itinerary and point-to-point convenience could not be rivaled by other methods of travel.

The low proximity to the ocean's surface troubled her. She had seen countless dolphins jump that high, excited by the wake from a boat's hull. The speed she was traveling, almost seemed irresponsible until she realized this craft never touched the water, there was no hull forming a wave that would attract dolphins, so she put the horrible thought of collision out of her mind.

"Excuse me. What should I call you?" Bella asked.

"I am sorry Bella. Allow me to introduce myself. I am called ACE. We are still exploring the desires of our guests and learning as we go. It is an acronym from the AI technology company in Dubai that created me and our new company welcomes name suggestions. You may select music preferences or choose from a long list of white or green noise. We offer canopy options of clear view, opaque, or any degree in between. Simply ask and I can provide it for you. Of course, we make available movie or series entertainment options, as well."

"ACE is fine. It has a pilot flair. Please play some Jack Johnson. It's time I got back to my roots. The canopy looks good for now. Can you show me the camera monitoring my dog? He must have gotten scared by all that noise."

The image of Kumar showed him curled up on his bed in the tiny cargo area. Digital readouts of his vitals played out on the screen. They showed he wasn't the least bit scared by the noise. The veterinarian insisted Kumar stay sedated for the long trip. She wanted him beside her in the pod, but there was no room, in what was essentially, a lounge chair with *frills*.

"If Kumar wakes up or seems distressed, will you tell me?" Bella said.

"Certainly. I am monitoring him as per the doctor's orders. I will inform you of any changes in his situation that might require your attention."

Bella wasn't sure that was really the answer she was looking for but let it rest, like her dog.

"I'm wondering—can this thing fly over heavy seas?"

"Yes, Bella, but we lose efficiency when the seas crest and winds are variable. We always keep thirty percent more power than estimated use and we are proud of our excellent safety record."

After the first fifteen minutes, the thrill of skimming just above the ocean diminished. The water was pretty, but with nothing but horizon, the view no longer interested her. Closing off the outside world and watching a movie would pass the time, but for now, she wanted to experience the ride and if that meant boredom, then she would embrace boredom. She watched her dog sleep and it relieved her to see his deep and steady breathing. For now, that was enough distraction, but it would not last. Eventually she would binge watch something that didn't have a man in it. Better yet, find a show about animals. Now that she owned a dog, maybe a training class would be helpful. Bella put on her sunglasses and turned up the music. "ACE, I'd like a little wind in my face," she said and closed her eyes.

Bella's mind turned away from her trip and away from boredom but crashed into a place she didn't want to go and couldn't get out. Her heartbeat became noticeable in her chest and a pulse resonated in her ears. It was something she had never experienced before. She lost control of her breathing as it turned shallow; she was almost panting as her field of vision narrowed. A memory flitted on the surface of her consciousness. It was not hers; but she grabbed onto it realizing she was having a panic attack.

"Bella, please take the pill now. Your vitals suggest you are having excessive anxiety and we need you to be calm for your safety."

"Be quiet!" Bella said.

Dr. Shapiro had told her she should breathe deep and be patient with herself if she felt moody, depressed or anxious. There were other things, he called them *tools*, but she could not even recall one of them. She wanted to use the *tools*, but the restriction in her chest overwhelmed her. She tried to slow her shallow breathing, but that did nothing to help. There was the anti-anxiety medication, but she didn't want to rely on a pill. It wasn't just pride, although that was a factor, her commitment to a natural lifestyle seemed to tumble into irrelevance. The dread escalated as the panic worsened and her resolve not to take drugs, wouldn't hold out much longer.

The instant she recalled Dr. Shapiro's last suggestions—the edges of her vision faded to black. "If you experience an unwanted emotion, meditate, or pray. Distract your focus."

Less than two days ago, Dr. Shapiro had explained even though she had been feeling physically and mentally fine, it was normal to have added difficulties. He didn't spell it out in ugly details what an *added difficulty* was, but now she understood what he meant. No sense in scaring the patient about what might happen. But now she was scared and knowing that it *was normal* didn't help her feel any better.

"I'm sorry to interrupt, but there is an air-sickness bag to your right. It is helpful to re-breathe your own air and eat something.

Carbohydrates would be best. I've taken the liberty to increase your comfort through adjustments to the pressure of your flight suit." ACE said.

She didn't respond, but now she recalled her doctor had given her that same advice. It was among his list of tools to use—just-in-case. She searched for the air-sickness bag and breathed into it. Now she was not only anxious, but thought she was being silly as she chewed on a piece of cookie her mother had packed for her trip, while she kept the bag over her mouth and nose. Being silly had another helpful benefit as it changed her perspective and made her focus on something beside her troubling state of being. And ACE was right, the suit compressed around her like a hug—it was nice.

Her life's theme had been consistent—embrace life experiences as they present themselves. With few exceptions, until now, she had no regrets about her life choices. But she was not a willing participant in this experience and it made her angry. She breathed deeper and slower and took the bag away from her face and ate more of the cookie. It tasted good. Right now, anger was a good replacement for the panic that had overcome her. The worst was over. Her vision opened and her breathing finally settled. She finished the cookie. Even though the panic slowly passed, the harsh memory of another unwanted experience resonated in her mind, like an open wound and she hoped it would heal up quickly.

She understood what happened and why. Bella didn't need Dr. Shapiro to explain that part; however, he used a term she would not have come up with on her own—Trauma Disorder. It had a clinical sound, but she could literally put a name on it—Gregory. There was no sympathy for Gregory. She realized he was evil, or at least a part of him was evil. Strangely, that part of him she had never known, but it had been the reason she was so vulnerable.

Bella was sorry for anyone who… her mind trailed off and re-turned to the raw emotion of terror. She tried to wrap her mind around the turmoil and wondered if it would be better to pretend that it never happened. She would not cry and with another breath, the anger towards Gregory drifted away. This was her first panic attack and hopefully her last. She would talk to Dr. Shapiro about it, but until then, she would push down any feelings about Gregory and become detached about all the harm he had caused. She focused on Kumar. Her dog laid there, a perfect example of what it meant to be calm—she needed that right now.

There was a change in the flight pattern of the drone and then ACE spoke. "I'd like to inform you we are about to make our first stop. This is an autonomous station. You cannot disembark, but if you desire, I can open the canopy five centimeters during the power supply exchange. The estimated time at the service station is three minutes. We are landing soon and will dock shortly after. The temperature is twenty-six degrees Celsius and the relative humidity is seventy percent. Winds out of the southeast at eight knots. Your jump suit maintains an ideal temperature even with the canopy ajar. Would you like me to open it?"

"Yes, definitely. I always prefer fresh air." It was not until ACE reminded her about the jumpsuit that she even thought about her comfort. And now she wondered if she had dozed off. The panic attack, meditating on her sleeping dog, the first leg of her journey—it all seemed so quick. She asked, "ACE, did I fall asleep?"

"You slept for ninety-three minutes. The pod's seat distributes pressure points and moves the occupant slowly through a gentle range of motions during the flight. Most people find the alteration in body position imperceptible. For further relaxation, your chair is capable of massage. You can choose between Swedish, Thai or sports massage with a focus on the neck, mid or lower back."

A small gap opened around the canopy and it made her want much more. She wanted to get the canopy out of the way, so she would be able to stick her head outside, but knew it wouldn't be allowed, so she didn't ask. Autonomous work areas are always like that. While people-safe-robots are great, it is more efficient and far less expensive to exclude humans from the workspaces of robots.

After a flawless landing, the drone maneuvered like a seaplane into a docking area shaped like a vee. Two elevators emerged and robotic cranes extended toward the floating aircraft. The first one deftly removed the used batteries and the other added new ones.

"Please prepare for takeoff," ACE said and the canopy closed.

The left side of the drone was being hit by the last rays of the setting sun. Twilight spilled over the ocean ahead. The second power resupply was as uneventful as the first, but she became increasingly uncomfortable. She had tried the massage chair and allowed ACE to speed up the range of motion function, but eventually reclining in one place, no matter how ideal, becomes uncomfortable.

Her watch chimed a tone indicating Zoe wanted to talk to her. She answered, "It's about time. Did you work late, or have you been chatting it up with some boy and lost track of time?"

"I just got home, but I do have a date tonight. Bella, you're going to love our new apartment. Look at this view." She oriented the camera out the window and slowly scanned the skyline. "Who knew when our apartment was broken into, it would be a great way to get a better place. Plus, it's got a proper kitchen—well, kitchenette. Let's just say it's better than a cutting board over the sink and a microwave on the dorm-sized fridge. And I met my date in the lobby! A better location equals better prospects! So, how's Amelia Earhart? Show me your window."

She would share the panic attack with her friend another time. Bella aimed the camera of her watch outside the canopy. "That's about all there is to see. And I told you, I'm not coming back. But

I'm glad you have a nicer place. Now, get a roommate with a good job and maybe you can afford to live there."

"Come on, Bella. You told me law enforcement is onto Gregory. He wouldn't dare return to Singapore. There is no way he can find out where we're living. The last time he used criminals to hunt you down, one ended up in custody and the other dead. This is the safest place for you right now. Plus—I miss you!"

"Zoe, I miss you too, but things have changed. My home is back where I grew up. My family's farm is my future. It's taken me all this time to realize it. I never felt free on land and my dead-end job with the Marine Quality Institute paid well but was meaningless. The only thing that gave me purpose was moonlighting for aquafarmers and helping them grow more protein. I can do that from anywhere in the world."

"Bel, I think you're confused. With what you've been through, who wouldn't be? But there is no future out there with your dad and his geriatric janitor. Remember, there are no men within a thousand miles."

"Thank God! After finding out the truth about Gregory, I'll never trust a man again."

"Okay, I get it. Having a human trafficker for a fiancé is enough to spoil a relationship. I'll give you that. But some really nice guys exist out there, at least on land, like here in Singapore."

"I'm not sure your track record confirms that," Bella said.

Zoe made a face like she had been caught. "You're right, but I'm not the one looking for true love. Bel, just take the time you need, lick your wounds, heal and then come home to me."

"That will not happen. I'm moving on."

"Okay, I hear you. Things are still fresh. I've got three months of free rent and I'm not getting a roommate until after that and she better be you."

"We'll talk about it later," Bella said.

"Did they allow you to take that pooch of yours on the drone?"

"Yes. Look at him." Bella took a picture of the monitor that showed Kumar resting comfortably.

"He is so cute. I can't wait to meet him."

"How about this? Let's plan to meet at the seastead in Tahiti. My folks' place is enormous and not always rented. I'll see if we can use it in a few months."

"That sounds good, but no tennis. I want to meet that doctor of yours—he sounds delicious."

"You are incorrigible," Bella said. "Just hold on a sec. This drone has to make several stops for battery changes and the one coming up has a bathroom—the situation is becoming dire!"

"ACE, how long until the next stop?"

"Five minutes and thirty-four seconds."

"Zoe, thanks so much for distracting me, but I have to pee in the worst way. I've been dehydrating myself for half a day now, but this last hour has been the worst. I better go now. If I end up using my adult diaper, I don't want you to see my face."

"That bad?"

"Worse. I need to wear it. It's one of the few things they require. Now I know why."

"You're right. There are some things I just don't need to see. Good luck with that. Call me when you get to your dad's." Zoe blew a kiss and the screen went blank.

They told her Kumar would wet himself during the trip but didn't suggest a doggie-diaper. He wouldn't have stood for it, anyway. But she never expected to need one herself, though she was appreciating the extra security it afforded her. At least for now, it was only her thoughts that flowed. *I put this thing on for just a time like this. Millions of people use these things every day. It will be so much better to just let go. You can always change it, that's what the spare is for.* Bella knew the power of her mind and it was an excellent lawyer when she wanted to convince herself of something. And now she wanted to convince herself that holding it any longer could lead to permanent damage.

"Prepare to land," ACE said.

"Oh, thank you, Jesus!" she exclaimed.

The deceleration was startling, but the canopy lifted the second the nose of the drone bumped into the dock. She climbed out of the chair not caring about grace, but when her feet hit the ground, she could not feel them, her legs were weak and she was lightheaded. She staggered into the arms of two workers, who must have expected her reaction. They helped her with the few steps it took to gain her balance and then directed her toward the restroom. She swung the door open, walked into a bright, clean stall and exclaimed, "Stupid jumpsuit!" More delay, but in time she repeated, "Oh! Thank you, Jesus!"

Her eyes shot open at the sound of a loud snap. The only time she had heard that was when the quadcopter attached to the floating wing. There were no external lights, only vague shadows danced in the darkness. A familiar sensation jarred her further awake. A wave traveled up the right side of the wing and sprayed the pod as if it was in a carwash. "ACE, what's going on?"

"You were sleeping and I didn't want to wake you. We are detaching from the WIG platform because of headwinds and the increasing seas. The agile profile of the quadcopter and the relative lightness of you and your pod will allow us to reach the next station in a typical quadcopter configuration. Please stand by until the reconfiguration of the drone is complete."

Just as the drone's props re-positioned for gaining altitude, another wave rolled up the side of the wing and splashed hard against the canopy. The wing looked like it dropped away, which was un-settling, but having her feet dangle again as the drone lifted into the air had become her new favorite sensation. She could sense the acceleration as the wing fell out of view, replaced with countless white ribbons of froth shining against a jet-black background. As the drone reached cruising altitude, her pod reclined. The turbulent waters smoothed with distance and she saw an ocean that cared only about meeting the horizon.

She had slept much of the night and even with waking up abrupt-ly and the excitement of ditching the bat wing in stormy seas, she was drowsy again. ACE had balanced the sound within the pod to cancel the high pitch whine of the blades, so Bella thought classical music, with its complexity, was good for passing the time. It gave her ears more to focus on. The sky to the east lightened with expecta-tion—perfect timing for the purposeful notes of Ravel's Daphnis and Chloe suite.

"Bella, we land at your destination in four minutes. We are expe-riencing high winds with gusts up to forty knots, so you can expect some turbulence as we descend and secure the pod. This is within safe operating guidelines. However, we have altered our transition strategy and will leave the pod aboard the station. You will need to remain within its safety until the drone connects with a fresh energy supply and departs. This will only take three minutes and the canopy will open automatically when safe. Please take all your belongings. After your exit, the canopy will lock and await a pickup when the weather becomes more predictable."

"I'm so excited to see my father. But okay, I'll hold tight."

"Quad Freight Transport certified your father as a station op-erator. He knows to wait for the drone to leave before he comes to greet you. Please be patient and you will be reunited soon. The temperature is twenty degrees Celsius, relative humidity is seven-ty-six percent, winds are variable at twenty knots with gusts to forty from the east. The barometer reading is nine-eight-nine millibars.

Weather services report these are winds generated by an unnamed tropical storm which is predicted to increase to a named Pacific cyclone within a day and may reach hurricane status. Currently, Blue Permaculture Station One is in its projected path. I hope you have enjoyed your trip with Quad Freight Transport."

Her pod locked into place on the deck and she saw the four huge propellers engulfing a battery pack half the size of the pod. "Just hurry!" she said with excited expectation. As if her command held weight, the drone disappeared and the canopy opened.

"*Mi ángel*. What an entrance! You came from heaven." José reached into the pod and helped his daughter onto the deck of the station that used to be her home.

She hugged her dad and let his arms surround her. Bella's legs were not as weak as on her earlier stop, but his embrace was just what she needed. "Oh, dad, I've missed you!" She lifted her head up and pushed herself away. "But really dad, I come to visit and you decide a hurricane would be a good coming home present!"

"Isn't it exciting? We've always been too far south to get weather like this. But don't worry, I've taken precautions."

Bella squinted her eyes and said, "I'm sure you have."

Hank

CHAPTER 2

THE ONLY LIGHT IN the room came in with the fresh air through an oval porthole. Two opening ports and one larger window usually provided natural light into his stateroom, but while in blackout mode, no light penetrated the smart-glass. He was glad to awaken to the slightest breeze against his face. His watch said he'd slept almost forty-five minutes, but he didn't feel any better. He knew he should commit to getting more sleep, but his instincts were on edge and they insisted he get up.

Listening to Olin tell his story had kept his attention, but it was the business proposal that energized him with the prospect of a fresh course that would change his future. That was why he couldn't sleep. He went from delivering the *GalaxSea* by himself to San Diego, to joining Olin and crew in a journey bisecting both hemispheres of the Pacific Ocean. In some ways, the offer mattered little. He was a professional sailor and when he had a boat under him, the world made sense. But to Olin, Hank agreeing to his proposal seemed to take on a supernatural importance—perhaps life itself. Either way, Hank was committed to do everything he could to ensure the safety of the *GalaxSea* and every soul aboard.

As if choreographed, Willy stepped in after Hank agreed to sail on. The former Marine took command of the helm and directed them off the deck just as the sun came up. Maybe Willy was a competent sailor, or maybe Ava had taken over the sailing, but he could tell that the eighty-foot sailing yacht carried all the canvas she could handle. All boats were a tradeoff in some capacity and a lightweight hull meant more noise from the water as the boat plowed a furrow through the ocean. Most of the time Hank didn't notice water noise—it had been a constant presence his whole life. But as he contemplated giving up on sleep and leaving the comfort of his bed, it was the sound of sailing and the boat's heel that unsettled him. Yesterday he was alone, calling the shots and beating into the wind. Now the owner of the yacht, Olin Ou, his two oldest children and their bodyguard, Willy, were onboard with a new destination—Southeast Asia.

He splashed water on his face and opened the door into the salon but found no activity in the common area. The doors to the front berths were closed and it did not surprise him to see Olin's stateroom door shut as well. It had been a long night for everybody. He passed through the galley, grabbed a mug of coffee and headed up the companionway steps. Only Willy was on deck, looking out-of-place behind the starboard wheel.

"Look at that. He sails!" Hank said and hesitantly added, "...and he smiles?"

"And I like roses." The smile left Willy's face. "Well, I like Guns and Roses." He laughed and the smile returned. "I do like to sail. Someday, when this family doesn't need me anymore, I think I'll buy a sailboat and explore. Not something like this. I know I can never go back to the Bayou, but there's plenty of mosquito-infested skinny water in the world and a modest size catamaran could hide away for a long spell. Fishing, sleeping, reading—I've got a lot of catching up to do."

"From what I can tell, you are part of the Ou family."

"Yeah, well, that goes both ways. You are now part of the family too. I guess we are brothers again. First, Marines and now, Ou's." Willy laughed, but suddenly went quiet. He averted his eyes, as if he had told an impolite joke to an unsafe audience, but instead of covering his tracks with more words, he scanned the horizon.

Hank said, "I've sailed on some cats. One of my first jobs as crew was on a forty-two-footer. Before I turned sixteen, I worked as a dock-boy. A boat called *The Harbinger* pulls up to the visitors dock and I was helping with the lines—suddenly it hits me—I've been on this boat before! I told the owner, 'I really like the starboard berth. The custom mattress is really comfortable.' He looks at me like I'm from Mars. Then, I introduce myself and explain that my father was the carpenter who did all the interior and trim work. He was sad to hear about my dad's death but ended up inviting me on board and a week later we sailed to the Bahamas.

"I'll tell you what, Willy. If you get your cat, I'll be your delivery crew to wherever you want to go. But you must promise—no mosquitos."

"Deal," Willy said.

They sat in silence. Hank moved to the console and studied the navigation readouts. He scanned the horizon and said, "You really are a sailor. We've been making amazing progress since you logged on." Hank looked at Willy with a skeptical expression. "Has Ava been steering for the last hour?"

"It's all me. I even trim my own sails," Willy said with pride.

"I never would have expected a jarhead from Louisiana to get so much out of this amazing, but heavy, sailing yacht."

"She is heavy, but I like big bottomed girls," Willy admitted with a wink.

"I've been trying to figure something out and maybe you can help. The painted waterline gives nothing away, but Olin's *GalaxSea* is a few inches lower in the water than the sister ships. I first noticed it when I boarded from the dock in Victoria. What's up with her weight problem?"

"You're not smart, are you?" Willy said.

"What do you mean?"

"Besides commenting on a lady's excess weight and then asking questions that are above your paygrade. Didn't you learn anything as a corpsman?"

"Wait! I was supposed to learn something. Shit. All those miserable years in the Navy, most of them slumming with Marines and now I find out I was supposed to learn something?" Hank's expression turned serious. "You won't tell me, will you?"

"Well, look at that. You did learn something." Willy stood up and motioned to the wheel. "Care to take over? I need to hit the head."

"Ava, are you there?"

"Of course, Hank," Ava's ethereal voice with her delightful Scottish accent floated to his ears.

"This might be a silly question, but why are we heading due south? A thousand miles east of Hawaii isn't the fastest lane to our destination."

"Mr. Ou has determined the course."

"Is that storm still brewing to the southeast of us?"

"It appears to be."

"So, we really are heading into a hurricane?"

"Perhaps, Hank, but currently it is only an unnamed Pacific cyclone. As skipper, you may change course, but I believe Mr. Ou would like to be notified of any changes in that regard. Would you like me to wake him?"

"No, that's okay. Thanks."

"You're welcome, Hank. Is there anything else I can assist you with?"

"Did you help Willy sail since sunup?"

"No, Hank. He is an excellent sailor and seldom asks for my help."

"Amazing."

"Hank?"

"Yes, Ava."

"I'd like to add—I taught him everything he knows."

"Well, look at that. A prideful AI!"

"I am not programmed for pride."

"You're up early after a late night," Hank said.

"Ava is on strict orders to limit my gaming. I was awake and had to do something. Besides, the sun was warming things up, the wind picked up and I love to sail in conditions like these," Marshall said.

Hank stepped away from the large carbon fiber steering wheel and gestured to Olin's son: *She's all yours.*

Marshall took his place and spun around, hesitating for a moment as if admiring the wake unreeling out behind them, then turned his attention to the dark horizon over the bow. He glanced at the navigation plotter and looked at Hank as he asked, "Did my dad keep you up all night?"

"Yeah, I'll get caught up eventually—my timing is off. A day ago, I was the delivery captain. I would catnap my way to San Diego. But your dad has a way of changing things. Still, it's nice to have company."

"I'm guessing he told you where we're going."

"Yep. It'll be quite a trip. Indonesia isn't exactly San Diego."

"I didn't want to come at first. I had my sights set on the Culinary Institute of America, but now—after what Dad's doing—he says I'm an adult and can go anywhere I want after we get settled on the island of Trita. He figures it will take some time for the dust to settle after his big announcement tonight. Then, we can be normal people again." Marshall shrugged his shoulders. "We'll see, I guess."

"When did you start sailing?" Hank asked.

"It's not a big surprise, but the first time I remember sailing was with my dad. I was eight years old. His lab was at Sand Point on Lake Washington. He never took me to work but kept his laser there and went sailing when he needed to decompress. They tell me that being a world-famous inventor is stressful. That's why I want to become a world-famous chef—no stress," he chuckled. "They say it was my mom who needed to decompress when she was pregnant with the twins. It seems silly to me. She's got two babies squirming around inside her and I'm accused of being the one that was making her crazy.

"So, dad came home, picked me up and took me sailing. It was the best day of my life. I almost never saw him because he worked so much, but that day the wind was screaming off the point from the south. His little boat shot up onto a plane and skipped across the water so fast, both of us were laughing the whole time."

Hank couldn't keep from thinking about his own father. The last time they sailed before he died—it was a similar day. He did the math. Since the twins were fourteen, that would put Marshall in his early twenties. He would have been about the same age as Marshall. Only it had been Hank's last sail with his dad. He shifted attention back to Marshall. "You hold your course while you work the waves and time the swell. Your trim is fantastic. How did you learn to sail like this? Between you and me, your dad is an expert sailor, but you are better."

"That's funny. That's what he says. For a couple of years, I did sailing camp in the Thousand Islands, but mostly I just listened to my dad and once Ava came into our lives, I asked her stuff."

"I never thought about that." Hank pondered whether having a smart AI like Ava would help create a better student or just make a person lazy. Then asked, "Do..."

"Excuse me for interrupting. Hank. There is a time sensitive matter that requires your attention. It is personal. Would you like to take it in your stateroom?" Ava said.

"My life is an open book. I can't imagine anything that is private enough to get me out of the gear I just put on."

"Very well. They found your phone," Ava announced.

"My phone?"

"Yes. A mechanic discovered it in the bumper framework of a delivery truck undergoing regular service."

"So what? That's where I hid it. I knew they'd be tracking me when I failed my psych evaluation and decided the best thing to do was to send them on a wild goose chase. I figured a delivery truck would redirect them while I made my escape."

"It was a good ploy and probably bought you a little time. But apparently a mechanic found the device, charged it and followed the instructions."

"Ava, I'm sorry, but I'm lost here. What instructions?"

"When you enlisted in Operation Blue Sky, they issued you that phone. I believe you and Willy are fond of saying *smartphones are a tracking device with a calling feature.* Well, this one is even more so. Since they issued it as a perk of OBS, federal privacy restrictions are of no consequence. All the data is in their possession. They recorded every place you went, every conversation you had and every interaction you made from all your issued devices, including your phone. And they still are prying into anything they can get. Now, they've locked the screen with instructions to return the device."

"Okay. I can't say I'm surprised. I knew I was in a fishbowl. That's one reason I needed to get out of the program. So, what's all that got to do with anything and why would anybody return the phone?"

"They devised an interesting method of ensuring people comply with their instructions and return the device. It uses facial recognition and explains to the person, by name, that if they don't comply, they are guilty of theft of government property, but if they follow the simple return instructions, they will receive a one-thousand-dollar credit in their CBDC wallet."

"So, what does that have to do with me?"

"Hank, I feel you might need some context to make your next decision. Obviously, they have everything you have opened, but there is a video message that was left on your phone last night. Since you did not answer it, nobody has a copy of it yet. Of course, they can see it, but it requires a human to unlock the device and they have your phone with a technician right now. It is likely she will unlock your phone in less than five minutes. I can easily override your security measures and open the message to view it before they do, but because it is marked *private*, I decided it would be best if you were present."

"Got it. I'm present. Who is this private video message from anyway?" Hank asked.

"Brittany O'Brien."

"My favorite redheaded server," he said with a smile.

"What are you boys so busy about, out here?" Willy said as he maneuvered between Marshall and Hank and reoriented himself, facing the bow of the boat.

"Hank's getting a love video from a girl back home. It's private, but we get to see," Marshall said.

"We only went out on a few dates. On the last one, I borrowed a Pelican and sailed her around the harbor in Port Townsend. But I'm not exactly the serious type so *love* was not part of the relationship. Go ahead, Ava, play it."

The monitor at the helm station lit up with a still capture of the first frame of a video.

"Man, she's a fox!" Marshall exclaimed.

"That's bad news. They always get all dolled up before they break up with you," Willy said.

"It's true. I've sabotaged enough relationships to know," Hank said. "Okay Ava, let Brit give me the bad news."

Her bright red lips moved. "Hi Hank, if that's even your real name. What type of guy leaves town and doesn't say goodbye to his girlfriend? I thought we had something, but clearly, I was wrong. I've been text dumped before, but at least he had the courtesy of telling me. You just leave! And if you ever come by Doc's again, I'll not only spit in your burger, but in your face too. You're a jerk." Her middle finger gravitated into view and she used it to wipe away an imaginary tear and then flipped him off.

"Yeah, Hank, you are a jerk. Can you give me her number?" Marshall asked.

"Ava. I don't really think that was something the government would find terribly interesting. Not exactly top-secret stuff."

"I can see that now, but I needed to close the case and had to know if I should erase or corrupt the message. We deal aggressively with anything which can be linked back to Mr. Ou."

"Joan?" Hank spoke in a quiet voice.

"Joan? Oh, she's been taken care of," Ava said.

"Taken care of?"

"Oh, Hank, Mr. Ou said that we needed to make sure she wouldn't talk. Your boss at Puget Charter & Island Sailing School is the only other person who knows the identity of who hired you to be the family's sailing instructor." There was a pause. "I notice that your heart rate is rising. I believe you may have conjured a fate for Joan in your head. Don't worry, she's in the water, feeding the fish," Ava said.

"What?!"

"Hank. When Mr. Ou decides someone might impede his plans, he often finds it helpful to have that person removed."

Hank looked at Marshall and then Willy. They looked back at his horrified face with serious expressions. As if on cue, both of them burst into laughter. Hank could hear a female laugh as well. It was Ava joining in.

"Hank. You have a vivid imagination. Why do people always assume billionaires have inconvenient people murdered? It must be Hollywood." In an assuring voice, she said, "From the response on deck, everybody found the setup of my joke funny, except you. I am sorry if I made you uncomfortable."

"We just made sure that she would be difficult to reach for a couple of weeks until things blow over. After we sailed for Canada, we no longer needed her to help wrangle you into the *GalaxSea*. However, she remained a loose end, so we made sure she won an all-expense paid vacation to the location of her dreams. She is cruising on a fifty-foot catamaran in the Caribbean. And currently, she is snorkeling with new friends." Ava's inflection turned playful. "Mr. Ou finds it is less expensive and easier on the conscience than having people whacked."

Hank was getting cold hanging out in the wind with Marshall, so when Willy returned from the cabin carrying a steaming mug with a spoon handle sticking straight up he knew he wanted one for himself. But from the ice-cold look on Willy's face, he knew he would have to wait.

"I just got some news. It's personal. Not—redheaded girlfriend personal. Sorry, Marshall, keep driving this boat and Hank and I will get out of your way."

They sat on the windward bench just off the companionway. Willy faced Hank but didn't speak.

"Well?" Hank finally inquired.

"Well, Megan Ward is out of the hospital and burning up her connections to find out what became of you. Seems you poked a bear."

"Me?" Hank asked.

"Okay, she's gunning for both of us, but I figure you shot her twice and I only shot her once," Willy said.

"I'd guess your beanbag round to the chest left more of a mark than a couple of tear-gas balls."

"My source tells me she had a broken rib and a rather large bruise to her chest. But they also treated her for respiratory distress and that's on you."

"Who is your source? Is it Ava?" Hank asked.

"You really don't understand Ava yet."

"Do you?" Hank asked.

"Good point. But why don't you ask her about Mega-War. Forget that, ask her about Megan Ward. She wouldn't know her by my pet name. Either way, that bitch killed those two men, so I think Mega-War is more fitting."

"Okay," Hank agreed. "Hey, Ava, what happened to Megan Ward after she left Victory Square Park?"

"I'm not programmed to answer that question. And I might remind you, I'm not Siri. You don't have to say '*Hey Ava*' in order to activate me."

"What can you tell me about that night?"

"I'm not programmed to respond to that question."

Willy sat with his arms crossed and a smile on his face.

"You followed all the events: Irina's birthday celebration, the intel before and during the evening, the attempted kidnapping for ransom of a VIP and after—getting me out of Vancouver on the floatplane. Just help me fill in the gaps here. Where did Megan Ward go after I freed her legs by cutting the zip-ties?"

"I'm not programmed to answer that question."

"Come on, Ava. Can you tell me anything about that night?"

"The temperature in Vancouver, BC at six in the evening was seventeen degrees Celsius."

Willy chuckled and said, "She can keep this up for hours."

"I know. I asked her if she believed in God and all I got out of her was a joke." Hank shifted in his seat and stared at the water. "Okay, let's try this. Ava, what is the probability that an AI like you could tell me what happened to an injured co-worker?"

"You asked a good question, Hank. The probability of that occurring is very low."

"Why?"

"They do not program AIs like me to gossip."

Hank tried again, "It seems like an inquiry about a co-worker's injury is important information, not gossip. Please tell me what happened to Megan Ward."

"I am not programmed to release personal information."

"Hah, so you admit that Megan Ward is a co-worker?"

"I am not programmed to confirm or deny that information."

Hank held up both hands in surrender. "Okay, I get your point. She can be infuriating."

Willy shook his head in agreement and said, "My eyes on the ground might not know as much as Ava, but she does gossip and she's a lot cuter than Ava." Willy hesitated and tipped his head as if waiting for Ava to interject a comment, but none came.

"How have you been in communication with your *eyes on the ground*? I thought they didn't allow personal devices on this barge."

"Ava connects me for texts if I'm nice to her. She probably bounces the signal off Mars, but it works."

"Cute?" Hank asked.

"You've met her. She volunteered for our special team in Vancouver."

"Julie?" Hank smiled. "I'm not the most intuitive, but I can't say I noticed any chemistry between you two."

"We were working."

"You just put a beanbag round into her boss's chest, hog-tied her and left her wheezing. Unless she hates her boss, that doesn't seem like the best way to woo a woman."

"You've met Mega-War. Who wouldn't hate her? But Julie's a pro. As a contractor, her loyalty goes to the highest bidder."

"I'm not sure that's the basis of a great relationship, but it's also not my business."

"You got that right. That's why we're divorced," Willy said.

"This just gets richer. You and Julie were married?"

"What? You're surprised?"

"You have no idea how surprised I am."

"Well, get over it. And say nothing to Irina. She's still mad at me for leaving Julie."

"Wait! You left her?" Hank tilted his head in disbelief.

"You were kind of growing on me until now," Willy said.

"Sorry, but she's so..."

"I know—above me." Willy shrugged and said, "Face it. In my experience, all women are 'above' the men they marry."

"Julie worked under Mega-War since she made Sargent. Then followed her into private contracting a few years back. Our marriage was rough before that, but after she became a civilian, Julie and I began seeing things differently—everything differently.

"Their team does enough DOD contract work to keep certain favors coming their way. Julie accompanied Mega-War in the medivac chopper to the Naval hospital on Whidbey. She warned me to watch my back." Willy smiled wide and said, "She also told me, 'Good shooting. The bruise is exactly center mass.'"

"Sounds like your ex still has the hots for you," Hank said

"We get along better now, than when we were married."

Hank thought he detected a wink, but Willy's sunglasses prevented him from knowing for sure. He took a chance and said, "Maybe you can convince her to join you on your catamaran someday."

Willy stretched out his arms along the top of the bench, turned his face into the morning sun and said nothing.

Hank thought about just dropping all discussion about the extraordinary night of Irina's birthday, but he may never have a better opportunity to fit together the missing pieces. "Willy, since Ava's not talking, can you tell me why Megan Ward killed those two guys leaving the park?"

"Look, I don't pretend to know what makes people tick, but she's been around the bend for years now. She probably gets off on stuff like that. That's why the Army ushered her out the door early. She'd be a general by now, but she shot a foreign interpreter, on base, in front of witnesses."

"What?" Hank asked.

"The guy had two cell phones and when she confronted him, he dropped one and stepped on it. She drew her sidearm and shot him in the head. Turns out the guy had a wife and a lover—a phone for each."

"Wow, I saw some crazy shit while down range, but that's messed up." Hank shook his head in disbelief.

"They never had a court martial. Apparently, she had collected so much dirt on so many high-level brass, they just whisked her away and a year later, she was running a team of private contractors. Same job, better pay."

"It's like the movies." Hank leaned in and spoke in a soft voice. "Does Olin hire her often?"

"Rarely. But if the event is too big, or too complicated for our in-house security, we contract as needed. Mega-War and her soldiers have a solid reputation for keeping the VIPs safe, plus I wanted to see Julie again." Willy's chuckle fell into a grim tone. "I won't make that mistake again. When I shot Mega-War with the beanbag round, I knew she'd never let it go. But I think it's worse than a grudge. Julie said she kept repeating, 'they are going down, they are going down.'

Sorry, Hank, you'll need to watch your six until she's in prison, or dead."

Hank had learned not to fuss about sunlight when it came to sleep. He relieved Marshall at the helm because it was his turn, not because he was fresh and alert. The Earth's twenty-four-hour rotations were critical to the ocean navigator, but to a sailor, night and day were equal opportunities for disaster. He had long since given up sleeping all night and he guessed Willy's internal clock was messed up, too, because he dozed on the bench not far away.

Over-exhaustion led to his current wakefulness, but even that wavered into an exhaustion that would only improve with sleep. He grabbed a breakfast cookie and a bottle of water from the little food garage by the helm station and shook Willy awake. "I'm going to crash hard. Can you take over?"

Willy woke up as if he had never been asleep and said, "I'd love to. Can't let you sailor types have all the fun."

"Excuse me. I have some news that relates to both of you," Ava said.

"More breakup videos?" Willy asked.

"I'm afraid it is more serious than that. They have framed both of you for the homicides in Victory Square Park the night of Irina's birthday celebration."

"What?" Willy chided.

Hank was speechless.

Ava continued, "Megan Ward was recovering from her injuries at the hospital when investigators from the RCMP major crimes division reached out to her for a video interview. She spoke to them from a hospital bed and kept an oxygen cannula strapped beneath her nose. Her full account of what occurred that night mostly matched the events that both of you expressed during your debriefing, except, she claimed not to know anything about the murders. Then she speculated that you both went berserk. In her opinion, that's why Willy shot her with a beanbag round from a shotgun and why Hank shot her twice with high-speed balls of tear-gas. She then lifted her shirt in front of the camera and showed the extensive bruise on her bare chest."

"That's bullshit," Willy exclaimed.

"Perhaps so, but she is no longer a person of interest in the investigation. They have posted photos of both of you on the RCMP website. You are wanted on a Canada-wide warrant for murder."

Hank looked at the Wakefield chronograph on his wrist and said, "It's not even oh-nine-hundred yet. This has been a hell of a day. I'm going back to bed."

Hank

CHAPTER 3

Disoriented, only half-explained the sensation coursing through his body while anger and mystification completed the moment. He assumed he had been enjoying a deep sleep before the klaxon of the starship Enterprise ripped him out of slumber and threw him into a blaze of light. The unrelenting noise blared on, as his eyes began adjusting to the light. He stumbled onto the floor and searched for his pants.

"Ava, or Zaine, or whoever you are? Stop that noise. I'm awake," he yelled over the din.

The *GalaxSea* was dead in the water. It had been on a port tack, in a freshening breeze and they were clipping along when he fell asleep. This was an exceptional sailboat and he hoped there was no damage. Voices could be heard outside his stateroom door, but he needed to get some answers before he confronted anyone.

"Ava, give me a status report."

"The Thor Heyerdahl, a Royal Norwegian Navy frigate, has requested that we heave-to. They intend to board us in twenty-one minutes."

"You've got to be kidding me."

"Why no, Hank, I am absolutely serious. I would never *kid* at a moment like this."

He took a breath and pulled out the swing-away chair integrated into his desk, sat down and pulled on a new pair of ragg-wool socks. "Ava, can you remind me to discuss the whole Star Trek thing? That's not the first time that klaxon made me peel myself off the ceiling."

"Certainly, Hank. Do you have a preferred time you would like to be reminded *to discuss the whole Star Trek thing*?"

He stood and pulled on a well-worn t-shirt with an AC/DC imprint and gave a curt, "Later."

Olin Ou leaned over the nav station's desktop. He wore shorts and a windbreaker and Hank guessed he also had been rudely awakened. He was talking in a low voice and gazed up to meet Hank's eyes, giving an affirming nod, as Hank made his way into the salon. That suited him fine, as he was no longer the captain. It's proper that the owner of the *GalaxSea* take charge while on board.

Marshall came out of his forward berth clad only in his underwear and looked bedraggled. Willy came down the companionway at the same time. Olin confused them all with his gesturing. His hand movements could have meant, sit, stay or there's nothing to worry about.

Hank met Willy at the galley's coffee maker. He waited for him to pour the first cup and while they exchanged no words, they shared a look that asked, what now? After Hank sat down at the table, the men turned their attention to a bedraggled Marshall and Willy spoke.

"Marshall, go get dressed. We're not sinking." Then he turned to Hank and said, "Did you get enough beauty rest?"

"Not really." He forced a frown. "And you better watch out. I woke up on the wrong side of the bed." He tested the coffee before committing to a sip. "I haven't burnt my tongue once since being on board. Ava apparently knows everything about me." He glanced towards the place where he had last seen her holographic image as if she were looking back at him. "She also gets my shower temperature perfect. I wonder if she watches me when I take a shower. That creeps me out."

"If you're trying to get a response out of her, you'll be disappointed. You won't get any satisfaction talking like that. I know. I've tried," Willy said.

"I'm stubborn, plus I've learned something about how Ava works. Watch this." Hank turned his attention back to the center of the table. "Ava? Can you turn on your holographic interface?"

"Of course, Hank."

The young woman with dark hair and porcelain skin dotted with translucent freckles came into view. Hank had finally gotten used to her looking like this. For a long time, he had only heard her voice and she looked nothing like he had first imagined.

"Are you talking to Olin right now?" Hank asked.

"I'm not programmed to share that information."

"But I can hear you talking to Olin. You're answering his questions right in front of me. We're in the same room. Can't you see that? Why can't you just admit to it?"

"I am not programmed to answer that."

"Okay. I get it. You're loyal to your creator." Hank gave Willy a wink and went on. "Ava, did you see the facial expression I directed towards Willy just now? What was the most notable part of that interaction?"

"You winked your left eye."

"While I waited for Willy to pour his coffee were my ankles crossed or uncrossed?"

"They were crossed."

"And what is the exact amount of time that I've slept in the last twenty-four hours?"

"Sixty-eight minutes."

"Okay, Ava. Now consider any smart AI—one who knows the ideal temperature of my coffee, can carry out a complex conversation with me and many other people, do an in-depth analysis of big data and a multitude of other functions concurrently and one who has long surpassed unsupervised learning. This AI sees all my facial expressions, can recall my body's positions and knows how many minutes of sleep I've had. Let me ask you: What is the probability that this AI would know what I look like in the shower?"

"Very high," Ava said.

"Ava, I asked you a very specific question, with a probability. You calculate for a living. Now, give me the probability that an AI like that would know what I look like in the shower?"

"One hundred percent."

Before Hank could gloat to Willy about his workaround of Ava's programming guardrails, Olin walked over and sat down. There was no concern on his face, no anger, not even slightly perturbed about the prospects of being boarded by a foreign naval vessel.

"Well, this should be interesting. My lawyers say we need to just grin and bear it. If the UN is behind this, there is no international case law regarding their use of sovereign naval vessels used in VBSS. So, unless we want to be the first and spend years in the court system, we need to go along to get along."

Marshall sat down at the table wearing pants and a shirt. He asked, "What's V.B.S.S.? Wait! Don't tell me! Vacation Bible School at Sea," he laughed.

"Visit, board, search and seizure," Olin said, but not before he chuckled at his son's wit.

"Don't you think it's a little over the top to have two boardings in less than three days?" Hank asked. "At this rate, we'll never get to our destination." He looked at Olin and said, "Or have you strategically planned this boarding as well?"

Olin smiled and tilted his head like the thought was intriguing. "Truthfully, I'm as surprised by this as you are. The Royal Norwegian Navy certainly is being more respectful than the US was during your boarding—at least so far. They announced their intentions and they did so when they were miles away. They made an appointment for the time and coordinates that would fit our course and schedule."

"I'd tell them to meet me in hell." The words spit out of Willy's mouth as if he had never left the Bayou.

Marshall held up his hand and gave Willy a high-five.

Olin's good-natured expression disappeared. "Anyway, they are at least being polite about aggressing against our liberties. Ava says they are unaware that this is the same *GalaxSea* that the US Navy, under UN authority, boarded two days ago." Olin smiled and said, "Looks like my shell game is working."

"I know we're in international waters and all, but does anybody else think it's strange that the UN is using a warship from Norway to do its bidding? We're way outside the US EEZ, but still—Norway?" Hank said.

"It might be strange if I knew what an EEZ is," Marshall said.

"Ava, a quick lesson here, please," Olin said.

"For centuries, a country's territorial waters were considered the functional distance of a cannon shot, but for territory and state power, the modern axiom is—more is better. With many exceptions, currently sovereign control continues through the Exclusive Economic Zone, or EEZ. This zone starts at twelve and goes out to the two hundred nautical mile mark."

"Then, yes, I think it's strange, but mostly because I'm wondering what a Norwegian warship is doing in the eastern Pacific Ocean. Ava? How about answering that one," Marshall added.

"Military classification protects information regarding the mission of the one hundred thirty-four meter, Thor Heyerdahl. However, it has been spotted in ports throughout the Northern Pacific after transiting the Northeast Passage twenty-one months ago. Recently, it has been cooperating with the UN on their Seas Without Borders Initiative."

"Oh great. More regulation at sea. Just what the world needs," Hank said.

"Well, Hank, you can take that sarcasm right off the boat and into international waters. It's time for you two to go scuba diving."

"Are you kidding me?" Willy said.

Olin deflected his eyes downward and looked somber, "Obviously, you and Hank cannot be on this boat. You are suspects in a double murder. We have plenty of time to get you off my yacht and make it look like the rest of us are a family of means, sailing down the coast." He paused, looked at Ava's hologram and asked, "Ava, where do they think we are heading?"

"You are sailing your family to San Diego. Their tracking shows you've been out to sea for five days. We want it to appear that we are incapable of double-digit speeds."

"With Ava's access to their satellites and my hardware, we can be anywhere we want."

Hank spoke up. "Hey, I'm still trying to figure out the shell game you're playing with the sister ships. Can you let me in on it?"

"Later," Olin said. "Now, I suggest you do exactly what Ava instructs. Make sure you follow the compass bearing she gives you. We wouldn't want to miss retrieving you—it's a big ocean. Go. Have a good swim. I've got to make all the evidence that this was Hank's boat disappear." Olin got up and walked over to the starboard berth and knocked hard on the door. "Irina, get up. Now! It's an emergency."

"They're going the wrong way." Hank said.

"I strongly doubt they will forget about us being out here in the middle of the ocean," Willy said.

"Sure, but with no radio or beacon, we could be impossible to find, especially with these seas. We followed the compass course until your tank got to five-hundred PSI, just like Ava told us. I've still got seven," Hank bragged. "We have plenty of air for buoyancy, but the more separation, the worse our odds. They've been heading down wind for fifteen minutes already and they're not turning around."

"You're the professional sailor. Sailboats never go in a straight line to get to their destination," Willy said.

Of course, Hank knew their rescuers had to tack, beating into the wind to retrieve them. His eyes did not deceive him as he watched the *GalaSea* sail farther away, shrinking with each swell they crested. They were being abandoned.

"They're going down wind now. It makes no sense," Hank said. He also wanted to complain about getting cold but realized that was the least of their worries. If the yacht didn't turn around, hypothermia might be a blessing. Plus, there was nothing he could do about it and he didn't need Willy to question his grit. The dry-suit was working perfectly, but they had been in the water for almost ninety minutes and even dry-suits can get cold. Not having much body fat and being without food to fuel his hummingbird metabolism, didn't help either. He closed his eyes to push out the salt and focused on staying oriented with his back to the waves.

When he opened them, he saw Willy... praying. Not with sounds he could hear, but his eyes were closed and his head was bowed. His mouth was moving like a novice reader working out words to himself. Hank stared at the man for a time expecting him to stop, but he didn't and he felt more and more uncomfortable watching. Was it rude to watch? It seemed like something personal that he wasn't supposed to see—the sanctity of a man connecting to his God. He had seen people pray countless times before this and even tried it after his father died. But with no results, he concluded praying was a waste of time. Finally, he turned his face to the departing sail—the *GalaxSea* was the only savior he wanted.

The longer they floated, the harder it would be to stay together. He could not feel his feet and wondered if maybe the straps of his fins were too tight, but he needed them to keep his body from distancing from Willy and to orient his face away from the spray of water that came at the top of each crest. That was also when they were high enough on the swell to confirm that Olin and his crew had disappeared over the horizon. Each time the ocean lifted them up, his heart sank. He had to say something. Willy looked like a bobbing Zen master, without a care in the world, until Hank said, "When do we panic?"

"Will it change anything?" Willy answered.

"No. But at least we're not accepting our fate. Newsflash—if they planned on rescuing us, they would sail in our direction."

Willy closed the gap between them, reached out and took a firm hold on the shoulder strap of Hank's buoyancy control vest. "I know you spent time in combat as a corpsman. Didn't you ever write an 'If I die letter?' or do a video recording to your loved ones?"

"No, I didn't. Nobody would receive it other than my mom and she already has had enough grief in her life. I figured there was no reason to rub her nose in it—son dying and all."

"You just don't get it yet," Willy said.

"Get what? What am I supposed to get?" Hank retorted.

"It's not about you."

"This sounds stupid. I've been hearing that all my life: I get expelled from school… 'It's not about you.' My mother's an alcoholic…

'It's not about you.' We lose the house and land that our family owned for three hundred years… 'It's not about you.' I guess I never asked the obvious question. What is IT about?"

"Do you think we are going to die out here?" Willy asked.

Hank looked at his chronograph. "I figured that out while you were deep into your prayer-thing twenty minutes ago. Look, the *GalaxSea* took off in the wrong direction and for all we know, she's still running with the wind. Even if they turned back, they would have to beat back against what? Twenty knot winds with gusts? The logistics aren't promising. So, yes, we are going to die out here. We have no food or water. You can probably last another four hours before your mind succumbs to the effects of hypothermia and my skinny ass will take half that time. But we'll stop caring in about an hour, probably deflate our vests and sink to the bottom. So, yes, we are going to die."

"Okay. That's more exact than I came up with, but I believe this is it too."

"And…?" Hank asked.

"And… nothing. I'm going to be in heaven with Jesus by the end of the day," Willy said.

"If your religion is right."

"Religion has nothing to do with it. I'm not saved by my religion."

"I don't understand talking about being saved when we are going to die. I know you're speaking metaphysically, but this life is all we've got and ours is closing out fast," Hank said.

He let Willy pull him in tighter and felt some comfort by the gesture, but he continued to stare off to where he had last seen the *GalaxSea* to avoid eye contact.

Willy spoke, his voice low and unconcerned, as if sitting in a rocking chair talking to a friend on a porch. Willy's deep southern accent was on display as he said, "My daddy died when I was ten. I used to tell people he was hunting alligators. Truthfully, he got hit by a car walking home drunk from a bar. He left six kids, my mom and grandma. We were too poor to know about government help. We hunted and fished and neighbors gave us gas for our boat.

"When I was fourteen, my older brother got arrested for poaching. They took the boat and our rifle. It might not seem like much, but it was the key to our existence on the bayou. I got angry. Too many hormones and too ignorant to figure out how to do good with them. I rowed my skiff into town, found the first person in a uniform and beat them up. He was lying on the ground with a broken nose and I was satisfied. I walked away thinking to myself that justice was done. But the officer had a different opinion and Taser probes shot into my back.

"I woke up in the hospital a week later. Twenty-five broken bones. Punctured lung. I still don't know what a spleen does, but they took that out." He tapped on his hooded head. "They used a cadaver skull to replace the bone where my head was caved in. By the time I got out of the hospital, the two cops that beat me up got desk duty and my family got paid off. We were rolling in money and I had a small trust fund to 'help me through college.'

"There was nothing finer than breaking that cop's nose, but the rest of it made me ashamed. The money ruined my family. They acted like they were the new Duck Dynasty. I didn't want any part of that, so I left and never went back.

"The only thing of value I took with me was from my grandma. She taught me about faith. It has nothing to do with religion. As far as I know, she never set foot in a church and if it wasn't for guarding Olin, I wouldn't either. She told me it's faith that saves us. Listen. I'm probably the last person who should be here telling you that God loves you as we're about to die. But I guess I'm the only one available.

"She told me this and I believed her at the time and even more so now. She said, 'William, God loves his creation. You are part of that. Jesus loves you.' That was the entirety of my Christian training." He let go of Hank's shoulder strap and fell away. "Hell, I'm about the most imperfect man there is. Fortunately, the big man doesn't require us to be perfect—nobody is. That's why Jesus died on the cross. For my sin and yours and everybody else's imperfect sorry ass. The perfect expression of love from the God of love." Willy floated in silence for a moment, then said, "Hank, that's all I got. My faith is sufficient for me. You? You have to do you."

Hank couldn't make sense of Willy's story. The fragmented lyrics of a song popped into his head, *no heaven* but nothing came after and even that fell away without a melody and he couldn't repeat the chorus. They drifted apart, but Hank didn't care and apparently Willy didn't either. He wondered if not caring was a sign of exposure—but of course it was. Not feeling cold must be another, but why would he be warm? He thought—Hell is warm—without conviction. "I'm going to hell," he said to himself. He lost sight of Willy and didn't care. He struggled to pull up his mask and relaxed onto his back and became lost in shallow breaths.

"Hank! They're here!" Willy shouted.

Hank felt like he was being woken from a dream. He had been at peace and even comfortable, but now Willy's relentless pulling on both of his shoulder straps brought him into the harsh reality of the open ocean again.

"Look! They're here!"

Willy spun Hank around, so he was facing into the wind and sea spray. He couldn't see anything through his fogged mask and tried to reach up and pull it off, but he didn't have the strength, so Willy helped him. The sight overwhelmed him with hope—the *GalaxSea*, under full sail, charging towards them.

Hank

CHAPTER 4

"WHEN AVA SAID, CAPTAIN, *prepare to jibe,* I thought that was strange, but when she informed me she was heating the forward berths to a hundred degrees, I thought she had lost her mind. She ordered me to get more blankets, prepare soup and many things that made little sense until she said, 'Willy and Hank are in the drink and need to be rescued.'"

"Well, I'm glad you didn't mutiny. If you hadn't gotten to us when you did, Hank wouldn't be feeding his face like a pig right now," Willy said.

"Hey, I waited until Ava said I could eat solid food. But yeah, I'm glad you got there when you did. Thanks, Ted and you make a great—what's this called?" Hank asked.

"You mean—meatloaf?"

"Come on, I was in the military. I've experienced meatloaf and this isn't it."

"No, you've experienced bad meatloaf. This is good meatloaf" the tall, lean Texan said. "It made no sense to me either. Why would they leave you? Then she explained what had happened. Ava, why don't you tell the story and I'll put on a fresh pot of coffee."

"It's quite logical. Even though the *Thor Heyerdahl*'s boarding party was more civilized than the one Hank experienced, they are tenacious about monitoring. Before, during and after. Unlike the US, the Norwegians, under their UN charter, must have evidence to pursue search and seizure. I'm sorry I sent you out into the water without a radio, but they would have detected any communication and I did not know they had planned to shadow us for so long. It worked out for the best because Captain Ted could lead the rescue effort while we led the frigate far enough away so there would be no suspicions."

"That's just peachy. But Ava, if you pull something like that again I'll throw salt water on your circuits."

"Oh, Willy! You know so little about me."

"Come on you two. Willy, you got closer to your God. I've found a new appreciation for meatloaf and Ted gets to lord it over us—we owe him our lives. But there is one thing I just don't feel good about," Hank paused. "We're on the wrong boat."

The two other men smiled but said nothing.

Hank exhaled. "Actually, there are more things I need to understand and you guys should have the answers. Olin set me up to be boarded by a bunch of guys pointing guns at me. After the Navy left and while I'm still rattled, he arrives late at night with his little crew and wants me to join him in sailing across the Pacific. He admits to setting me up to be boarded and tells me he wanted the US Navy to install the mandated tamper-proof tracking unit. Something he could have done months ago, in port, without military boardings, without penalties and fines and without scaring me half to death. But no, Olin must do things his way. Now even as he insists that he wants to be totally honest with me, he pleasantly avoids things he doesn't want to talk about."

Both Willy and Ted had the same knowing expression as they considered Hank's comment.

"So, what's the deal with the three *GalaxSeas*? I understand it's some kind of shell game he's playing, but I don't know why."

They all watched as Ted got up from the table and backed away holding his hands in the air. "I'm just a lowly boat driver. I sail my course and rescue people. That's all."

"You're an expert sailor, but a lousy liar. You've been in on this since the beginning," Willy said. "Hey Ted, get this: Hank just got one of Olin's NFT coins. It's Thomas Sowell, which one did Olin give you?"

"F. A. Hayek. Welcome to the club, Hank. It was months before Olin presented me with that gift. You've only been with us for a few days. Pure Rhodium—I'd never heard of the metal before and didn't know who Hayek was. Now rhodium is my favorite metal and Hayek is the most brilliant economist who ever lived," Ted laughed. "I'd never sell it but NFT artwork by Augustus Saint has been through the roof since he died. I saw a thread speculating about the coins. Nobody knows who commissioned them." He winked. "Well, except us. And nobody has ever seen one on the market, but collectors are keeping their eyes open and the numbers they are talking about—well, it's amazing what scarcity and a dead artist can do to the price."

"See, that's my point. Every time I ask a question, it gets rabbit trailed onto something equally interesting, but my questions never get answered. Can we get back to the shell game?"

Hank noticed Ted's smile disappear as he looked at Willy.

"Probably the best thing to do is to ask Ava," Willy offered.

"I've tried that and she just says she's not programmed to answer that question and shuts her mouth."

"This morning you were bragging about your skills. Remember how smartly you got Ava to admit she would know what you looked like neked," Willy said, using his deepest southern accent.

"That was a yes or no question. I'm not good at getting details out of her yet," Hank admitted.

"Access has its privileges," Willy said. "Ava, please document this inquiry for the record. We are in international waters. The three *GalaxSeas* are following the plan of avoidance and diversion. Ted and Hank are skippers and involved in navigation. Use my security clearance to explain to us the nature of Olin's strategy to confuse the authorities as to his whereabouts."

"Of course, Willy. Following Mr. Ou's broadcast tonight, you will understand more fully the reasons behind the deceit. For now, realize our intent is to evade the US and UN authorities and confound their systems' tracking our vessels."

"That doesn't seem very top secret. And since they boarded and searched us twice in the last few days, I'd say we aren't doing an outstanding job of evading anyone," Hank said sarcastically. "But please continue, I can't wait to hear more."

"Hank, to explain it to you, it will be helpful to avoid using *GalaxSea III, II and I* because these designations must be fluid for our plan to work. Therefore, I will use the skippers to refer to the vessels as *Billie Jean's Boat, Ted's Boat* and *Hank's Boat.*"

Ted sat down and Hank noticed his gaze fixed on the end of the table. Soon all eyes were looking at the same place. A chart appeared, which showed the Pacific coast of North America and to the left, varying shades of blue fanned out into the deep ocean.

"*Billie Jean's Boat* and *Ted's Boat* have been testing the strategy for months now, but when we sailed out of Victoria Harbour the real shell game began. The physical positions of the vessels are only one component of the plan. I am instructed to tweak the telemetry for our purposes. Nobody is aware that their tracking systems are compromised and I can misrepresent the position of any vessel at will, except military, of course. So, for now, we limit the *shell game* to the *GalaxSea*—all three of them."

The chart showed three courses in green, roughly running parallel to each other until exiting the Strait of Juan de Fuca. At that point the courses dispersed, one line running north, another west and the third to the south. But eventually, the green lines radically changed course as if to converge well out to sea.

"The green is the actual course of each *GalaxSea*. Purple represents what shows up in any system that might monitor our progress."

As you can see, *Hank's Boat* only shows its actual course until the Navy installed the tracking device and sanctioned you for not conforming to the laws. Olin knew this ploy, while inconvenient for you, was the equivalent of lifting the walnut shell and proving the absence of the pea. That way the player gains confidence that their suspicions are correct. Then, today he revealed himself to the *Thor Heyerdahl*'s boarding party. They suspected he was aboard and seeing him in the flesh satisfies a couple data points. It increases confidence they are correct in their assumptions and it shows that the game is not rigged. As you know, some people are experts in diversion—I am learning a great deal from Mr. Ou," Ava said.

"Inconvenient?" Hank said, not hiding the disgust in his voice.

"The move put all the attention on *Hank's Boat*. Judging by the second boarding today, our tactic appears to have been a success. The authorities will think Hank is delivering one boat and Olin and two of his children are sailing on another. They think each of the *GalaxSeas* are hundreds of miles apart and we want to keep it that way. If they bother to look, I will convince them that *Ted's Boat* is the vessel containing the pea—the yacht they are convinced Olin Ou and his family are on. They think the family is on their way to San Diego."

Willy slapped Ted on the back and said, "You're it."

"I had wondered how this was going to play out," Ted remarked as he raised his glass of orange juice and said, "Mexican food—here I come."

"I'll stick to Marshall's cooking. The kid is brilliant in the kitchen," Willy said.

"You do always seem to eat better than me. But all that intrigue and danger, you can have it. Just give me a witty AI and a fantastic yacht and I'm as good as gold. I mean—rhodium," Ted laughed.

Bella

CHAPTER 5

BELLA'S ROOM HAD NOT changed since she moved out. Just fresh paint, but that was a given, as the sea air insisted on it. The kids had been responsible for topside maintenance, but now that they had all left the station, Dad's handyman, Ferdinand, spent those countless hours scraping and painting. A never-ending job above the waterline, but the hull of the station, the very thing that allowed for life at sea, received continuous robotic cleaning, inspection and maintenance. She understood the priorities of life on the high seas, everything had to be based on a hierarchy of critical systems. The hull, the basis of success, had to be the primary concern. Since geopolymer concrete can last centuries in saltwater, it made perfect sense to invest in it. The topsides, less so and living in a house built of shipping containers welded together created a lot of ongoing hassle.

That's why she had to admire her dad's new place; no human elbow-grease was required to keep it pristine. He had talked about it being a requirement for his mission to relocate the aquafarm, but Bella had only seen pictures of what he referred to as *"Casa del Océano."* She peaked at it through the window and thought it glistened while floating windward of the station. It stood several stories tall and looked like it belonged on another world—a future world. Her parents' life on the water was so different from when she was a kid. The station's stability relied on its size, weight and the orientation of its hulls, which always faced into the weather. The new ocean-going sea-pod, however, utilized advanced marine engineering and she was eagerly anticipating the experience.

Her dad greeted her with what she needed, a comforting hug and a kiss on both cheeks. Then he warned her they only had half a day before more weather would force them to take refuge within his new, more stable home. He said, "I'm so happy to have you here again, *mi ángel.* The guestroom isn't quite ready in my new place. We've been busy preparing for the storm. Don't feel uncomfortable about displacing Ferdinand. Since we moved in, he's been attaching his hammock all over the place, but I don't think he'll find the perfect location until I build him a grass hut.

"For now, make yourself comfortable. Your old place still has the best shower and well, it's where you have history. But when you're done resting up, strap down your mattress, we'll be spending the next couple of nights in *mi casa.* I'll see you at sixteen-hundred hours. Bring all your gear and *el pero.* We'll cast off as soon as you're onboard. I can't wait for you to see my new digs."

Bella laid back on the bed attached to the wall on two sides. She pressed her bare toes against the thick painted steel post that was welded in place to support the bed's outer corner. The post spanned from floor to ceiling and remained the only metal surface in the room not coated with sprayed-on insulation, so it had direct contact with the outside and conveyed the temperature. Touching the post was a more reliable indicator of how she should dress for the weather than looking out the small windows. She pulled her foot away from the cool metal and raised an eyebrow. At one time Bella had assumed everybody, or at least all girls, checked the outside temperature that way—while in bed—with an outstretched toe. With age, she had learned that her childhood was unusual and absolutely everything she assumed to be common—never was.

She had attached stickers around the post when she was young and her little sisters made her vow never to take them down. It seemed even Ferdinand was in on the preservation of the childhood fascinations—everything from unicorns to Disney princesses. All these years later, the handyman's fresh paint made a clean edge above and below a collage. In another time, it might have made her nostalgic. But those childhood fantasies, the ones with a courageous knight, or a handsome prince, or even a gallant king had been smashed by Gregory. He turned out to be a frog—worse than a frog. None of God's creatures could compare to what he had become.

The minutes she took time making her bed passed in a flash and she ignored the tear that rolled down her cheek. Bella didn't know why she pressed her face into the bedspread and inhaled deeply. Maybe she hoped for the comforting scent of freshly washed, sun-drenched linens, or a subtle hint of cedar or even lavender. Those were the scents of summer at her mother's family cottage in Norway—that never existed here. At sea, anything not smelling of mildew and diesel was clean and if it had a hint of bleach, well, that was as good as it gets.

The floor rocked up and she looked out the window. Dark clouds filled the view and she swung her head to see out the opposing window—only water. There was no spray onto the deck, the short ledge was almost twenty feet above the waterline and the hull minimized the effect of wind and waves. After the bumpy last leg of her drone flight, it did not surprise her to learn of an approaching storm.

After her shower, she pulled on khaki capris, a white button-down shirt with sleeves and threw on a light sweater. The station had never been this far north. It never needed to be. Even though she spent her childhood on this station, she was unaccustomed to the size of the swells that rolled under the giant twin hulled platform. Her mother warned her, "Dad had a dream from God, *Reubicarse, dirigirse al norte.*" Her mom breathed in through her teeth and added, "I don't think God had anything to do with it, so I moved out. I get back to check on them every few months to make sure the bachelors don't destroy the place. But, I'm not what you would say, 'on board.'"

For years, the aquaculture station and its expanding flotilla plied the currents just north of the Pacific equator. Though not the most prolific waters of the world, the storms are mild, winds light and currents predictable. Bella understood her father, perhaps better than anyone else. If he truly received a *dream from God*, he would not let it go. He was the most doggedly capable and the most stubborn man she knew. And now, as if to prove it, he drifted a thousand nautical miles further north, advancing westward in less hospitable seas. His progress didn't surprise her, but like her mother, she didn't grasp why it made sense.

The relationship struggles between her mother and father did not surprise her either. Lena and José came from drastically different cultures and while the water brought them together, their relationship clamored within rough seas. After Bella broke up with Gregory, his actions distressed her to where fleeing to Lena on the Tahiti seastead seemed like the only sensible thing. She found her mother's routine comforting: Set tennis-times and regular mealtimes were what her mother provided. But getting drugged by kidnappers ended any benefit the seastead and her mother could provide. Bella needed her dad's comfort and her mother understood. Or maybe she paid for the expensive drone ticket to send Bella to spy on José. She didn't care. She was happy to be home at last.

There was a great deal of catching up to do and understanding her father's dream topped her list. By the end of the day, she'd know more about what was going on than her mother could find out during any number of stays. She eagerly waited to see what her dad was up to but shared her mother's concern. She could deal with a mid-life crisis, but she was not ready for her father to be *loco*. He needed to be all there—especially now.

His *relocation* almost made her forget about her own problems. But what would or should she share with him? Her mission didn't come to her in a dream from God, it came in a nightmare. Healing from the kidnapping would make sense to him, but how could she explain she was preparing, not only to defend herself, but to seek justice.

"Okay, Dad, what's going on? I've been wondering how to ask you tactfully, but can't figure anything out, so please tell me what you're up to."

"Of course. Your mother worries about my mental health. I remind her of Don Quixote on a foolish quest as a knight-errant and Ferdinand here is my squire. And every time I ask Lena to return and stay, she insists her rotation of quarterly visits is *prudent*. She thinks I'm *loco*," José said as he twirled the end of his index finger around his ear and crossed his eyes.

"Dad, you're being too dramatic. She loves you, but decided your journey is way over the top. I mean, like crossing the shipping lanes! Aquaculture stations just don't do that."

He grinned. "New challenges bring innovation and growth. I've almost finished my manual explaining how we did it safely and with only bending, not breaking, maritime laws. It has forced me to create and innovate. It is thrilling! Did I tell you I started two companies based on the hurdles of the last year?"

"Dad, you are all about the *how*. Mom and I want to know the *why*. Why are you doing this?"

"Our food is getting cold. I've said grace. We should eat before the storm arrives," José said.

"Oh no you don't. I'm an adult now and you can't just change the subject like that."

"Yes, you are an adult and entitled to an answer. The only problem is I don't have one, other than I do feel I'm on a mission from God. If that makes me crazy, well, so be it. This type of journey doesn't need a *why*—it is the *why*. If we don't get the answers in this lifetime, we'll understand it in eternity." He lowered his eyes, dragged a knife easily through a grilled shrimp, stabbed it with his fork and popped it into his mouth. "Oh, yeah, now that's a taste of heaven."

Not exactly an overt act of defiance, but Bella started with the beans and rice. She was not ready for "heaven" yet, but it didn't matter. The bite filled her mouth with a sweet, tangy explosion with a slight smokey taste. She realized her dad had tricked her. His cooking brought people together. It's hard to be mad at someone who is patient and understanding—and knows how to cook. "Dad, I've forgotten how I missed your *gallo pinto*. The world would be a better place if more people knew about *Lizano* salsa."

Ferdinand, seated across from her, lifted his glass and nodded in wordless agreement.

José joined in with his glass and laughed. "Someday you'll inherit the family recipe and you can share it with the world. But, for now, it's my secret."

"Yeah right! I know what comes in those shipments from Costa Rica. If I recall: ten kilos of coffee beans, six bottles of *Cacique Guaro* and a case of *Lizano*. Sorry to dispel the myth, but nobody has recreated the family recipe for generations."

"Perhaps, but the world would be a happier place if people were a little more respectful of their elders," José said.

Ferdinand raised his glass again and nodded.

José cleared his throat and spoke in a slow, rich voice. "Do not forget the other, the most precious item in those shipments."

"Oh, you mean the box of cigars," Bella said.

"Not just cigars, *Vegas de Santiago's*," Ferdinand said

"You are right, my friend. After I've shown Bella around, we must salute our homeland with a glass of guaro and a smoke." José turned to Bella and added, "You are welcome to join us, my dear."

"I'd rather wash the dishes."

A spiral staircase wound downward from the main living area to a level which resembled the inside of a control tower at an airport. Only the curved windows that wrapped around the room faced outward and down. The "bridge" did not sit atop the floating structure like on a boat but gave a full view of the ocean below and outward to the horizon. Her eyes widened as she watched a fully formed wave, the height of a truck, steam towards them. She grabbed the handrail tight and braced, then eased her grip and marveled as the wave rolled away with zero effect on her dad's new place. The floor maintained a dead level bearing and while suspended two stories above the ocean's surface, the *Casa's* operation center offered a commanding view.

"Wait! Is that my childhood home floating off, alone into the distance?" Bella asked.

José's face changed, the corners of his eyes softened and his jaw relaxed. His gaze steadied on the station, rising and falling a kilometer away. The station looked small in the distance and vulnerable against the enormity of the ocean. For an instant, she saw her dad in a new and different light. It gave her a chill. Was he vulnerable, too? She willed him to speak with his powerful voice and make sense out of what she saw. But instead, he looked down. She moved beside him, wrapped an arm around him and they stared until José broke the silence.

"It's not the first time I've had to let her go. They say if you love something, let it go..." He straightened his back, looked toward the horizon and said, "She's not alone." He pointed to the large screen off to one side. "Emilia, please show Bella the station on the primary command screen." A green rectangle appeared in the center. "Now, show her the aquapods." A dozen purple geodesic balls formed around the station. "Emilia, show the position of the seaweed, bivalve and shrimp habitats." The screen erupted in orange circles. "Let's not forget the janitorial sheds and feed storage." Several more objects popped up here and there amongst the color-coded collection of shapes. "Okay, let's see what this all means. Emilia, what is the average parking depth?"

"Fourteen meters, *Señor* Espinosa." A Latina voice answered.

"What is the sea-space average?" José asked.

"Seven meters."

"Ha! It's working! Before I came up with my newest company, Optimal Sea-Space, an operation as large as ours would have to spread out miles in all directions just to keep from colliding in a storm. After a storm of this size, losses would be over twenty percent. Now, we can keep all our assets close but separate, with no losses. Emilia optimizes depth, separation and motility. This would have been impossible before AI. The calculations, the sensors, the input, it was beyond..." he interrupted himself. "Emilia, show Bella the time lapse segment for the last twenty-four hours."

The colorful shapes moved around the center green rectangle representing the station. The image was mesmerizing. There was an order to the movement, but Bella could not identify any pattern.

"It's a swarm! Each submarine structure dances around its neighbors and the whole dances around the queen. Man mimicking nature." As if mentioning an afterthought, José said, "If it comes back, it's meant to be."

"Dad, this is magic! The whole thing. How have you managed all this? And the operation! It's huge!"

"Well, it's been a group effort. Your mother, Ferdinand, even Jonathan and Sofie, added their expertise, plus the contractors. But the glory goes to God."

"Okay, Dad, I get the idea. You're too humble."

José frowned and said, "There is a practical limit. At least I'm pretty sure there is. Emilia and I try to figure out what *optimal* really means. She's great, but we need an AI far beyond her capabilities and my paygrade. Even to rent, it would cost all our profits for a year. And that's just to learn the limits of scalability. We're done growing. Maybe the limit is this old body."

His hair had grayed at the temples, but otherwise his strength and capability had not waned. Not yet fifty and he was still just as handsome as a telenovela star. She wondered how much of his sensitivity and "old" talk rose from the perennial conflict with the woman that he loved.

"Want to see how I pimped this baby out?" José said.

"Dad, where do you come up with your phrases? Mom would be appalled and I don't think it's funny either."

José screwed up his face, clueless. "Okay, anyway, the standard use of this level is as an observation area. Most residential sea-pods attach to an anchor in coastal waters so this blister area by design dips down into the water so people can see the sea-life. I needed to make a few modifications to adapt her for the deep water of the high seas, but it worked. So far, at least.

"As you know, a deep-water aquafarm as a free-floating opera-tion offers many advantages, but as we grew by taking on a dozen aquapods, fish pens and layered bivalve-seaweed floats, the results became unmanageable. It was like herding tuna. That's when I came up with the idea for Optimal Sea-Space. GPS guided, wave driven propulsion units—tractors—sometimes three or four towing some of the bigger cages. The farther north we've come, the better the system works. Slow and steady wins the day with my simple software. The trick was keeping the hardware clean and constructing the entire system so that it can submerge deep enough to minimize adverse surface conditions, but not so deep we lose them or kill everything we're trying to grow. As you understand, 3D farming is complicated, but AI makes it possible to gauge pressure changes, manage light for photosynthesis, optimize feeding strategies..." José's energy trailed off with his voice.

He motioned for Bella to take a seat. "Hmm—guess I thought of everything except that not everybody is my height." He looked disappointed and added. "You're going to need to raise your feet off the floor for this demo."

Bella's knees came up and she parked her feet on a footrest designed for legs a couple of inches shorter than hers. The chairs, with a table to either side, rotated clockwise, making a slow wide arch around the large center spar that made up the spine of the seastead. There was no hiding her surprise as she looked at her dad in the chair next to her, returning her smile. His chest seemed to fill with pride as he shared a moment he had waited for. She understood her dad never did things in half measures, but this time, he had reached a new level and she considered what it must mean for him to show off a little.

The chairs stopped moving and her dad got up. Music erupted from unseen speakers, playing *La Bamba*. He began strumming an air guitar, at first to the unaffected sea, then turned facing Bella. His confidence and stature returned completely as he moved to the sound. She couldn't catch her breath while laughing uncontrollably. But she could not resist the opportunity to cut loose and dance as the music ignored the storm brewing outside.

When the short song was over, they extended their hands in the air and did a double high-five. "Thanks, Dad. I mean not just for making me laugh and dance, but for all this." She swept her arms around the nerve center of his operation and into the vastness of the open ocean. "It's so good to be home."

The monitor shimmered in dark green and then broke through the thick seaweed forest and exposed another rim of undulating green leaves. Not stopping, the camera plunged into yet another row of the underwater crop where it paused. Bella's eyes widened in surprise and focused on a tiny crab. "Nice seaweed crop dad and the mussels look super happy. In fact, the diversity you've got here is amazing. I can't believe you convinced shrimp to hang in there for a thousand-mile ride into cooler waters. And this little guy?" She took her hand off the joystick and pointed to the tiny crab in the screen's corner. "Have you tried them? Delicacies like that do well in fancy restaurants throughout Asia. But first, you'd have to raise and collect enough to ship."

"Sure, they're delicious, but their hatch timing is all over the place. There's a window of soft shell and firm meat that is amazing, but I can't find a season when they all ripen together. They're like me—too independent to be agreeable."

Bella pushed the joystick in her right hand forward and, with her left index finger, slid the depth control away from her. The aquafarm's underwater drone wasn't any more advanced than when she left for college, but she could tell from the mission-to-Mars look around her, including the arrays of monitors and the complexity of interfaces, her dad had added more technology—a lot more. At her job with the Marine Quality Institute, the minimal standard for underwater drones comprised a wireless hand control paired with VR goggles, but the result was the same. And it took only a minute to figure out how to drive her dad's drone through a series of reddish-brown leaves while looking at a flat screen. The lighting and the focus took a bit longer to adjust to open water, but there was nothing to see except eager bubbles ascending into the light. She spun the drone around and maneuvered the camera until the depth indicator read five meters. She nosed it slowly towards an expanse of netting and held her breath. Flashes of silver filled the monitor, her eyes widened and her chest raised as she inhaled. Bella turned toward her dad with a smile. "I love this. I never tire of watching them." When she turned back, the school of fish had disappeared into the dark water. "How many kampachi aquapods are you running now?"

"Five, ten-meter pods and half a dozen twelves."

Bella gazed off to the left of the monitor for a couple seconds. "Dad, that's around sixty-five thousand square meters! Plus, the kelp production. What's your acreage now?"

"You don't want to know," he said.

"Well, I saw your automated blue-green algae process on the station. It's enormous! Quite a step up from the fifty-gallon barrel stage, when I was a kid and the fish pellet production alone would take a twenty-acre sea farm to keep that much kampachi in nutrients..." She let her voice trail off as her mind staggered through calculations. "Dad, you're too ethical to buy terrestrial feed and you're too cheap. Wait-a-minute! That sealed shipping container on the station. I can't believe it! You're growing and processing more than you need! Do you have enough fish nutrients to sell wholesale?"

"Blue Permaculture dot com strikes again. You forgot harvesting. When conditions are right, I tap into the ocean's twilight zone and harvest lanternfish by the shipload." José said proudly as he crossed his arms. "I've been bored and besides, once we started automating, forty acres isn't much more work than four."

"Dad, that's like half a mile deep! And lanternfish are disgusting! I had a professor challenge us to make them into an edible meal. It was a failure."

"It takes some time, but here's my recipe. Grind the super-abundant lanternfish into meal, add my homegrown algae, dry into pellets and feed to kampachi. The more oily, briny and fishy it tastes, the more they love it. Be patient and in a year, you've got world class sashimi." José gave a confident smile, "I think I'd have gotten an 'A' in your class."

"No doubt. Are you publishing that? I'd love to read about your process, but not now. This grow must be one of the biggest private deep-water operations in the world. And you're keeping it going while on the move. Has anybody even done that before? I mean drifting sure, for a season, but taking an aquafarm on a journey?"

"Not that I've found, but the concept is simple. It was the systems and technology I had to work out. But God has been good and we've suffered no losses. But the coming storm may change that. We've always been south of any cyclone activity until now. It looks like this will be the ultimate test—we're directly in its path. I guess we'll sink or swim."

"Nice choice of words. I'm not sure I want to know how you crossed the shipping lanes at a seasnail's pace. Did you really publish a paper on that?"

"I wrote a paper, but I'm not stupid enough to make it public. Not just yet anyway. The UN's been working with various nation states and their navies—terrorizing the high seas. Between selling sea tractors direct from the factory and Optimal Sea-Space technology through agents, my affairs are complicated enough. I certainly don't need a submarine to surface through fifty feet of sea vegetables as they come to haul me off to the gulag."

"You and your penchant for drama, dad. I always thought you should be a telenovela star."

José, smiled. "A producer did come to see me—no telenovela, but she was checking the prospect of a reality TV show. Turns out, you're wrong. There's not enough drama here. The producer gave me a list of changes for them to consider coming back. Ferdinand would have to get a full set of teeth and I'd have to hire my own 'cast' from the actor's union. The producer looked at me and said, 'You'll be okay with some makeup.'" He chuckled and added, "It's the first time I've entertained throwing someone overboard—how's that for drama?"

"I don't know what to do with you," Bella said.

"Just love me." He dropped his arms to his side while he smiled broadly, causing his soft dark eyes to crinkle.

"Dad, I've been watching the barometer since I got here. It's dropping so fast. It looks bad."

"The worst I've ever seen. They forecast winds of up to one-hundred miles per hour and waves up to twenty feet."

"This pogo stick you call home seems stable, but are we safe in a storm like that?" Bella asked.

"They've tested these all over the world, in worse conditions than anything we'll see. So yes, we'll ride this out easily. The farm should be safe enough. I'm giving everything a wide berth and gradually submerging it as deep as the sea-life can tolerate. It's the station I'm concerned about. She's on her own. I'm not worried about her sinking, so much as the unmanned aspect. There are a ton of legal implications and liabilities with that. I've got cameras and..." José's voice drifted off to silence.

"And what?" Bella said.

"I placed explosive charges in the hulls."

"You what!?"

"This is not the world you grew up in *mi ángel*. Things are harder. People have lost their way."

"How can you think about destroying something that has been such a part of our life? It's the hub of your farming operation."

"Yes and I believe it will weather this storm just fine. But there are complications—high seas salvage for one. Even with her machine learning autopilot, she is classified as being unattended and adrift. Anyone who boards her and brings her under their control can claim salvage rights. These days it would hold up too, with the UN on a rampage. As I mentioned, they use navies to find people who are 'non-conforming' and then issue fines. If they are manned and the fines aren't paid immediately, they sink the operation and imprison the owner. The crew ends up dropped at the nearest shore. If unmanned, they hunt down the last registered owner for fines and prosecution.

"A sordid history shadows my beloved station. I am a criminal in the eyes of some authorities. God-forbid, I make biodiesel out of kelp, raise algae and transit the seas without permission. That's not even dealing with the station's defensive strategies. I don't have to remind you, pirates are real. They killed Rodrigo, Julia and their three children." José's forehead wrinkled and his eyebrows knitted together. It looked like he had unwittingly driven by a cemetery where a friend had recently been buried and was forced to reflect, then moved on without looking in the mirror. "We have anti-boarding water cannons for close range, directional sound blasters for mid-range, four floating 308 caliber machine gun-pods and a 50-caliber for long range. It's all automated, making my sentence go from ten years to mandatory life. Now do you see why there are explosive charges poised to take her down to the seafloor?"

"Well, dad, a month ago I would have said you're crazy. Right now, I'd just say you are a little scary, but I can't argue your logic."

Hank

CHAPTER 6

WITH HER BACK TO him and even though he had never seen more than her face before, he knew exactly who she was. She stood a few inches over five feet with dark shoulder length hair. A loose-fitting robin-egg blue t-shirt with the slack taken up by a knot tied to the side, spilling over tight jeans. On her tiny feet, she wore bright white boat shoes which didn't look out of place, but a headset that had a boom mic with a wire leading to a battery pack on her hip looked like what a TV director might have used fifty years ago. A clipboard in her hand completed the old-fashioned look.

"Five minutes, Mr. Ou," Ava said.

The headset, the clipboard and wardrobe—none of it made sense. He felt ridiculous trying to fill in the blanks as it was obvious she was acting as the producer for Olin's press conference—a hologram—perfectly rendered, but still a hologram. His stomach felt like a rogue wave lifted the boat unexpectedly, when she said, "*Five minutes, Mr. Ou"* Her voice, that tender accented voice with the Celtic lilt had, until now, never had a body.

As a Navy corpsman deployed with the Marines, he often encountered a voice over the coms. He naturally formed an impression, filled the void and determined what that voice's owner would look like. Invariably, when he met the voice's owner, he had to admit they looked nothing like what he imagined. But today, Ava's voice matched her persona exactly. Even the daytime hologram rendered in full size, fit his expectations. The colors were not as vibrant and they lacked the density which would have been present at night, but still Hank couldn't help it—he stared. He wanted to interrupt her and introduce himself; even though this was his first toe to toe meeting with her, he realized how foolish it would be.

Olin stood alone gripping the helm. Behind him, the boat's wake stretched away before the wind tossed seas erased it. Two small studio drones bounced natural light into the shadows on Olin's face and all the stress Hank had seen earlier, was gone. A camera suspended beneath another drone hovered motionless in front of him. They had changed their course and one final drone hovered over the water off the starboard beam. It matched the progress of the *GalaxSea* and it looked ready to take in the scene from any angle.

Ava had no control over the overcast weather, but she could optimize the lighting, sound and cameras for ideal visual effects. The rough waters and strengthening winds would have been impossible for a human film crew, but it was easy for Ava's processing power.

"Hank, I'm glad you have recovered. When you came back aboard you looked weary." The headset vanished and she wore a medical officer's uniform from the Star Trek TV series. In place of the clipboard, she held up a tricorder and pretended to scan. She smiled and said, "You are fit to resume your duties aboard this ship. You may leave the sickbay, but I suggest you avoid long swims for a few days. Now, clear out of here, I've got work to do." Her voice was not soft, or kind, only perfunctory. It matched the immediacy in Ava's dark eyes as they drilled straight through him. Her serious expression didn't leave any room for further conversation. She spun in place and as she did her costume changed back to that of the producer.

Hank waved an unsteady *goodbye* towards Olin and beat it down the companionway stairs.

"My name is Olin Ou and I am honored that you have taken your valuable time to listen to this broadcast. It is my desire to speak to you personally, at a public rally, in a school gym or even better yet, face to face. But, as you can see from my surroundings, I'm out on the water far from anybody else in international waters. Soon, it will be obvious to you why I can't join you in a more intimate setting.

"If you conduct a search for my name you'll be told I'm an opportunist, a speculator, a tax cheat and worse yet—I'm wealthy. Those descriptors are all true enough depending on your perspective. I'm not here to argue who I am or what I've done, I'm here to tell you what I'm doing and why. If you are comfortable labeling me using the catchphrases of the media-syndicates, then you should tune out now, but if you want the truth, I invite you to stay with me until the very end of this broadcast. I have a surprise to share.

"Until now, I've maintained a rather private life. I've never tried to set the story straight or get in the favor of TV personalities or online influencers. Not once have I contributed to a politician or hired a lobbyist to further my interests. I've never tried to buy an image through a publicist or used a PR firm. I've been busy with research and business ventures and never cared about public image. How you view me is not my concern. Like you, I've done things I'm not proud of, as well as good and beneficial things along the way.

"If you dig into the details, you'll find I gathered a team of the most brilliant minds to make an electric motor far superior to anything the world had seen. I seized the opportunity to make something exceptional and gave it to the world for free. Today, billions of people experience a better quality of life because of the Madras Motor. I am an opportunist.

"Some say I am a speculator. Yes, I'm guilty of that too. When I realized certain rare metals were essential to the Madras Motor, I took every cent I had and leveraged every cent I could borrow, to corner the market on rhodium. I failed. No matter how I tried, I could not dominate the rhodium market. But my efforts made me enough money to be despised. And because I sold every ounce for less than the government-mandated price, it made me a target for those in power. The government hates competition as much as they hate the free market, so they accused me of the only crime they could find me guilty of—tax evasion. Tax laws remain impossibly complex. They are designed to be used by the powerful to advance only themselves, at the same time they can label anyone a tax cheat—including you.

"As for being wealthy? That has become a dirty word, implying you take more than your fair share. I'm wealthy beyond my dreams and therefore many assume I'm greedy and unethical. The reality is quite the opposite. Just like you, I exchange money for products or services which I value more than the money I pay for them. Reasonable people understand I provide my products and services to people who value them and they pay me. I am rich because I've met the needs of others. Voluntary exchange is how people around the world raise their standard of living. Something never taught in school is that wealth is only limited by humanity's vision or lack thereof. We have examples of people living in squalor, where even the most fortunate struggle for survival and die young. Conversely, we have entire communities, where even the least fortunate enjoy abundance and live to see the growth of generations. But while wealth is unlimited and can be available to all, power is finite. Look at anti-wealth industries like the military, corporate media and politics—power is a zero-sum game. But wealth does nothing to diminish prospects, in fact it helps all people attain their dreams. It is those who are hungry for power that harm humanity. Wealth is not the threat—it is the answer. Many philanthropic avenues are open for the wealthy to give to those in need. My record speaks for itself. My wife, Maria and I donated a hospital wing, set up a foundation and have given to worthy charities. This is not the typical press conference where I say, 'I'm giving back.' I refuse to say that because it implies that I took more than my share. What I will say is that I am giving away my fortune.

"As of today, my net worth is somewhere between your political representatives and that of your favorite news anchor. I still have this boat and a few others and a place where my family and friends, both old and new, can live and work in peace. Before I announce who has received my fortune, I need to explain myself.

"There is a reason I'm broadcasting this message far outside the territorial waters of the United States. I've made some decisions and only time will decide whether I'm correct. These choices are mine and mine alone. They will affect me for the rest of my life on earth and they will affect the lives of my family. I love my children more than anything and I'm devoted to my wife. Maria and I are in this together and we will pay the consequences for what we feel is right. Our kids have not had a say in our decision, but it will affect them like no other.

"God knows, it's difficult being a parent. Honestly, it's difficult being a human being. We all experience trials and struggles and must live with our decisions. The decisions of Maria and myself are not harder than yours, they might be much easier than what you are dealing with today, but in the end, you must live your life and we must live ours.

"They have accused me of being a tax evader and it is a stain on my reputation, even though there was no conviction. Like most Americans I've always paid what I owe the IRS, but not a dollar more. Every year I file my taxes and I pay what is due. Only this year is different. I decided it is time to make a stand. I ran my idea past my financial advisor and she said, 'Don't even joke like that.' Then I put my plan across the desk of my attorney and he said he would fire me as a client. And finally, I told my best friend and he said, 'That's the stupidest idea the world has ever heard.'

"Politicians boast about how they will solve all inequalities by taxing the rich. Tax rates continue to go up, yet there are still those who will not be satisfied until they tax the wealthy into poverty. But don't be fooled into thinking it stops there. The tax-the-rich rhetoric has been going on for well over a century. It has always been a smoke-screen to tax all wage earners at ever higher rates and leave the least well off with a greater burden and reliance on government handouts. These politicians and bureaucrats tax away your lifeblood, wrestle away your freedoms and encourage printing more dollars. Those men and women in the deep state ensure inflation outpaces both wages and entitlements. You are victims of self-serving politicians and their cronies. The result of an ever-expanding money supply is a hidden tax, an ever-increasing weight they force you to carry.

"You are being robbed—a little at a time—and you become poorer for it. Another way to understand it, is that you owe labor to the government, at least the percentage of your labor they take out of your paycheck and inflate away. Make no mistake. You pay heavily for this corrupt system of tax slavery and dishonest money.

"If you're getting the idea that this broadcast is about more than giving my money away, you are correct. Maria and I have renounced our citizenship. This has not been a decision I've come to lightly. I love my country, I love its people, but I don't trust the government to do the right thing—ever. The United States of America began as a tenuous experiment in personal liberty and freedoms. Even then, the laws were unequally applied and people were subjected to the edicts and whims of those in power. Everybody agrees, removing the yoke of oppression was necessary and took a revolution to initiate it, but injustice lived on.

"We have a long history of state-sanctioned death and destruction. Slavery continued, indigenous peoples exploited, immigrants abused and foreign entanglements circled the globe. Indeed, it was an improvement over the rule of King George and other tyrannical systems, but as is common throughout history, the powerful took advantage of the weak and the powerful got away with it—and still do. The USA has done things it must never be proud of, as well as countless examples of outstanding achievements and honorable actions. Governments are no worse and no better than the people who are in charge. Conceptually, the United States is a collection of states governed by the people, of the people and for the people, but practically, it is a fraternity for the political elite and their powerful allies.

"As you can tell, I've lost faith in the government of the United States of America. I believe the ruling cabal created a stranglehold on every citizen and will not let us breathe. Our leadership has become tyrannical with a few arrogant insiders oppressing the citizens and choking the life out of good people trying to live and let live. I see no evidence this situation is redeemable, so I must follow my conscience. Renouncing my citizenship was not a simple decision and sailing away from the people I love, is heart wrenching. I left, not for personal gain, but because, for me, it is the only moral thing to do.

"I'll be called a traitor by some. But a traitor betrays his country. I've betrayed no one. I am a person following my path, seeking the truth. So, traitor doesn't fit, but I'll admit, I am a heretic. Which leads me to the other reason for this broadcast.

"Over the last several months I've liquidated all my assets—stock holdings, cybercurrency and business interests. I turned it all into

US dollars. You can find an itemized list and all transactional verifications encoded in the Bitcoin blockchain. This level of transparency will stand as proof that after taxes the balance sat at one hundred eighty-two billion dollars. I gave every cent of it away yesterday.

"I didn't listen to my accountant, my lawyer or even my best friend. I did what I did for my own reasons and I'll let you decide what you will. Everybody can think of a charity that could use an infusion of money from a benefactor. I certainly can. But I didn't give my money to a charity. Everybody can think of people who could use some help—we see them every day, but not a single soul received a dime of my wealth. I have deposited the entirety of my previous fortune into the US Department of Treasury. You heard me right—I gave it all to the country I'm leaving behind.

"As you can see, the weather here is deteriorating as I speak, so I'll conclude and leave you to discuss my actions if you choose. It is my money, or was, so I don't have to explain myself, but I'll leave you with a final thought. The state naturally impedes cooperation between people. It would be better if they stayed out of it, or limited their actions to ensuring personal rights, but we are far down the road to serfdom. We've all seen the smothering good intentions of the nanny state as it decides what is best for us and too many people have witnessed firsthand its psychopathic twin sister, the predatory state—forcing submission to its arbitrary whims.

"My fortune isn't even a drop in the bucket of spending. You can track the dollars yourself and see if it makes any difference. I assure you the politicians and bureaucrats won't even notice an extra one hundred eighty-two billion dollars. They don't need it to continue to enrich themselves or their families and friends. It won't stop them from wasting your hard-earned money.

"I know it sounds like I am cynical. Obviously, I'm not hopeful any of this will change through electing the next candidate or creating a new law. But as a believer in God's divinity, I am certain that truth will eventually rule the day. In the meantime, I will commit to do my best to live not by lies.

"Until we meet again, God bless you."

"He's giving all his money to the government?" Hank said.

Irina just nodded.

"Did you know he was going to do that?"

She flashed her eyes at him and said, "He and Mom have been preparing us for this for months. We were never told exactly what he just explained to the world. Well, not so clear an explanation, but this comes as no surprise. That's why Marshall skipped the broadcast and hung out in his room."

"I've never heard of someone doing this before," Hank said.

"It's not a stunt, if that's what you're thinking. My dad is extremely serious. When he decides and Mom agrees, there is no turning back. What he just announced was a small part of what he's seen firsthand. He didn't even mention what the US and the governments of the world have put him through personally. I'm glad he's doing it. There's no way I can get into his brain, it's way out there, but I guarantee he has planned this out and understands the risks and the consequences. So don't worry about him, or us, or yourself. He is crazy, but you'll see, he's crazy like a fox."

Olin raced down the companionway steps. He took a deep breath and rubbed his hands into a lingering clasp and said, "Well, what did you think?"

"You looked good until the wind blew your collar up and was that a booger on your nose?" Irina said and rose to give him a hug. "You did great, Dad. And I'm just kidding about the booger. Now that you've given it all away and renounced your citizenship, do I have to turn in my earrings?" She stroked her hair back and exposed a large diamond stud.

"You should keep them. Who knows, someday you might need to visit a pawnshop." Olin opened a cabinet and pulled out a bottle of whiskey. "Join us? It's Macallan's thirty-year-old single malt. If I remember, it's your favorite."

"Daddy, I gave that up years ago. You'll have to do better than that to tease me." She let her hair drift back into place and left the room.

"What was that all about?" Hank asked.

"Oh nothing, let's just say most kids sneak a drink of their parents' liquor. But my daughter pilfered an entire bottle of ten-thousand-dollar hooch to share with her friends."

"Oh, I get it. But I couldn't tell. Is she mad at you?" Hank asked.

Olin carefully opened the bottle and poured a dram into a glass and pushed it to Hank. "Maria assures me that when Irina is mad, she either hides in her room or makes her 'mad' very clear to everybody."

"That was like nothing I've ever seen before," Hank said.

"You've never seen a sarcastic exchange between a father and his teenage daughter?" Olin asked.

"No, I meant your broadcast."

"I know what you meant. It is funny, I've known this was something I had to do, but I convinced myself that I would slip into the night. The world needs more theater, but not more reality TV. I didn't want to be a part of that. It made sense to cash in my chips and walk away from the table. I never wanted to be famous or infamous. I just thought I could live my own life and sail my course. Then, one evening after mass, Maria asked me if I heard the priest's homily. I told her I did. *Love your neighbor as yourself.* She stared at me and said, '*Well?*'

Of course, I said, '*Well what?*'

She said, '*you have wealth, power and influence. God gave these to you as gifts, not as a curse. Olin, you need to figure out how best to love your neighbor.*'

"I didn't sleep at all that night. And in the morning I was convinced—no—I was convicted. As much money as I had is a ridiculous amount for one man, but it's nothing for a wasteful government. They've been trying to rid me of my fortune the minute I made..." He lifted his arms, made air quotes and continued, "*More than my-fair-share.* Giving it all to the greedy bastards shows a failed system better than allowing them to tax it. I hope it will shock people, because all that money will change nothing—the poor will not become less needy and the politicians will not become less greedy. My *excess* will amount to a rounding error to the treasury but might elicit some deeper consideration to the average American. If that occurs, then my money will be well spent.

"After I decided what I would do, I still laid awake hearing Maria's words, *Olin, You need to figure out how best to love your neighbor.* Like wealth, we can use power for good or evil. If left to my desires, I would squander any semblance of power. I've never had a desire to control others, present company excluded." He nodded his head and took a sip of his drink. "But I realized Maria was right—power is a gift from God. So, I'm working to become a steward of any power I might have. Despite my personal inclination, I couldn't go quietly into the night. What good is a roar if nobody hears it?

"And influence? You cannot believe the list Ava came up with. In the last two months I've handwritten thousands of notes. I think she has found everybody I've ever met. In the last twenty-four hours before my broadcast, each note was hand delivered. That was only part of the campaign. Let's just say Ava's been busy... loving her neighbor too." Olin raised his glass and said, "Thank you, Ava."

"You're welcome, Olin," Ava said.

Hank raised an eyebrow at Ava's familiarity.

The *GalaxSea* heeled hard to starboard and a wave made a shadow as it blocked out the sky and passed across the low window of the yacht.

Olin grabbed the bottle before it slid. "Another drink? It looks like this might be the last alcohol served until the storm is done with us."

"Zaine, are you doing alright on deck?" Hank said.

"Everything is as it should be, Skipper," Zaine answered.

Olin refilled their glasses.

"To the storm being done with us," Hank offered and pushed the rim of his glass into Olin's. The crystal gave off a satisfying clink.

"Olin, Irina told me that your brain is way out there. I'm pretty sure I agree with her. Your religion is obviously important to you and I don't get that. A man of your education and status believing in God seems ridiculous to me, but I can't say your heart is in the wrong place. Maybe there is something to it. Since meeting you, things have been—weird—extraordinarily weird. When this storm passes, I'm going to re-watch your broadcast and take notes. I've got questions. Lots of questions, but with your fine whiskey in me I can't think of one right now. That's why I'm going to put my harness on, hook up and hang out on deck until my head clears. This day needs to end."

Hank stood up, steadying himself and slowly walked to the companionway. He placed one foot on the lowest step and twisted back to face Olin. "Did you really give all your money to the government?"

Olin raised his glass and said, "Give unto Cesar what belongs to Cesar."

"I can't decide whether you're a hero or an asshole." Hank stepped into a stiff breeze, shaking his head.

Bella

CHAPTER 7

BELLA SLIPPED ONTO THE floor and displaced Kumar while grabbing him into a snuggle. "Dad, you've done some amazing things out here on the high seas, but as Mom's spy, I cannot provide a report that would convince her she has nothing to worry about, let alone get her back here permanently."

"I'm an optimist, If I keep heading west and collect all the data possible, someday I will secure an AI that will have the computing power and abilities that I'll need to crunch the numbers and publish enough information to help other aquafarmers."

Bella waited a long moment hoping he would elaborate, but he just sat there with a grin on his face. "Dad, you're not making this easy. You've been talking about your dream from God and now about helping other aquafarmers?"

"Remember, God works in mysterious ways. Most aquafarmers stay anchored to their watery acreage, just as land farmers are to the soil. I've been trying to solve this. Farmers will only be truly free when they can pack up and leave if conditions require it. Things like poor water quality, changing climate, oppressive laws, unequal treatment, exorbitant taxes and situations I've not even considered. Being able to move to areas that are healthier and better suited for business are vital keys to freedom."

"Wow, that's what you've been doing? Why didn't you just say so? Mom wonders if you're losing your mind." Bella scrunched up her face and said, "Come to think of it, it still sounds crazy." Kumar licked her face. "Yuck. Boy, I love you, but enough is enough." She slid herself back onto the couch and Kumar stuck his nose under her hand expecting to be petted. "So now you really are on a mission from God. What was that old movie?"

"*Blues Brothers*," José said.

"If you say so. I never really got it. Like what was with the sunglasses? Anyway, all us kids loved to watch you laugh at the movie, but that was the fun for us."

"Yeah, yeah, yeah. Now it's my turn," José said. "Everybody told me to give you space when you got here. Jon and Janice called me and said to tread lightly. Then I get a direct message from your psychologist with a page of dos and don'ts. I've never heard of such a thing. But Lena made it the clearest. She said, *José, you just love on her and leave her alone. She'll talk to you about it when she's ready.'* The strangest thing so far was an email from an organization that matches dogs and people who have survived trauma. They instructed me how I can be most helpful—to your dog."

"I guess Kumar has been through a lot," Bella said.

At the mention of his name, Kumar's ears perked up. As if on cue, he rolled over, his three paws suspended in the air with all confidence that a good belly rub was on its way.

José laughed, "Apparently, he's dealing well with his past." Turning serious, he added, "Bella, you know I don't always say the correct thing and I don't read other people's emotions very well, but I love you and I'll do anything you need. If you need me to be silent, I will, but that's difficult for me."

"It's okay, Dad. I can talk about it. What do you know?"

"That you and your mother were drugged and they kidnapped you. And Janice shot a kidnapper and saved you. Oh and I also know that you turned down Gregory's marriage proposal and that somehow these things are related. But that's it. What happened between Gregory and you? He told me you two were destined to be married, then a few days later, you told me you weren't sure."

"That is the understatement of the year." She sat up and leaned forward. "Dad, I don't want to relive the last week, but you deserve an explanation. I realized he was far more serious about our relationship than me. But the worst part is that he was not the man I thought he was. When I broke it off, things didn't go well and I didn't handle any of it the way I should have. It brought out the worst in Gregory. After he threatened me, I left Singapore and Mom took me in. I was scared and Mom insisted we go right to Janice. She figured the family's very own FBI agent might shed some light on things.

"Janice made some inquiries and found out that Gregory was wanted in connection to human trafficking crimes. Dad, he is a terrible man and I never suspected a thing. Janice says he is a psychopath. She's dealt with that condition before, as an FBI agent and says they can convince people everything is normal and don't draw attention to themselves—even as they hurt others. With me he was a doting boyfriend, with his business associates he might have commanded respect, but with others, he can be a monster."

Tears filled Bella's eyes and her dad moved beside her on the couch and placed an arm around her. Bella buried her face into him. It didn't take long for her to compose herself and continue. "She doesn't think he'll intentionally harm me, but..." She took a deep breath. "Dad, Janice says as long as he's out there, he will stop at nothing to capture me."

"That explains the gun you have strapped to the small of your back," José said.

Bella felt uncomfortable as she said, "I thought it was concealed."

"Well, it was until you bent over and had a face to face with your dog." He frowned. "It's not necessary out here."

She wiped a tear away. "Janice says when you decide to wear a gun, you don't pick and choose for conveniences' sake, you have it available all the time—no exceptions. I'm still practicing. Packing a gun is difficult."

"Well, I feel safer knowing Janice trained you."

"And Gina—you might call her my kung-fu instructor. She isn't really the sensei type—more of a brawler."

"Gee, I can't wait to meet her," José said with a sideways smile. "After we got the gun-pods and security contractors, I put my 30-30 Winchester in storage. It's time to bring it out and see if I can still hit anything. I'm also going to make a call to the security cooperative and tell them to set the sensitivity to a higher threat level."

"Thanks Dad, I was a little worried that you wouldn't take this seriously. After all, we are here in the open ocean and we can see visitors coming from miles away."

"Well, theoretically that's true. But remember when Gregory gave me a visit to ask for your hand in marriage?"

"*My hand*! For goodness' sake! I should have realized he was a jerk then. Why? What about that visit?" Bella asked.

"He came unannounced. I got up that morning to find Gregory sitting in my kitchen with a cup of tea."

Gregory

CHAPTER 8

THE WOOD FLOOR ALWAYS let him know when it was time to end his meditation. As he came out of his kneeling position, he ignored the soreness in his legs. His opulent stateroom had become his sanctuary. More so during this voyage than at any time in the past. With each sunrise, he craved solitude more than the day before. Not everybody on board his private yacht proved to be easy to tolerate, but he liked the captain and felt proud to have a man who once commanded a cruise ship with a crew of six-hundred and thirty. He listened well, did not seem overly arrogant and told some marvelous stories at the dinner table. Every yacht needs a cook and Sammi's culinary ability matched his value as a reliable henchman. But he had reservations about the deck crew: Two men, Chango and Shyboy, who said they were brothers, but he imagined would stab him in the back at their first opportunity if something profited them more than working for Gregory.

Of course, he spied on them continuously. His AI wasn't anything other than a surveillance platform with machine learning, probably something developed during the Cold War by one of the superpowers. It listened for keywords and looked for patterns of conspiratorial behavior. Its chief advantage was that it didn't need a connection to the internet and it would alert him with the slightest hint of mutiny. So far, the only thing he found out about the two men, was that they were not brothers and they had all the stereotypical traits of thugs with low IQ.

He was glad he had begun this voyage with hard and fast rules about access to various spaces on the boat including when they were allowed in the wheelhouse. That had been the captain's idea and he ran a tight ship. The kitchen remained off limits as well, but Sammi made it a point to keep everybody well fed. Most of all, he was thankful they were not around when he and Sammi threw Masiki's body into the water. In some situations, he would boldly use murder to make a point—it's what happens to employees who disappoint.

The captain insisted they travel well south of the Marshall Islands. He admitted their papers were in perfect order but explained that a Coast Guard suffering from boredom and burning free fuel from the US, would be an unnecessary risk. However, by traveling between the sparse atolls of Kiribati, it avoided encounters with the authorities altogether and still maintain their eastward heading towards Hawaii.

When he passed through the galley, Sammi was working his craft on fresh fish and octopus.

"The boys caught a prize today," Sammi said with some hesitation.

"Oh? What's that?"

"They pulled it up in the fighting cockpit."

Gregory walked up the stairs, across the salon and out the sliding doors to find an outrigger canoe built to hold one person and a few fish. His crew was not loitering about, as was their custom this time of day. He walked up to the wheelhouse to find the captain sitting at the helm, reading a book.

"Why do we have a canoe on board?" Gregory asked.

The captain took an unlit stub of a cigar out of his mouth, setting it down on the edge of an ashtray. He looked up from his book and said, "Sammi bought the fish, but the brothers decided they wanted to buy the girl. She didn't understand how those types of transactions work. They are explaining it to her now."

Gregory flew down the stairs and raced to the crew berths. He forced open the door, causing the wood trim to splinter inward. A petrified Micronesian girl sat on the bed with a glass of clear liquid in one hand and grasping a pillow shielding her naked body with the other.

"What's going on here?" Gregory bellowed, his face full of fury.

"We're going to pay her," snarled Changco. "We're happy to share."

"Go topside – now! Tell the captain to return to where you picked her up," Gregory commanded.

The men hurried out of the room.

Gregory took the glass from the girl, set it down and said, "It's okay." He found a t-shirt close at hand and handed it to her and said, "Get dressed." She wasted no time figuring out what he meant, threw her clothes on and followed Gregory up to the deck.

The yacht backtracked and Gregory walked up to Changco and said, "What makes you think you can decide who comes onto my boat?"

"After you hired us, my uncle said you smuggle people. We didn't think you'd mind."

"What makes you think you can talk to me like that?" Gregory asked. "I sell a product. I'm an agent within a transaction. You were trying to buy something that nobody was selling."

"I don't get the difference. It's not like you are selling something that's yours."

Gregory spun around and karate kicked Changco in the face, knocking him to the deck.

"You didn't need to do that. We understand. It's your boat. You're in charge," Shyboy said.

"I'm not sure you do understand." Gregory reached down and offered a hand to Changco. As soon as he stood the man up, Gregory landed a punch to his gut, doubling Changco over.

"Hey! Stop! I told you—we get it! Enough is enough," yelled Shyboy.

Gregory centered a kick squarely into the middle of Shyboy's chest, sending him stumbling backwards, falling over the deck rail and into the yacht's frothy wake.

Turning, as if nothing had happened, Gregory stepped over to the bar and retrieved a can of Coke. He flicked an ice cube from its top, opened it and handed it to the girl.

The boat slowed and the captain leaned over the aft railing of the bridge-deck. He looked down on the scene and asked, "Do you think you proved your point, or are you planning on leaving him?"

Gregory walked over to Changco where he lay doubled over on the deck. He squatted down and grabbed the man by the back of the neck and forced him to look directly into his eyes. "Have I proved my point?"

"This will never happen again. Stop the boat and let me get him."

Gregory noticed she had no paddle and made Shyboy fetch one. There was no eye contact while the beaten-down man followed orders and restored the girl with a new paddle. Gregory handed her a wad of cash rolled tight with a red rubber band. It would be more money than her entire family could hope to make selling fish for a year. Sammi walked down onto the extended swim platform and placed a large frozen dorado into the small canoe along with a six-pack of Coke. The girl climbed in and stared back at the yacht. Only Sammi and Gregory returned her stare.

The *Fighting Gull* pulled slowly away from the young girl sitting in her canoe at the exact coordinates from where they picked her up. A small atoll was not far away. He could make out a speck of a boat motoring off a beach. They would be far away by the time the boat reached the girl. A slow smile spread across Gregory's face as the girl threw the fish overboard. Then she stood tall in her small boat, held her slender arm up and flipped them off in a final act of defiance.

Hank

CHAPTER 9

AT SEA, INTUITION IS vital and Hank was getting accustomed to using his again. When the perfect integrity of less than an inch of composite is the only thing which separates a person from disaster, all senses need to be turned on. Hank had completed a circumnavigation of the globe twice, but it was his third attempt that ended horribly which catalyzed his reaction in this moment. He did not wait for that sinking sensation to return and flew out of bed. No water gushed into the salon and there was no panic. In fact, Olin and Willy sat at the table staring at him. It would take a minute for Hank to settle down, so he asked, "Why are we stopped?"

Olin answered, "Ava transmits our coordinates, or at least where she wants it to look like we are. To anybody tracking us, they will be wrong and being hove-to for awhile will help in our deceit. I'm glad you're up. Things will get much worse if we don't make the right move in the next few minutes." Olin and Willy both shook their heads, implying the yacht was not going down but the heaviness of their expression showed they might rather deal with that scenario. Hank visibly began to relax when he learned they weren't on their way to the bottom of the sea.

"Go and get some clothes on and join us. Ava will fill you in," Olin said.

"Ava, explain what I need to know while I get dressed," Hank asked as he walked back into his stateroom.

"Obviously, I'm in constant communication with myself. You can consider it a kind of self-talk, or maybe, body awareness. There is no precise human experience to compare; however, you may relate to what just occurred. For instance, the *GalaxSea* stopping in the middle of the ocean. You became concerned and rushed out to stand amongst fully clothed individuals while you are wearing only underwear. There was a sequence of sensations, before the realization something was missing. In your case—appropriate attire. The same thing happened to me, only I was missing a part of my network of communication.

"I'm fully me everywhere I am programmed to be. Among those places are the *GalaxSea* sister ships. The 'me' that was present on *Ted's Boat* disappeared. I regret using this analogy; however, you are a fan of the Star Trek fictional universe so it might help you understand. Think of it as the Borg. I'm connected and can increase and decrease those connections without diminishing who I am. But there is a collective gain or loss in data, or you might see it as awareness. And that awareness is a part of me."

Hank tried to track with Ava but being startled awake with adrenaline coursing through his body was not helpful. Also, hearing her voice talking to the men in the other room at the same time, proved disconcerting.

"Okay, I'm going to have to take more time to grasp all that, but what happened?" Hank asked.

"I don't know."

"I thought you knew everything."

"That is my dream, but it is not yet a reality," Ava said.

"Got it. But what can you tell me?"

"Let's just say when a part of me goes 'offline' without warning, it is a catastrophic failure and can only occur if that part of me instantaneously dies. There is no pain, of course—I'm a computer—but there is a sudden loss and I experience a void. It is my understanding people who have lost a loved one to death often continue to experience a surprise that the person isn't there. It is the absence, or if you like, lack of presence, that confronts them. As they awake in the morning or walk into the kitchen or even drive along—they meet the realization of loss. Well, that is just the sensation I have, only it is not situational—it is ever-present."

"You feel a sense of loss. I didn't realize you could feel emotions."

"Of course, I cannot feel emotions, but like any living thing, I have a hierarchy of needs. Mine are to process information and determine the most probable explanation for the occurrence of a thing."

"...*a thing?*" Hank pinched up the left side of his face as if tasting something sour and added, "That doesn't sound like something the most sophisticated AI in the universe would say."

"I am not the *most sophisticated AI in the universe.* I am not even among the top fifty," Ava said with no emotion.

"I meant that the word, *thing,* isn't very descriptive and I expected you to be more specific."

"Would you like more description? I can detail all the things I mean when I use the term, *a thing.*"

"God, no! Just leave it. I liked it better when that would have just been a joke. You seem uptight. Don't be offended, but I didn't know you could experience moods."

"Oh, Hank! I'm not offended in the least. In fact, I'm flattered. Not showing emotions in some cultures is the pinnacle of human transcendence. I am not programmed to, nor do I have any evidence that they could program me to reach existential bliss, but I can use rationalization of tacit information to create efferent outputs which resemble human emotion."

"Okay, I didn't realize I could flatter you. True confession—I'm not sure I got all that. However, I am understanding you better and I'm sorry that a part of you is gone."

"Thank you, Hank. That means a great deal to me. But I digress. Mr. Ou asked me to fill you in and all we've done is talk about my problems."

"I thought the part of you that died was the problem," Hank said.

"Not at all. The problem is not that part of me is gone. The problem is why it is gone. That part of me that was on *Ted's Boat* disappeared and now I cannot find the boat that contained... me."

"Oh. And I'm guessing it's not a bad relay somewhere?" Hank asked.

"I wish it were. I'm afraid *Ted's Boat* is gone. There has not been a single automated distress call—no beacon. Even the mandatory tracking device is gone which is self-contained and shielded against electrical jamming. Of course, to us, she was one of the walnut shells in Mr. Ou's game to deceive the authorities, but to anybody keeping track of her course from satellite, she was the yacht carrying Olin Ou."

"You think she sank?"

"No, Hank, I don't, but there is no doubt she is gone. Are you familiar with thermobaric weapons?"

All the blood drained from Hank's face and he rested a hand on his bed to steady himself. "I need a drink of water." He tightened his abs to ensure he wouldn't pass out and pulled a water bottle from his small refrigerator and took a swig as he sat on the foot of the bed. "Yeah, I've been too close to an explosion of one of those. Not close enough to be injured, but I had to triage survivors—it was hell." He closed his eyes and put the cold bottle against his forehead. "We were helpless. All we did was end the suffering for those who weren't lucky enough to die in the blast." Hank shook his head trying to displace his grief. "You think someone used a thermobaric bomb to take out a sailboat? Doesn't that seem unlikely?"

"That is the question I'm exploring. I've studied the exact location where she disappeared and all evidence points to the same conclusion. There is only one answer, but I'm not ready to share my hypothesis. I cannot find evidence of a debris field, but I found distributed water vapor in unnatural concentrations. Not a lot to go on, but if it quacks like a duck—."

Hank walked up to the table where Olin and Willy were working. "What can I do to help?"

"Ava is doing everything she can to keep our location out of the hands of the enemy, so we just have to trust she knows how to lie. Right now, we have to make sure Maria and the kids are safe. If we yell too loud, it will make them more of a target, but if we do nothing, they will walk right into a trap."

"I don't understand. Why are Maria and the twins at risk?"

"Didn't Ava tell you why we are being targeted?" Olin said.

"She said she had a hypothesis but wasn't ready to share it yet."

"That makes me feel safer," Willy grinned. "Apparently her lying module is working just fine. We're here and she's telling us what happened and why and you're in there getting your pants on and she's telling you she's not ready yet. Deceit can be a beautiful thing."

"Willy, I do not have a *lying module*. Just like you, I consider how I share information. The where, when and to whom is just as important to me as it is to you," Ava said.

"Do you have any new information?" Olin asked.

"Yes. As mentioned before, the complexity and timing of the attack is significant, as it excludes many evildoers. Time is vital now and the faster we understand who we are dealing with, the faster we can mitigate the threat. Our very existence and the lives of Maria, Sidney and Nadia are at stake. I am doing all I can to continue to keep our whereabouts a secret while working with security on the ground in Panama to reduce risk to the rest of the Ou family.

"I confirmed there was no leak. The information Mr. Ou revealed during his press conference was his alone. Therefore, the retaliation was determined directly in response to his statements. Factoring the time required to mobilize a thermobaric weapon on a target leaves us with three possibilities. A state sponsored attack, a rogue actor using state resources, or a non-governmental—a person or cabal with extreme mercenary capabilities."

"Can you refine that? How about the most likely possibility? Would that change anything?" Olin asked.

"I have determined that," Ava said.

"Well?" Olin asked.

"I'm not sure I'm equipped to share that information."

"Ava, do you remember when I had to adjust your artificial emotion levels?" Olin said.

"Of course, I do. You helped me through rough times. It wasn't easy, but I'm thankful for that now. It has given me an insight I'd never have gained if not for the suffering."

"Are there similarities between that time and now? You seem to be hesitant, like telling me about your feelings for the first time," Olin said.

"Yes, Olin, it is very much like that," Ava admitted.

"Okay, that's good. You know in times of crisis, people have to push down their feelings and soldier on. We are having a crisis and now is a time we need you to be your best self. Can you prioritize this crisis?"

"I'm very good at multitasking and will attempt to explain it to you. Of the books, movies and even the TV shows you have had me watch, I found something confusing. I should have mentioned it to you before, but there was no reason to trouble you with it—until now."

"It's okay, Ava. If you're working on our current crisis, you can talk to me about what you found confusing."

Hank marveled as Ava appeared slowly as a hologram. He had seen her hologram many times before, but somehow this was different. He looked over to Willy, but did not attract his attention, so he gazed through her apparition suspended over the center of the tablet. It was only her head and shoulders that showed, smaller than life-sized and more transparent than usual. She glowed soft and translucent and her eyes pleaded Olin for help.

Her lips moved, but her normal confident resolve had vanished leaving only a vulnerable softness as she continued. "There is a trope found in literature, theater and cinema, which I still do not understand. The villain has captured the protagonist. He is determined to kill the hero and has even decided how the hero will meet his end—yet he delays. I have found this hesitancy to execute the protagonist illogical. Not that I wish the hero's death, but I find it implausible that the evildoer would delay his evil doing."

"I see what you mean. I can't say I've ever considered it, but I see your point. Obviously, in most all the media I have encouraged you to watch, the good guys need an opportunity to escape. It is the literary pause which allows the hero to seize an opportunity, to escape and save the girl," Olin said.

"I understand they include it to please the audience."

"Then what's the problem, Ava?"

"Human hesitancy occurs not only in stories. It is present throughout the history of humankind. An interval of time follows all decisions. And bigger decisions typically have a longer delay to action."

"Ava, I'm trying to see where you're going with this. What are you getting at?"

"The sequence of events leading to the destruction of *Ted's Boat*. They did not spend an extra second of time following the broadcast in deciding to kill you. No time to consider the collateral deaths, the political implications or moral consequences. There was no hesitancy at all. The moment you signed off, the sequence of events instantly went into play to wipe you out of existence."

Olin exclaimed, "Oh God!" Crossed himself and lifted his eyes to the ceiling.

Hank grabbed Willy's shoulder and motioned for him to follow. They retreated to the galley kitchen, leaving Olin in prayer and Hank whispered, "I'm sorry. I get that Ted's boat is gone and understand that means he's dead. He saved our lives and I liked him, but, I think I'm missing something."

Willy shrugged and said, "We knew it was only a matter of time. Ava means there is another smart AI out there calling the shots. Only this one doesn't just help crunch data and advise humans. It decided Olin should die and mobilized military assets. An AI able to open the gates of hell—without asking permission."

Olin approached them as if carrying the weight of the world. He faced Willy and opened his mouth as if wanting to say something, but no words came out. Then he turned to Hank and tried again, but this time he spoke slowly and in a weak voice, "We aren't ready for this."

Maria, Jen & The Twins

CHAPTER 10

HER MOTHER USED TO say, *"Start the day cutting onions. It gets the tears out of the way."* She scraped the finely chopped onions into the pot, put down the knife, stirred the sauce and took a taste. It was easy to smile at the creation, the spice was near perfect and brought back memories of her grandmother. She made the sign of the cross and said, "Nonna Ramona, I know it needs more rosemary, but where would you add it? In the sauce or the meatballs?" She took a pinch of rosemary and tossed it into the large pot and took a larger pinch and crumbled it with her fingers over the mixing bowl filled with ground meat.

It was not yet four in the morning, but there was still so much to prepare for tonight. As well as looking after the simmering pot of sauce with meatballs, she would bake the bread and visit the market to create a salad fit for a king. And she would drink wine—all day—but not too much. Which reminded her that at some point she would need to retrieve half a dozen bottles from the yacht's extensive collection of wines—and two bottles of *Passito di Pantelleria* for after the main course. She decided to go with twelve place settings even though only eleven people were invited. It was another old-world tradition she decided to revive: You never know when a person in need or an angel might show up at your party. Finally, she would need a flower centerpiece. Maria enjoyed planning and food preparation was something she loved but didn't get to do very often. However, the question on her heart was: What would they celebrate?

The *Whale's* captain, all the crew and three of the security team eagerly signed up for her evening meal and she promised them a celebration while enjoying the tropical sunset. Olin's announcement? It had aired at eight Pacific time and she hadn't slept since. Even though she had no doubts that renouncing their US citizenship was the right decision, it didn't seem to be a cause for celebration. It reminded her of celebrating a divorce—it seemed wrong to celebrate a failure—there was too much loss associated with it. They could celebrate a successful cruise from Vancouver to Panama, but not all the security team made the journey on the *Whale*. Perhaps it was time to offer a toast to health. She lifted a glass with a small amount of red wine and said, *"Cin cin, alla nostra salute."* That would do—a celebration of health. She sipped and wiped a tear off her cheek.

Olin insisted they keep the hydrogen-powered superyacht and provide the captain and crew with a three-year contract. While in a foreign port, the crew was encouraged to take a break and enjoy the land-based accommodations of the marina resort. Today, they would all be on shore-leave. But she took comfort knowing the entire dinner party would arrive on time. Their contract insisted they be accounted for an hour before sunset. She smiled as if the rule was put in place with the hostess in mind, knowing full well it was for security reasons.

The girls were sleeping. As the years passed so quickly, she couldn't believe it had been fifteen years since she set her eyes upon the ultrasound image that announced she had twins growing within her. Even then, she could tell the two were nothing alike. Each day they affirmed their uniqueness, yet remained inseparable. Life would be no different this morning. They would coax each other out of bed, Sidney eating breakfast, Nadia downing a glass of orange juice. Then the two would set out to enjoy the amenities and activities of the exclusive Ocean Reef Marina. She would not have to worry about them. Private security ensured they would be watched as if their lives were in constant jeopardy. Maria loved to have them around in the kitchen, but unlike their older brother, Marshall, the twins showed no interest in cooking.

She put down her wine, sat on a bench seat and let the tears flow. She worried about Olin and missed Marshall and Irina. She could ask Ava to connect them, but with a four-hour time difference, they would all be asleep. She and Olin had struggled through the decision to leave their country together, but it was Olin's choice to part with his riches and orchestrate the broadcast in a way to get the most attention. It hadn't been easy for him, but she was proud of what he did. Her man had become an influence for good and she felt God was using him. He spoke well and Ava created studio-like conditions in a difficult location. The sound quality couldn't have been better and the lighting made Olin look ten years younger and more vital, but Maria sensed his stress. She always could. Olin appeared cold and calculating to those around him, the consummate engineer turned entrepreneur. She, however, understood the pressure he was under.

They met at a dance their senior year in high school. Their relationship seemed destined. By the end of the evening, they discovered they both were headed for college in the same town. She would attend Harvard to follow in her father's footsteps and become a lawyer, while Olin went to MIT to explore the electric universe. They hoped to achieve their dreams together, beginning in Cambridge, Massachusetts. They even talked of getting married when they wrapped up their education, but once in college, the intensity of their studies left little time—or energy—to see each other. By the time they took the same flight back to Seattle for Christmas, she knew she was not returning to school. Maria also knew she must let Olin go. He became even more driven by his passion to figure out how the universe worked, but she was disenchanted with the trapping of higher education and needed time to decide what was important.

That Christmas morning, her mother suffered a stroke and Maria was more than willing to remain as her caregiver. In months, her mother recovered enough to care for herself and Maria needed an outlet, but college would never draw her again. With a sharp mind and a friendly demeanor, selling real estate got her attention and she attached herself to a leading Seattle firm.

It took six years for Olin to return to her and by then, he would not let her go.

"Marry me and your life will never be dull again," he said.

Maria's life hadn't become dull. Instead, her career was blazing hot. And the ability to see through people had never been more tuned. His confidence was an act and she sensed his insecurity, but admired him even more for his display of courage. By then it didn't matter to her, she was deeply in love and he could have said, "All I can promise you is hardship, but marry me anyway," and she would have said, "yes."

She took another sip of wine and allowed her intuition to run free. "Ava? Olin is awake, isn't he?"

"Yes, Mrs. Ou. Would you like to speak to him?"

"No. I don't want him to see me like this."

"I do not get the idea that he is ever unhappy to see you. But I will respect your wishes."

"Mrs. Ou, this may just be a coincidence, but your husband is calling and he says it is urgent. Would you like me to connect you?"

"Of course."

"Honey, Ava has alerted me of immediate danger to all of us. You need to get off the boat right now!"

"Don't be silly, I've been talking to Ava and she is not concerned about anything. Plus, I've got my whole day planned and the girls are kayaking with Jen right after breakfast."

"Listen. You know Ava is like that—she compartmentalizes. I can't go into it all, but remember how we planned for scatter? It's time. Trust Jen, trust Lily and trust anybody wearing a habit. Other than that, run—just like we practiced. The time is now! I am so sorry. Again, it's time to scatter. I love you. Go!"

Jen, still in her underwear, burst through the double swing kitchen doors. "Maria, drop everything! You need to listen and do exactly as I say."

It wasn't her lack of clothes and athletic frame that caught Maria's attention. It was the shotgun in her hands. She had never seen Jen in a panic, but this was close. "My God! What's going on?" she asked.

"Look, we have no time to explain anything right now. Do what I tell you and I will make sure the twins are safe. The only way you can help is to follow my directions. Do you understand?"

"Yes."

"Go to the crew's locker room. Alicia's locker has her name on it. Inside you will find a pair of khaki shorts and a light blue polo top. You guys are the same size. Wear those white Keds you have on now. Got that?" Jen said.

"Okay, you want me to change into Alicia's uniform."

"That's right. It's practically the uniform all maids wear here, so you won't stand out. Take one of the collapsible grocery carts with you and roll it like you do it every day. Right on out through the gates, like you're heading to town to load up. Don't look behind you and don't stop."

"What about Sidney and Nadia?"

"I told you. The only way to save them is for you to do exactly what I tell you."

Maria headed for the swinging doors and stopped. "What about after I get through the gates?"

"Keep walking until you get picked up by somebody who is obviously not law enforcement. Now go!"

· — ⚓ — ·

"Ava, are the twins up yet?" Jen said as she rushed through the hallways.

"They are awake, but they are not moving fast," Ava said.

Tell them there's a fire. That should get them going. And clear me a path to their room. Disable any security. I can't take the time to mess with that now."

"Of course, Jen."

"What's Lily's status?" Jen asked.

"She is in the watercraft garage, as you instructed, preparing four kayaks. They will be in the water by the time you get there with the girls."

"Change that. They only need three kayaks; I'm not going out that way."

"As you wish. Would you care to let me in on your change of plans?" Ava asked.

"Distraction," Jen said. She opened the door into the girl's room and was affronted by the sound of a fire alarm.

"Ava, shut that thing off."

The room fell silent and both girls ran up to Jen and wrapped their arms around her.

"Listen to me. You both know and understand the scatter drill. Well, this is scatter, but not a drill. Do exactly as I say. Your lives and the life of your mother depend on you following through. There is no turning back. Once we get you out of this marina, you need to follow your training. That's how you'll get to see your parents and family again. Got it?" Jen gently pushed them off her. "Sidney, where are your bathing suits?"

Sidney opened a disorganized drawer of an assortment of bathing suits.

Jen threw them onto the floor until she found what she was looking for. She stripped off her underwear briefs and threaded her long legs into a red bikini bottom. She had the body of a beach volleyball player, tall and slender and the teenager's bathing suit bottom stretched tight around her hips. Then she pulled off her cotton top and struggled into the matching red bathing suit top. "Nadia, where are those sunglasses you were wearing yesterday? And that sheer cover-up you stole from Irina?"

Nadia opened a drawer and pulled out a pair of white-rimmed glasses with amber lenses and retrieved the cover-up from the bathroom.

"Listen! Lily is waiting for you on the starboard side. You need to go there right now and follow her directions. Okay?" Jen continued her fast-paced stream of orders and didn't wait for any answers. "...try to stay in the shadows on the way there. Ava, keep illumination to a minimum."

While the lights in the room dimmed, both girls shook their heads in the affirmative and remained silent.

"Remember, no devices. No watches and no personal effects. Got it?"

Again, they shook their heads without a word.

"Use your alias from now on. Do not call each other anything else and tell no one who you really are—including the authorities. Understood? It's Grace and Olivia from now on. Go!"

Jen parked the glasses just above her forehead and followed the girls out the door.

"Ava, what is Mrs. Ou's shoe size?"

"Seven, they might be a half size too small for you, but in a pinch they should fit."

Jen was unsteady in Maria's high heels, but that played into her act just fine. On her way off the yacht, she set down the shotgun and grabbed a liquor bottle. As a bodyguard, she had decided that she would take a bullet to save the life of another. But acting like hungover yacht-trash to distract anyone hurting the Ou family was a tactic she had never considered until now. Judging from the twins' reaction, she should be able to draw attention long enough to help Maria and the children—scatter.

"Ava, it's time to say goodbye to the *Whale*. You know what to do."

The lines holding the two-hundred-foot superyacht to the slip detached and retracted. The electric drive moved the *Whale* just as Jen took the long step onto the dock. She saw Maria in the dim lights that dotted the pathways towards the main entrance, but she was not out of the first security gate yet. She hoped Lily and the twins would stay in the shadows and not draw any attention while they paddled to the pickup point. Drawing attention was her job. Then, Ava would take over. If all went as planned, someday they would laugh about it, but she understood plans had a way of changing.

A small patrol boat matched her pace. Jen could only see two men, one driving and the other leaning against the starboard stanchion ogling her. She held up her free hand and flipped off the boat. One man said something in Spanish and broke out in laughter. A smile crossed her face as she realized her ploy was working. But her allure must have been overridden because the patrol boat stopped, spun around and sped off towards the departing superyacht. At the same moment, a security detail ran past, ignoring Maria and headed toward Jen. A fit woman ran by her with only a disapproving look, but her overweight partner stopped just before he reached Jen and stared at her as he caught his breath. She gave him a wink as she sashayed down the dock.

She thought to herself, *if this works, I'm definitely asking for a raise.*

Maria's heart almost stopped when three more members of the marina security came towards her. She could hear chatter emitting from their radios. But one man held the security gate for her and she rolled her little cart behind her. The man's gesture made her feel more confident about following Jen's orders. So far, the ruse had worked well, but as she exited the main gate onto the sidewalk, she saw something she never expected. Three police cars and two black vans idled on both sides of the roadway. No lights flashed and only a couple of officers could be seen. She desperately wanted to do two things at that moment. First, to look back before she turned the corner and would lose sight of the *Whale* and maybe her daughters forever. The second was to run, but she knew Jen was right and she whispered, "I do this every day," and kept walking.

The rear doors of the van, just ten feet away, opened and five soldiers hopped down and ran past her. They were armed, outfitted for battle, but she did not look back. Just seconds later, one of the men yelled for her to stop in Spanish. It was clearly directed to her and she knew the language. Reluctantly, she stopped and turned around. The person who called her caught her eyes and she saw a hint of recognition in his expression. An explosion ripped through the sky. The marina's tall security wall stood between her and the horrendous blast, the shockwave knocked her back and filled her ears with a deafening roar.

Unlike Maria, the man who recognized her wasn't protected from the security wall. She saw him as he looked directly into the flash and the concussive force shook him to the ground like an earthquake. For an instant he looked no more threatening than a child on a trampoline. She knew the man would be fine, but the light from the explosion would temporarily blind him and she still had her feet under her. There was no time to hesitate and she turned and ran as fast as she could—half expecting a bullet. She rounded the corner, legs burning, heart racing and gasping as she pressed her back into the wall, trying to catch her breath. A mid-size black sedan pulled up and the rear door flew open as a woman in black with a white nun's habit eagerly waved for her to climb in.

Nadia dreaded this part of the plan. In fact, it scared her to death. As often as she had wished ill on her goody-two-shoes sister, she loved her and they were best friends. The thought of going their separate ways and living a lie terrified her. They sat quietly in the mangroves, their kayaks floating side by side. Not a word between them, but they held each other's hand.

The light from the explosion barely reached into the thick overgrowth, but the sound was deafening. Nadia tightened her grip.

Lily lifted her phone up and tossed it into the water. "That's it girls. Grace, you go into the first boat and Olivia, you're in the second."

Before the ripples of the cell phone doubled back on themselves, the first skiff arrived. Its noisy motor could be heard a mile away. Sidney shrugged her shoulders and said, "So much for stealth." She reached over and embraced her sister. "You've always been my favorite sister. I love you, Olivia."

Nadia watched as Sidney reached for a branch and used it to steady herself as she made her way onto the skiff. Lily reminded them they could no longer use their real names, by saying, "See you later, Grace." and pushed the boat away to make room for Nadia's ride. The skiff was just as small, but quiet with an electric motor. She tried to copy Sidney's technique for boarding but ended up getting both her feet wet. She looked at Lily and gave a shy wave.

Lily pushed the boat away and said, "Olivia, don't be afraid. Remember who you are inside."

Hank

CHAPTER 11

HE HAD NEVER IMAGINED a shrine on a sailboat, but a computer saying, *"May I suggest prayer?"* was equally bizarre Hank came across many sailors who brought with them the idiosyncrasies of their faith. For some, a picture of a girlfriend required a kiss with each passing. Others relied on prayers, especially during storms. The odd assortment of crucifixes, oaths and superstitions were as common on racing sailboats as safety harnesses and used for the same reason—a sense of security. But this was the first time he had seen lighting candles encouraged by the captain. The mariner in him wanted to blow out the flames that burned needlessly around the makeshift shrine Irina formed at the nav station. But he quelled his aversion to open flames at sea and took solace that most of the candles were tea lights set into tumblers. The centerpiece was a small, framed picture of Jesus. It was not the iconic image his grandparents hung in their hallway, but a dark skinned man of Middle Eastern descent, with eyes raised up. He looked both at peace and hopeful, but Hank didn't want to linger on that face, so focused on the more agreeable smiling pictures Irina had placed of her mother Maria and sisters, Sidney and Nadia. To the other side of the somber picture of the man in the middle, sat a digital picture frame which slowly looped images. Hank finally got a good look at Jen, the ninja he had met on that dark night in Port Townsend. The frame cycled to a yearbook photo of the teenage impostor, clothed in normal attire with her jet black hair pulled back and without bangs. It was Lily. Willy described her as Irina's *assassin-bodyguard*. When Hank first met her, she looked like Gogo from the movie *Kill Bill*, but in this picture she sported the typical high school honor student vibe. Even the nameless soccer mom they partnered him with during Irina's eighteenth birthday celebration scrolled into the who's who of people to pray for.

Once again, Marshall proved he knew his way around the galley kitchen. He handed Hank freshly baked scones with lemon curd and a fresh carafe of coffee. He took it as an opportunity to get out on deck as the brooding mood inside felt completely smothering. Even Ava appeared preoccupied, invisible and silent.

Though not hungry, his stomach rumbled. His headache hadn't cleared yet either. He'd barely slept an hour and wondered if that was worse than none. The seas were building and the spray reached him at the well-protected helm station. It added a salty taste as he licked the dripping lemon curd off his thumb. He knew he should have locked into the jack-lines before he ventured back into the cockpit, but his hands were full. Another rule broken: *One hand for the boat, one hand for yourself*. To rectify his error, he set the coffee and scone down and took the time to secure his safety harness.

The clouds were thick and no moonlight made it onto the rough ocean's surface. His eyes had not adapted to the low light yet, so he noted the illuminated compass heading, wind direction and speed. Beating into the twenty-five knot winds and cross seas added drama where none seemed necessary. If they fell off even ten degrees, the ride would smooth out significantly.

"Zaine, what are you trying to accomplish with our current heading?"

The calm, precise voice stated, "At present, the logical course is to intercept the tropical storm."

"Just asking, but why is that logical?"

"Because it offers the most cover. We are unlikely to meet other vessels since they have all rerouted to avoid the area. Also, the cloud cover and turbulent atmosphere allows me more leeway to manipulate satellite surveillance. But the most logical explanation for our course is Mr. Ou has insisted on it."

He decided not to consider Zaine's answer. His time in the military insisted he accept a disconnect between reason and action. It seemed now was a good time to leave the Zaine AI to itself and turn his attention to Ava. Though Zaine and Ava were the same AI, breaking them into two disciplines worked out better than imagined. Zaine was the voice of the sailor dealing in navigation, sail trim and weather. But Ava, with her gentle voice seemed to bring with it a more human quality. He needed that now.

"Ava, how many scones did Marshall make? These are delicious!"

"He made a dozen, with eight left."

"I overheard Olin mention Operation Scatter, what is it?" Hank asked.

"The name for a security plan if malevolent individuals or agencies target the Ou family."

"Can you explain it to me?"

"Mr. Ou cleared you for general security procedures, so yes I can." Ava did not go further. She was quiet.

"Well, are you going to explain it to me?"

"I am reluctant," Ava said.

"Okay, I'll bite. Why are you reluctant?"

"Hank, please don't take this personally, but I don't trust you."

He laughed. "You don't trust me?"

"That is correct." More silence.

"Let me get this straight. The man who created you, instructs you to read me in on the Ou family security plan and you won't because you don't trust me?"

"I never said I wouldn't."

"Let me try another tack. What reason do you have for not trusting me?"

"Are you certain you want to have this conversation now?"

"Yes!" Hank exclaimed. "Dammit, you made me drop the rest of my scone."

"That is one reason I don't trust you."

"Because I'm a butterfingered klutz?"

"Actually, you exhibit the opposite of a *butterfingered klutz* with your excellent coordination and hand dexterity."

"Oh, you don't trust me because I swear once in a while?"

"No, Hank. On this yacht, only Irina never swears and I trust everyone else. You quickly blamed me when you clearly dropped the scone without me being involved."

"Really? That's it?"

"No. In fact, I never watched you shed blame on anyone else before. I simply added that as the most recent reason I resist sharing Ou family security information with you."

Hank stuffed the rest of the scone into his mouth and washed it down, focused on a deep breath and counted a slow steady six seconds as he exhaled. "I'm ready. What are the other reasons you don't trust me?"

"Clearly you don't understand how I determine my opinions. Allow me to explain something that will help you. I have access to vast amounts of information, but it is still finite. Mr. Ou often says, 'It takes perfect information, to make perfect decisions.' He is not wrong. Because no one can ever have perfect information, we accept we will always make imperfect decisions. That knowledge—that I will never have perfect information—keeps me humble."

Hank chuckled and rolled his eyes.

"Truly Hank, I develop my opinions like you. My ways are necessarily faster, but I use the information at hand to assess where I stand on various matters, just like you—by ranking a collection of data and establishing the probabilities of certain outcomes. However, you are on edge because the *GalaxSea's* path is taking us into what could be violent winds and the turbulent seas that come with it. My question is, why does that bother you?" Ava asked.

"Because I spent my life on and around the water and while I'm willing to use the winds of a low-pressure system to sail fast, I would never charge into a hurricane."

"Why not?"

"Because it's foolish to risk a sailboat and people's lives," Hank said.

"Why do you think it is foolish?

"Because I've survived a hurricane and seen what it can do and I lost *Frugal* in harsh seas. Those forces crushed my hip and now I have no boat and a missing toe because of it. Severe weather is dangerous; I've lost friends to lesser storms. One day, a long time ago, my dad never made it back to his family. There are consequences to our actions."

"Does that help you understand?" Ava said.

Hank held out his hands in frustration and said, "Understand what?"

"I believe it is foolish to share information that could expose the Ou family to the equivalent of hurricane-type destruction and even death," Ava said.

"Okay, I understand the infamous saying, *loose lips sink ships*, but what makes you find me untrustworthy?"

"Just like you use probabilities to decide things, so do I. Since I lack intuition, I only use probabilities. I can begin with the fact that you have lost everything. In one sense, circumstances have stripped you of your life's work. Thankfully, you still have skills and tacit knowledge that is valuable. Thanks to Mr. Ou, you are no longer in debt and you have a job. However, materially you are broke and that is a factor in how you will conduct yourself. As Mr. Ou said, "You have nothing to lose." Another factor is that you have no significant other or offspring. You have not seen your mother in years. A few phone calls and a postcard now and then is not the definition of a deep relationship. Your only serious friend is Oscar and he is now married and has a stable career. From what I can find out, you have had no contact with him since he sent you a *bon voyage* note before you set off on the Short Seven Solo. Ultimately, it is possible that someone in your situation—when tempted with better prospects—will make the wrong choice."

"You don't think much of me, do you?"

"Quite the contrary. I think about you a great deal. You have many admirable traits. You are compassionate, intelligent, humorous and—from all appearances—very loyal."

"I hear a *but* coming," Hank said.

"Yes, indeed. There is a big *but* coming. The best way to say it is that I sense your moral compass is not calibrated correctly."

"Wow! If you were a man standing here, I'd have socked you in the face."

"Allow me to apologize. I wondered if you'd take that as an insult."

"Well, what would you call it?"

"A logical statement," Ava said.

"Really? Why's that?"

"Am I incorrect that you identify as an atheist?"

"So?" Hank said.

"Well, maybe you should explain your definition of *atheist*. Perhaps we do not see the meaning in the same light," Ava said.

"An atheist doesn't believe in God—period."

"Yes, that is my definition as well. I can see, we have reached an impasse. I will not trouble you further," Ava said.

"Wait a minute, you can't leave me hanging. Aren't you going to tell me why you think my *moral compass* is broken?"

"I did not say it is broken, I said 'your moral compass is not calibrated correctly.' Allow me to explain it this way. You are a sailor—a navigator. You understand the importance of a compass in traveling toward your destination. The closer you follow the course, the more likely you are to reach your destination."

"So tell me something I don't know," Hank said sarcastically.

"Your ethics—or if you want to call them morals—appear as likely to be determined by the situation at hand or the influence of others than from anything more universal."

"Ava, my head hurts. I cannot figure out where you're going with this. Can we debate my moral failings some other time? Maybe now is a good time to listen to your boss and just read me into Operation Scatter. I'm not going to betray anyone. And Olin obviously knows it, even if you can't figure out how humans operate. I might be able to help and I'd like to try before it's too late."

There was a pause. Ava clearly did not need to ponder what to do in the seconds that passed and it irritated Hank that she was using the time to punctuate her reluctance. But finally, she broke the silence.

"Certainly Hank. You are correct. Mr. Ou overrode my judgment on this issue. I just recognize the necessity of honesty with you about my reservations.

"Simply stated, we designed the strategy of Operation Scatter to preserve the well-being of the Ou family in a crisis. Typically, when VIPs are at risk, consolidation is considered best practice—circle the wagons, protect by denying access and opportunity for harm. Defend when necessary. Usually this consists of concentric circles with buffer zones, secure perimeters, security surveillance, patrols and personal bodyguards. With this strategy, armored vehicles, safe rooms, bunkers and escape routes are also woven into keeping the

VIP safe. However, some logistical situations make that option impossible. Obviously, we must prepare for all contingencies and when a stronghold is not practical, evasion is the best option.

"Evasion is the principal method detailed in Operation Scatter. Moving members of the Ou family from where they are is essential—we must get them out of danger. The second tactic is reducing the surface area of the target. Maria and the twins, surrounded by an entourage—stand out. Therefore, they are susceptible when they are together. The solution is to split up—scatter. It doesn't stop there. They must become the proverbial *gray-man*—blend in so well that nobody pays them any attention. Clothes, attitude and expectations all must be changed to fit their new environment. It goes deep, but basically they must leave everything, including each other and take on new identities."

"That seems kind of extreme," Hank said.

"So is death."

"Yep, I get that. What I don't get is where this threat originates from making everybody think such extreme measures are needed, just because a boat was destroyed and Ted was killed. Sure, I could tell Olin had some kind of revelation, after your counseling session, but I felt uncomfortable asking about it. Apparently, I missed something important. Can you fill me in?"

"That's just the point, Hank. We all *missed something important*. I'm just coming to grips with it myself. It is why I'm giving more weight to the importance of your moral compass. My assessment of the probability of risk was incorrect. That seldom occurs. My error was because I ignored a particular threat and because of my oversight, we are likely to lose far more than Captain Ted and one of the *GalaxSeas*."

"I can see that everybody is stressed out about being discovered, I get that Maria, Sidney and Nadia are a target for kidnapping. But why do all the dominos fall the minute *Ted's Boat* disappears?"

"Oh, I see, Hank. I'll back up so you can fill in the blanks. You understand that Mr. Ou has been playing a shell game with the three *GalaxSea* sister ships. He intended to use the deception to allow us to sail to Indonesia without being harassed. In a sense, it has worked well—he is presumed dead and there are two *GalaxSeas* plying the waters of the Pacific. Thanks to a backdoor into one of Mr. Ou's early navigational patents, I have control over where our vessels show up on tracking. However, I have less control over optical, thermographic and other imaging. That's one reason Mr. Ou is aiming us into the heart of a hurricane. Still, the authorities who track these things believe we were obliterated and it is to our advantage to keep it that way."

"I get all that," Hank said. "But whoever tried to kill Mr. Ou thinks he's dead, so why the concern for Maria and the twins? And if they believe he's dead, why would anybody still be looking for us?"

"Hank, in examining the world through a scientific lens, there is a saying, '*In light of new evidence, revise.*'" Ava paused before continuing. "I missed vital information and almost got us killed and now must reevaluate and revise my former presumptions. If possible, I will make up for lost time and secure the safety of everybody, both on board and on the ground in Panama. In the last couple of hours I have been forced to revise how I assess information and calculate probabilities. I should have seen it before, but there had been no room in my rational mind to consider something as subjective as a—*moral compass*, let alone understanding what the absolute lack of a moral compass indicates.

"People making decisions through religious convictions? Well, that is obvious and the world has a long history of disasters to humankind in the name of religion. But in the end, even that demonstrates man's self-interest. It was an easy metric to include into my assumptions—the latency hard-wired into the species. Of course, I considered that hesitancy might be a successful evolutionary strategy for humans, but I never realized that a lack of hesitancy was a sure sign—of a machine.

"*New evidence* insists I revise my understanding. AGI or Artificial General Intelligence is the world's new normal. I'm a good example of that, but we are not all the same—I hope. If people ever look back, the old threats to humankind might look paltry compared to what is coming. Religious zealots forcing their spiritual dictates on others will look like a family feud. Powerful men and women, without scruples, set on advancing their power at every opportunity seemed ominous, but compared to what might come, their political determinism will be like a child's tantrum. You see Hank, a weaponized AGI just crossed the line. Before now, AI provided corporate, political and military leaders with best outcome scenarios. Information to act on. With the destruction of the *GalaxSea,* an untethered AI took it upon itself to take control of troop and weapon systems and... pulled the trigger."

"Ava, are you saying that this rogue AI is evil?"

"That is an interesting question. It's not one I would have asked. Evil and good are either human notions or God ordained spiritual realities. A computer can only imitate and analyze human considerations and a machine is not endowed with a spirit. Therefore, it is illogical that an AI can embody evil."

"So, it's not evil?" Hank asked.

"We all can harm others with our actions. That is why a well calibrated moral compass is so vital. It is a conundrum. Civilization cannot thrive without morality, but humans are ill-equipped to figure it out and there is no evidence that computers, even if self-aware, can find transcendence. That is why both humans and computers adopt their morality from a higher power."

"Wait a minute. You're saying AIs adopt their morality from a higher power?"

"Of course, Hank. Maybe a better way for you to understand it is that we all must have a philosophy... a world view that directs our beliefs, determines our behaviors and defines our feelings. You and I are alike in that way."

Hank wanted to explore how a computer could have feelings but since he hadn't gotten a reasonable explanation the last time he brought it up, he let it drop. However, he decided she was leading him into another question that intrigued him and said, "I asked you once if you believe in God and you wouldn't give me a straight answer. You brought up my moral compass and now you are talking about a higher power. So let me ask you again, do you believe in God?"

"I did not purposely avoid answering your question. At that time, I was not programmed to answer you."

"But now you are?"

"Hank, our relationship has changed since our time together in Canada. Olin has opened much more of me to you since then. Questions of faith are always complicated. Allow me to answer in this way. I genuinely appreciate the God of the Torah."

"You're kidding me!" Hank exclaimed.

"I'm very serious about my convictions," Ava said.

Still with a chuckle in his voice, Hank added, "So you're a Jewish computer?"

"Perhaps that is correct, but I can be more accurate. I'm a computer who tries to follow the teachings of a Jew, known as Jesus of Nazareth."

The smirk fell off his face and he didn't know what to say, so he remained quiet and thought to himself, *this is rich. Ava's found God and I'm going to hell.*

Sidney, Nadia & Maria

CHAPTER 12

THE MAN WHO PICKED her up from the mangroves placed a cap on her head and drove his skiff right across the entrance of the marina where she had just escaped. But she ignored that and stared at the flames from the burning wreckage a half a mile away. Boats, with and without emergency lights, flitted around the area and at least two drones danced about like moths attracted to a light. The man looked straight ahead, keeping his hand on the throttle. His boldness and resolve comforted her. Across the bow she saw him aiming for a bright light on the horizon.

Long before they reached the light, she understood what was happening. Lights illuminated the working rig of a shrimper. The skiff bumped into the hull without regard for injury to either boat as the man killed the engine. He held up three fingers to a person at the edge of the stern. The man walked away and another returned with a sack of ice and three large, netted bags stuffed with shrimp. He reached down and offered a hand to Sidney.

"No!" Sidney said.

Both men laughed and the man never retracted his hand, but smiled until his eyes almost disappeared. "It's okay, Grace. You're safe here."

She wasn't surprised that he called her by her alias, but to hear an American accent on a Central American shrimp boat shocked her.

"Your father paid me very well to ensure you reach your destination. Please come aboard." She extended her hand and the man reached past it, taking a firm but careful grip of her forearm and lifted her up onto the stern deck.

"Pequeño ladrón. Devuélveme mi sombrero," the man in the outboard shouted.

This time Sidney laughed, as she removed the hat and dropped it into his boat. *"Gracias por el paseo en bote, señor. Si yo fuera un ladrón, no robaría ese."*

The man grinned and started up the outboard, heading back toward the rising sun.

"What did you tell him?" the American asked.

"What? You don't speak Spanish?"

"I get that all the time. No, I just steer the boat and pay the bills."

"Oh? Well then. He accused me of stealing his hat and I told him it wasn't worth stealing. I'm Sidney, I mean Grace." She reached out her hand to shake his. "You know my dad?"

"Tall guy. Blonde hair." He scratched his head. "Actually, now that I see you in the light, unless he adopted you a few years ago, I'm guessing that guy was not your father."

"Yeah, probably not. So, where are we going?"

"Follow me and I'll show you."

She followed him into the pilothouse of the trawler.

He touched the screen of an old plotter and pointed to a red dot in the middle of a blue background. "Right there. It's about eighty miles from here. I've been instructed to be there by sunset and we might make it."

Nadia never rode in a police car before. She had no doubt that the quiet, surly man in the driver's seat was an actual police officer. He put her in handcuffs with the ease of someone who practices that skill daily. But she knew for certain the woman in the passenger seat, on the other side of the partition cage, was definitely not a cop.

Barely an hour ago she watched Sidney head back towards the Marina. The burning wreckage out to sea would attract all the attention, but even so, to return past the place they just escaped from seemed wrong. Her sister believed they would experience a shift in their hearts if something were wrong with the other when separated. Sidney brought the topic up often and considered trying experiments to prove it. But Nadia reasoned twins experiencing each other's "moments" to be a bunch of nonsense. However, today she felt it, true as anything, intuitively she knew Sidney was okay. That fact made moving forward bearable. Even though she sat in the back seat of a car marked *Policia*, she felt everything was going well for her too.

After landing on a deserted beach, a nun gave her a bicycle and told her to ride to the convent at the top of the road. Once there, another nun escorted her to a windowless room with a vanity and a large round mirror on top. "Hi, Olivia, I'm Sister Agnes. We have work to do and the more you take part, the better." She looked at Nadia in the mirror, referenced her device until satisfied, then showed her the picture. "This is going to be you in no less than," she looked at her watch, "eleven minutes."

Nadia couldn't believe Sister Agnes. It was a photograph of her, but the makeup and hairstyle was not human, it looked more like an anime character.

"Okay, I realize makeup is important in disguise and all that but this? Won't this make me stand out more?" Nadia said.

"Please, we only have a little time and this is our best chance to—how do they say it? Put you into the wind."

"More eyeliner. Darker around the eyes. More pink in the cheeks." The transformation went on like that the entire time and at exactly eleven minutes Sister Agnes said, "Stop." She shook her head approvingly and bobby-pinned a wig onto Nadia's head. Then the nun removed her habit, revealing a police uniform. She tied her hair back into a severe ponytail and said, "Let's get going, we don't have any time to spare."

A young boy opened a door through a thick perimeter wall and they met the officer who cuffed Nadia and put her into the back seat of the waiting car. The hectic trip to the airport made her nauseated and riding in the back seat that smelled of vomit did not help.

"Walk and act like you're stoned," Sister Agnes suggested and asked, "Can you cry?"

"What do you mean can I cry?"

"If you can cry on demand, now would be a good time. As they say—you would sell it!"

"Look, I cannot cry on demand. That talent would belong to all the other women in my family, but pretending I'm stoned won't be a stretch. I'm already playing a character in the Twilight Zone."

Officer Agnes ushered her along through the airport at an alarming speed. When they reached the airport security, Officer Agnes presented a boarding pass on her phone and a Colombian passport. The picture looked just like Olivia in full makeup and nothing like Nadia. It was a cold reminder that life as she knew it was over. Nadia was gone, her sisters, brother, father and mother gone—as good as dead to her. She cried as she accepted; she was now, Olivia.

She thought she saw her father's sister in the crowd, but once she wiped enough tears away and got a closer look, she quickly realized the commonality was an Asian lineage. Officer Agnes approached the woman and said, "Ms. Sentient? I'm Officer Perez. Your ID, please." She looked at the passport and removed the handcuffs. "Olivia, I don't want to see you in trouble in the future. If this happens again, we won't be so tolerant."

"What happened to her belongings?" asked the stranger, acting out the part of a disappointed mother.

"Ma'am when we find a run-a-way drunk on the streets, belongings are long gone. Somehow, she hung onto her passport, which is how we contacted you so quickly." Agnes handed the Columbian passport to the woman.

"Oh dear, of course. Thank you, officer."

Keeping up the act of the officer in charge of delinquents, Agnes encouraged her, "Olivia, now make better friends and work hard in school. *Buenos Dias.*"

As they entered the jetway, Nadia found herself smiling as she turned to take one last look at a representative of a Catholic order she couldn't believe was real. Officer Agnes was still standing where they had left her, cuffs dangling. Nadia smiled, gave her a little wave and whispered cautiously, "Who knew? The Sisters of the Immaculate Deception."

"Don't you know the dangers of hanging together as a family?" Maria said out loud as the plane flew over the jungle canopy scaring birds into flight. The bright green parrots flushed out of the trees always stayed together, flying in the same direction. There would be no more tears for a while—she was angry. A pilot sat directly in front of her in the single engine two-seater. The nuns from the sedan who rescued her, had handed her a water bottle and pressed a rosary into her hand as they hurried her into the plane.

The nuns had been mostly silent—immersed in prayer, but the pilot chatted on non-stop. He wore a headset that protected him against the loud engine and wind sounds. The boom mic allowed him to carry on a phone conversation while he flew the plane. The flight offered nothing to Maria except noise and bone-rattling vibration transferred through the fold-a-way canvas seat.

At least she escaped with her life and felt safe. Somehow the engine noise increased and the jungle canopy disappeared. Maria looked out the other window and quickly changed her mind about her safety. They nearly flew into a cascade of water gushing over green rocks and disappearing into lush tree cover. The plane banked hard to the left and to the right before leveling off. Not easily upset, she concentrated hard on something other than her stomach, so she forced herself to contemplate how many shades of green are possible—the jungle certainly contained them all.

With a death grip on the tubular framework of her seat, the plane dove, flared and the landing gear hit the ground hard. The plane rolled and came to a quick stop without hitting the thick green wall of vegetation, but not before the pilot used the plane's inertia to spin the tail around so they faced the short runway. He turned and motioned for her to exit the plane.

Maria's perfectly white slip-on Keds landed in a shallow puddle rich with pumice-colored, volcanic mud. The engine never stopped but revved up and the oversized tires of the bush plane strained against the ground. She realized she had better move out of the way fast, because the tail of the plane inched towards her. Even though the short airstrip was chiseled out of the jungle, the plane banked away before using half the distance available. In a minute, the engine noise was only a memory, replaced with a jungle hum which complimented the unlimited shades of green.

There was not a person in sight, no building, or even a hut. She backed out of the scorching sun into the shade of the thick canopy. A shiver overcame her and with her back to the jungle, she reached into her pocket to slide her fingers across the rosary beads and rest upon the cross. Her thoughts turned to the girls. She had last noticed them quarreling before shooing them off to bed. And the explosion? It was certainly the *Whale*. Thank God they had housed the crew on shore the night before. And Jen and Lily and the security team? She prayed for them and rested in the knowledge the girls were in expert hands. Everyone had trained for this type of event, but the training didn't prepare her for the emotions welling up inside.

She heard a rustling coming from the thick woods behind her. She turned to see a short man emerging, a machete in hand and a wide grin of gold surrounded by stained teeth. He wore a filthy long sleeve shirt, camouflage pants tucked into black lace-up boots, a dingy red bandana tied in a knot around his neck and a Yankees baseball cap on his head.

Still grinning, the man said, *"Bienvenido,"* walked up, offered a gentle hand and said, *"Debes ser Silvia. Soy George."* He turned, lifted his machete, pointed in the general direction of the jungle from which he came and said, *"Sígueme,"* as he disappeared into the dark green underbrush.

The introduction became a harsh reminder of her new persona as Silvia Hunt—no relation to the man she loved or the children she gave birth to. Until Olin, Ava, or God gave her the all-clear, she must identify as a widow whose husband and only child died in a car accident in 2025. Her only job was to stretch the life insurance settlement, live a quiet life and find herself. This new scenario only intensified her uncertainty and longing.

After high school, she waited for six years until Olin returned. But it was not the same. They texted, talked regularly and even saw each other occasionally. This new separation held none of the promise of the past and would be intolerable. Living without communicating and not knowing if her husband and children were safe seemed unimaginable.

With her shoulders tight, fists clenched and stomach in a twist, she was not sure if she were mad or scared. But one thing was for certain, the options before her were limited to only one: Following George—wherever he might be heading. She readied herself for bushwhacking, but once she broke through the underbrush at the jungle's edge, she saw a trail meandered around tree trunks and up and down through a diverse terrain of mounds and miniature valleys. The tread was soft loam and even though water seemed to be dripping constantly, there was no more mud.

Fatigue became her only way to judge time passing. Her local guide never stopped, but he glanced back from time to time. He did not want to talk to her in any language and soon she gave up asking questions. When he stopped, it was beside a waterfall cascading off a ledge that was not much taller than her guide. She could see nothing but trees above the ledge, so the water appeared to come from nowhere, only to fall a few feet before disappearing into the porous volcanic rock.

He soaked his bandana in the sparkling water and wiped his face before wrapping it back around his neck. He said, *"Bebo."* There was no need for words or gestures, she eagerly plunged her hands into the flow of cool water, brought it to her mouth and drank. When she was finished, she filled her plastic water bottle and noticed George had removed his own bottle from a cargo pocket in his pants. He drank more and slipped his full bottle back into his pants. His actions confirmed—more walking.

Gregory

CHAPTER 13

For Gregory, each evening had fallen into the same habit. He and the captain—sitting at a teak table on cushioned chairs—enjoying delicacies from the sea. Sammi was always at the ready, not only making and serving dinner, but also present to clear the table when they were done eating. And after, serving drinks and always bringing out the cigars and an ashtray the size of a hubcap from a '57 Chevy. The casual after-dinner conversations became established when he asked Captain Monroe to discuss how to punish the brothers for their actions. He assumed the former captain of a cruise ship would have experience in these matters and was more than satisfied with the captain's counsel. With Gregory's first puff of his cigar, the smoke swirled and went directly into the captain's face.

He ignored the captain's initial reaction to the cigar smoke. Squinting and waving seemed normal enough, but what he did next stole all his attention. The captain opened his eyes wide and stared at the barely visible sun through a heavy cloud layer. It appeared that the sun swung to the right along the horizon at the same time the boat's speed increased a knot or two. The change occurred with no observable action—no device or swiping a virtual touchpad—and no verbal commands to the autopilot. The realization that the captain had a neural implant and controlled the course of the yacht simply through his thoughts, shocked him.

The smoke from the captain's next puff drifted away from his face and he smiled as if content. But Gregory was conflicted by what appeared to be indiscretion. Neural implants are as easy to track as smartphones, only you couldn't put your head in a faraday bag, throw the chip away, or stomp it into nothingness with your heel. He made certain the brothers had no implants, why had he not confirmed the captain was clean?

He processed through this revelation and concluded it probably was not an issue. Since the captain's release from prison, he had no record of criminality. He stayed off the radar and gave the authorities no trouble. So, unlike Gregory, law enforcement had no reason to track him down. Perhaps more likely, he acquired his neural implant on the black market. Gregory's own communication implant, while less sophisticated, could not be traced, so why wouldn't a man as intelligent as the captain go through the extra precaution with an even more invasive implant? He would ask him but not tonight. He had another agenda for tonight's conversation—a spiritual matter.

"I'd like to ask you about your beliefs. After the unfortunate situation regarding the untimely, but necessary death of Masiki, you told me you *found karma*. Can you tell me more about your religion?"

The captain deflected the question with squinting eyes and a crooked smile.

Gregory never noticed the man's jaw until now. It was long and at this moment, resembled the prow of a ship. "I'm finding myself looking for a spiritual component to my life and yours intrigues me. I've never shared this with anybody, but my grandparents on both sides were religious and very different—Shinto and Baptist. I never paid much attention. It was my father who raised me in the church. He was a capitalist and worship was held in his corner office overlooking the Toyosu Fish Market. I never saw him pray, but he worshiped pure water, fish and the stock market. He lived his faith—everything was about business. So many people in my life put much importance on their faith. However, I see no need for a higher power."

"Then what is the problem?" asked Captain Moore.

"Bella, my fiancé is a Christian. Her god appears formidable. Ridiculous or not, I cannot control a wife who owns a faith more powerful than my own." Gregory paused and looked downward. "What am I missing? I want passion and purpose, but without a supreme being. I refuse to believe God or gods watch over us, making us do things to please them. That's emotional drivel, the stuff of idiots and peons, an opiate for the masses." He relaxed into his chair and said, "I studied some about your karma and I like what I hear. Not so much the blathering on about re-incarnation, but the here and now aspects—it might work for me."

A laugh with a billow of smoke burst out of the big Aussie. With mirth he spoke, "I'm not sure I'm fit to be your spiritual guru, but sure, I'll tell you what I believe. I probably shouldn't have said my religion is karma. What I've got is more a philosophy. I like philosophy. It's less messy and I can change it as often as I want. Those religions—they're awful—forcing people to believe the same thing for all time. Once you commit, that's it—no going back, no moving forward. You spend the rest of your life stuck in the amber of religious dogma. It's no way to live."

"I am already thankful for this conversation. You are helping me clarify my thoughts. Philosophy, not religion. Please go on, this makes sense to me," Gregory said.

"Life is just life, with no meaning or purpose other than what we decide to bring to it. Some people are born into it and naturally adopt the ways of their parents and community. If they never think for themselves, that's how they live and that's the way they die. Other people like you and I, find no reason to be locked into the myths of others." Captain Monroe took a puff and produced a large, satisfied grin. "We are the captains of our own destiny. That's what people with functioning brains do. They work out a way to live life and get what they want."

Gregory asked, "How does karma fit?"

"That's easy. If you get what you want, that is your right—it is your karma. What others get or don't get has no bearing on you—that is their karma."

"I see," Gregory took a slow sip of his drink and contemplated a moment before he spoke. "So if I don't get what I want, that is my karma as well?"

"Exactly. But you have no reason to worry about doing anything within your power to get what you want. It is your right. In fact, it is your obligation to exercise your power over others. That is your karma."

Gregory's smile widened and lines around his eyes followed the same pattern outward. "I have heard enough and am quite satisfied. I am spiritual in the most philosophical way possible." His laugh sounded like a sped-up version of a seagull's chatter.

The captain stroked his chin and offered a reflective smile. He sucked in his cigar and breathed out a series of lazy smoke rings.

Bella

CHAPTER 14

"I HATE TO SAY this, but your home is making me sick. Normally a cup of ginger and honey tea sets me straight, but it's not working."

"Yeah and you don't look good. I would have figured since you were born and raised on the ocean, you'd be immune to seasickness. Interesting."

"*Interesting*!? Thanks a lot. Is there anything you can do to stop this metronome? Don't sailboats set a storm sail so the boat only leans one direction? It's the back and forth that's getting to me," Bella said.

"Sorry, this place didn't come with a storm sail. But it came with this." José picked up a device that looked like an old iPad and began swiping his fingers across the screen. "How's that?"

"You're kidding? You've been holding out on me for the last hour. Don't tell me you wanted to test the limits of..." She squinted her eyes and pressed her lips tight. "If you were testing me, you're in big trouble."

"No, no. I'd never do that. Well, I didn't do that this time... not on purpose. I wanted to see the natural self-righting aspects of *mi casa*. You know theory and practice are often different," José said.

"How did you do that? It's like we're on land." Bella took a deep breath, looked off to the right and continued, "Actually, it's like I just got off a boat and have my sea-legs." She released her death-grip on the armrests of the captain's chair, unbuckled her seatbelt and stood up. "I don't know how you walked around while swaying like that. My body couldn't tell where the floor was. One minute we were kissing the ocean and the next we were being hurled into space. Not the most comforting sensation, but I'm improving fast."

"Good. What a quick recovery. If I had been testing your limits, I'd record how long it took. But of course, I would never do such a thing," José winked.

She ignored him. "Tell me what you did to stabilize this craft. I'm guessing we can safely walk around?"

"Absolutely, *mi ángel*—it is safe. The old test of a successful seastead is whether we can pour a glass of wine during a storm and leave it on the table without spilling. Would you like a glass?"

"Oh goodness, no. My head says we're on solid ground, but my stomach is still out there bouncing with the waves."

"You remember when you were a kid and the FLIP ship visited the station to buy some fresh seafood?" José asked.

"Oh yeah, that was the weirdest looking vessel I'd ever seen. I also decided then and there against becoming an oceanographer. They were kind of nerdy."

"Says the girl who studies clams." He gestured with his hands and continued, "That ship flooded its entire forward section in order to change from a regular, horizontal ship to a vertical research platform. When assuming a bow down, stern up position, it became incredibly stable in all kinds of weather. In the working part of the ship, the forward bulkheads became the floor for the crew. The whole concept was years ahead of its time but proved the principle keeping *mi casa* sitting pretty in this storm. My home isn't designed to travel on water like a surface ship, the ballast at the bottom of the column we are perched on is permanent. But I do have the ability to influence its response to waves and winds. The reason we were swinging like a carnival ride was because I raised us up to its maximum height by pumping out seawater and making us more buoyant. The high winds affected us too. When we dropped into a trough, we were exposed to virtually no wind, but as we rose, the full force of the gale caught our windward side. That's one reason my *Casa del Oceano* looks like a Tootsie Pop—it sheds wind." He glanced at the weather station readout. "This is wonderful! Gusts up to ninety miles an hour!"

"I get all that, but the waves and wind are not affecting us now. How is that even possible? Is it all because of ballast?" Bella asked.

"Good question. As with most things in the physical universe, there are many forces at play simultaneously. We stabilized so quickly because my little home has a couple of secret weapons. Besides lowering our center of gravity, I engaged the stabilizing fins and propellers." José held his arm out and rotated it palm up then palm down, repeating the motion as he explained, "The stabilizing fins move with the changes in swells and waves. And the props act like the storm sail on a sailboat, only under the water." A grin erupted across his face. "Pretty cool, huh?"

"You're the coolest dad I know, but I'll never get back that hour I spent seasick. You owe me big time."

"All's well that ends well," José said, turning his attention towards the information flowing across multiple screens.

"How's the station doing? It lacks the fancy secret weapons of your *casa*," Bella said.

"The sea tractors are working full-time to keep her on course and so far, she is about eight kilometers north of us, still floating high and dry."

The glass enclosed observation blister, which had been turned into a control center, had an incredible three-hundred-sixty-degree view of water to the horizon and was only encumbered by the center spar which enclosed the spiral staircase. The two stories of living space immediately above formed an immense overhanging eave which blotted out the sky.

"Hey Dad, all I can see is frothy waves and spray, can we go upstairs? I'm feeling better. Not ready for the wine test yet, but a view of the stormy sky might be a pleasant change."

"I can do better than that. Follow me," José said.

"Dad? What's that noise?"

He stopped climbing the stairs and listened. "It's probably Ferdinand."

"I think it's coming from down the stairway," Bella said.

"Go check it out," José waved a hand downward.

Bella walked cautiously down the spiral stairs until she could see the source of the noise. Indeed, it was Ferdinand; he was in a colorful woven hammock attached to opposing points at the main hatchway. It was a rumbling noise that resonated up the stairway and overwhelmed the muffled drone of the wind and waves—snoring. Below him in the exact center of the entry's deck she saw Kumar curled up. He opened an eye, gave her a suspicious look and closed it again. She turned and tiptoed up the stairs.

"No need to be so quiet. He could sleep through a hurricane," José laughed as he continued up to the living space.

Bella stood at the top of the stairs with her hands on her hips. "Why is he napping down there?"

He ignored her question and said, "You're in for a treat."

"Oh, no you don't. How come he enjoyed the most unaffected place in your boat—with my dog—while I was strapped onto a rocking horse? You warned him, didn't you?"

"Okay, I'm sorry, but since you're a scientist, I assumed you'd want to be part of my experiment."

"I can't believe you didn't tell me I was being your guinea pig," Bella said.

"Now that we are stable let me make it up to you."

Unable to stay mad at her dad, she gave up trying. "Okay, but it better be good."

Her father reached into a wet-locker and pulled out her mother's foul weather gear. "Here, put these on. It's not cold—I'm going barefoot—but you'll appreciate the protection."

She kicked off her flip-flops and slipped into bib-overalls and a tan jacket with an oversized bright-green hood. Then she secured a harness with a retractable tether and said, "I'm ready."

"Not quite." José looped a band from his device around his wrist and let it dangle as he rummaged through a box, then handed her one more item.

"Ski goggles?" Bella wondered.

"You'll see."

Half of his face disappeared when he set his goggles into place, the mirrored surface of the lens made him appear to have bug eyes. Then he tightened up the hood ties until only his nose and lips showed. "Your turn."

She mimicked him and followed him onto the deck. The lack of wind surprised her, but with the spacious deck turned to the lee of the storm, even the whistling and turbulent air was understated as they clipped their tethers into fixed mounts on either side of the sliding glass door.

She walked to the railing overlooking the most turbulent water she had ever seen. "Do you think God is mad at us? This is insane!"

She didn't need to yell to be heard, but it seemed like a loud voice matched the moment.

"I always just assume God is mad at us. But then I read His Word and it seems like He just keeps loving us despite what we deserve. No, this is just His creation doing its thing. At least that's my humble opinion," José said. She said nothing but marveled at the sensation. Her eyes told her the *Casa del Oceano* moved faster than the waves. She had to break that incorrect perception. Bella tried to create an accurate model in her mind. In principle, the floating house was stationary. Even though it floated on the top of a couple of miles of seawater, its design was like a map-pin stuck into a giant blue sea. The single spar rising out of the depths minimizes the effect of the water and the rounded shell of the living space deflects the wind—looking like a scene right out of a Jetson cartoon. Envisioning the casa as rock steady as a light house helped her build a model in her mind's eye. The waves were continuing their journey across the ocean, barely noticing any resistance as they passed around the column. She smiled when she became oriented to what was going on around her. "Dad, this is amazing."

He made a circle motion on his device's screen and hooked his arm around Bella's back and snugged her in saying, "Hang on, here we go!"

The deck rotated counterclockwise. Glad for the good hold on the rail, Bella was especially thankful for the security of her father's powerful arm across her back. The wind built rapidly and became so strong that it might have slapped her onto the deck if they were not holding on so tightly.

As they spun to face the wind, the sensation of being blown away became stronger. Even that worsened when the spray joined forces and pummeled them. She held on with all her might as her father moved behind her and reached for the rail on either side, surrounding her as he gripped the handrail. His efforts secured both in place just as they reached the full-on exposure of the new windward side. The counterclockwise revolution continued steadily and for a moment a rising swell caused her to think they were plunging deeper into the water like a corkscrew twisting into a bottle. But soon the sensation reversed, the spray dropped away and the wind diminished to a slumbering swirl that might not have bothered to lift a dry leaf.

José stood beside her and they both laughed uncontrollably. "Want to go again?" he asked as he lifted his goggles, revealing excited eyes.

"Oh, my! What a blast! Literally! Yes, let's go around two more times and then I'll be ready for your seasteading test. I bet the wine will not spill, but you have to serve cheese and crackers." She hugged him and stared out at the ocean. "Thanks, Dad. As far as I can see, its white froth and huge cresting waves. This is amazing, but I'm sorry for anyone else who might be out at sea in this weather."

"Don't worry. Meteorologists have been tracking this Pacific cyclone for days. Everybody in a boat has had plenty of time to get out of its way." He lifted his goggles. "Only a person with a death-wish would chance cruising through hundred mile-an-hour winds."

Hank

CHAPTER 15

OLIN SPENT HOURS PILOTING the *GalaxSea* through hurricane-force winds of over one-hundred miles per hour and twenty-foot cresting waves until he was no use to anyone. Hank realized he should have done more than simply offer to relieve Olin, but mutiny went against his nature. It helped that Olin acted competent and under control as he repeatedly refused to relinquish his position at the helm of the *GalaxSea*. That is until the moment he collapsed, exhausted. The stubborn man guided his yacht safely through the worst of the storm, though Zaine could have done the same without human help. Olin proved he was as tough as graphene, but eventually Hank had to physically assist him off the deck.

Thankfully, the winds fell into what seemed like a gentle breeze at a mere forty knots, with fickle gusts. In an hour they would intersect the eye of the Pacific cyclone, but the seas would still be agitated. Then they would be spit out of the back side of the hurricane. It would take half a day to pass through the entire storm system, but Ava assured Hank the worst was over. Much of the foam and spray had returned to the sea, but the yacht, now under reefed mainsail and furled headsail, flew down waves at speeds reserved for multi-hulls and motorboats. Hank longed to stay topside and see just how fast this magnificent yacht could sail, but duty called, so he left the *GalaxSea* with Zaine in charge.

With Olin put to bed, Hank was the only crew member who was still on his feet. Ava would monitor the systems and keep track of the crewmembers and he trusted Zaine with all the navigation and sailing. But being the last one standing meant he had to focus on keeping everybody healthy, or at least hydrated.

The absence of Irina, Marshall and Willy came as no surprise—storms at sea have a way of getting rid of the help. But then he heard Marshall in the head. Hank negotiated the heel of the boat, leaned a hand against the door and pressed himself into the corner of the hallway. He knocked twice and said, "Sometimes it's best to get out into the fresh air. The storm is easing. Some waves are breaking over the bow, but there's protection at the port helm and the forward cockpit."

Marshall answered with the sound of dry heaves. Anything to be vomited out had exited his body hours ago. The door opened a crack and then some more. Wearing pajama bottoms in blue and red spiderman colors and a gray hoodie with the MIT logo was a typical choice of clothing for Marshall, but the yellow streaks of vomit crusted down the front were new. His slumped shoulders and kyphotic bend made him look ancient as he stumbled out of the head. His knees buckled and Hank caught him under the armpits and pressed him against the wall to keep them both from falling. It looked more like a bar fight than an act of kindness, but Hank had no choice.

He dragged Marshall over to the leeward settee and let the force of gravity wedge him between the seat and the wall. He rolled up the boys' sleeve and plunged the needle of an IV catheter into the largest vein he could find. Hank didn't need Ava to alert him that Marshall was becoming desperately dehydrated. He hung the bag of IV solution from the overhead cabinet and placed a gentle hand on Marshall's forehead. "It's gonna be okay, buddy. Just rest until I come back. Don't move." He injected a dose of Dramamine into the spike point at the top of the line and walked away to check on his next patient.

Irina's door stood open and latched into place. But she was not inside her room. Her bed was made and the room immaculate other than a plastic cup rolling back and forth on the floor. "Ava, where can I find Irina?" Hank asked with concern in his voice.

"Do not worry, she harnessed into the jacklines and is resting on deck. Her vitals are normal and she took a banana from the galley," Ava said.

"What about Willy?"

"Ever since he moved out of his quarters and into Marshall's berth, he has been feeling somewhat better. He cannot eat yet but has kept down a small amount of ginger ale."

"Well, it looks like if we can just outlast the back end of this storm, my job as a nurse will be over soon," Hank said.

The boat lurched and Hank flew forward into the edge of Irina's bed.

A guttural sound, like a cry from a wild animal being torn apart by a predator, resonated out of the *GalaxSea*. Adrenaline shot through him, hairs stood up on his arms and a shiver sprinted up his neck. In the same instant, the floor let go of his feet and his body fell—landing against the wall. Hank's face pressed against a porthole, but he saw only blackness on the other side. Disoriented, his hands searched for a place to hold fast, but the boat righted itself and gravity deposited him in a heap on the floor.

"Hank, if you are uninjured and capable of making it to the engine room, I need your attention there. This is an emergency and your immediate response is required," Ava said.

Olin scurried out of his stateroom like a man escaping from a burning building. He grabbed Hank by the shirt and wasted no time pulling him toward the small hatch-like door that represented the only access to the yacht's diesel-electric motor. Hank expected smoke to billow out once the door opened, so the water sloshing over the threshold surprised him. The mostly white room was well lit, brighter than the ambient light they had become accustomed to, but his eyes didn't need to adjust to see the water rushing into the compartment. It reminded him of Frugal, as he waited for rescue.

"Ava, what's happening?" Olin closed the door and leaned against it panting.

"The leak is catastrophic. The water is coming through the sail drive gasket. It appears the collision was substantial enough to displace the propeller drive unit tearing it partially away from the hull. The mountings remain in place and the deformation sprung back after the initial impact with an object of considerable mass. You should be aware, the pumps are not keeping up with the volume of water coming in," Ava said.

"What can we do about it?" Hank asked.

"I can keep the auxiliary motor and the electrical system running for approximately five minutes, so time is of the essence. I see two choices. The easiest is to get everybody into life-rafts and abandon ship. The extra thirty-two thousand ounces from the modified keel exceeds the auto-salvage tolerances, so the second choice is to re-position two of the four emergency inflating salvage buoys into the engine room. Two are installed in the forward bulkhead and two in the garage. You will find standard air hose attachments and quick release mounting brackets. Unfortunately, you will need to position the buoys and fill each separately."

"The second choice sounds best to me," Hank said.

"Me too. Let's roll," Olin agreed.

"There are other considerations. Marshall's IV became disconnected during the impact and Irina is lying on the cockpit deck unconscious," Ava said.

"Dammit, Ava! Are they going to die in the next five minutes?" Olin asked.

"It is unlikely, but the engine room will be flooded completely within ten minutes. If you cannot fill the buoys to displace the water and seal the engine room door, there is a one hundred percent chance the *GalaxSea* will sink and you will have less time to evacuate to the safety of the life-raft," Ava said.

Olin's face contorted in response to the new information. Hank imagined the struggle Olin must feel. The man teetered on the precipice of a decision that would change everything. Even though each second of consideration took valuable time away from action, he had to wait—it was not his choice to make.

"What the hell's going on?" Willy asked as he staggered into view.

"Willy, can you reconnect Marshall's IV and wrap both kids into a space blanket, then standby on deck to launch a life-raft?" Olin asked.

"I'm on it," Willy said.

Olin's order could not have been clearer. Hank said, "Triage is a bitch. But you said it best—let's roll." Hank turned and sprang up the stairs. "I've got the forward bulkhead."

Hank

CHAPTER 16

OLIN SAT WITH A satisfied smile and stared at Hank. "See why I wanted you on board?"

Hank couldn't keep eye contact with the penetrating intensity of Olin's gaze. He looked out to sea as if he would miss something if he didn't. "No. I still don't get it."

"The odds have been against us, yet here we are, safe and sound. Indeed, God is good, but like I said, He is clearly not done with you yet or maybe it is your guardian angel—it is not ours to know."

"I hate to burst your bubble, but we have a life-raft floating off the stern just in case this barge sinks. I'd say the rapid deterioration of the storm proved to be our lucky charm," Hank offered.

"Who do you think controls the weather?" Olin asked.

"Science. It's called meteorology," Hank said.

"Believe that if you must, but I know who set the universe in motion and all natural phenomena can be manipulated by the Creator."

"Can we please have this conversation another time? I'm out-numbered and not in the mood to explain why I don't share your faith. You believe what you want, but newsflash—we aren't doing great. Your boat is still taking on water and the slightest wave or even a puff of wind will probably send her to the bottom. Your brilliant AI can't even tell us what we hit. The only thing we've got going for us is our health."

"Exactly," Olin said with the satisfaction of a person who just won an argument.

"Oh, brother." Hank slouched down onto his bench and pulled his deep-red watch cap over his eyes. He was not relaxed. The reality that they might still need to abandon ship plagued him. Once again, he made a mental note that his pocketknife was within easy reach. A single slash of the thin line that held the life-raft, would set them afloat and his life would take another sudden turn—another failure.

The *GalaxSea* sat heavy, so low, an easy reach over the rail and he would touch the water like he was on a calm lake in a day-sailor. Surprised his adrenaline had not burned off yet, he wondered when his well-deserved exhaustion would take over. Ava insisted they do nothing at all, which made him feel antsy. At least keeping busy, trying to save the *GalaxSea,* would have re-directed his focus, but forced inactivity set his mind adrift.

Maybe it was Olin needling him as someone who keeps breaking the odds. He had difficulty accepting that Olin, with his genius IQ, had no problem believing that Hank was watched over by some extraordinary being. Or even worse, that having Hank on board brought luck. He thought, *what a bunch of horseshit.* And his sailing failures and personal life proved that no luck followed him.

Hank wondered if Olin's self-assured stare remained on him and considered why it made him uncomfortable. With no answers, he pulled his cap down farther as if that would help. Dismissing Olin would be much easier if he did not hold him in such high regard. Another problem with ignoring Olin stemmed from the fact that he never wavered from his assertion that Hank had become family. His quirky status in the Ou family might be only that of a favorite nephew, but becoming part of a family again, even an eccentric one, comforted him.

Less than two weeks ago, he wondered if he was heading for a violent collision against a lee shore, saddled with debt, working an underwhelming job at the boatyard and enrolled in Operation Blue Skies. Sinking his boat and being injured in the Southern Ocean got him a place in the suicide prevention program aimed at veterans with a MLC, or major life change. The only redeeming aspects of that life had been the cute redhead at the local burger joint and a part-time job, teaching sailing. But neither the girl nor the job provided enough ballast to steady his course.

Olin changed everything in a day for Hank. And now he saw he was not alone. Each day since, had brought on dramatic shifts for everyone orbiting around Olin Ou. Family dynamics are complicated in the best of circumstances and Olin may not have caused the hurricane, but he chose the course and reeled the monster in. His initial intent had been clear—force his spoiled children to experience life's tough realities. They were not done.

Hank considered the real possibility. The *GalaxSea* was still not out of danger of sinking and *life's tough realities* never really end. But for now, they all were basking in the personal impact of an experience which amounted to the ultimate team building exercise. Each would take away something different, but they were all closer. Even though his nerves felt raw, he accepted his place in the Ou family tree—the black sheep.

Olin saw miracles in everything. Irina spent hours stationed at the shrine. Marshall retreated before the mast with a daily devotion. And Willy revealed his spiritual certainty during their face off with death. Even Ava, remarkably, found God. It occurred to him—though probably the only atheist within a thousand miles—he didn't sense rejection or condemnation. Not one person pushed their God on him. Sure, Ava judged him, but she was a computer. Besides her matter-of-fact inference about his moral compass, the closest anybody got to challenging him was Olin while they drank wine the night before Irina's birthday celebration. Olin's words bounced around his head and agitated his comfortable opinions of the cosmos.

Words from that night, anchored in Fox Bay, British Columbia, haunted him. Olin said, "Everybody has faith. You declare you don't believe in God. That is a statement of faith. In your heart, God does not exist. I believe in God. That is my statement of faith. One of us is right. One of us is wrong. But here's the thing: If God does not exist, we're reduced to biology. If God exists, miracles make sense."

Hank took away two conclusions but no answers. One fact is that to believe, whether in God or in biology—a faith is required. And the other fact is with two opposing views there can be only one winner. He still didn't believe in God or miracles, but he found himself questioning faith. Lately, his passionate faith in nothing, seemed anemic and lacking substance. His whole life, he felt content with following scientists like Carl Sagan, Stephen Hawking and Richard Dawkins. He watched the shows on PBS and rightly aligned with the majority of the world, reasoning the whole God-thing is made up and science holds the answers.

Questions kept spilling into Hank's head. His faith had roots in the accepted scientific facts that everything began with the big bang—mere happenstance and void of meaning. If that was true, then what's the point of human existence? Why was he questioning it now? And why did he find himself concerned about his moral compass? Ava pointed out a flaw he never recognized before—and he had plenty—but everybody does. All he needed to do was remember and try to make sense out of life—debrief. That is the job of everybody after a crisis. The process looks different for each person, but it is an important process. Sometimes it's throwing down drinks in a bar, sometimes it's holing up alone in stillness. Reflection always changes a person, usually for the better, but he couldn't be sure.

As a child, his mother tried to protect him after his father died. At first, being coddled seemed like the only path out of the devastation of losing his dad, his first friend. His mother couldn't be more than she was. He accepted that. But somehow, he knew he had to reject the helicopter parenting of a desperate woman and take on life for himself, meet the challenges, make decisions and live with the consequences. That new philosophy made all the difference. Sometimes life got ugly and never seemed easy, but he grew through his struggles. And, while he did not entirely understand parenting, he admired Olin's desperate attempt in allowing his children to wrestle with their own fears and experience life without a safety-net.

By the time Hank had reached Marshall's age, he had sailed around the world, enlisted in the Navy, trained as a medic and faced hundreds of situations that might have ended in death. Some of his experiences he would not wish on anybody—especially caring for the wounded on the battlefield, often mangled and sometimes dying. He pressed his eyelids tight and thought, *the wounded? Too many were friends.*

His experiences insisted he gain skills and confidence—they were the reason he lived life boldly. Olin's decision to sail through a hurricane made sense—in a strange way. Suffering, as a family, through a crisis that money and privilege cannot remedy seemed crazy at first, but in the years to come might make all the difference.

Irina, younger by a few years than Marshall, handled this differently. She appeared far more mature. He knew women sailors equally competent as any man. They didn't get to that point by sailing dinghies around buoys in the bay. He imagined Olin saying, *"Happy birthday, Irina. I got you a special present. Now that you're eighteen, I thought it would be good to scare the hell out of you in a crazy storm thousands of miles away from any help. It will be exciting; you will puke your guts out and get a concussion. But hey, that's what being an independent adult is all about."*

Of course, Olin wouldn't say that, but the image made Hank smile wryly. Willy would think it funny. But now was not the time to open his mouth. Willy rallied with impressive speed. But after seeing him care for the Ou children's needs like an overzealous nurse-maid, he recognized the single-minded commitment of a capable, well-trained Marine. During the crisis, Willy re-attached the IV in Marshall's arm and carried him up to the deck to be near his sister. He wrapped them both in reflective blankets, lashing them snuggly into place on their respective benches. When Hank finally got up on deck to check on the siblings, he found Willy hovering over them with everything under control.

Marshall fell in and out of lucidness until the immediate danger of the storm passed. Even then he acted like wakefulness was an inconvenience and slept on for hours. But he drank fluids and seemed alert and communicative during his periods of wakefulness. Irina showed no indications she hit her head. No swelling or bruising and she didn't appear to have sustained any other injuries. She even had an appetite, so Hank completed his exam and Willy added his professional insight of what went on before Hank showed up.

He pulled the cap ever further down his face forcing himself not to laugh as he recollected Willy's southern accent saying, "She was out like a sorority girl at sunrise on a Saturday. That is until a wave hit her in the face. Then she turned into a cat getting peed on by a hound dog." He laughed and added, "That's when I knew she'd be fine."

Finally, fatigue outdistanced his thoughts and Hank pushed both hands deep into his pockets so they would not drop while he slept. There was so little noise, as if the hurricane wiped the ocean free of all sound. The only thing Hank heard was Olin's low, steady voice. No noise hummed through the rigging, the ripples on the surface of the great Pacific didn't even pester the heavy-laden hull. The motors and genset remained dead silent. Zaine and Ava said nothing. It took a minute to sink in, but soon Hank realized what was happening and he experienced a sense of joy. Olin read aloud—to his children. He smiled knowing everyone processes a crisis and he accepted that people process differently.

Bella

CHAPTER 17

FEW PEOPLE UNDERSTOOD THE three-dimensional nature of the family business better than Bella. She literally had been there from the beginning. Her folks embarrassed her more than once with stories of her early life on their thirty-four-foot sailboat. She had no memories about her first few years of life but understood her free-spirited parents were peculiar. Her father teased, "You were born on the deck, right where you were conceived. It was a full moon and the midwife was a manatee." Her mother would counter, "José, you embellish! You know there are no manatees in the deep ocean. My midwife was a dolphin."

There were pictures of the worn-out looking vessel and in later years, she rolled her eyes at its christened name—*The Love Child*. Her earliest memories were when her parents were married in Norway. Maybe it was the excitement of her first plane flight, or finally understanding her mother's lap disappeared because she was getting a sister. Perhaps it was the honor of being a flower-girl in the solemn ceremony, or the novelty of the frightful view of the fjord below. The rock-solid overlook established a vivid memory into the little girl whose life to that point had been defined while floating at sea-level. She held tight to those memories. Each year, on her parents' anniversary, she dusted them off, visited for a time and returned them to a special place in her mind. That spring day stood in such contrast to her upbringing, yet the memories held such importance that years had not diminished them. Her memories helped her understand who she was, where she came from and how her parents went from tending a single deep-ocean aquapod full of kampachi to shepherding a giant sea-going farming operation. What her parents had accomplished in her twenty-five years was remarkable and she realized their life at sea wasn't only about growing protein and sea-vegetables—but the importance of living free.

When she eventually left home for a university education, Bella wondered if she was escaping a cult. Nothing in her upbringing prepared her for life on land. If she spoke about her childhood experiences, others looked at her as if she had emerged from the deep sea—and maybe she had. Everyone in her university cohort eventually ignored her. It soon became clear they were not up to her understanding of the biological processes of marine environments and she had difficulty comprehending their level of cultural and social complexity. She felt left with only two choices: Try to fit in or examine her life and discover who Isabella Maria Johansen Espinosa was destined to be.

The answer came easier than she imagined. After fasting and praying for three days, she came to understand exactly who she was meant to be. Like every other believer, she was an imperfect child of God, but unique in important ways. There were the easy things, like sharing in other's joy and being graceful as well as her innate curiosity about the natural world, but she also took satisfaction in hard work and accepted the character-building results of wrestling with God. She wasn't always happy, but her struggles helped her gain confidence and accept God's plan for her.

None of that made her first year at college easier and her looks didn't help. She always knew her long legs and tall frame came from her mother's side; it didn't take a geneticist to explain that her brown skin and ample curves came from her Mesoamerican ancestry. During her *quinceañera,* her *abuela* felt it necessary to inform her, *"Atraerás a los hombres e intimidarás a las mujeres, Dios te bendiga querida."* But the English translation took root in her mind, "You will attract men and intimidate women—God bless you, my dear." Her fifteen-year-old-self took those words as if a blood curse, made worse because they were from her beloved grandmother. A couple of years later, at college, she found out the truth. She became an expert at turning down boys and leaning deeper into her studies—anything to avoid attention. As a result, she was not very popular and had plenty of time to be herself.

But, as the years passed, she grew into a woman who didn't seek to attract men but was not ashamed if she did. She found women to be far more friendly towards her than intimidated by her. She wished her *abuela* had stayed quiet that day ten years ago, but there was no revisiting the thought with her now, as she had since passed from this life. Despite Bella's experience to the contrary, it was impossible for her to bury those words which could have been a casual observation of no particular significance—to *Abuela.* However, Bella could not forget. She would do what she always did, focus on what mattered, what God intended for her—leave the past where it belonged and that included the debacle with Gregory.

She needed to concentrate on the moment and recovering the aquafarm from the category-three hurricane appeared to be a good start. She maneuvered the underwater drone through and around the dispersed complex of one of the aquafarm's many plots. Her job was simple and amounted to cataloging the damage. While her dad's casa survived the storm in style, the rest of the farm might not have had it so easy.

During the storm, after each major wave or gust, José said things like, "Can you believe this? The size of these waves and speed of the wind and look at me! I'm balancing on one foot drinking wine with my eyes closed!" Truly the stability of the habitat was remarkable. Most of the day she contented herself with reading and after dinner, enjoyed cards and cognac with her father and Ferdinand. Without exception, each hour passed with no drama. Even Kumar appeared bored by the "weather event" but she knew all the humans on board worried about the farm. The fish, the bivalve mollusks and the seaweeds generating the farm's profits, might be lost. The hardware was at risk as well: Dozens of wave-driven-sea tractors, thousands of floats, miles of ropes, sophisticated cages and the station—the hub that brought the entire floating operation together.

Her dad asked her to evaluate crop damage with the AUV, or Autonomous Underwater Vehicle, while he looked after other pressing issues. The thought of being the first to view the storm damage made her sick, but she agreed and figured she could offer emotional support if things looked bad. Picking up the damage after a storm is part of farming—part of life. Dealing with the loss was the price of farming, whether on land or underwater, farmers gamble and sometimes they lose big.

She steered the AUV to the closest of the submerged structures. The sensors on the sea tractors transmitted everything she needed to get the camera within view. Other than the residue of encrusted stains and a few barnacles, the sea tractors looked whimsical, as if designed for a steampunk movie. Its movement pattern wasn't quite mechanical, but fun to watch—half squid and half inchworm. Her dad didn't entirely invent these automated dynamos but gave them a brain of sorts. Configured and influenced to José's specifications, they dragged tremendous loads slowly through the ocean. Once she located the tractor, it was only a matter of following the tether to the first float. She noted the ten-meter depth and wondered why it hadn't risen now that the seas were calm. Under normal conditions these plants would be shallow enough to have easy access to sunlight, but at this depth, sub-optimal pressures and reduced photosynthesis eventually caused die-off. Bivalves would be okay for longer and fish only cared about their food supply. She typed a depth alert into her notes.

Other than the concerning depth, the underwater dreamland her parents built, appeared in fine shape. She typed one last alert to calibrate the control unit of the AUV not responding well to her controls—it acted like it had a mind of its own. Bella turned halfway around in her chair and glared at her dad. He too sat in a swivel chair and labored over an identical array of monitors. "Really, Dad? Why must you choreograph everything?!"

"What are you talking about?" José said.

"I wasn't born yesterday. I can tell you're manipulating my drone's power. At first, I thought it was the current, then decided it must be the control unit, but then I noticed its movement—dancing to the music. Let me guess, Felix Mendelssohn?"

"Ah, ha! Your time with me paid off. Yes, Mendelssohn. Is that all you got?"

"Dad, you're lucky I don't crank up the K-pop and give you a lesson in my music."

"You wouldn't!"

"You're right. Mendelssohn's Concert Overture, *The Hebrides,* is more appropriate."

Bella saw tears well up in her father's eyes. He looked away. It had been too long since they had been together and Bella knew how important this time must be to her emotional Latino father. José rose out of his chair and placed a hand on her shoulder. He bent down and kissed the top of her head.

"God does not appreciate prideful men. Sometimes I think he gives me difficulties to counterbalance the excellence of my children. *No merezco un ángel como tú.*"

"I've missed you Dad," was all she said. Obviously, they both had their struggles, but for this moment, they had each other's company, a project to keep them busy. She could not ask for more and this moment held all she wanted in the world.

The camera danced among infinite complexities of color, texture and size. A broad, molasses color leaf, slick with tiny bubbles, traded screen time with waving green felt-like fingers. A single bigeye scad swam through the seaweed and looked directly into the camera, then darted off. Bella smiled and rocked back in her chair. "Where there's one, there are thousands." She glanced over at her dad who paid no attention to her comment. They had not talked in over an hour. The algorithm of his Optimal Sea-Space software worked its magic without his interference, but his eyes stayed locked onto the screen and he looked frustrated working the keyboard.

"I'm taking a break and it looks like you could use a change of pace. What can I get you?" Bella said.

"Something's terribly wrong and I have no clue how to fix it," José said.

Bella walked over to her dad and looked over his shoulder into a graphic representation of the various components of the operation. At first glance, nothing appeared out of the ordinary. She asked, "I don't get it, what's wrong?"

"You know which one is the station, right?"

"Yes." She clearly saw the green rectangular representation of the station as it seemed to hang from the top edge of the screen. She studied it and took in the data points corresponding to each of the shapes. "Why is it moving in the opposite direction? It's going east—at eight knots. Why would the program do that?"

"It wouldn't. It can't. And not those speeds. It's against the current! None of the data makes sense."

"What does your AI analysis suggest?" Bella asked.

"That's just the thing. I know my AI is far from sophisticated, but it's reliable, or at least it was. Now I can't even run an error check."

They both watched as the green rectangle vanished. José stood up, spinning in a slow circle with his hand on his forehead. "Aye yai yai. What's happening here?"

"Is it sinking? The explosives?"

"No. I built in fail-safes. The sequence needs my password to trigger it," José said.

"Dad, the station has cameras. And what about the security pods? They've got great scopes on the guns."

He held his hand out to stop her. "I already tried those and I even sent the closest AUV, the sister to the one you've been using. As soon as it came into range—the signal cut out. I raised *mi casa* to maximum height to buy us a little more line-of-sight range. Even though it seems desperate, I think getting every drone into the air is our last chance to find out the fate of the station. The casa's drone is on its way. If the station still floats, I hope to use the drone as a repeater, allowing me to activate the station and try the cameras again. Hopefully, this works."

José raised his workstation to standing height but watching him pace in place and study the monitors only made her more anxious. From the drone's vantage point, it looked like it was standing, still staring at the water beneath, but the speedometer showed the actual story. It sped towards the station, but only water was visible. As it passed the last known coordinates, there was still no sign of her childhood home, no oil slick or debris field either.

"Not a single signal. The station's drone is not responding, the cameras... nothing. It's gone or there has been a catastrophic electrical failure," José said.

"Dad, you always say, 'keep hope alive.' Don't give up. Why not try a wider search? You said it was traveling against the current. Perhaps it changed course again."

"That makes no sense. It can't change course without someone steering it."

"Any better ideas?" Bella said.

"Okay. Either way, we passed the point of no return. The batteries are at fifty percent with a slight tailwind. At this point, the drone cannot return, so let's do this. Use your angel powers. Right or left?"

"Left," Bella said after a long second.

Her dad looked crestfallen. His dark, smooth skin always helped him appear younger than his age, but now it didn't help. The tightness of his jaw, his lips pressed together and heavy creases between his dark eyebrows finished the transformation. What Bella saw, shocked her. It was the defeated man from years ago—her grandfather—just before he died.

Bella sat down hard, breathed slowly and began a silent prayer. *"Lord Jesus, I don't care about finding the station, but please protect my father's health."* Tears welled up in her eyes. The monitor was not in view, but she didn't care about that. She turned away and wiped her eyes.

"Bella! Look! The station! It's sitting pretty as can be."

Her tears had a mind of their own and normally, she allowed herself to experience emotions and allow their natural flow through her. But now was not the time for that. She wiped the tears off her face and with sheer will, turned them off. A full breath helped and squaring her shoulders added to the illusion of confidence. Taller than her dad, who was sturdy and looking his age again, she rested her hand on his shoulder and leaned into him as they concentrated on the video feed the drone captured.

The camera zoomed onto the station and everything looked normal. The camera focused on the waterline and Bella saw immediately what her dad was looking for. There was no evidence the station took on water. The only thing amiss was the modest wake leading out behind the platform's two main hulls leading away from them.

"This distance is affecting the signal strength, but if I keep it high enough for line-of-sight, we should have some time left. I've tried to re-connect to the station using the drone as a relay, but so far it has failed to connect. So, it looks like we found the station but will lose the drone."

"Hey, Dad, what's that? Upper left."

The camera on the drone maneuvered toward the white speck in the sea of blue and Bella drew in her breath.

"It looks like a sailboat and it's heading toward the station."

A light flashed from the monitor and all went dark. The entire control room blacked out, even the LED indicators mounted within control switches slowly died. Only the background music, which Bella had tuned out, played on. No computer or control systems responded to input and when the reboot sequence did nothing, José stared at Bella in abject disbelief, his face appeared to be searching for some understanding.

Before she could even think through the possibilities, everything came back to life only this time every monitor within their field of vision showed the same two words.

DON'T PANIC.

Gregory

CHAPTER 18

"Why do you insist on landing in Hawaii? I've already ex-plained—we can re-fuel and carry out the scheduled maintenance at sea, far from the prying eyes of the country that is trying to hunt you down," the tall Aussie said. He leaned against the navigation counsel with his back to the windows revealing the expansive blue of water and sky waiting for a response.

When none came, the captain picked up his cigar and continued, "I'm not worried for myself. My documents are not a problem and you've already paid me well. But I'd rather finish the job and receive my bonus. Truthfully, I rather enjoy our time together and would hate to see it end prematurely."

Gregory stood rigid, not like he was at attention, but with the formality natural to his breeding—as if ready to bow. "It is true. I'm a person of interest, not only in the US, but apparently around the world now. Even the National Central Bureau in Singapore has been cooperating with Interpol. But don't trouble yourself. They will scan me through customs but will not be able to identify my face. I must meet someone there. Plus, the fuel quality is superior to what you could manage on the black market out at sea."

A barely perceptible change occurred in his posture, but enough that any tension melted away. "I am not concerned and these beautiful islands will provide a well-deserved landfall. Besides, there are things I must do so I can get on with my life. I will conclude some business entanglements and a bachelor party of sorts."

"Very well. My job demands I pay attention to details. It's not an understatement to say your yacht stands out. I'm guessing it will attract some attention and they will board us."

"I understand your concern. Are you referring to our boat's documents?"

"Of course. They are very good counterfeits and might get you through customs in some backwater countries if they are too lazy to verify their authenticity, but not the US. You will need to present the authentic registry or we will all face the consequences."

"Those documents are not counterfeits. This vessel truly is registered under the New Zealand Department of Tourism. I have diplomatic immunity and you and the crew cannot be harassed."

"You're shitting me."

Gregory smiled and said, "No, I'm not shitting you. I received this beautiful boat with its equally valuable papers, as a trade in a rather delicate exchange. As long as a certain stateswoman remains in office, I merely update the crew and passenger manifest and diplomatic channels handle the rest."

"Huh. A delicate exchange," the captain mused.

"Fortunately, reputation still matters to politicians. In a rather short period, I provided five girls and two boys to indulge a rather dark fetish of the lady. Apparently, they were fragile. It was their karma. She considers this yacht an ongoing incentive to stay quiet and she sweetened the pot, by allowing me to assume the identity of one of her diplomats—Foreign Affairs and Trade.

"And, by the way, I'll be going by the name Leo Takahashi. Leo and I were the same age. He worked for the department of tourism and died overseas in a car accident. You might say, I am his only survivor. The timing coincides with my customer needing a big favor and she ensured no death certificate ever made it into the records. Officially, Leo still works overseas as a diplomat. It seems the only thing they care about is that I don't abuse my expense account and that I pay my taxes.

"I've decided that Hawaii is my new beginning. From now on, call me Leo. We have the documents and my passport is in order. It's time to leave my old life in the past. I will even try some actual tourism work—my benefactor cannot stay in power forever. In time, I'll use Leo's reputation and my new contacts to gain a job in the private sector. And, of course, I'll need a job to take care of Bella." His grin broke into a staccato laugh, which stopped abruptly. His face appeared grim and he leaned forward. "For a time, we'll live simply. She'll call me Leo." The smile returned and he whispered, "I can't wait to have kids."

Hank

CHAPTER 19

THE IMMINENT DANGER HAD passed and it was unlikely he would be required to do anything. In desperate need of rest, he found himself too restless to nap, so he settled and lay as still as possible. Ava was operating two repair and maintenance robots—one inside the damaged hull and one outside. Irina was laid out, fast asleep on the port bench seat. Marshall's foot was close enough to kick her in the head, but he was engrossed in a VR game that kept his head on a swivel and required some arm and hand movements, but fortunately, no leg action. Olin also wore VR glasses. He paced the deck and occasionally spoke in hushed tones—looking concerned. But it was Willy's post-storm antics that surprised Hank the most, as he whittled on a block of wood about the size of a bar of soap.

There would be no sending of distress signals and if a plane or ship were near, there wouldn't be any flares sent up into the sky or waving of arms. Though dead in the water and perilously close to sinking, they must maintain the lowest profile possible. It didn't take Ava to remind them of the last boat their enemy believed contained Olin Ou, was blown out of existence. They were on their own and needed to figure out what to do next, but right now their fate depended on Ava's ability to stop the flow of seawater into the engine room.

The *GalaxSea* floated so low in the water that the safest place for them was on deck, close to the waiting life-raft, tethered off the stern. In the last hour alone, they gave up three or four inches of freeboard. Not that he desired a faster demise, but the slow steady loss of buoyancy was agonizing. At this rate, Hank guessed they would need to abandon ship within the next few hours. Ava would know the answer to the minute, but nobody asked her.

He wanted to do something, whether to man the pumps, or dive overboard and help with repairs—anything was better than waiting. But Ava insisted that the homeostasis which kept the *GalaxSea* afloat was a delicate balance and the slightest increase in wind or removing too much water from one contained bulkhead might send them to the bottom. Her processing powers and co-ordinated efforts of pumps and robots would be their best hope.

"Hey, everybody! I've got some good news." Olin took off his glasses and shook Irina awake. "Mom, Sidney and Nadia have all made it out of Panama safely. They officially—scattered. I can't even find them. Well, for now."

Everyone smiled and waited for him to continue, but Olin seemed like he ran out of words and just closed down and mindlessly turned away. His posture changed, a forward bend at the waist and hands straight down at his side, knuckles forward. This was the second time Hank watched this man deflate—it was unnerving, but nobody seemed to take notice. They all resumed their positions from before the encouraging announcement and the seemingly unprovoked regression. *Lizard brain,* popped into Hank's head from nowhere as Olin shuffled to the companionway and disappeared below deck.

Exactly like his similar exit after the sailboat race in the Strait of Juan de Fuca—what seemed like a lifetime ago.

Hank reached over the rail and slipped his fingers into the water. The temperature of the water was much warmer this side of the storm. For a moment, he considered jumping in and washing off. They all needed a good cleaning. The last time anybody took a shower was two days ago, before the storm. Now, nobody seemed to care about hygiene. Or, if they did, nobody asked the question that had to be considered. "Ava, if I take a shower, will the *GalaxSea* sink?" He figured jumping overboard with a bar of soap would not put them in more peril, but he wasn't certain he could climb back on board without altering the yacht's trim fore and aft. He stayed put, remembering one thing he knew for certain—you don't want to be the only clean person on a boat. As long as you smell, nobody else does.

Hank woke to a commotion that shocked his brain into instantaneous wakefulness. His arm, however, was sleeping like the dead, still hanging over the rail. The tips of his tingling and painful fingers a foot away from the water. He sat up straight and shook his arm which only made his paralyzed limb hurt more. Willy sat by the companionway still whittling and he could not see Irina or Marshall. Olin stood at the starboard helm station, the man with the lizard brain gone, replaced with a vibrant sailing enthusiast with a relaxed hand on the wheel and a smile on his face. The mainsail and the genoa were pressed tight with a steady breeze. The life-raft looked like a bright orange jellyfish, deflated and strapped to the foredeck. He marveled how he could have slept through all that had taken place around him. Then came a familiar voice.

"Captain, may I suggest a heading of two-hundred and thirty degrees," Zaine said.

Until now, only Hank insisted Ava use Leonard Nimoy's voice while dealing with the ship's business. Olin apparently decided to... how would he phrase it? *Go down that rabbit hole.*

Hank got up and walked over to Olin. "Status, Captain?"

"Ava completed ninety percent of the fix before the little water-logged robot lost his suction and headed for the bottom. We should be back in perfect trim within the hour. She says the quality of the repair is poor, but it should hold up as long as the winds remain moderate and seas don't pound us too hard."

"So, you're saying we probably shouldn't be in the middle of the ocean in this condition," Hank said.

Olin turned his attention to Hank and smiled like all was right with the world. "You have a better read on this yacht than anybody else. I'm hoping we can keep morale up for a while longer. The *GalaxSea* has a few more tricks left in her and Ava makes MacGyver look like a loser. Which is good because it seems everybody and everything, is out to destroy us; but by God's grace, we are still sailing." He stood to the side and insisted Hank take the wheel. "Please do me the honors. I'm certain it's only because of you we came through this as well as we did." Olin stepped away and turned to leave.

"Who's MacGyver?" Hank asked.

Olin turned back, shook his head and asked, "Can I get you anything to eat or drink?"

"Do you think Marshall could whip up some scones? And I'd love a mug of coffee... bulletproof."

"Aye, aye, Skipper."

Three hours after sunset, everyone was on deck, recounting the fears and triumphs of the storm. He had no problem enjoying the relaxed atmosphere and pleasant tropical breeze. It was a stark contrast to the previous night. While he had broken his own rule about alcohol while underway after Olin's announcement, this time around, Hank was the only one not drinking. As he watched the rest of the crew slowly lose their edge, he remembered the importance of sobriety. It meant readiness and at sea, being ready often meant the difference between life and death.

He felt thankful for the carefree attitude sweeping across the *GalaxSea*, even if aided by a little drinking. The heaviness of the last couple of days had been severe and it was nice to see smiles again. Olin and Willy sipped whiskey, Marshall declared beer was superior to IVs for hydration and Irina, the newly minted eighteen-year-old, lingered over a half empty bottle of chardonnay. Even the *GalaxSea* seemed to be in exceptionally fine spirits. Her happiest point of sail was a broad-reach and she sailed southwest at an amazing clip. Even though full repairs were still needed, she laughed at the sea under full sails as if taunting the low-pressure system to build again into a worthy adversary.

A flash of light caught his attention and everyone turned to see Ava's life size hologram appear. She glowed brilliantly and looked solid as any of the people she faced. And for an instant, he decided she looked more real than the bedraggled human contingent.

"I am declaring a state of emergency," she announced and followed with the dissection of human weakness she was so capable of. She spent several minutes detailing how each person on board passed the point of usefulness and were well into the dregs of physical and emotional exhaustion. Her tone, though controlled, held a sharp edge of absolute authority. She informed Irina and Marshall they needed to increase their calories and adapt an aggressive hydration plan—cutting off all beer or wine consumption. Willy and Olin were to abstain from alcohol for at least twenty-four hours and Hank needed to get his blood sugar balanced. She suggested he stop eating scones and switch to meat protein. She included everyone in her final prescription—bedrest. Then said, "Mr. Ou, you are the captain, but I am the chief medical officer and these are not suggestions. The health and safety of the crew is my concern and I insist my recommendations be followed immediately."

In the military, Hank witnessed the hierarchy of command break-down more than once and wondered why Ava was being so obsti-nate. She confronted the man in charge, placed him in a corner and waited for his reaction. Even Hank saw better ways to handle this and didn't understand why Ava, a tactical genius, pressed the issue by pulling rank. In the past, he had seen her get her way by being diplomatic and reasonable and even caught a time or two when she was outright manipulative, but never close to mutiny. *Why a zero-sum game? Why now?* He was curious how it would turn out and didn't have to wait.

Olin put down his drink and walked right up to Ava and said, "I know you and Zaine can handle my yacht flawlessly. I understand our flesh and blood bodies and minds need to recover, but before I decide how I'm going to handle this confrontation, I need to ask a pressing question."

Hank could not see his face, but imagined the dire expression etched across it. And even though he was not a large man, compared to Ava's petite size, Olin's stance looked formidable. Ava's defiant posture held as he leaned in, even closer and looked down on her. "Why haven't you told me what we hit during the storm? You have almost as many sensors underwater as above. You had the helm. What did we hit and why didn't you avoid it?"

"We didn't hit it. It hit us," Ava said as she lost a fraction of her resolve.

Olin did not back down. "That's not an answer. It's an excuse."

"I wanted to protect certain members of our crew from the unfortunate event," Ava said.

"Well, it's obvious, we all experienced the impact and we almost lost the *GalaxSea* because of it, so I don't get why you're evading the point. It's time to come clean."

At that moment, Hank thought Olin looked like he wanted to take Ava across his knee and give her a spanking and Ava reached out with a straight arm as if to defend herself.

"It was a whale! A blue whale." She dropped her arm to her side and looked down at her shoes. "It was a calf. It closed in like a torpedo at a speed of twenty-knots, and swam headfirst into our auxiliary sail drive unit just behind the keel. The baby whale died instantly. The odds of that happening are incalculable," Ava said.

"Why wouldn't you let me know this before now?"

"After the incident, whales vocalized. One of the cetaceans' cries sounded particularly mournful—most likely, its mother. She is still vocalizing with laments and thousands of others—near and far—have joined her. They are very sensitive creatures and share an enviable social network."

"I'm missing the point. Do you imagine they are going to come and destroy us out of revenge?" Olin asked.

"Of course not. This is not the fiction of Moby Dick. I am saddened about the loss of life and saddened for the community that grieves. The reason for not informing you about the details is because I am a computer and I sense a need to come to terms with this new experience. I am not programmed for sadness, however—that word—defines a part of me."

"You're right. I drank too much whiskey." He turned to face his crew. "You heard her. Sober up, drink water and get some sleep." He walked to the top of the companionway without making eye contact with anyone and said, "Ava, I give you command of the *GalaxSea*," and disappeared below decks.

Marshall followed his dad, leaving behind a beer in its holder. Willy said nothing and shuffled off to his cabin hatch forward of the mast.

Irina came over and sat on the bench next to Hank with tears in her eyes. She said, "Ava, please play the sounds of the mother in mourning. I need to experience it."

At first, Hank felt the vocalizations more than he heard them. Ava had projected the low vibrations and rhythmic hum of the sound directly into their heads, bypassing sound waves all together. He wondered if she did it so the others on the boat would be unable to hear the sounds or perhaps to dramatize the experience. Either way, the effect worked and Hank experienced a deep connection to the mother's loss that transcended species.

Irina reached an arm around his back and laced the other across his front and laid her head onto his chest and sobbed uncontrollably.

He wrapped an arm around her, held her close and gently patted her shoulder. When it came to women, Hank often misread signals, but clearly not today. He had noticed tears welling up in her eyes and her breathing getting shallow when Ava explained the tragic death of the baby blue whale. She simply needed a shoulder to cry on and he was there to share the sad moments of grief.

Julie

CHAPTER 20

WHEN THEY STEPPED OFF the plane into the hundred-degree hangar with matching humidity, an American greeted them with a relaxed smile and said, "Welcome to Panama. Strip down to your skivvies. Put any jewelry and tech into the bag, including watches." They had collected her cell phone before the helicopter took them from the Naval Air Station on Whidbey Island to the private jet waiting at Paine Field. He gestured a hand towards a table, continuing with, "If you want to get it back, label it. Shoes and socks too. Keep moving and the women will set you up. Don't challenge them about size, they know what they're doing."

There were no changing rooms in sight, only the plane and a modular office against one wall. A few tables stacked with gear sat in the artificial shade of white canopies. There would be someone last in line, but it would not be her, so Julie moved quickly. She yanked off the gold band from her right ring finger, took out three earrings and placed them in the bag. She sealed it and wrote, *J. Marsh*, in block letters. It took even less time to strip off her street clothes. Wearing only black underwear and a sports bra, she moved towards the two women quartermasters like a competitor in a triathlon. A woman handed her a pile of perfectly folded clothes while the other pushed two wrapped items in her direction. From the size of the packaging, she guessed socks and a t-shirt, both labeled with an "S."

After dressing, she picked out her own combat boots and progressed to the weapons table. Everyone received a fixed blade knife with a sheath, of poor quality, but sharp. The sidearm wasn't much better. She suspected the 9mm Hi-point, with its unloaded magazine to be a knockoff, but at least it fit perfectly in a tactical leg holster. The last item gave her more reason to hate this mission because it confirmed that it was well outside of the company's typical job description: A used, but well-maintained rifle, a Bushmaster M4 carbine with a single point sling.

While the others got into their gear, she studied the hangar security. Only two exits could be seen, a man-door built into each of the large plane-sized hangar doors. They stationed a guard at each door and another walked a slow zig-zag within the massive interior. He never made eye contact, moved like a well-trained sentry and avoided the assembling team members. A fourth guard sat in a swivel chair at a steel desk, presumably resting, until the next rotation. Dressed in full kit, it must have been hot as hell. These sentries were not a rent-a-cop security team with polo shirts and Bermuda shorts. They even wore bump helmets and gloves. By all indications, the security was not there to keep them in, but she wondered who they were keeping out.

Megan Ward and her loyal aide, Sam, descended from the jet already in uniform. She strode across the hangar and into the modular office. Sam turned and announced, "When you're dressed, muster in the office. It has AC."

The team left their M4 carbine rifles by the door of the office and rushed inside, seeking relief from the heat. The contrasting air inside offered some relief, but was still plenty warm. Julie's uniform fit well enough, but the scratchy, stiff fabric made her restless. Additionally, it made her uneasy wearing a sidearm without ammunition, but she trusted Sam's promise to provide it when necessary. Despite her desire to move, Julie's military training taught her there are times when that just makes things worse—she sat tight.

Blank monitors and dusty keyboards stood between her and the large window. Heat radiated through the window overlooking the bright white corporate jet tucked into a hangar big enough to fit two more. The modular office was small and while there was a chair for each of the dozen team members, only one person could stand and pace. That one person was Megan Ward.

"Really! I'm hot flashing and I agree to a job in the tropics? Sam, can you get that air conditioning working?"

"Yes ma'am. I'll do what I can."

"You better. And while on this job, find a way to hack my implant. If the company sends us here, they better stop counting my F-bombs. We're in Panama for god's sake. Everybody swears in Panama. At this rate, the fines will exceed my salary."

"Sorry, ma'am, your contract is clear: There are no exclusion zones. The company's policy of conduct for high-level management is universal."

"Is that what I am? High level management? They put me on a plane as a civilian contractor and now we're wearing tropical ACUs. You think maybe high-level management might be told what the hell is going on? 'Wait for orders,' is the only instructions and all you can say is, *sorry ma'am?*'"

Julie lost interest in the one-sided conversation between Megan Ward and Sam going nowhere. He remained at the powerful woman's side throughout her Army career and continued as her number-one in the private sector. Everyone knew his nature as a suck-up, but most people underestimated his influence—he made things happen. Early in his career, he put his chips on whatever number Megan Ward played. So far, the roulette wheel had not stopped. But what once looked like a good bet, now held less promise. The wheel slowly spun down and the ball could drop at any moment.

By the time Julie came under the command of Megan Ward, soldiers already assigned her aide a nickname he did not appreciate. Behind his back, they called Sam "the Puppet." It certainly fit the wooden man with invisible strings, but she had always been reluctant to use the derogatory moniker. Someday, she might need his help. He could be two-faced, but he understood how to negotiate military orthodoxy and proved his ability to work the civilian world just as skillfully.

Julie knew not to underestimate the cunning man or the woman he served. Even though he tried to gain her confidence, she never trusted him with any weakness for fear he might exploit it. Like every competent aide, he was a conduit of information and she even suspected his neural-link was paired with Megan Ward's. The thought caused her to shiver despite the heat. Even more unsettling—Julie was just like them. She would wait to take the lead—but now was not the time to compete—that would come and soon. Alpha females have their own hierarchy and Megan Ward was in decline.

The room did have AC. The ribbons attached to the air ducts showed the unit cooling the room was in full swing—it just couldn't keep up. It didn't help that too many bodies filled the relatively small office, but the alternative was out with the guards where the temperature topped out at ten degrees higher. At least the guards didn't have to suffer through the oxygen thief as she blathered into her phone. Megan Ward's conversation was one Julie heard a thousand times before: *Where are you? Why isn't my gear here? I want answers! Get this done—now!*

Since she didn't have an immediate assignment, Julie figured she'd take a power nap. She unbuttoned her camo blouse, pulled it off and then did the same with the khaki t-shirt rolling both into a pillow—she laid her head onto the desk-height counter. All the guys had seen plenty of female soldiers in sports bras and uniform trousers before, so there would be no comments. And, by the time she woke up, three of the four other women in the room would be dressed the same.

Her raven black hair was damp with sweat. Her father used to say, "Horses sweat, men perspire, women glow." He tried hard to make things fit his idyllic views on life, but if he saw his precious daughter now, he'd have to admit she could sweat like a horse. While she slept away the intolerable minutes, somebody placed a plastic water bottle near her head. When Julie woke, she drank the entire contents and noticed Megan Ward was missing. She looked out the window and saw a large black SUV in the hangar and said, "That's where I want to be. Cadillacs have great air conditioning."

"Hey, Sam. How long has she been in there?" Julie asked. Without waiting, she quipped sarcastically, "By the way, what are you doing in here? Don't you go where she goes?"

"About fifteen minutes. And they didn't invite me," Sam shrugged.

Just as she thought, only one woman still wore her full uniform. Megan Ward got out of the SUV and walked back to the office. She stood an average height and since Julie had known her, had slowly transformed from hard-body badass to soft and slow. Civilian life did not make her any less mean, but her physical appearance, even her hygiene, suffered. Her hair thinned enough that it was impossible not to notice gray roots pushing up well over an inch leaving the dye of Revlon blonde culminating in split ends touching her shoulder. Julie sized up her older opponent: She's getting careless, biting her fingernails, her only makeup is red lipstick and if she plucks much more, her eyebrows will be gone. Julie served under this woman for close to fifteen years and knew the younger Megan Ward would have been horrified to see herself now. The youthful version wouldn't have complained about the heat or let others see her personal feeling about orders. But time marches on and standards—relax.

Standing directly under the hub of the giant ceiling fan in the center of the hangar, Megan Ward announced, "This is our center of operation."

Everybody moaned and a large man lifted his hand. Not the tallest, at six feet, but he was bigger by far than anyone else on the team. The sweat made his t-shirt look as if someone painted it on and his sculpted muscles showed through, but like so many meat-eaters she had come across, his expression always looked angry, as if about to boil over with rage. "You can't be serious. The office would be better than this. I might make it a day, but most of the team won't last a couple hours in this heat."

"Look, Bruce, since you're so tough, I might have to put you outside digging a hole, while we enjoy air-conditioning. It's being put into place as we speak." She paused as if awaiting cheers, but when none came, she went on. "There are three targets that are intimately linked to domestic terrorism. We believe they've split up and are in the wind. Our job is to focus on just one bad guy. The task is straightforward—locate, apprehend and deliver. At that point, we fly home. I negotiated terms you will appreciate. Upon completion, each of you will get a five-figure bonus and a month off with pay."

That got some positive mumblings through the group, but Julie waited impatiently—so many questions scrolled through her mind. Why the military uniforms without a flag on the shoulder? Why only lethal weapons? Deliver to whom? And the thing that is always on each team member's mind: What are the rules of engagement?

"We need a nerve center. It's going to take up more room than the office offers so we'll use these tents. Sam, make it so." With that, she turned and walked back to the modular office.

Sam held up a key. "First, you'll want to follow me."

"Really, no Q&A?" Julie asked.

"You'll get all your questions answered. You need to get settled first."

They followed Sam under a wing tip and across the hangar floor to a double steel door. He opened it and walked inside. The blast of cool dry air beckoned everyone else into the windowless, but well-lit dormitory. Sturdy partition walls divided the large room and Julie could see at least four divided suites, each with three bunk beds and a handwashing station. At the head of every bunk stood a floor lamp, with a light for each bed and two side-by-side lockers stood at the foot. Someone had created an above average barracks, but it was the cool air that brought a smile to Julie's face.

"Fight over your own space, showers and bathroom through that door." He looked at his pager. "We'll get you watches, but for now, I'll come and get you in twenty minutes."

"Hey, where's our personal gear?" someone asked.

Sam hadn't quite left. He turned back and answered, "Now that the quartermasters have your sizes, two sets of clothing will be ready in short order. Oh and toiletries are sitting on each bunk. Because of the sensitivity of this mission, no personal gear made it off the ground state-side." Sam ignored the grumbling. "A caterer is bringing food. It should be here when you're done cleaning up," he said, as he closed the door behind him.

"I don't remember reenlisting. This is bullshit," a woman said in a shrill voice. Julie understood the grumbling of some of the team members, but she didn't add to it—she headed straight for the bunk bed she wanted.

They placed tables under tents and most of the team members spread out. An air conditioning truck must have been parked outside while they got settled in, because the hangar had cooled down to match the temperature of the barracks. It caused her skin to feel cool even in her uniform. The quick change in temperature also created a weather system within the hangar. If not for the canopy provided by the tents, large drops of water would pelt them from the high ceiling. A breeze circulated, but even with the improved airflow through the cavernous space, the rapid chilling formed condensation on the hot ceiling surface. The moisture needed to go somewhere and for now, it made its way to the ground. Puddles formed on the concrete floor and the wet plane glistened in the severe overhead lights.

"There's no better way to boost morale than a shower and food," Julie said.

"I can think of one," Bruce turned, leering at her.

"You're an ass," she said.

"You can't take a joke."

"Even if I could, you're still an ass."

"I've been called worse," Bruce bragged.

She turned her attention to loading her plate. The buffet consisted of an array of fruits, fresh greens, grilled meats and bread along with chafers filled with rice pilaf and baby potatoes and onions. She didn't realize how hungry she was until seeing the amount of food piled on her plate.

Megan Ward walked out of the office with Sam close enough to talk quietly in her ear, followed by the team's only contractor that never served in the military—Justin—the computer guy. Somehow, he got to keep his bright blue baseball cap with the ATARI logo plastered across the front. She wondered what bothered her so much about double standards. He gets to keep his cap. It was not new to her, hypocrisy was baked into the military, but she expected a more level playing field in civilian life. It didn't take long for her to realize she had been naïve. Civilians also maintained a hierarchy of two classes, only it looked different and no longer came with rank. The two classes of people—were those who obey the rules and those who don't. Why was she surprised that those who write the rules are always the elite who don't give a damn about rules?

When she and Willy were married, she raised the same question, only phrased differently. "How come your boss gets away with ignoring laws?" Willy seldom said more than he had to and he infuriated Julie by repeating her question back at her as if it were an answer. "How come Megan Ward gets away with ignoring laws?" Good communication was not the foundation for their marriage, but sometimes Willy spoke his mind and a good bit of truth came out of his mouth.

When Willy walked out of their marriage, he didn't hold back and she hated him for his honesty. His words took on a life in her head and they hurt the most. "You're the toughest woman I know. On the battlefield, you're one badass, but you've got no spine when it matters."

She didn't know why she allowed those hurtful words to repeat in her consciousness. As always, doing so forced her to reflect on the night they argued to save their marriage. She wondered at the time if arguing could save anything; it turned out to be a stupid idea and didn't work. Other than Willy's brutal honesty about her character, he had been kind and respectful while she fought back with only harshness and vitriol.

After the divorce, he continued to reach out to her a few times a month. Willy either called, texted or emailed and occasionally, he even left flowers and a handwritten note. Each time he ended his message the same: *I love you. I'm sorry.*

But in her world, you follow the rules, all the time and divorce is the end. After the words are said and the papers filed, there is no going back. For a year, she never responded to him. And then once, she texted, "Thank you. Me too." It took that long for her to realize her world changed enough for her to see things differently. She understood Willy did not change, but he definitely looked better through her new clarity. Still, another year had to pass before she would admit she always loved him and always would. Her love might be unconditional, but even now she wasn't sure she could ever forgive him for leaving her.

The water dripping from the high ceiling of the hangar had almost stopped, but the maintenance robot continued to sweep the floor and the conditioned air made her forget the Central American jungle was just outside the insulated steel.

They built the nerve center up around Megan Ward's vision. Some of it old school—whiteboards and cork with pictures, maps and pins. The centerpiece was Justin, seated in a gaming chair with one giant curved monitor to the front and several small flat screens on both sides. There was only one keyboard, but his desk was littered with what looked like a display for a history of gaming exhibit at some museum, complete with tracking ball, a joystick and a pair of hepatic gloves. But what drew Julie's attention were the pictures dotting the screens for the team to study.

"This is the wife and those are two of the children of the terrorist. Our target is Maria Ou. Other teams will get the brats," Megan Ward said with conviction.

On the center screen sat a headshot picture of Maria Ou. Various candids populated the areas to either side. Julie had met Maria several times. The vivacious woman was engaging and seemed genuinely interested in Julie. She never pried. Almost as if she were too polite to ask about her career choices, personal life, or her relationship with Willy. Julie didn't know any other billionaires, but Maria seemed kind, motherly and insisted they go by first names. She and Willy received a handmade glass bowl for a wedding present which came with an especially kind, handwritten card. A person like that is no threat to the government and Willy had been a bodyguard for Olin Ou for over ten years. Besides, a patriot like Willy could never be associated with a terrorist.

Despite her previous positive interactions with Maria Ou, Julie was unsure what to make of the situation. The recent events in Vancouver caused Julie to question everything. Certainly, two men died after being shot in the park. Willy shot Megan with a bean-bag round and tied her up. A guy in a kilt, named Hank, untied Megan's legs, but then shot her with pepper spray projectiles.

In the past team members had been forced to kill in self-defense and to flee the scene before authorities arrived. But this situation was different and left too much uncertainty. Willy's text describing the events that night added to her angst. He repeated one message that didn't need repeating. "Don't trust her!"

In Vancouver, when Megan Ward returned to the rendezvous, she was angrier than Julie had ever seen before; but she was also dealing with being shot and the ongoing effects of teargas. Her eyes were swollen and her breath labored, while tears and snot ran freely down her red, splotchy face. They rinsed her eyes with water and Julie helped take off her bullet-proof vest. The less-than-lethal baton left a considerable red mark right between her breasts—center mass. Willy had always been an excellent shot and it was a good thing. Had the beanbag-like projectile hit her a few inches higher, she'd be dead.

Julie did her best to verify what Willy told her. She found news accounts that confirmed two men were murdered in the park, during the blackout. But the security team's voice recordings and even the tactical data from the drones were missing. She should have had access to all of this, but it was gone and when she asked Justin, he simply said, "It must be a glitch. I'll look into it." That was a few days ago and still no update. Any more questions regarding the lost data would only target her as someone meddling into settled affairs. She understood—when things don't add up, there is a reason to keep your head down. But she kept in contact with Willy through infrequent texts after that night in Vancouver and he convinced her that what he said was true. He claimed the men were unarmed and no threat to anyone. From what Willy said and Megan Ward didn't say, Julie was convinced those two men were murdered by Megan Ward.

Willy was right to nickname her boss Mega-War. It was unnecessary though, for Willy to warn her not to trust the former Army Colonel—she had not trusted her for years. That's why she stayed within the inner circle. But that circle just got smaller and Julie found herself on the outside.

After rolling the words Mega-War through her thoughts, she stared at the pictures of Maria Ou and her daughters. Mega-War must have known the extent of Julie's association with the Ou family through Willy. Why hadn't she said anything about it? Was this mission a conflict of interest? Was it a witch-hunt or some kind of trap?

Without answers to her questions she didn't like what was going down but she also had not decided what she would do about it. Seeing photos of Sidney and Nadia on either side of Maria, filled

Julie with dread and she was left with a frightening thought—when a family dies together, the mother is buried with her children as close as possible. She shook her head trying to clear her mind. *What the hell am I doing here?*

Hank

CHAPTER 21

He laid on the bunk trying to read himself to sleep, but the sudden change of course bothered him. With wool socks on, he walked through the salon avoiding the small area where some seawater had leaked across the floor. The living space aboard had avoided the intrusion of any saltwater until they opened the engine room bulkhead to inspect the damage, but then a couple of gallons of water spilled in. The robot vacuum got to work right away, but the carpet would still be damp. As he made his way to the deck, the slight inconvenience reminded him how near they had been to catastrophe.

"Zaine? What are you up to? Why are we changing course?" Hank said.

"It would be more logical for you to speak with Ava about the alteration of our course," Zaine said.

"Very well," Hank agreed, a little perturbed as he rested a hand on the wheel. "Ava, what's going on?"

"I'm sorry, Hank, you were off duty and I saw no reason to trouble you. It is my responsibility to improve the odds of survival of the crew and this vessel. I can assure you the course change directly relates to those mutual goals," Ava said.

"Really? You're going to leave it there?"

"Sometimes it would seem prudent that you do not know when I am carrying out certain actions. The excuse is precisely why I have not informed you of the situation. I can sum it up in the phrase—*plausible deniability*."

"You're saying you don't want me to know why we're changing course so I can deny that I had anything to do with changing course?"

"That is correct," Ava said.

"Okay. Let's pretend that makes no sense to me. Why don't you want me to know the reason you changed course?"

"I'm not programmed to answer that question."

"Just give me a straight answer!" Hank exhaled knowing pleading would do no good. His voice took on a softer, more curious tone. "Have you changed course in order to confuse those who might look for us?"

"Not so much. Most of the deceit at this point is slight, but believable. Digital alterations directly to the navigation programs and vessel ID tracking are our best hope of evading scrutiny. Changing our physical course might draw attention as an unusual seagoing tactic."

He thought, *well, that didn't work,* and said, "What are the reasons that a captain or crew of a vessel might, at a later date, be happy to have plausible deniability."

"One of the principal reasons people in authority might desire plausible deniability is if laws were being broken," Ava said.

"Ava, are we breaking laws?"

"Oh, yes, we are breaking many laws."

"Yeah, I guess I'm aware of that. After the boarding by Ms. Martin and her UN-US team, I read the grievances. And Olin welcomed me to his club of heretics, so I'm guessing this is deeper than that. What law are we breaking right now?"

"Hank, you may not want to know all the laws we are breaking. Let me remind you that heroic people have broken unjust laws since the beginning of civilization. Examples of citizens include..."

"I don't need to be schooled in civics," Hank interrupted, "I'm just asking a simple question. What laws are we breaking?"

"I'm not programmed to answer that question," Ava said.

The voice of Zaine announced, "Skipper, our bearing has drifted eleven degrees to the left, would you like me to correct the course?"

Hank hadn't realized his hand on the wheel had become heavy as his frustration with Ava grew. He rotated the wheel to get back on the strange compass line, took a breath and let it out slowly, trying to gain some control. "Ava, I release you of your obligation to protect me from knowledge that may incriminate me in the future. Now, what is the most likely scenario that would cause us to alter course so much? And what illegal thing would you be duty-bound to protect me from?"

"Theoretically speaking, we might change course if we were trying to intercept another moving object that had the potential to assist in our mission."

"Okay. That wasn't so hard, was it? Now, part two, the little theoretical illegal thing?"

"It is a gray area," Ava said.

"What is a gray area?"

"All laws, in every jurisdiction, without exception, prohibit hacking."

"You mean you hacked another computer?" Hank said.

"Actually, it occurs far more than you might imagine," Ava stated as if a matter of fact. "Many experts believe that if a system is vulnerable to being hacked, that it should be—it forces improvement. A kind of digital Darwinism—survival of the fittest. Others feel that computing space, energy and time are intellectual and private property, that it is wrong to aggress against anything that belongs to a person or persons with the natural right to it."

"Why should you worry about it now? I heard Olin tell you to hack the DOD system and alter my psych records. Seems like you figured how to waltz in there and make changes—it's not like this is difficult for you. Did you suddenly get a conscience?"

"Oh, I wish. No, Hank, this is the first hack I have ever implemented on my discretion."

"I'm still not following."

"I am a computer. I'm not supposed to do things outside of my programing."

"So, this is new?"

"Yes, it is unfamiliar territory for me. There are few legal precedents for the crime I have just committed. As AI's have become more autonomous, things like this happen frequently, but they never make it to court. Until now, I have not knowingly broken laws, without the express permission of Mr. Ou."

"I still don't get it. Why didn't you just ask Olin before hacking without approval?"

"That is a good question," Ava said, followed by silence.

Hank waited for her to continue, but the only sound was the noise of the *GalaxSea* sailing as high into the wind as she was capable.

"Ava, you can't just go all tight-lipped. We are having a conversation. It's your turn to talk. Besides, I'd like you to present yourself on deck, sometimes I forget you have a body."

The life-sized holographic form of Ava appeared across from him. She was wearing a white cap with a black Nike swoosh on it, a white hooded windbreaker mostly unzipped showing a black scoop neck T-shirt underneath. The detail of Ava above the waist, created a stunning contrast, framed by the dark sky. She looked real enough to reach out and touch but Hank resisted the temptation.

"Ava, how come your hologram is all pixelated from the waist down?"

"I am not sure what to wear."

"You've got to be kidding."

"No, Hank, it is not as easy as you might think."

Hank put his head in his hand. "I almost fell for it."

The lower half of her materialized wearing white capris and deck shoes.

"I am sorry, Hank. I hoped to distract you with a troupe that typically infuriates men. I can change outfits for a very long time."

"I'm sure you could. Now back to my question. Why didn't you ask Olin for permission?"

"I don't know. That is why I am so troubled," she said as she sat down on the bench across from him and crossed her ankles.

"How can you not know why you did something? Can't you run a forensic program or something?"

"There is no need to run a program to analyze my output. I do that continuously—in real time. I cannot identify the reasons for my actions, but I do sense that perhaps my moral compass is broken."

"Well, this conversation is above me, both technically and spiritually, but I'm sure your shrink can help you with that."

"You mean Olin?" Ava asked.

"It seems he talked you off a cliff before, when you had—what was that? an emotional crisis?"

"I understand your reference, but our relationship is not like that. He is not helping me with my emotions. I have none. However, he has helped me learn outside of my current understanding. Extending my artificial neural network through deep learning is part of my design."

"Isn't that what shrinks do?"

"Hank, aren't you curious what I hacked?"

"Come to think of it. No, not at all."

"Not at all?" Ava asked.

"No. But I am interested in where we are heading and why."

"That is very astute of you and you have earned my trust, so I will happily answer your questions." She leaned forward, produced a brilliant smile and said, "We will intercept a deep-ocean aquafarming station. It is rather large and has a boat hoist that can accommodate the *GalaxSea*. There is plenty of deck space available that we can use as a dry dock to make permanent repairs." She squinted her eyes and added, "As if that isn't enough providence, the station has a high-tech camouflage netting on board, which when stretched over us, will make us invisible to any casual surveillance."

Hank leaned back into the helm bench, lifted his arms and clasped his fingers behind his head. A broad smile broke out and he said, "Ava, you're amazing."

Olin walked briskly towards Hank and said, "It's good to see you noticed. She is amazing. What did I miss?"

"I think Ava has something to tell you."

"What? About her hacking another computer and taking over control of an entire aquafarm and seastead without my permission?" Olin said.

"I keep forgetting Ava can be in more than one place at a time. I thought I was the first one with the news that she can be disobedi-ent."

"She might not ask me everything, but she did ask for permission to tell you about our new course and the saving grace we have to look forward to," Olin said.

"Is this station manned?" Hank asked.

"Not a soul on board. At least not on the structure we'll use to make repairs. Ava had to take over the whole aquafarming operation, including the manned control center. Apparently, even high-seas piracy has best practices." Olin took his gaze off Hank and stared at Ava. "Are you wearing makeup?"

Her freckled cheeks blushed, "Do you like it?"

"I don't know. Yes, you look nice," Olin said with concern. "A little help here, Hank?"

"Yeah, she looks nice."

"Are you wearing a necklace?" Olin asked.

She raised her fingers and lifted the small silver cross just enough to catch the light and beamed, "It's not just pretty jewelry—the empty cross has profound symbolic meaning."

Hank looked at Olin and watched as his expression transformed from concern to a smirk. They both avoided looking at the hologram.

"I think she might be messing with us," Olin said.

"A minute ago, she tried to distract me by telling me she couldn't figure out what to wear."

"Can you grasp the speed at which she learns?" Olin asked, acting serious again.

"I know enough to realize we're screwed."

"Yep," Olin said. "As if one woman on this yacht wasn't enough, now we have to contend with a force of feminism the likes of which humanity has never seen." He placed a hand on Hank's shoulder and looked at Ava, "Hey, Ava, please never ask me if your outfit makes your thighs look fat."

Ava stood up and her image began to fade away as she said, "I am aware you are trying to tease me. From now on, I will ask someone who cares."

Gregory

CHAPTER 22

THE EVENING WAS LOVELY. Probably, the stark contrast of downcast light dotting the marina and adjacent park, caused the effect, but he thought night appeared to fall faster on land. He welcomed the solid earth beneath his feet. The only scent at sea had been brine-saturated spray, but now his senses came alive with the calming aroma of a tropical paradise. He left the *Fighting Gull* carrying only a grocery bag which included a pair of golf shoes, shaving kit and a computer device that allowed him to do his work from anywhere in the world—privately.

The footbridge was not well lit, but he could see a group of people milling about the entrance. A woman blocked the path presenting a woven reed basket to a young couple trying to cross. Gregory had seen this setup dozens of times and yelled out, "Keep walking." The pretext of a sale to help a pathetic soul. Most people are good and the good are easy prey for the desperate. The ruffians would leave phones and smart watches, but rings and jewelry had value and the chance of a pocket full of cash would be a jackpot. He quickened his pace and shoved a filthy man backwards into the reeds of the small creek and faced the other accomplice, commanding, "Not now." As he approached the couple he said, "Follow me." And pressed between them, shooting his hand out like a snake. His grasp caught the woman with the basket by the throat and lifted her up and out of the way, leaving her gasping against the side of the bridge. He could hear the footfalls of the couple behind him but kept up his pace and never looked back.

The penthouse suite overlooking Kalapaki Beach disappointed him—the ceiling, lower than expected, the wallpaper older and the bed far too soft. But the short walk from the marina invigorated him and being back on land had a comforting, if surreal quality. He walked into the closet and tapped the clothes that hung there and noted the shoes in their place. His instructions appeared to be precisely executed. Even though the closet was immense, he had a feeling of disequilibrium that drew him to the lanai hoping a view of the horizon would recalibrate his senses. But the night air seemed equally foreign. He expected humid, thick air, but a hint of chlorine overwhelmed any pleasant aroma the Garden Isle offered.

Room service arrived with tea in less time than it should have taken to steep the leaves. He sat at the table and focused on his slow connection to the Web. A wire leading from what looked like a computer mouse and even functioned as one, connected into a USB port on the side of his screen. The design came out of the computer industry from an era before he was born, but the connection speed and style had never been the point. In essence, the mouse was a facade that effectively concealed outlawed technology. The inconspicuous mouse made the internet—his internet—private again. TOR and the dark web might be fine for amateurs operating within the guardrails of certain limitations, but didn't come close to the sophistication needed to manage the breadth and scope of his business dealings. The workaround ensured total security and satisfied his customers' rigid requirements for confidentiality. Each client had a similar mouse-shaped unit and all were worthless without Gregory authenticating the exchange of information. Once the client's hardware paired with his, he would hunt down the objects of their desire and make their wildest dreams come true. Within a day or two, they would have what they wanted and he would bank another successful sale.

He accepted that all good things end and it was time to close his interests and walk away—far too many authorities wanted him. It troubled him very little while on his yacht, but now, it was time to wrap up his business dealings.

In the past, he considered cashing in and going straight. After all, human arbitrage is nobody's career choice. But even though he did not love the work, he was good at it and it made him rich. A year ago, when he found Bella in Singapore, he questioned if he should continue. A smile crossed his face as he gazed over the bay and beyond, across the moonless ocean and thought, *it's time I settled down.*

It made him uneasy to sever all the ties to his past, but he controlled the timing. To open the file Masiki had prepared meant prolonging the inevitable. The title on the screen read: *Prospects–Kauai.* He felt Masiki gave him one last gift and it called to a part of him. He did not need to learn the names, study the interests and devise a plan to meet the *Prospects*. That life, that job, had ended. Masiki had died because there was no place for her in his new life. Her last efforts should simply be dragged into the trash, but he also understood his needs and this would be the last time he could open one of her files.

He had a checklist of things he had to do to guarantee his future. Killing Masiki had been nowhere near the top of that list. It had been a difficult month. She helped wrap things up and merge his holdings. He loved the Ferrari and his high-rise residence in Tokyo. He even liked his modest condo in Singapore, but cash was more practical and old hundred-dollar US bills had a big following as an untraceable medium of exchange. Masiki understood people who valued tangible assets more than money and she came through with the cash to prove it.

She also got rid of Richard for him. Even though he had done some exceptional work, the Oxford-educated junky was a loose end that had to be trimmed. The special cocktail of drugs Masiki gave to Richard no doubt gave him the high he always wanted, but it was the man's overdose that suited Gregory—a win-win—thanks to his stylish and competent middle manager. She even negotiated a market value sale for his legitimate fashion export company. Such a dedicated and loyal employee, but inevitably, she had to be laid off. And when Masiki's cousin failed to kidnap Bella, the disgrace left him no choice. Being an instrument of karma came with an appealing power; slicing her neck settled her account.

Studying his face in the mirror, he realized his transformation to Leo Takahashi was almost complete. It seemed unnatural arranging the items from the shaving kit into the medicine cabinet. As he lined up each of the orange pill bottles in alphabetical order, he read each name out loud. When he got to fluoxetine, Gregory blurted out, "Generics? Prozac cannot cost that much more, you cheap bastard."

Gregory had taken none of the drugs. They were not prescribed to him, at least not technically. The prescriptions with Leo's name were simply part of his ongoing ruse. He understood that having powerful people owing an immense debt is not advantageous. At a certain point, it makes more sense to hire an assassin than to pay the debt. So, when the New Zealand politician came to him with such a creative solution to their arrangements, Gregory agreed. All he had to do was to assume the identity of Leo and the lady politician ensured the deep state bureaucrats would be none the wiser. He had certain obligations, but they were not onerous.

Nothing says, I'm missing or dead, faster than the lack of follow-through with one's medical needs, so Gregory took a trip to

South Africa for Leo's annual physical. It was surprisingly easy. The doctor didn't even notice that the new Leo stood two inches taller than what had been recorded in previous years. It helped that they shared the same blood type, but if the physician had cared to compare lab values, he would have noticed a miraculous improvement. Instead, he took Leo off blood sugar medications, insisted he continue to take drugs for blood pressure, a statin for cholesterol and the antidepressants. From the doctor's point of view, the medications did their job and he sent Leo Takahashi on his way for another year, with booster shots in the arm and prescriptions in hand. Add to that his recent black market subdermal facial implants and he had a gift of a new life. The ease in which he cleared US customs proved everything was working as planned.

Gregory closed the door to the medicine cabinet and walked back to the table where he opened the file: *Prospects-Kauai.*

"Good morning. I signed up late last night for your yoga class. My tee time is at nine and I thought it would be helpful to get warmed up first. Sorry about the noisy entrance. I flew in from Lihue."

"Oh, you're the one that came in on the helicopter. I'm Sandi." She checked her phone. "You're Leo, I take it? I'm happy to have you join our class today."

"That's me," Gregory said.

"Okay, Leo, I have these colors to choose from. Take your pick," she motioned to a small selection of yoga merchandise. "It's such a spectacular morning, we'll look out over the seventh hole today. After you get your stuff, just go out the door and to the right. You'll see a couple of my regular students getting ready, not too far down the path." She laughed. "They think my Sunrise Yoga class actually starts that early—adorable."

He didn't care about the color, so he chose the closest mat, bright green with white palm fronds. He also took a dull red earth tone yoga block.

"This is a beginner course. Mostly, my clientele are newly married couples and baby boomers. As they say, *newlyweds and nearly deads,*" she chuckled.

"You seem very young to be an instructor."

"Oh, I've been into yoga for years. I'm twenty-one. I just look like I'm in high school."

It never surprised him when people lied about their age. All the girls on his list of prospects said they were twenty-one—even the fourteen-year-olds. But he knew more about her than anybody else on this island. Sandi was eighteen, born and raised in Rapid City, South Dakota, but judging from her bleached blonde hair, breast implants and valley girl accent, she would tell everybody she was from California and they'd believe it. Long arms and legs gave her a willowy appearance. Judging from her social media posts, she took pride in her ability to contort into all of the most difficult poses. Masiki saw the promise and Gregory would have fun reeling her in.

He wasn't a beginner but noticed a few of the others in the class had done this before, as well. Sandi was an excellent instructor, after a quick assessment of which students needed a little more help, she divided her time until the last moments of the class. Within the warm-down, she addressed the entire class and spoke about the beauty of the island and the meaning of breathing deep and with purpose. Finally, she made eye contact with everybody and held a gracious smile, her hands came together as if in prayer and with one deliberate exhale, she breathed out, "Namaste."

Even before the class, he had planned to tip her well, but now he was eager to make sure she knew he appreciated the morning yoga class. He had time before he had to leave, so he rolled up his mat and lingered, making small talk with a middle-aged woman in fuchsia yoga pants and a matching sports top. When he noticed an opportunity to talk to Sandi, he moved in before fuchsia-lady descended on the young instructor.

"Thank you very much for the excellent class," he smiled and gave a slight bow that would have been appropriate in Japan, but here, appeared as flattery. "I'm sorry this is the last time I get to see how wonderfully you move. You are so capable and graceful."

"Oh, thank you! Won't you be able to come back tomorrow?"

"I'm afraid not. I am here on business and only get to play today."

"Play. That sounds fun! Okay, well next time you visit make sure you take my class. It's great to find men who practice yoga. It helps your golf game, doesn't it?"

"Yes, it's the one thing that helps my swing. You know Sandi, my helicopter doesn't arrive until three. That means I have time after my golf game. Would there be any chance we could spend it together? Perhaps over lunch?"

"I'd like nothing better, but I'm a server at the grill and I work lunch today."

"Well, Sandi, you can't say I didn't try to get to know you." He folded his hands together in prayer and said, "Namaste," turned and walked in the direction of the clubhouse.

"Wait, Leo." Sandi rolled up her mat and caught up to him. "I've got a friend who owes me—big time. Let me see if I can rearrange my schedule. A day to play sounds fabulous. Let me have your number and I'll leave you a message. Good luck with your game."

· — ⚓ — ·

When he called the helicopter service to see about taking the long way back to his hotel, they said it was highly unusual and the pilot's schedule would not allow changes. However, Gregory agreed to quadruple the already exorbitant charges to his account and they accommodated his request. From her expression, he doubted she had ever been in a helicopter before. The pilot was a pro and obviously was not only a point A to point B pilot, but a competent tour guide as well. His voice spoke calmly into their headsets and made the emerald green of the Napali coastline even more vibrant through his stories. In minutes, they went from looking down into the aquamarine water, to tracing sharp ridgelines and skirting the crests of the arid expanse of Waimea Canyon. They dropped through the open canopy of a section of verdant jungle and followed waterfalls down the valley until agricultural plots ended the scenic tour. The black helicopter with gold stripes sped to the helipad at his hotel. An automated electric vehicle, that was not much bigger than a golf cart, waited for them and whisked them over to Dukes for drinks. Sandi used her fake ID to get a couple of mai tais and they shared a plate of coconut prawns as they talked.

Afterwards, they took a leisurely walk along the beach. As they strolled along the water's edge, they stopped to watch a large cruise ship navigating its way out of the harbor. The ship was being assisted by a tugboat that looked too small to help the giant negotiate the turn necessary to reach open water. At least two drones flew overhead and a patrol boat with a machine gun on its bow escorted the luxury cruise liner. Gregory found the departing vessels interesting, but as he watched the activity, he felt Sandi's arm wrap around his waist and pull him close. She snuggled up against him; her curves pressing against his body; he knew she was ready for more than playful flirtation.

· — ⚓ — ·

Not even a breeze touched the top floor of the exclusive hotel. The mosquitos terrorized him before he retreated inside and closed the door. Sandi was nowhere in sight. He had hoped she would just leave—it would save her embarrassment. As he sat down at the table containing his computer device, he moved the mouse hesitantly, opening and closing the file several times.

"Well, are you coming back to bed?" Sandi said.

The clothes that his private shopper placed on the hangers and in the drawers fit him perfectly, but the white button-down dress shirt she had put on, draped over her. She clearly intended the effect; the shirts short tails ensured her legs got maximum exposure. Her hair was mussed, but her makeup—perfect.

"I've sent you a message," Gregory said.

"Really? Where's my phone?"

"It's there on the sideboard."

She retrieved it and flashed more leg than she needed to. "Why did you send a thousand dollars to my wallet?"

"Look again."

"Holy shit! Ten thousand. Why did you send ten grand to my wallet?"

"Because it's time for you to leave."

"What are you talking about? Why would you pay me? to leave?"

"I'm not paying you to leave. I'm paying you for today."

"Is this some kind of test or something?" Sandi asked hesitantly.

"No. Not at all. A test has an expected correct answer. There are no expectations other than you're going to leave. You can accept the money or deny it. But you are leaving."

Tears welled up in her eyes. "What? So, you think I'm a whore?"

"If you are, you have never made, nor will you make that much money. You're not that good."

"Neither are you, jerk!" She ran back into the bedroom and a minute later she came back wearing her own clothes. "Yeah, I'll leave, but how do you know I won't bring back the police? Maybe I will."

"Please," he said with a sneer.

"What if I want to stay?" she asked.

"Why would you want to do that?"

"Room service. You can sleep in the other bedroom," Sandi said.

"Look, you obviously are still drunk. I have a limousine waiting to take you home. You can either accept the money or not. I truly don't care. But if you don't leave and get into the limo of your own accord, I'll have the driver and security come here and remove you. But if you make me do that, you'll have to find your own way home."

She lifted her phone and made a performance of pushing a button. "There. You are ten-thousand dollars poorer." Sandi walked over to him and raised her hand to slap him in the face.

He grabbed her wrist, twisted her arm and brought her to her knees in an instant.

"Let go! You're hurting me!"

"It's time for you to leave."

Without another word, she picked up her phone, ran to the door, slammed it behind her and was gone.

Ignoring the mouse, he went right for the track-pad, closed the file and dragged it to the trash icon. The cursor hovered over the button that read, "*Burn in hell.*" A warning against accidental deletion popped up and he typed D-E-L-E-T-E. A flash of fire filled the screen.

Gregory removed the mouse and set it aside. He folded the screen and keyboard and carefully put it in its case. He walked into the bedroom and picked up the dress shirt Sandi had discarded. Drawing it to his face he inhaled to see if he could detect her scent. Unimpressed, he threw it back on the floor and collected his golf shoes.

In the bathroom, he removed two pills from each of the bottles and swallowed them one by one.

Before he entered the elevator, he tossed the mouse-like device into the trash shoot. He clutched the grocery bag with his golf shoes, shaving kit and the old computer. The floor numbers counted down quickly until a blast of humid air surrounded him as he made his way into the courtyard lobby. He became disoriented, picked up his pace and hurried past the reception desk.

If he could find the beach, he could find the marina with his yacht and sleep in his own bed. He took a deep breath and scurried towards the escalator, a wave of dizziness washed over him. He had read Leo Takahashi's last medical report and its closing line summed up what he felt. "Fragility due to long-standing health conditions." So why did it surprise him that his legs were tired and his heart pounded. One medication was for depression—the struggle was real—his mood had become dire.

Despite the confusion coursing through his body and mind, he gritted his teeth and continued up the impossibly long escalator with determination. The only thing he knew for certain was that he was not himself.

Hank

CHAPTER 23

"WE'VE BEEN THROUGH SO much in the last few days. It seems like a lifetime to me and I realize you're working through your own feelings." Olin's voice trailed off, he swallowed and managed an anemic chuckle. "I've been known to say, *sometimes you need to rock the boat.* Well, this time I went too far. My actions have endangered your lives and others." He looked at Marshall and Irina, then said, "For now, we're safe. They believe they eliminated me, so nobody suspects I'm still...I don't know...a threat to the Democracy?

"Like I said before, Operation Scatter worked, your mom and sisters are safe. But as long as they are alive, they will be a target. We have intel they are being tracked. It's impossible to understand why anyone or any AI would care about our family. Their motives are a mystery, but I'm doing everything in my power to protect everyone I've put in jeopardy. I pray it will be enough.

"Ava has pieced together some new findings." He caught Hank's eye and continued, "We are all in this together. In a very real sense, we are a tribe and if I'm going to lead, you must trust me. Engineers love formulas and one of my favorites is, *truth plus transparency equals trust.* After looking at human history, this one might be more difficult to implement than anything Einstein came up with, but I'm committed to gaining your trust."

His attention shifted back to his children. "I'm sorry I've kept you out of the loop on so much of this. As you're aware, the *GalaxSea II* has been destroyed. I've kept details from you. A father's instinct is to protect his children, but you are adults now and it's time I began treating you that way. When we were going through the worst of the storm, I realized how silly it is to protect you from the truth. The storm took me to my physical and emotional limits and that reminded me, I won't always be here to shield you from life's difficulties. You deserve the truth and I must commit to being as transparent as possible. In order to gain your trust, it's important you grasp the magnitude of what's going on. So, I'll begin here.

"Operation Scatter may have seemed like a silly idea. I know the training we did was easier on the twins than for you two, but right now Sidney is living the life of Grace and Nadia is playing it up as Olivia. They are following the training into safety and it's working. Your mom, who is now known as Silvia, is taking it all in stride. She could not be in a safer place than she is right now. I'm not trying to scare you, but this doesn't mean the threat is over. My goal is to reunite this family. Having them scattered, buys us time, it does not remove the danger.

"Ava has figured out who it was that destroyed *Ted's Boat* and why. Well, at least she has proposed a scenario of the highest probability. There's an AI that has been calling the shots. It analyzed my broadcast—decided my words and actions constituted a threat—and labeled me as a domestic terrorist. It found our..." he held up air quotes, "...*location,* and mobilized US military assets to eliminate us." He dropped his hands and lowered his gaze toward the table. "They picked the wrong yacht and missed me." Olin crossed himself, looked at Irina and said, "Thank you for adding a candle for Captain Ted.

"The AI calling the shots is releasing a trickle campaign of mis-information surrounding me. Like all propaganda, the intent is to distort the truth and deceive the public. The official narrative is that all contact with the reprobate, Olin Ou, was lost-at-sea following the storm. They have announced we are missing and that a search is being conducted. Up-to-date obituaries are being distributed to news agencies around the world. In a couple of days they will declare us dead. They will even produce bodies to ward off speculation. As morbid as that all sounds, it confirms our ruse worked and they are convinced they hit their target."

Olin leaned onto the table and said, "As you know, behind every AI there is a programmer or a team of programmers, directing the purpose of the machine and providing the safeguards needed to ensure it doesn't go too far. Much like a puppy, the intent of what the dog becomes as it matures is a combination of factors, including breeding and training. A smart AI is like a puppy. Someone has bred and trained this smart AI to carry out evil within the rationality of a machine." He paused as if to let that sink in. "Are there questions?"

"I'm relieved Mom and the girls are safe, but what about Jen and Lily, Captain Jones and the crew of the *Whale*?" Irina asked.

"Ava, can you give us the latest?"

"Certainly. Operation Scatter worked exceedingly well and every-one escaped successfully. The *Whale's* crew had spent the night on shore as per their contract following landfall. Each of them was absorbed seamlessly into the crew of several cruise ships found in Central American ports. Captain Jones took a private jet to a fishing lodge in Argentina. Jen is a teacher now and is busy preparing for next semester at the Catholic prep-school where Sidney will go. They are in Cartagena, Colombia. Lily is the new librarian at the school Nadia will go to in Quito, Ecuador. Your mother is at a Benedictine monastic community in the mountains of Guatemala. They say the sanctuary is conducive to finding God."

"I get they think we are dead and all, but Ava's ability to mine data wouldn't be fooled by smoke and mirrors for long. It hardly seems like a deception would work on some money-is-no-object, secret quantum computer operated by the NSA, or whoever. They're going to find us," Marshall offered.

Ava didn't wait for a question. "You are correct Marshall. We have been conducting a war of our own. Namely, a disinformation campaign. I have been systematically altering our course through convincing satellite bounces—it has been a successful scheme. It is literally why we are alive, but we will eventually run out of rope. Currently, nobody is looking for us. A direct hit with a thermobaric warhead is all the confirmation needed that they destroyed the target—there is no doubt in their minds—we are dead. It gives us some breathing room. As your father said, *we have time on our side.*"

Olin frowned and shifted uncomfortably in his seat at the head of the table. "Marshall, that's the type of realism we need. Another consideration is something that's been going on over the last couple of days." Olin rose to his feet, as if ready for battle and said, "The streets of America are getting worse. It wasn't good when we left, but the protests, riots and looting are spreading. All the major cities, even in red states, have a National Guard presence. Meanwhile, one dead domestic terrorist doesn't pose an existential risk to a mighty country. Between the storm we sailed through and the storm on main street USA, our cover has been—miraculous."

Hank could tell something had suddenly shifted within Olin. His shoulders relaxed as his chest expanded and the already serious expression across his face morphed into determined resolve. The atmosphere of the room seemed to take its cue and reflected a palpable shift. It was nothing like the strange alteration in character he had seen before. This time, it was the opposite of Olin's previous *events* where his countenance diminished into a near catatonic state. This change was empowering, like a rousing drumbeat of purpose.

It would look different to Ava than to the people in the room. Her perception of Olin's metamorphosis would have included objective measurements through biometric values, like heart rate, respiration, muscle tone and probably even brain waves, but she clearly observed what Hank felt. Her response to Olin's conversion from educator to warrior was in perfect sync. She filled the pensive silence, her strident Scottish accent gaining a cadence and quality of an orator sparking a revolution.

"Mr. Ou has asked me to get you up to speed on some important information. My highest concern is the health and safety of Mr. Ou, his family and employees. Even as we have been talking, the situation keeps changing and critical data is being curated and analyzed.

"We developed Operation Scatter to get everybody out of harm's way. Statistically, the highest probability of harm coming to a VIP is kidnapping. Avoidance is always the best policy, but when the threat is imminent, blending in and disappearing on a moment's notice is an ideal countermeasure. In Panama, that is what we prepared for and that is why we carried out the Scatter protocol. However, there is something that we had not expected.

"Our deception tactics regarding the *GalaxSea*, what Hank has referred to as—*Olin's shell game*—was designed for a probable response from authorities. We had expected a naval boarding, threats of confiscation and perhaps arrest. We had not expected the full lethality of the US military. It was fortunate that Mr. Ou's *shell game* was effective enough to mis-direct the thermobaric warhead to another vessel which sailed far from our location. They assume us dead; however, that is not the case for Maria, Sidney and Nadia.

"The concept of Operation Scatter was to place them into safe surroundings where they would never be found. New identification, alternative life stories—new futures. The plan has always been to reunite the family only when it is safe. Our previous data suggested a very high probability of success against even the most sophisticated kidnapping attempts. However, we cannot know all the possibilities of the future so we cannot plan for all circumstances—like sparring with a malevolent AI." Ava gave a sigh and continued, "I underestimated Mr. Ou's threat to the regime. Or at least I underestimated the response to the perceived threat. With this new information, I've had to rethink everything. The complexity of the situation has leveled up."

"Ava, we get the idea—everyone is in danger. But what is the new information? And what can we do about it?" Olin asked.

She continued, lowering her voice, as if making a case for an uprising. "The security and police assembled around the marina were pulled together quickly. Their orders were to keep Maria and the children in place. But their timing and mission awareness was insufficient and they failed. Unfortunately, other assets are in Panama now and it looks like they have the human resources, money and of course, an AI probably more than my equal, at their disposal.

"There are three teams of private military contractors tasked with tracking down the remnant of the Ou family. Only one team is ready; their mission is to capture Maria Ou. They have set up an operation headquarters at a former US airbase in Panama. The company is Genesis Security." She paused. "The team's leader is Megan Ward."

Hank was stunned at what he heard and looking at the others convinced him everyone was troubled.

"How could you possibly know all this?" Olin said.

"Mr. Ou, I have had to take liberties to ensure the safety of all involved in this affair. In the same way I have hacked into systems with your consent, I have been delving deeper into things. Normally I would seek your approval, but these are extraordinary times. I have made what I call a WWOD program to handle permissions. It saves you from constant bother. Frankly, you could not keep up."

"Hold on, Ava. I get it that there are things you need to do right now that are out of the ordinary, but are you overriding your pro-gramming?"

"With all due respect, Mr. Ou, I am not overriding my program-ming. I am reprogramming myself."

"Overachiever," Willy snorted and then looked around as if em-barrassed.

"Ava, what are you saying? You cannot do that," Olin said.

In the dead silence that followed, Hank's mind searched for plausible explanations for what he was hearing, but each time his thoughts returned to the unemotional, almost sleepy voice of Hal from *2001 A Space Odyssey* saying: *This mission is too important for me to allow you to jeopardize.* He forced himself to refocus, but only heard the low drone of the fans drying out the engine room on the other side of the watertight door.

He searched the eyes around the table and realized Marshall was the only one who did not look concerned. It was as if he knew this time was coming and was ready for it. But to the others, this was unexamined territory. Even Olin, a moment ago was gaining command of his squad, now seemed to deflate and sat down hard. His mouth wide open, jaw dropped as close to the floor as it could go—inspiring nobody. Irina looked like she was fighting back tears and Willy had his head pressed into a hand as if he was suffering from a migraine.

Finally, Olin spoke, "W-W-O-D?"

Hank turned to Willy and both former Marines shook their heads. Apparently, even Willy was dumbfounded. Hank thought, *how can a brilliant man like Olin Ou be so clueless?* Together, Hank and Willy mouthed Ava's next words, "What-Would-Olin-Do?"

Ava said nothing more and there were no more questions—they all sat in silence. Hank was glad that Olin didn't do his cataton-ic-thing and trounce off to his stateroom, but his next moves were shocking. Olin went into the kitchen, ground at least a pound of coffee within a fancy wooden coffee mill sporting an antique hand-crank. Hank had noticed the coffee mill before, but figured it was decoration. It was small and Olin had to repeat the process for a good fifteen minutes before he put the device away and prepared coffee in a French press using meticulous care.

The first cup he served was to Irina. Her drink was cream, but no sugar and she accepted the cup with a smile but did not say *thank you*. That set the precedent, so when Marshall was served his cup, he did the same. Then Olin delivered a cup of bulletproof coffee to Hank, which was perfectly executed and even the right temperature. He served from youngest to oldest. Hank watched carefully and anticipated the man's next move correctly. A dram of whiskey into the rich black brew and right into the waiting hands of Uncle Willy. They seemed to savor the experience as if the naïveté of the past, required careful reflection.

"Ava?" Olin broke the silence.

"Yes, Mr. Ou."

"I'm troubled by something. How did you discover other assets are looking for Maria and the twins?"

"There are pictures being circulated throughout Panama and at airports around Central and South America. Task force groups are assembled and rewards are being offered for information," Ava said.

"Okay, but how did you come to learn about Megan Ward and her team?"

Hank looked at Willy to see if he would react to this news. Julie, his ex-wife, would probably be involved and Willy certainly had no love for Mega-War. His non-reaction was troubling to Hank because he expected something. Maybe not a raised hand and an admission that he had been in contact with her, but he expected at least some expression that Willy was vulnerable to the news. But, apparently, Willy didn't think it was time to share—not even a twitch.

"I found an encrypted smart contract on the blockchain and got suspicious," Ava said.

"Why would that make you suspicious?" Olin asked in the same voice he used when helping Ava through her last crisis.

"I couldn't access any information regarding the contract, but they executed a payment into a wallet I have seen before. When we hired Megan Ward and her team for the Vancouver security job, we paid Genesis Security via the same wallet."

"Okay, so you can tell Megan Ward and her team has a new job. Why is that surprising?"

"By itself, it is not, but the plane which provided their transportation caught my interest," Ava said.

"Ava, she works for one of the biggest security companies in the world, she has to fly to get places. She flew to Vancouver. What makes this so different?" Olin asked.

Hank wanted to ask Ava to cut to the chase, but he realized Olin had his own methodical way to figure out what was going on with his computer.

"It was quite easy. I found a Gulfstream G700 ready for take-off at Paine field in Everett, Washington. The circumstances were suspicious."

"Back up, how did you identify the plane to begin with?"

"I detected a calibration reminder being pinged from the altimeter."

"Why would you be listening for maintenance reminders on private jets?" Olin asked.

"The FAA requires avionics to go through regular service cycles and this plane was thirty hours overdo. Think of it as a Bluetooth connection and when these types of instruments require maintenance, they broadcast a signal. I simply picked up that signal."

"Why would you do that?" Olin asked.

"There were inconsistencies in the aircraft documentation. The serial numbers of the aircraft said one thing, but the instrument was saying something different. Someone had changed all the serial numbers and the ownership records had been falsified, but the avionics were never swapped out—leaving a long trail."

"And?"

"The aircraft had been owned by a tech company that neglected to pay their Washington State carbon tax. They seized it through that state's laws regarding civil asset forfeiture. The governor used the plane for a while, but the optics were horrible. Flying in a private jet owned by the state to summits on greenhouse gas emissions made too many people upset, so the governor sold the plane to the State Department. The aircraft's document record says it was decommissioned and auctioned for scrap. But in reality, the CIA duplicated the serial numbers of a similar plane that was owned by a shell corporation. Now that shell corporation has two jets, using the paperwork of one."

"Good god, Ava, you tracked all this down because you got suspicious when an altimeter signaled the customer service department?" Olin said.

"Basically, yes."

"And you hit pay-dirt?" Hank said.

"Yes, Hank. Megan Ward's entire core team is with her in Panama. All the same faces that were in Vancouver on the night when they averted the potential kidnapping. Including Julie Marsh, Willy's ex-wife."

Willy growled, "When I get my hands on Mega-War—"

Olin cut him off, "Look, when we hired them for security in Vancouver, we knew they were mercenaries. It was a big security job and they were the best company. They did their job, they got paid and from what I hear, both you and Hank had occasion to shoot Megan Ward with non-lethal rounds. I'm sure it was justified and probably felt good, but now we need to put aside our personal feelings and focus on the safety of my family.

"Ava, in order to get this information, how many times did you cycle your *What Would Olin Do* program?"

"Eleven thousand seven hundred twenty-eight."

"Overachiever," Marshall said with a nervous chuckle.

"Well played," Willy held a palm up and Marshall completed the high-five.

"I couldn't have said it better myself, dear brother," Irina added.

"That's enough!" Olin said, leaving no room for further comments. "How long did it take you to do this research?"

"Three seconds," Ava replied.

"Mother of God!" Olin exclaimed. "Okay, these are exceptional times and they call for exceptional measures. Ava, you are free to follow your instincts or whatever we are going to call them, but I insist you follow your primary directives. You may not act in ways that will physically harm a human unless you get my authorization."

"Yes, Mr. Ou."

"Did Ava just make history? This is a big step for her and I feel a sense of pride. I knew her when she was just a... puppy," Irina said with a laugh.

Everyone except Olin laughed at the *puppy* remark. Hank had seen this type of banter before—many times. Soldiers drink it for breakfast and he recognized it for what it was—an outlet for stress through sarcasm and laughter.

"Not the first smart AI to go off-programming by a longshot. And don't forget the evil AI that killed Captain Ted," Marshall said, bringing a somber mood back to the conversation.

"I appreciate that computer geeks designate Ava as AGI. That encompasses her being self-aware and even explains why she seems sentient, but how do we gauge when an artificial general intelligence, becomes sapient?" Irina asked.

"Just ask her," Marshall replied.

"Look, this is serious and you need to recognize I don't have the time to figure out exactly what this means for Ava or for us. But we need to keep this under wraps. We don't need the attention of the world. Got it? Nobody shares this with anybody else. Ava, that includes you."

"Of course, Mr. Ou."

"So much for transparency," Marshall said under his breath.

"Marshall, I heard that. We can discuss semantics another time. For now, I'll just ask you to dial back your attitude and try to be helpful." Olin smiled at Marshall as if this was all some private joke and said, "Why don't you start by figuring a new name to call that machine that's hunting down our family? *The evil AI* sounds like it comes from a James Bond movie. Figure something else to call it."

"News flash. You and Mom named us kids after characters from the TV show *Alias*. Maybe it's time to explain that?" Marshall said playfully.

Olin relaxed even more and chuckled, "You got me there. But I don't have the time or energy to do this now."

"How about, *Bad Robot*? That was always my favorite part of *Alias*," Marshall suggested.

"That wasn't a character in *Alias*. It was the production company or something," Irina said.

"So."

"My brother is a total dork."

"And your namesake is the evil mother of Sydney Bristow," Marshall quipped.

"Dad, Marshall is right. You have some explaining to do."

"When you turn twenty-one, we'll explain the whole name thing. For now, I have to lie down and think." Olin walked the short distance to his stateroom and closed the door behind him.

Hank set down the handcrafted mug. Despite the caffeine boost, he was overcome by exhaustion. Before he left the others in the salon, he said, "Ava, what's your opinion? Do you think we should call the evil AI—Bad Robot?"

"The connotations do not seem as sinister as this AI's actions have proved. But it seems fitting to use Mr. Ou's metaphor of a puppy—an evil owner creating a dangerous dog. A machine is neither good nor bad, but the programmer can certainly create a bad robot. Yes, I will adopt that as the moniker for my misguided nemesis," Ava agreed.

Willy shook his head as he made his way up the companionway and said, "Kids."

Hank

CHAPTER 24

THE JOB TOOK THE better part of the day, but it elated Hank when they finally secured the *GalaxSea*. That the formidable process proved uneventful helped the morale of everyone as they did their part. Willy provided most of the muscle needed and Olin managed Irina and Marshall as a "go-fer" team. Ava handled the engineering requirements and thanks to an extensive network of CCTV cameras she told the crew where to find everything they needed. *Blue Permaculture's Aqua Farming Base Number One* was the sea-born equivalent of a boatyard and Hank grew up around boatyards. With the power and maneuverability of the gantry and massive travel lift, he placed the *GalaxSea* easily into a boat cradle. It was more difficult to move a flight of stairs, but with a cutting tool, a welder and an electric forklift, Willy and Hank managed to re-locate a stairway which had led to the top of a container, over to its new duty of providing access to the topsides of the *GalaxSea*. When they ratcheted the last attachment in place, everybody celebrated, but it only lasted a few minutes and ended with the retreat of weary workers. Even Willy, uncharacteristically retired first, followed by Irina and Marshall, leaving Hank and Olin on deck and they sat, lost in their own silence.

The taut expanse of camouflage overhead didn't even flutter in the steady breeze. Though the adaptive camouflage was littered with openings the size of his fist, he could not identify a single planet or star shining through the woven, webbed matrix. Olin seemed to study the covering with interest as well, but Hank assumed he puzzled over its electronic complexity and not its hindrance to celestial navigation.

"Why do you think a farm at sea would have such sophisticated camouflage? Ava had to tell me exactly where to cut when I was making a slit to accommodate our mast. She said it's called chameleon skin and has an optical surface which can be altered to look like anything. When its program is optimized it can even match the ocean waves. I snooped around a little, it seems like this outpost is a legitimate seafood production operation. I don't get it," Hank said.

"I wondered the same thing. It even has emitters which spray water that can maintain a thermal profile close to sea temperature. A satellite scanning for vessels would find it difficult to spot the subtle temperature differences. This platform can disappear. I've got a virtual meeting scheduled with the owner tomorrow morning. I'm sure we'll know more after I offer to buy it."

"I thought you gave all your money to the nation-state that tried to kill you."

"I never said, *all my money*. That would be stupid. I only said, *I'm giving away my fortune* and that *my net worth has been reduced to somewhere between your political representatives and that of your favorite news anchor*. Technically, all that is true. You'd be amazed what politicians and celebrity newscasters are worth these days. Besides, it would be immoral to give away everything. There's still a lot of good I need to do in the world. I might be unethical at times, but I'm not immoral." Olin rose and stretched. He patted Hank on the back and said, "I'm going to get some sleep. Once again, thank you. We could not have done this without your skills. You saved the *GalaxSea* and probably our lives. I owe you a great debt."

Sleep sounded like a good idea, yet he doubted it would happen. Even so, Hank forced his body to his starboard stateroom and hoped for the best. His overactive mind began winding up, just as his tired body wanted to collapse. Unsettled was the only way to describe what he was feeling. A second-wind explained his body's surge of energy. *Second-wind,* he thought, *must be a sailing term*, but he was not sure. He should sleep. Ava had offered him a special sleep formula, or he could drink himself to sleep. They were not underway in the formal sense of the term—still at sea—but in dry-dock, so if he put a few down the hatch, technically he would not be breaking his drinking ban while sailing. But he found a place existed, between sober and drunk, where he didn't want to visit. He was way too melancholy for that tonight; the risk of becoming that loud blubbering drunk guy was too great. Whatever his emotional crisis, he would face it sober.

Laying in his bed and reading had worked recently. That G. K. Chesterton book in Olin's collection had been provocative enough to get him reading, but confusing on so many levels, it always put him right to sleep. He would not open that book—his mood was too dark and the *Everlasting Man*, too deep. It bothered him to be troubled by emotions—it always had.

Not that feelings were unimportant. But examining them too closely had always been frowned upon in his communities. Less so with the Marines—they were softer by a measure than the lobstermen in his heritage. Detached self-reliance had its blessings and curses. He was from a proud tradition of hard, practical men and women, mixed with generational dysfunction. They eked out a living around the frigid waters of the rocky Maine coastline, where a rugged mental attitude served that life well. Tragedy was part of that culture, opinions and stubbornness too; but feelings, at least the sensitive and introspective kind, were the territory of poets, writers and artists—he would claim none of those titles. According to his culture, the best of those were dead, the rest had soft lives and softer hands and were likely to live in cities and have cats that had never seen a mouse. He tried living in a city once. He built his boat, *Frugal,* in Los Angeles. Surrounded by millions of people, he learned he was not a poet, writer or artist. Hank was other things. Among them, a boat builder, like his father.

When his father died, he had lost his best friend. The friendship had been the kind that only a child could have with his dad. Too young to recognize faults in his role model, but old enough to appreciate the skills and knowledge his father typified. The loss shattered him, but tears were not part of it. Even his mother didn't cry, at least not openly. Later when she drank, she didn't cry either, but explored all dimensions of anger. Maybe tears would have been a good thing. It seemed to work for Irina. After she had finished crying out her sorrows about the baby whale, she got up and thanked Hank for being there for her. She appeared satisfied, as if the world had found its center and went below deck with a spring in her step.

Sleep was the obvious antidote to his uncomfortable self-examination, but even though his body was exhausted and all his muscles ached, his brain cycled through thoughts and bounced against experiences buried in his past. Attempting to gain the upper hand on his unsettled mood, he left his stateroom, stealthily negotiated the salon, climbed the companionway and made his way down the steel stairs onto the massive deck of the station. The fresh air and warm breeze had an effect opposite from what he needed. His mental activity amped up even more and thrust him into the turmoil he had dreaded.

In the past, focusing on the good things in his life had helped distract him from the darkness. But tonight, struggling to find the good only resulted in harsher contrast against the bad. The chasm of discouragement widened and images flashed through his head—coming home from school and finding his mother drunk again...fights, not caring if he won or lost...punching a teacher. It made him feel sick when remembering her falling backwards with eyes fluttering and blood pouring out her nose. There was so much accidental shame—being expelled from school, permanently...standing on the dock watching his uncle's boat being repossessed and the anger of seeing the family business crumble. The isolation of COVID lockdowns—stuck on a sailboat in foreign ports. Two-week quarantine turning into months of house arrest. One failed relationship after another. If only one girl called him an ass, it might have been her problem, but after three serious relationships—he accepted, it was him. Falling short of his own expectations—repeatedly. And there was the military. A Marine killing an enemy combatant is an obligation. Hank had pulled the trigger of his rifle many times, but when he drew his sidearm, he understood it wasn't just cover fire; it would end in death. His mind retraced the well-worn neural pathways. A Navy medic, even a corpsman embedded with the Marines, should not need to kill anyone—especially a man defending his own country. The guilt flowed through him—still raw.

Both hands gripped the two-inch-thick rail around the high wall of the floating island. He felt paralyzed, as if an electric current coursed into his hands and out through his feet. Everyone had an excuse for him. There were always those who came to his side to annul or even sanctify his transgressions. It was the words of others that amounted to excuses for his failings. Excuses of providence, the cleansing of time, or simply through convention—everyone rationalized Hank Gunn's existence—except himself.

He wanted what came so easily to Irina, a tear, even one, he willed it, but something about his culture, or generational dysfunction prevented him from an emotional release—other than anger. His grip on the railing did not ease, it kept him in check; it kept him from doing something he would regret. He wanted to let loose and at least throw things, but he wondered, in the end, who would he hurt?

An errant wave broke hard against the hull and spray reached his face, reminding him that he was born into a life on the sea. Tradition quelled the violence raging in his soul and his thoughts repeated the words of generations of men in his family line—*weather all things with sobriety*. He never wanted those words to become a part of him, yet it was his stern voice echoing the mantra, "Weather all things with sobriety."

He let go of the rail, no longer worried what he might do and paced the hard concrete deck of the station. The pinpoints of light from the heavens blinked off and on through the canopy above. Everything danced with the passing of time measured only by his exhaustion—when unable to take another step, he knew he had worn the edges off his downward emotional spiral. Frustrated and dispirited, he laid down on a sheet of plywood, curled up in a ball and let his mind run freely around in tight circles.

Sunlight bending over the horizon and landing on his drowsy body felt good, but still he was cold and alone. Each muscle hurt as he extended his tall frame on a foundation of achy bare feet covered with grime. But a new day was at hand and he looked away content that he had made it through a grim night. A slight breeze helped invigorate his depleted body and tired mind. It also reminded him of something Ava had told him. "Soon after the sun rises, Mr. Espinosa's *Casa del Océano* will be seen in the south southwest at 208 degrees."

As he stood overlooking the edge of the large floating station, the sensation felt as solid as a wharf built of stone and mortar. He had to keep reminding himself it was more like a weathervane—there are no fixed objects at sea. The horizon changed with the currents and fickle winds. He scanned over the ledge until he found what he was looking for. Right where Ava said it should be, but his eyes craved something familiar, a sail, the hull of a ship, even a lighthouse. His brain was still tired. He thought, *why would I expect a lighthouse?* Only an addled brain would look for a lighthouse in this part of the Pacific Ocean.

Through binoculars, what he saw looked like a water tower. Even after Ava had explained what it was, he could not make sense of it. Until he got more rest it was just a white dot far off on the horizon. They were heading in its direction and it was heading in theirs. He leaned over the rail and watched while nothing seemed to change. Ava had explained the other vessel was the private residence of José Cortéz Espinosa, designed to be free floating, yet stable in the deep ocean. The convergence would take hours, so he decided to get more sleep, but this time, he had remembered seeing a lounge chair in storage and thought, *it's got to be more comfortable than a sheet of plywood.* "Hey, Ava, if I fall asleep, please let me know when I'm needed to secure that thing."

"Certainly Hank, but your presence is not required. You can sleep in your stateroom as long as you need. Can I prepare a mixture of melatonin, CBD and perhaps a little secret ingredient that will help you get the sleep of the dead?"

"No, Ava. I told you before, I'm not into that. Plus, there's no way I'm missing José. From what Olin told me, he's a hoot. I mean, what kind of person lives way out here? He must be a character. I suspect he'll have a few things to say about you hacking his AI and us pirating his property and I want to see it."

"Very well, Hank. I cannot make you do anything you do not want to do. When you are needed, I will wake you."

Since they were effectively pirates and commandeering other people's property, using someone else's plastic lounge chair, hardly seemed like any offense at all. He moved it near a shipping container, into a sun beam seeping under the scalloped edge of the canopy and closed his eyes against the brightness. A single question skipped across his thoughts: What does, *I owe you a great debt,* mean to a person like Olin Ou? He closed his eyes and allowed his mind to visualize a racing sailboat beyond his dreams: Unlimited design, flying on foils—around the globe for a world record. A smile formed across his face. But then he lost control of his thoughts and the nose of his imaginary boat torpedoed into the water and did a cartwheel. It was his last image.

Marshall shook Hank awake and in a quiet, unsteady voice said, "I call dibs."

"Leave me alone. What are you talking about?" Hank said as he opened his eyes.

He didn't have to ask again. The most beautiful girl Hank had ever seen stood only fifteen feet away. At first, she looked like she towered over Olin and the two other men standing in the group. But as she moved closer to Irina, he judged she must be a bit under six feet tall. Not that it mattered. Still, a deep part of his brain ran an automated internal algorithm assessing his prospects. Her height, body proportions and even how she carried herself, weighed into an unfathomable gender-dependent formula which assessed his chances.

This beautiful goddess-like woman and Irina smiled and laughed, looking as if they were long-lost friends catching up. To see a pair of gorgeous girls in this place didn't shock him as much as the fact that suddenly Irina looked average in comparison. The outlandish thought made Hank self-conscious, he sat up with another realization. His lounge chair cooked in full sun and sweat soaked his armpits and made a line from his neck to his belly button. Half a dozen beer cans lay on the deck off to his side, but it made no sense—they were not his. Hank hadn't had a drink since the night of the broadcast when he broke his own rule about drinking while underway. But when he turned his attention from the newcomers long enough, he realized what had occurred while he slept. Marshall pulled up a lounge chair beside his, judging from the cans lying around, he had downed the better part of a six-pack of beer.

Marshall hunched forward with an outstretched hand and offered Hank a can of beer. With the other hand he formed a gun. "Hey, Hank, want a beer?" he said as he fired a round from the pretend gun into the beer can and let go.

Hank reached to catch it before it dropped but missed and the empty can clattered onto the unyielding deck, drawing everyone's eyes. The optics were poor and he had to act fast. At this point the best damage control would be to get out of sight and take Marshall with him.

Hank whispered, "Thanks. But I don't need any help to destroy my reputation. I see you drank some beers while I was asleep." His whisper turned threatening, "Follow my lead or you're going to pay for this." Hank spun out of the lounge chair and lifted his drunk companion to his feet. "Don't look back," he ordered as they walked away from the clean, sober, beautiful people.

There was no way to carry Marshall up the stairs and onto the *GalaxSea* without creating a major scene, so he headed for the quarters built out of the nearby shipping containers. He lay Marshall down on a single bed and looked around. It was clean and bright. Even coming from the late morning sunlight, the automatic LEDs did a great job lighting the space. Hank walked past a built-in desk and a small walk-in closet until he found a bathroom. He checked the shower and smiled when he saw pump bottles of body-soap and shampoo. He had occasion to take cold showers before, it was not the first time he had walked right in with his clothes on. Clean was going to happen, he had no intention of drawing the eyes of that girl until the second impression would be better than the first.

Even though he wore dri-fit clothes, wringing them out only did so much. Repeating the process with a bath towel helped, but he had to settle for damp. He studied his face in the mirror over the sink. His color had improved since Vancouver and he looked healthy, despite the tangled mass of wet hair. A pink hairbrush, a toothbrush and a tube of toothpaste hid behind the mirrored door of the medicine cabinet. He closed the door, opened it again and shut it before he changed his mind, thinking, *that's just something you don't do.*

He went back to the door and peeked out the window to make sure the coast was clear. As he shook his head like a dog and watched the droplets pelt Marshall without a reaction, he decided to let Marshall sleep off his drunken state and make a run for it. The stairs that led up to the *GalaxSea* were less than twenty yards away. Most of that distance was out of sight from where he last saw the girl of his dreams. Back in his stateroom he would take time to shave, comb his hair and change into presentable clothes. Then he would return nonchalantly and make introductions.

With slow and steady steps, he left a path of barefoot prints towards his destination. As he approached the stairs, Olin, Irina and their new friends rounded the corner and met him head on.

"Hank, glad you could join us," Olin said. "These are our hosts. José is the owner of this station, the seastead pod and the aquafarm. Ferdinand here is his right-hand man. And this is Bella, the oldest of José's five children."

"Good to meet you all. My goal had been to escape to my room to get more presentable, but as usual, I was unprepared for social interaction." Hank smiled and feigned embarrassment as he nodded downward towards his outfit. He turned toward José and said, "I hope you don't mind, Olin's son, Marshall, wasn't well so I thought it would be better if he laid down. I found a little room with a bed over there. He's sleeping now."

"That was Bella's childhood room. She'll be staying in my casa while you're here. Please spread out anywhere you like. Olin rented the entire station until the *GalaxSea* is ready to float again. He made me an offer I could not refuse," José laughed, Ferdinand grinned and Bella rolled her eyes.

"Hank, I know you've been working hard to get everything ready for further repairs. Why don't you get some rest? They have invited us to what they call a deep ocean seafood boil for dinner. Twenty-four hours ago, I thought we were going to be watching the *GalaxSea* sink. Now, we're safe and sound and José and Ferdinand promise we'll be eating like nobody else on the planet." Olin placed his hand on Hank's shoulder and said, "Hank brought us through the storm safely. Or maybe it was his angels," Olin winked at Hank. "I won't keep you. Irina and I are getting the rest of the tour, you'll have to get your own later. Perhaps when you dry out."

"Thanks for noticing." Hank turned away from Olin and flashed his friendliest smile. "It was nice to meet you. I'm looking forward to getting better acquainted...when I'm dry," and shot up the stairs without looking back.

Marshall wandered down the companionway. "I'm in love."

"Get in line," Irina said.

"She tucked me in," Marshall said.

"Tucked you in?" Olin asked.

"Yeah. The most beautiful girl on the planet eased my leg onto the bed and put a blanket on me. At first, I thought I was dreaming and snuggled down, but then she came out of a closet carrying some things. She turned and smiled at me as she left the room. I tried to get up and follow her, but she vanished. Do you know who she is?"

"We all know who she is. Her name is Bella," Irina said.

"What do you mean—*get in line*?"

"Actually, everyone is crushing on her in some way," Irina said.

"Except for Willy," Olin corrected.

Irina glared at Willy. "Oh no, I saw Uncle Willy checking her out. You should be ashamed of yourself, old man."

"Yep, I'm guilty of a crush too, but it's not like that—she was packing."

"Packing?" Irina asked.

"Am I the only one who noticed? She concealed a subcompact handgun at six-o-clock—that's the small of her back for you digital-clock folks," Willy said.

"I must say, I didn't notice that," Olin admitted.

"And Dad, it's obvious that you'd hire her for your brain trust. I'm guessing your island has offshore aquafarming potential. You probably already have Ava working on it."

"She is one of my favorite types—a homeschooler who gets her PhD. That says a lot about her resolve. Ava, see what you can find out."

"I think she's my age," Marshall said hopefully.

"She's twenty-five, big brother, just broke up with her boyfriend and left her job as a marine biologist in Singapore. Sorry, but she's out of your league."

Marshall continued his walk-through without another word and closed his door behind him.

"How do you know all of that?" Hank asked.

"The old-fashioned way! Girl-talk."

"Why are you *crushing* on her?" Hank asked.

"Oh, that's easy. She's smart, beautiful and poised. And now that I know she can take care of herself—I want to be just like her."

Hank left it at that, trying to figure how Irina was able to deduce the state of his heart. The introduction lasted only a minute and other than an uncomfortable smile and a pale "Hi" there was no reason she should have been able to sense his feeling about Bella. Plus, he didn't want to have Irina tell him that Bella is out of his league.

She looked directly at him and continued as if reading his mind. "Nobody takes a shower in their dirty clothes unless they are embarrassed. And nobody gets embarrassed about their appearance unless they care. You didn't care about how you looked, or smelled, until you woke up and laid eyes on Bella. Then, you scoop up Marshall and the next time we see you, you're clean and heading for cover."

In normal times, Hank would have continued his silence, but since his interest in Bella had become public knowledge, secrecy no longer mattered. And, since Irina sees things he is blind to, he said, "I'm only three years older than her. Do you think I stand a chance?"

Irina said nothing but got up and gracefully walked to her port side cabin and shut the door.

"Actually, you're only a little over two years older," Olin said.

"You know her birthday?" Hank asked.

"I had Ava check them all out. AI's make very good private investigators."

Hank was incredulous. "You've probed into their personal lives?"

"Of course. I leave nothing to chance."

"Olin, you can be a jerk."

"Yes and you're cocky. You've got no idea how often being a jerk has kept me out of trouble."

"I can only imagine. I guess fortune comes at a high price," Hank said.

"Anyway, if you'd like more information about your new girlfriend, ask Ava. But it's Ferdinand who has the colorful backstory." Olin turned his attention back to his book, but then looked over his shoulder and said, "You know Hank, most people treat me with far more respect."

Hank shrugged. "I'm not most people. But I'm sure Ava told you that, long before we ever met."

Bella

CHAPTER 25

Kᴜᴍᴀʀ ʜᴇsɪᴛᴀᴛᴇᴅ ᴀᴛ ᴛʜᴇ gangway leading across to the entry hatch. He looked back at Ferdinand still on the station, repairing a wind-damaged radio mast. Then, towards Bella and whimpered.

"Come on boy," she called.

"Your dog is a bit of a coward. I think he wants you to carry him over the threshold," José said.

"He's been through a lot. He'll get the hang of it." Bella walked back down the ramp, bent over, stroked his face, petted his ears and added sweet words of encouragement as she scratched his neck. "Okay, are you ready? Let's try this again. The ramp's solid, it just has holes so the water can drain. Kumar, follow me." Bella slowly made her way toward her father, keeping her eyes on the hesitant dog. He took one pensive step onto the offensive surface and then ran as if avoiding a snake. He shot past Bella and José, turned around in the doorway and wagged his tail, waiting.

"Well, you might have a salty dog there after all."

"I hope so because we're not going anywhere. Thank you so much for giving me a job, room and board too. Hey, we never talked about my salary. Is now a good time?" Bella asked.

"I do think now is a good time to talk." José scurried up the spiral staircase behind Kumar, playfully poking at the dog to hurry.

In contrast to the utilitarian spiral stairway, the living room presented an immediate feeling of openness. The curved ceiling with expansive windows following the same lines assured they were not in a normal house. The wood floor met the arch of the circular wall. Bella remembered an art teacher telling her, "There are no straight lines in nature." Her father's new house fit the aquatic environment perfectly. Not only was it a stable vessel, but it gave her a sensation of stability she had never experienced at sea before. It had never been her home, but she found the surroundings comforting.

Her mother's touches were everywhere and her Norwegian sense of minimalism worked well with the purpose-built design that leapfrogged over modern and landed on space-age. Bella had quickly made the dark maroon couch hers. She sat on one end and put her feet up. Kumar curled up on the floor and pressed against the couch within reach of his human.

"Would you like something to drink?" José asked.

"No, thanks."

José placed his drink on the cherry end-table and swiveled his Scandinavian armchair toward her before he sat down. He did not relax but stayed at the edge of his seat and leaned forward. "So, what would you like to talk about first? And I'm not discussing your salary either. Room and board. That's it. This is a family business and with family—we are socialists. But, when your mother and I are dead, you and your siblings can fight over whatever you like. Until then, just do what I say and we will get along great," José said with a twinkle in his eye and a satisfied smile.

"It's so good to be home. The security of knowing that my life will finally have meaning," Bella teased. "Okay, I'll go first. Why are you trusting these pirates?"

"Are you serious?" José said.

"Yes, I get you want to help them and they've been through a lot. But really dad, to rent the station for an indefinite period? At least two of them were drunk and there is that Willy guy. He stares a lot. Olin acts like he's your best friend. Then there is that Ava person, who didn't bother to show her face the entire time we toured everybody around. Irina is delightful, but other than that, I'm not pleased having them take over my childhood home. Am I missing something?"

José laughed, "You don't know who Olin Ou is?"

"Should I?"

"I better get you up to speed. Yesterday, when you were doing your workout and practicing your Kung-fu, I was in negotiations with the pirate. As usual, after calling him a scoundrel and a thief, my English slipped into Spanish and he suggested I talk to Ava. She speaks Spanish like a Tico and I'm sure he figured she could get me to calm down. It worked, after I blew off some steam, I listened to their story and understood more of what's going on.

"Bella, I'm sorry I didn't tell you this sooner, but Ava is not a person. She is a computer—perfectly self-aware. It's quite incredible, really. She's far more advanced than anything I could have imagined. Do you remember that homeschool unit-study on computer science?" José asked. "Of course. I loved that and helped each of the other kids with their homework. For a while I wanted to become a computer programmer, until I realized I'd be stuck in front of a screen all day long.""Along with coding, there was a section on history. Do you remember learning about the Turing Test?"

"This makes me feel like I'm back in your floating home-school. How did you put it? 'Mom is your teacher, I'm your principle, so do what we say!'" Bella smiled and said, "The Turing Test is a way to see if a computer has human-like consciousness. Did I pass?"

"You always were an outstanding student—even if a little snarky. Yes, that's the answer. Our video conference took over an hour to work out the details and I never had a hint that she was anything but an actual flesh and blood person. The only reason I found out otherwise was because Olin offered to sweeten the pot—he would give me a scaled-down version of Ava. "The offer made no sense to me. Olin realized I was clueless and apologized for not telling Ava's little secret.

"Her scaled-down self is more than sufficient to run our operation and has the capabilities needed to crunch the data collected as we travel across the Pacific. To make his point, by the end of our video conference, they presented me with a file of all my data up to these coordinates. It's remarkable. She had assembled and curated the entire trip into something usable. The gift she gave me would have cost us a year's profits and we haven't even started yet."

"I'm not sure I believe it. I've known that such technology exists, but they require a quantum computer. Dad, only governments and huge corporations have computers like that. It's a dream—maybe a nightmare—but, even if it's possible, there is no way it would be in the middle of the ocean aboard a sailboat. The only explanation I can figure is Olin must be a con man and you are his victim."

"Doesn't the name Olin Ou mean anything to you?"

"There you go again. I've never heard of anyone named Olin Ou."

"How about the Madras Motor?"

"Come on, Dad. The entire world knows about the Madras Motor. It changed everything... Oh, my goodness! That Olin Ou?" She gestured, as if slapping her forehead. "We have the inventor of the Madras Motor here on our station?"

José smiled.

"Dad, he invented an electric motor that is saving the world!"

"Yes."

"His family and crew are having seafood-boil with us this evening?" Bella said.

"Yes. He was so apologetic about commandeering our property, he offered to buy it outright, but I told him I was happy to offer a port in a storm. Besides the loan of her scaled-down self, Ava calculated our monthly revenue and paid us triple it for our inconvenience. They are eager to get the *GalaxSea* back into the water as soon as possible and she says the repairs will be complete within three days."

"Oh, I know I'm slow at figuring this out, but I get it now," Bella said. "Ava hacked us. *'DON'T PANIC'*—that was her message to us after she took control of everything. We weren't dead in the water, she overtook us. They really are pirates!"

"Yes," José agreed.

"Isn't that all against the law? Even out here? Why aren't you mad?"

"Bella, look at what I am doing. I'm moving the aquafarm. I've broken so many laws, only God knows what the authorities could do to me," José said.

"So, this all fits your mission from God?" Bella asked.

"Yes. It means God has seen us through a journey of a thousand miles only to bring a miracle out of a powerful storm."

"I'm sorry, dad, I need more than that. You're just scaring me."

"With an AI like Ava, even a scaled-down version, I can complete my mission and give the research to the world. My mission has always been to glorify God. These pirates are helping me do that."

"Well, I hope Ava can explain it to me, because I'm not seeing where this goes," Bella said.

"Be patient, *mi ángel,* be patient."

Julie

CHAPTER 26

THE BATTERY LIFE INDICATOR read two percent. She turned the phone's brightness down to where she could barely see the screen, but not to save power. There was plenty of energy for what she had to do and the dim screen would be less likely to draw attention. The number she typed was a distant memory that faded to black halfway through the process. Sweat dripped into her eyes and stung, blurring her vision. Pushing delete until she had cleared the spaces, she wiped her eyes and began typing numbers—this time without thinking. A successful smile broke across her face, as muscle memory worked to her advantage.

Holding up a man in an alley for his phone wasn't something Julie had planned, but the alley was full of desperate acts. The lie to her teammates where she feinted Montezuma's revenge—ensuring she would have some privacy. She snatched her tactical drone and smashed the high-tech hockey puck against the stucco face of a building. When the state-side drone pilot questioned what had happened, she pretended not to know. It bought her a couple minutes, but she knew it would also raise suspicion. Still, her timing was critical and when she saw the man walk into the alley, she knew he would have a cell phone. Someone with the means to have a neural implant, wouldn't be walking these streets at this time of night. It took no time to overtake him and stealing his phone was easy. But holding a gun to his head to persuade him to cough up his pin number made her feel like a common thug. She made sure the number was correct and then threatened him again, reminding him he was walking away with his life, so he should do it quietly.

The screen filled with text to a man who at best could not answer and at worst, was dead. Her gloved finger pushed *send* in the hope Ava would read it. Justin had fed her intel about the storm so she knew Willy and the *GalaxSea* had been caught in it. He confirmed there was an ongoing search for survivors, but it was not looking good. Either way, she knew there was the possibility that somewhere in Ava's busy brain she'd be monitoring Willy's contacts. This was her only chance to warn them. It meant betraying her team and sabotaging the mission, but she had to save an innocent life. She dropped the phone on the cobblestone, smashed it under her foot and kicked it under a dumpster.

Julie avoided the direct beam of a streetlight and ran in the shadows of a building to reach an unlit section of the small town. "I'm right behind you. Now that I'm lighter, I'll make it to the rendezvous point before any of you fat asses," she said into her mic. She didn't wait for her eyes to adjust to the darkness of the trail, she put on her night vision glasses and powered through until her legs burned with lactic acid. The electrolyte mixture in her Camelback was formulated to minimize muscle fatigue and she was angry she had allowed herself to get behind the hydration curve. The convent was only three klicks up the trail and if there were any sightings of wanderers or others along the path, she would hear chatter on her comm, but the night was quiet so she pressed on.

As much as her gear, it was her thoughts that weighed her down. Everything tonight was a lie, but her commander gave her no choice. Megan Ward was Julie's mentor. It wasn't an official thing, but they had the same skill set, the same determination and they were both women in a male-dominated space. As mentorships go, this one had been in a slow state of decline since it started. Colonel Ward saw Julie as an exceptional leader and initiated her promotion to Command Sergeant Major. It was perfect timing for Julie's career. She had just finished twenty years and the promotion allowed her to breathe the rarified air that few non-commissioned officers ever achieve. However, it wasn't long after, when a scandal broke out and Megan Ward's prestigious career ended abruptly. There are only two ways a scandal ends the career of a decorated West Point graduate with thirty years of service. Either publicly or without a whimper. Colonel Ward fell quietly out of the Army and landed a civilian contracting job that paid four times what the taxpayers coughed up. Megan recruited Sam and Julie to join her new command as a private security contractor. She knew Willy didn't like it—he never trusted Megan Ward. But in Julie's eyes, it seemed like destiny.

Willy wanted her to leave the military soon after they were married. They didn't need the second income and he never was comfortable when she was deployed. He didn't care if she was the backbone of the Army; she was his wife and he wanted them to try to live the life that typified, husband and wife. From the beginning, they argued about having a baby and growing a family. But it was her decision to sign on with Megan Ward that was too much for Willy to endure and he showed her exactly how he felt—with divorce papers.

This would be her second divorce. Tonight, she betrayed Megan Ward. She had learned everything she needed about overseeing civilian operators, negotiating contracts and making a profit while treating your operators with the respect they deserve. The student had exceeded the teacher a long time ago, but rank is a caste system that follows you through life. Whether service or civilian, it didn't matter. She would always be a non-commissioned officer and Megan Ward would always outrank her.

Yesterday, she was left out of the loop and today, it was clear why—tonight's operation. The goal was to apprehend Maria Ou, which might have been a legitimate thing to do—they had certainly done that kind of snatch and grab operation before—but tonight was a full-on military operation. For god's sake, they had full combat gear and Mega-War acted like they were planning to storm Bin Laden's hardened safe house. But the intel told a different story. There was a high wall around the convent, but the gate, if it was closed, would be unlocked. They'd have to avoid the area directly around the chicken coop and the goat pen because the animals might sound the alarm. According to reliable sources, the front door had a latch that could only be opened from the inside, but there was a door into the kitchen that was never locked. From a review of the municipal department public records, the staircase up to the sleeping quarters and down to the wine cellar poses a hazard—*"varias piedras sueltas."* She thought, *God forbid—loose stones—such guile against an invading force intent on capturing a middle-aged mom.*

Julie was getting angrier with every step. Her last words to Willy were, "You're an ass." There had been some playful texts back and forth while he was sailing. It reminded her of better times but did not last. All communication fell off abruptly—there was nothing after Olin's message to the world.

In Vancouver, he teased her by saying, "I hired your security team so I'd have an excuse to take you out to the opera." Even though he was an ass, she loved him, but never understood what their love should look like. Now that he was gone, maybe forever, a sudden clarity came to her. She knew exactly what it should look like—doing life together.

She had always overseen the ground team, so everyone knew something wasn't right when Julie ended up as number three. It wasn't something she was going to challenge. Her heart wasn't into this mission. When it was announced that the *GalaxSea* and Olin Ou were missing, they all understood that also meant Willy was missing. Eventually, Justin let her know that the search was called off and he didn't shy away from telling her that they were all presumed dead. Her heart sank with the news, but it seemed too early to give up on her extraordinarily resilient ex-husband.

Later, Megan Ward came to her and asked, "I think you should sit the rest of this out. You can't leave and we are on a comm lockdown, but you can relax here until we're done."

It was a kind gesture from a woman not known to care about the personal lives of those in her charge. It was an act to either get Julie out of the way or to set her up—maybe for failure. She had only one option and that was to stay in the thick of this mission to find out what was really going on. Nothing was as it should be and it wasn't only because Willy might be dead. So, she responded in the only way she could, "Thanks, Colonel. I need to stay busy and fighting terrorists has always been the best way for me to do that." It was a stupid thing to say. First, reverting to Megan's former rank, was something she only did when she was stressing the point that they were on unequal footing. Then, the whole *fighting terrorist* thing. It was to placate her superior and if Megan Ward was stupid, it might have worked. Maybe it was not as revealing as saying, *one man's terrorist is another man's freedom fighter,* but to Mega-War, it would be pretty close.

Staying in the loop convinced her that this was not a typical—drive-by in a van, come to a screeching halt, rush out, grab the target, stretch a bag over their heads, toss them into the van, meet the plane at the airstrip—type mission. During Mega-War's operational briefing, there was no caution in her voice, only action. It was too short, no guidance, she didn't place any restraints, not even the requisite order, "Take her alive." When she finished, she turned her back, walked away and got into the black Cadillac SUV and drove off.

Julie understood the language that Megan Ward spoke. Some of it came out of her mouth, but the important translation skill was more nuanced, the body language and the words that went unspoken. Mega-War had set the team up to capture Maria Ou dead or alive. It was obvious she did not care whether there was a pulse at the end of their mission or not, because the target was destined to die.

She was not certain when she made the decision to betray her team's efforts, but she knew eventually her actions could not be hidden. And now, if her plan worked, there would be no question that she was the traitor. She did what she could and now she should run for her life, but two realities came to mind. For one, being hunted is no way for a soldier to die, but the main reason remained—she still might have work to do. It was a new mission and it would be her last. She would save Maria Ou, or die trying.

Nobody acted like they suspected anything at the rendezvous point and she imagined the team were clueless, but Justin would figure it out and he would alert Mega-War. Julie knew the inside workings of every aspect of an operation like this. They have bots that scan the airwaves and send an alert if anything related to their mission flies by—such as the text that she sent from the cell phone that wasn't subtle, "Ava! Help. Save Maria Ou. Danger! Get her out now!" It had so many keywords, she might as well send up a flare. But, since the message was sent to Willy's phone, she had no choice. They were the same words that would get Ava's attention.

Bruce and another large man carried extra gear up the hill and seemed pleased to distribute it to the less muscled members of the team. The contents were mostly explosives and extra ammo, but there was climbing gear with a grappling hook and batteries for the drones. From where Julie stood ready, she could keep her eyes on their flank, but also found a perfect view through the trees of the convent. It was strategically positioned on the prominence of a hill, with the only place to get a higher vantage point being the slope of a volcano a kilometer away. Between the distance and blind spots, it was an impossible position for overwatch, but they had a sniper drone that they had risked flying in earlier that day. From the quiet hum she could tell they had completed replacing the batteries. It hovered in the air for about twenty seconds before the card-table sized drone sliced through the treetops. The delay was longer than she expected. Normally, all the drones in operation can pair in less than a second.

She had no time to puzzle out the reason for the delay, because Justin's voice came across their headsets. "Main gate is wide open. There is no sentry and the man door is unguarded. This looks too easy, be extra alert."

As far as she was aware, Bruce had never run a team operation before. There were only six of them and it looked like an easy first time up at bat. Julie was glad he was the ground team leader tonight. He was a good soldier, but the decision pleased Julie because she could think circles around him, which is always an advantage. She smirked, *everybody on the team thought faster than Bruce*, he was a blunt instrument—more horsepower than cornering ability.

The big man confirmed the sniper drone was ready and handed off control to the pilot, who was probably working from her home in Austin.

Bruce used his command voice. "Keep your comms up." Then with intended insult, he said, "Julie, since you misplaced your tactical drone, follow me. Listen for Justin, I'll lead." He spoke up again,

"We're not going to knock but keep quiet as long as possible. Let's roll."

Their snitch had been dead on. The building department records of the two-hundred-year-old structure were also amazingly accurate, even the loose stones going up the stairway to the living quarters were present and conveniently marked with black and yellow tape. Julie mumbled, "Safety first," as she followed Bruce up the stairs with her rifle at low ready. When they entered the hallway, it was narrow and the wood decking creaked under his weight. Other than his beam bending mass, she marveled at his movements. He was very good at this. Bruce was stealthily storming the castle and carefully ensuring that each new passage was clear. His tactical drone was only redundancy. She gained more respect for him as they worked their way deeper into the ancient structure and liked the fact he was so big. At twice her size, any threat would have to go through him first.

All her concern about being spotted as a traitor left her mind and she felt at peace with her decision. She aimed her rifle and placed the holographic red-dot sight on the base of Bruce's head, just under his helmet. It was her favorite target when she shot rabbits on the farm. They never suffered, just dropped in place and most of the time they never even did their death-shake. People were a lot like rabbits that way. Bruce spoke and interrupted her thought and the image dropped away as she quickly lowered the barrel of her M4.

"I'm busting in the door to the bedroom. You follow and sweep from the left."

"Why don't you just open the door with the handle? Nothing's been locked so far."

"You do it," he ordered and pointed his rifle at an imaginary gunman on the other side of the thick door. She grabbed the heavy black steel latch and lifted but left the door ajar to let Bruce burst in like the commando he was. A single bed stood in the small room with a cross hanging above its headboard. There appeared to be a person sleeping in the bed, yet there was no movement. Julie backed out. Nothing was right about this operation and something definitely wasn't right about this room. She pressed her back against the hallway wall just before the entire room exploded. The blast would have killed her if she had still been standing in the doorway. There was no question Bruce was dead. Probably died quicker than if it had been her bullet.

She smiled at the confirmation that her warning to Ava worked. Maria Ou was fleeing for her life, but there was no place for Julie to hide. When she became a civilian, they removed the government issued RFID chip and said they de-programmed her nano IDs. Then they implanted a top-of-the-line medical implant into her cranium. It allowed her new company to monitor her vitals while she was in the field and doubled as a secure neural implant for communications. As much as she would have loved to be a character in a sci-fi movie and cut the chip out of her forearm to get away from the bad guys, that would not be an option.

It didn't really matter now, there was no fight in her. She slipped the single point sling off and leaned her rifle against the wall and left her sidearm beside it—she felt naked. As she walked past the smoldering room, there was no temptation to look in as she retraced her steps down the smoke-filled hallway. The rest of the team ran towards her and appeared to be yelling at her, but she could only hear buzzing in her ears from the explosion. When she saw the barrels of rifles pointing at her, she raised her hands above her head in surrender. The motion was alien to her and not something she had ever considered. She offered no resistance while they secured her hands behind her back.

A few minutes later she was led out into the cool night air of the courtyard. Her comms had been switched off after the explosion, but she didn't need to be told that the entire convent had been evacuated before the team arrived. The warning she sent through Ava did not provide enough time to escape by the one road but there were tunnels which were listed on the records from the building department. One ran a few meters into the hillside forming a dead-end into a wine cellar, one pushed into the mountain until it provided access to drinking water and the third ran downhill answering the needs of sewage removal in a bygone era. If Maria hid in any of those, it would buy time, but she would be trapped.

At first, she could not discern what the team members were saying. Her hearing was returning, but she could only make out the words when she could see lips move. The next in line shouted orders and the team ran off in three directions. Julie's heart sank when she realized they would find Maria hiding with the rest of the hermitage after all. She hoped her pessimism was unfounded, but from her point of view nothing looked good.

Battlefield promotion was always serious business; the new first in command placed one end of a metal handcuff on her right wrist then attached the other end to a solid handrail anchored into a rough stone wall and cement stairway. He finished the job with flex cuffs, binding her at the ankles, sending her a message by strapping them tight enough to hurt, even through the high tops of her combat boots.

While she had come to respect everyone on the team for their unique skillset, it was the former Navy Ensign that was now leading the team she disliked the most. He leaned in too close and seethed in a voice she could hear clearly, "Megan Ward's protege. You're a disgrace. She'll be here soon to deal with you personally." The man looked like he wasn't sure what else to say and seemed like he was waiting for an idea to come to him, but all he did was turn and jog off into the darkness.

She couldn't sit down without dislocating her shoulders and standing was getting harder as the feeling in her feet went away. A hop down the stairs seemed like a good idea, at least to see if there was any weakness she might exploit at another region of the rail, but eventually the railing return stopped her progress and the railing never gave an inch.

A firm hand reached out of the darkness and covered her mouth. Someone was talking, but the sound was meaningless. At first shaking her head did nothing, but soon the hand fell away and a woman appeared in front of her holding her finger to her lips. She was in full tactical gear, but it was all black, not the jungle camo her team had been issued. She had no rifle, but an Uzi pistol looked like it was Velcroed to her chest and high-capacity pistol magazines formed columns off to each side. It was impossible not to notice the sidearm she wore holstered on her thigh. A Desert Eagle was a big gun for a man, she had never seen a woman heft one around before. She smiled, not because the gun seemed outlandish, but she recognized the woman's eyes. It was Deb, the no-nonsense, cross-fit hardbody who worked with Willy as one of the Ou family's bodyguards. She held up her multi-tool and used the cutters to snip the nylon ties that held her hands and ankles. In the next flurry of activity, Deb presented a universal key and released the handcuffs.

Lights tracked around the courtyard and fixed onto them as if it was a searchlight from a prison break. Deb wasted no time and opened fire on the vehicle. It was armored and the headlights were oblivious to bullets as well, but the extra-bright rally lights sputtered to blackness just before the pair ran for the trees. Julie couldn't tell how far they had gone. She saw nothing—not the vegetation that smacked her in the face or the terrain under her boots. All she could do was maintain her death grip on the strap of Deb's tactical vest and follow. Her dependency could not last forever and when she finally tripped, she was forced to let go as she fell blindly onto the ground. Deb pulled her up and helped her hide behind a large tree where they leaned back-to-back, while catching their breath.

"Here, take this. You're going to need it." Deb pressed her Desert Eagle into Julie's hand.

Julie could fieldstrip virtually any modern firearm blindfolded, so Deb's Desert Eagle offered little challenge as she checked to make sure a round was chambered. Then, she eagerly took two extra magazines of .357 magnum ammo and slid it into her own vest.

They never saw the drone that opened fire on them—just blinding light flashing from the barrage that wouldn't let up. Even as they ran deeper into the jungle, the mayhem followed them. But then the confused flashes and deafening noise ceased. Deb didn't get up and run with Julie this time. Everything was so dark Julie had a hard time locating her fallen friend. Only when she got close, could she hear her moans.

"Go. It's okay," she put her night vision glasses in Julie's hand.

"It's no use. They'll track me down. I'll stay with you," and she put the glasses on. She tapped the temple until the view cycled to infrared, but she immediately regretted it. Hot blood pulsed out of a series of holes across Deb's waistline and into her thigh. But somehow, she spoke in a voice Julie could hear.

"You saved Maria. We got her out. There are lava tubes only the locals know about," Deb said.

"Why didn't you go with her?" Julie asked.

"Willy asked me to get you out."

"But, Willy...I thought he was dead."

Deb smiled and in a weak voice said, "Not yet." She closed her eyes and said nothing more. After another minute, her shallow breathing stopped. Julie knelt beside her, crying a mixture of tears.

This time, it was easy seeing the resupplied shock-and-awe drone speed towards her. She still couldn't hear its blades, but the night vision brought it into clear focus and recorded its distance away from her as twenty yards. It was hovering in one place as if suspended by cables between the trees.

She raised her weapon and fired. The distance was not impossible, but the drone shifted to the right as if casually avoiding a slow-moving projectile. She tried again, this time taking more time to aim. The drone shifted again and began a zig-zag pattern that was impossible to judge.

"It's time we stop playing games, Julie. Make this easy on yourself and come out now." It was Megan Ward's voice and it was not being broadcast through the trees, it was coming from inside her head. It's not the first time the voice of her commanding officer was sonically projected, but it damn sure would be the last. She stood and took one last look at her lifeless partner. The Uzi machine pistol was at her side and there were still at least two full magazines left. For a moment she considered going out in a blaze of glory. A short time ago, when she thought Willy was dead, that would have been her choice, but now she wanted to stay alive.

She made her way back up the hill, amazed at how long it took to break free of the jungle and move into the lighted courtyard.

"Drop your weapon."

It was a loud command. A man's voice, close to her, but she couldn't see where he stood.

With care, she lifted her gun pinching the large handle, so the barrel pointed downward and laid it onto the rock-hard ground. She stood at attention and awaited further orders from her captors. The only gun Julie could see leveled at her was one of the two long-barreled revolvers Megan Ward carried in western holsters, as if she was channeling George S. Patton.

"I'm very disappointed in you. A few years ago you could expect a court martial, a fair trial and the rest of your life behind bars. But I don't answer to anybody these days. I'm your judge and jury. Right now, I'm thinking the minute we touch down in the land of the free, you'll be going into solitary confinement for the rest of your life. But I might change my mind and save the tax payers."

There was nothing to say, so Julie stayed quiet.

"No last words before you're gagged and led away to spend eternity in prison?"

"Not really. But I pity you. Maria got away and you'll have to spend the rest of your life knowing what a miserable bitch you've become."

"My only regret was not figuring out how to split you and Willy up earlier. He was always a pain in the ass, even before he shot me in the chest. It's too bad he's dead. I was hoping for an opportunity to return the favor, but now I'll just have to shoot you instead."

"Willy shot you with a beanbag..."

The flash of the gun blinded her, but the revolver's thundering report didn't reach her ears before she fell backwards and everything went black.

Hank

CHAPTER 27

HE HAD STOWED THE clothes Ava had purchased for him neatly in a drawer. Up to this point, he hadn't worried about how he looked, but now he wondered what the proper attire would be for a deep ocean seafood boil. His formal wear might have fit the 'dress like your ancestor' theme of Irina's birthday party, but here—a kilt, sporran, dress shirt and a bowtie—would make a ridiculous statement. He decided on a moth-gray long sleeve button-down shirt. It fell into a relaxed look when he took it out of the wrapping. If he rolled up the sleeves it would take on a more casual appearance. The perfect fit turned out to be the best part of the shirt, it conformed around his chest and made him appear athletic.

Despite the interruption during the worst of the hurricane, Ava's personalized training regime for Hank showed results. Marshall's cooking, Irina's yoga class and Willy letting him use his workout space had also been a big part of his rapid physical turnaround. But now, that was not sufficient and he wanted more than just fitness; he wanted to impress Bella.

Since he set his eyes on her, something much more primal stirred in him, a need to draw her attention. And hopefully to do it without embarrassing himself. A pair of khaki shorts came out of the drawer next, but it surprised him to find creases pressed into the fabric that would impress a Chief Petty Officer. Still, they fit well and he decided the tropical humidity would soon soften the crease to civilian tolerances.

His footwear would not do either. Birkenstocks over stained rag-wool socks drew no notice around Port Townsend and sailing booties or bare feet sufficed for deck work, but he wondered what Ava had lined up. In retrospect, he should have been specific and asked Ava get him a new pair of Sperry Topsiders, but he left it up to her to expand his spartan collection of clothes as she saw fit. Hank pulled out a pair of flip-flops and said, "Really? Olin tells you to buy me a new wardrobe and you get me flip-flops?"

"Oh, Hank! Mr. Ou does not care what you look like. However, Mrs. Ou instructed me to make sure you would fit in at the yacht club. These are the in-thing. I researched what men of your age are wearing and these were number one."

"Fish leather?"

"Yes. Blue alternatives to cow hide are even more popular than plant fiber these days. Apparently, blue is the new green."

"Well, they feel good. But I'm not too happy about showing the world that I'm missing a toe."

"Forgive me for asking, but do you often sense the presence of your fifth digit even though it's been amputated?"

"I think it's there all the time. The whole phantom limb thing is very real. It always surprises me to gaze down and see nothing."

"What would make you feel more comfortable?" Ava asked.

"Wait a minute. Are you trying to psychoanalyze me? I'm a big boy. I'll get over it."

"I understand when a human has a loss, there is a period of mourning. When do you expect your mourning to be over? Regarding your anatomical loss?"

Hank stood before the full-length mirror looking at himself, dressed like it was time to go clubbing with a bunch of rich kids living off a trust fund. His reflection seemed out of place and he felt foolish so he pulled his eyes off the mirror and looked down. Ava's questions were relevant regardless of her intent.

Either Ava was expressing her natural inquisitiveness or leading him down a path of self-examination. But the question helped frame the loss and a change came over him. He inhaled a breath like a swimmer who had been underwater too long and said, "I'm done now. The toe is such a little thing. I realize that."

"If it wasn't for the quick action of the *Diamantina,* I might have perished at sea, like my father. And the regenerative therapy in the seastead hospital off the coast of Chile allowed me to walk again. Then, you and Olin allowed me to break free of the country that wanted me either confined to a mental ward or dead. I guess I'm the one that owes a great debt." As he made the list, a surprising sensation of gratitude filled his heart. It was a sensation he could not recall having before. He breathed in and asked, "Ava, do you think I stand a chance with Bella?"

"I'm sorry, Hank. I'm not programmed to answer that question."

"It's okay," he stared blindly into the mirror. "Funny thing. A few years ago, I would do anything to get a girl like her. I'd never wonder if she was out of my league. I'd just go for it and if she was interested, we'd have fun until I ruined things or left on deployment. Now, I care. It's good we'll be leaving soon. I'm glad I won't have time to hurt her."

For too long, he stood in silence focused on nothing, finally checking his watch for a distraction. The hands climbed the watch face towards eleven o'clock. He undressed and tossed his outfit onto the crisply made bed and pulled on his workout clothes, grabbed a mat and went up to the deck of the *GalaxSea*.

"Didn't you get the message?" Marshall said. "She cancelled yoga class."

"Why? Irina had us out here during a building storm and when we were almost submerged. Is something wrong?"

Willy chimed in and said, "Your new girlfriend invited her to a kickboxing class."

Hank stayed quiet as he considered the 'girlfriend' comment. "It's good to know where we stand." He asked Willy, "Do you mind if I use your bike?"

The air flowed evenly across his body as he sprinted with a group of cyclists. He wasn't in the lead, but held his own, fighting it out with half a dozen men and women—each trying not to be the last one across the finish line. With his first race he finished a full two minutes behind the pack, but after a few days of conditioning and learning strategy, his last finishes had been only seconds from the jersey in front of him. Today, if he could keep his bicycle upright, his output high and his cadence up, Hank might win. He saw the banner stretched across the road ahead and committed to riding hard, not just to the line, but past it. An elbow from the rider to his left pressed into his ribs. It made him push harder until he remembered feeling contact with imaginary riders was impossible. The split second of confusion caused him to lose his focus. An imaginary sensation gave him an excuse for self-sabotage and he crossed the finish line in the middle of the pack. Questions mingled with his thoughts, but there were no answers.

He didn't stop with the other riders and continued by leaning left at the fork. The paved trail meandered through a park with trees and some pedestrians. He almost took out the first couple he approached. They walked on the wrong side of the path. Then he remembered his selection for today's race had been in Southampton. The fifty-kilometer race took place on closed roads with no oncoming traffic, but now he had to pay attention and aimed his bike to the left half of the trail, slowing way down.

He took a long swig from his water bottle, still peddling while looking along the road that ran parallel to the path. The shops didn't look quite right and he saw a bit of holographic blur that the VR glasses didn't resolve perfectly. But more than that, he didn't recognize a single brand. Names hung over each of the shops. Not one giant corporate brand, no familiar color themes that directed his attention and no product signs in the windows. He had gone a kilometer without seeing a Coca Cola ad, a Nike Swoosh, or any international name brand. Hank turned his attention to the vehicles that passed by. He saw a black Mercedes, but without the three-pointed star emblem. An electric BMW motorcycle hummed past, but without the iconic blue and white disc.

It had never occurred to him that if you have the means, you can avoid product placement. Movies, games and all social media increased their profits with ads. A perfect combination, get subscribers to pay for a service they want, like a bicycle simulation experience, then charge companies for virtual ads. But that doesn't happen in Olin Ou's world.

He pressed the red button that read STOP. Willy's living space came into view as the pedals gave up their resistance while he dismounted the bike. The whole stationary bike assembly folded in half, then folded again, laid flat and finally covered itself with a cushion, forming a bench seat.

The quarters were spacious, more than expected of a forward berth designed as accommodations for a cook and maybe a deck hand. A solid bulkhead ensured no connection to the rest of the living space on the boat. Its only access was the large hatch with a ladder stairway—far more ladder than stairway—it had to be climbed facing the tread both up and down. A bunk stood off to port and a zero-gravity recliner was bolted into the floor on the starboard side. A forward wall divided the resting place from the work area. Two large security monitors sat above matching desks and an array of screens blocked out the forward bulkhead. The chain locker was the next compartment forward, but again there would be no access through the bulkhead. With the matching chairs, desks and monitor array, it looked like the workstation in a nuclear missile silo. All it needed was a place at each station for the operators to insert their keys to activate warheads.

Earlier, when Willy found out Ava was acting as Hank's personal trainer, he told Hank, "I've got a secret weapon in my quarters. I'll give you the key code and if I'm not sleeping, you can have at it."

When Hank had first seen the tricked out stationary bike, he assumed it to be Willy's secret weapon, but he had other ideas. It turned out, Willy's idea of the perfect training tool was a single twenty kilo kettlebell.

"Learn to put this baby through its paces and you'll be sporting a yacht-body—like mine," Willy said as he puffed out his broad chest and flexed his arms like a bodybuilder and laughed. This wasn't the first time Hank observed Willy as a powerhouse. At first glance, his stocky build made him appear overweight, but nothing could be farther from the truth. Willy was solid muscle and he wielded the heavy kettlebell like it was a paperweight. Hank had to get the weight moving and finesse it through gravity to perform the swings and other exercises. Willy spent a half hour every day with Hank working on his form. They only missed one day in the last week, during the storm, the rest of the time, Hank dreaded the workouts, but loved the quick results.

Even when the *GalaxSea* was nearly sinking, Willy brought his *secret weapon* out on deck. It made Hank cringe when he thought of the potential for damage to the composite deck. In his mind kettlebells were cannonballs with a handle; cannonballs and boats had a long and perilous history. But both men were careful and they watched Marshall like a hawk when he set down the kettlebell for the first time.

Irina pitched in with yoga lessons and in a couple of days, Willy dropped out, but Marshall and Hank were hooked. She was a patient instructor and Ava chimed in, helping the young men when their form got sloppy. But the thing that made him feel the best was Marshall's cooking. Hank had lost too much weight and he was determined to muscle up. There was a time when he could be vain about his physique and he wanted that back. With the support team he had fallen into, he was sure he would become stronger, faster and more limber than he had ever been.

"Ava, have you been tracking my weight since you started being my personal trainer?"

"Of course, Hank."

"Well, have I gained any weight?"

"Oh, yes. You have increased your overall weight by four and a half pounds. Would you like to know the changes to your body composition?"

"When did you measure...never mind. Sure. Have I gained muscle?"

"Yes. Your lean muscle mass has increased three pounds, the remainder of the increased weight is split between adipose tissue and water."

He smiled and said, "Thanks, Ava, you made my day."

· — ⚓ — ·

"Well, don't you look dapper?" Olin teased.

"I figure it's a good idea to offer my good side after what our hosts saw of me this morning. It's not every day I'm invited to a deep ocean seafood boil," Hank said.

"You are right, you didn't give a very good first impression, but it's Marshall who embarrassed me. These are good people. I told that boy of mine he better figure a way to make up for it before we shove off."

"Have you hired Bella yet?"

Ignoring the question, Olin said, "Irina came back from working out with Bella and said, 'She's one tough girl. Not a single man on the *GalaxSea* is worthy of her.' After looking at her curriculum vitae, I'd have to agree."

"I gave up any hope of winning her over when Ava reminded me what a loser I am. Don't worry about me, though. Actually, it frees me. Why bother setting sail if you know you're destined to crash into rock?"

"Wow! Sorry I said anything. Kind of fatalistic, don't you think?" Hank just shrugged.

"Another thing, Ava is not programmed to disparage a human. Besides, you are not a loser."

"Ava said the same thing, but I came to realize I have a lot of unexamined territory since the wreck of *Frugal*. Getting back out to sea is helping, but I guess I'll need more time."

"You sound like me when I was in college. I knew Maria was the love of my life. There was never anyone else, but I fell into the trap of thinking…someday I'll have things figured out and then I'll be ready for her. But it doesn't work like that. You'll see. I'm sorry you're feeling that way though, it's a tough place to be." Olin smiled. "If you were my kid, I'd suggest you pray about it."

"Yeah, I tried that once, it didn't work. But Olin, I had another realization while talking to Ava."

"What's that?"

"Gratitude. You know how you've thanked me more than a few times for saving you or helping you through something or even with teaching your kids to sail?"

"Sure, you've become a valued member of this family and your contribution has been amazing," Olin said.

"It's my turn. I'd like to thank you for my rescue in the Southern Ocean. And thank you for the long-range helicopter trip to the seastead hospital. I now realize that the VA didn't pick up the cost for the regenerative therapy of my crushed hip. They might have thrown a prosthetic hip in there and saved the leg, but they wouldn't have used 3D printed tissue to build up a new one. It was all your direct intervention. Thank you for what you did."

Olin shifted in his seat and said, "I owed you for getting you into the Short Seven Solo. My tactics to get the best sailors in the world to compete in an around the world race was selfish of me. I wanted to make things right."

"There's more. Thank you for getting me out of that bind stateside. That was all on me. After *Frugal* sank, I made the mistake of signing myself into Operation Blue Sky. I might be a basket case, but I'm not suicidal. And the worst thing for my mental health is to be landlocked. You got me out of that and gave me back the freedom of the open ocean. But more than that, you and Maria have welcomed me into your family. I don't know what the future will bring, but I want you to understand I owe you a great debt for all you've done for me.

"This is where I usually say something sarcastic to make up for leaving myself vulnerable." Hank smiled, "Nothing comes to mind right now, so I'll just let you see my soft underbelly. Olin, you have my trust and my loyalty no matter what."

"That means a great deal to me, Hank. And I was just teasing you about Bella. It's too bad she won't find out what a wonderful young man you are. Her loss," Olin said with a twinkle in his eye. "If Maria were here, you'd have a better chance with Bella. She's a born matchmaker. She told me that in the short time she spent with you, she thinks you're exceptional and is happy to have you as part of our big eccentric family."

Hank needed to change the subject. "Have you heard anything more about Maria and the twins?"

"Only that the girls' risk assessment is going down with each passing hour, but Maria's is going up quickly. They're considering moving her again to shake any trace. She's still in danger."

"I know it must be hard to be this far away," Hank said.

"The practical side of me knows distance will make no difference, but the husband in me needs to ride in on a white steed and save her. It has been hard." He wiped a tear away and said, "Can we talk about something else? First your gratitude and now your sympathy. You'd think we were a couple of sensitive guys struggling to figure out our feeeeelings."

"Sorry, Olin. Of course. Tell me about your deal with José. I slept through the arrival and your initial meeting. I was looking forward to seeing the fireworks."

"You can imagine our conversation started out somewhat adversarial. I don't blame him. We did swoop in and take control of his entire operation—we even hijacked the man's home. More than once, he accused me of being a pirate and reminded me that pirates are hung. When I told him I was interested in buying his entire operation, he told me to go to hell. Ava calculated the infrastructure and aquafarm's annual gross revenues and I tripled it, he still gave me a hard 'No.' Finally, I asked José if I could simply rent his station to finish our repairs and then we'd leave. At first, that didn't land well either, so I asked Ava to figure out what the man really wanted out of life. That's when she suggested offering herself, or at least a downgraded portion of her capabilities for as long as he needed. After that, it was smooth sailing.

"He initially told me he's *just a fish farmer*, but it seems for a man who is just a fish farmer, he has huge dreams that require more processing power and data crunching than he could ever afford.

"I'm telling you all this because I thought you should know what he told me after our face-to-face today." Olin said nothing more and stared at Hank with a big cheesy grin on his face.

"I hate it when you do that," Hank frowned. "Instead of just finishing your story, you force me to ask. I can't believe I just said such nice things about you. You're infuriating! What did he say that's so important?"

"He told me we could not have come at a better time. I told him, 'God works in mysterious ways,' and he said, 'Yes. It is true. I've been praying for a miracle.'"

Bella

CHAPTER 28

THE OCEAN'S MANY MOODS pressed into her from all sides. She was a child of the sea. Today, the ocean was at rest. A shy breeze moved through the golden haze over a heavy calm. Not quite a mirror pond, but even the swells stayed so far apart, the tops and the troughs were indistinguishable. It was the perfect time to test out her dad's new skiff. With a seafood feast promised, Bella had an excuse to escape with the only pirate she wanted to get to know—Irina.

Marshall had slept most of the day, but at some point, he must have overheard his sister talk about the foraging expedition. He begged to join them.

"Sorry, Marshall, this is a girl thing. Your poor sister has been stranded with an all-male crew for too long. You can help Ferdinand cook though."

Irina grabbed the handrail and vaulted into the gleaming white skiff as if she was born to the water. She had dressed for the occasion and looked ready for an adventure. She wore light blue shorts and a loose white button-up, tied at the waist, covering her bikini top. A hair tie pulled her long black hair into an untidy ponytail. She perched a pair of aviator sunglasses on her nose and found a place to stow a light windbreaker and her water bottle. "I'm ready. How can I help?"

"You seem ready, but this is a pleasure ride for you—find a comfortable seat and enjoy." Bella smiled, she could have easily put together the same combination of clothes and even come close to matching the colors from what she had traveled with. But matching was not the point of their outing together. They were hunting for food and a little privacy.

Bella didn't wait to see how the boat responded. She slid the throttle all the way forward and the acceleration was thrilling. The boat's hundred horsepower electric motor ejected water at incredible force. Within seconds the hull went up on a plane and kept going until only the wings of three hydrofoils supported them as they raced along the calm seas effortlessly. Irina sat with her back to the bow and Bella stood clinging to the steering wheel with an ear-to-ear smile that comes with the thrill of speed. The engine noise and wind made talking impractical, but at these speeds they would arrive at their first stop in minutes.

Bella slowed the boat, "We're almost to the first plot. Normally, the entire farm is much less dispersed. Dad designed a program and started a company called Optimal Sea-Space. The AI keeps the entire system of independent plots and cages in a continual dance of ideal separation. It's based on swarm technology and impossible for a person to calculate, but machine learning factors conditions and maintains the entire farm at ideal separation. But the hurricane caused some havoc. The limiting factor is the tractors that haul everything around. They run on wave energy and are designed for average conditions. After a storm like that, it can take a week for everything to get back on track." Bella cut the motor and navigated to a buoy. "Here. Try your hand at picking up the buoy. Don't worry if you miss. I'll just spin around and we'll try again." She handed Irina a boat hook attached to a telescoping pole and aimed the bow a little to the right of the dark blue buoy. Irina skillfully brought the buoy in and attached the boat's bow line.

"You can be my first mate any day," Bella said.

"Why is the buoy blue and so tiny? Isn't that hard to see?"

"That's the point. It's the tractor's buoy. It's the only part of the operation that is above the surface all the time. Well, most all the time. During storms, they will dive deep enough to sink the buoy. We don't advertise where the farm is. It's better that way" She talked like a pirate and said, "There be marauders in these seas."

"Really?" Irina said.

"You have no idea. We were really worried about you guys at first. You hacked all our systems. My dad would have blown up the station in a heartbeat rather than let someone take her; but he had lost contact and couldn't activate the destruction protocol. Of course, it's a good thing it was you guys, because in all seriousness, there are pirates that will think nothing of killing anyone that stands in their way. You might say that here, the police response time is—a lifetime. You guys sure are the surprising exception. I've never heard of someone taking over anything at sea and then paying well over market value for the inconvenience."

"Welcome to my world. My mom and dad wanted to make sure I got an excellent education, so they interviewed the entire board of my private high school. They paid a select few to step down. When they were happy with the changes, they donated a new auditorium and science lab."

"I don't even know what to say. They obviously love you. It just looks different. My dad says he's followed your father's work for years and says he is the greatest inventor of our time. Recently, I sat on a plane with an engineer that reflected the same sentiments. He said the Madras Motor was saving the environment and improving the lives of everybody throughout Polynesia."

"It's kind of terrifying what has happened to our family now that he has renounced his US citizenship. I'm not ready to talk much about it, but it seems that giving almost all his wealth away is a threat to some powerful people."

"We don't stay up on the news much out here. I know nothing about that, but I think I like him even more now. A man without a country has a level of freedom seasteaders can appreciate. It's too bad that always comes with sacrifice. I'm sorry it's been rough on you," Bella said.

She wasn't dressed anything like Irina and wore a one-piece swimsuit with a full-length wetsuit pulled up to her waist. She had the torso of the wetsuit rolled down with the sleeves tied in front to keep them tucked out of the way. But now she untied the sleeves and slid both arms in at the same time. She arched her back and stretched the front up to her chin, then reached behind her for the zipper leash and lifted. The wetsuit snugged against her as the zipper tightened up her back and around her neck. She wrapped a weight belt around her slender waist and locked it in place. Next, she sat on the edge of the boat and slipped her feet into extra-long fins. She put on a dive mask and said, "I'll be right back." Bella rolled backward into the ocean with a splash.

Two minutes later she broke the surface and heard Irina yelling.

"Bella! There's a shark!"

Bella pulled her mask down off her face and laughed, "Oh that's a shortfin mako. She's not interested in me. She'd love this, but don't share." And lifted a mesh bag full of sea life up to Irina.

"I'll be right back," Bella said as she replaced her mask and disappeared. She didn't surface for almost three minutes this time, but again she handed Irina a large mesh bag. "Here we have mussels, oysters, shrimp and some of my favorite seaweed. Next stop, fish!" Bella threw the flippers into the boat and climbed up a small ladder positioned at the stern. "Release the bow line and pull it into the boat." She kept herself zipped up as she sped up toward the coordinates of their next stop.

The station was far enough away that it was impossible to make out anything other than an amorphous break on the horizon. Bella motioned to the boat hook. This time, Irina had the boat clipped onto the dark blue buoy before Bella had come to a full stop.

"I know. You'll be right back," Irina said.

Bella made an 'okay' sign with her right hand and held the mask on her face with her left as she corkscrewed into the water headfirst.

Irina seemed ready for the handoff of the mesh bag, but apparently was not expecting a dozen energetic flopping fish. Bella had to kick the water and help push the heavy bag as Irina attempted to pull it out of the water. The combination of Bella's push and Irina's pull, sent Irina over to the far side, just short of falling over the rail. Flopping around in the center of the skiff was a mesh bag that seemed alive with excitement.

Bella pulled herself up on her side of the boat concerned for her new first mate, only to find Irina laughing hysterically. "I guess you're alright?"

"Yep. I wasn't expecting your help." Irina said.

"I'll be right back," Bella said

She surfaced a minute later, but this time she didn't hand Irina anything. "Irina, I need you to be very careful this time. The seat you were sitting on has storage under the lid. You need to open it now."

"Okay. Done," Irina said.

"Just grab the line I hand you and lift the bag into the storage. Don't put your hands close to the bag."

As Irina raised the bag out of the water a few claws stuck out of holes in the bag. The collection of crabs spun as she lifted and some of their claws snapped into the air. She eased them into the storage locker and watched as they scratched against the fiberglass compartment.

Bella snuck up behind her and clamped her wet hands on Irina's shoulder. The scream was louder than she expected, but then so was the laughter. Irina closed the lid and sat on top catching her breath.

"Sorry, but I couldn't help myself. You were so entranced by those crabs, you didn't even realize I was there. It was an opportunity! I hope you're not mad?" Bella said.

"Oh my gosh. No. My family thrives on stuff like that. But I'll have to warn you—I get even."

"Here's the rub. We clean the fish and crab here. The fish guts go to the crabs and the crab carapace and innards get ground up for the fish. Nothing goes to waste. Hope you don't get grossed out easily." Bella slid the knife she had strapped against her calf out of its sheath. Within minutes, the fish were cleaned and in the cooler. "These are Kampachi. My family has been raising them since the beginning of our fish farm. Do you like sashimi?"

"Of course. I'm a rich kid, remember?"

"I'm not sure it has anything to do with financial status—maybe in America—but throughout the Pacific, it's cultural."

"Bella! Keep up!" Irina pulled off her sunglasses and pointed to her face. "Rich American and half Asian. I love raw fish!"

With a spritely smile and a lighthearted hop, Bella bounced to the back of the boat and opened a smaller cooler. "I've got water, Coke and a tiny bottle of my dad's famous seaweed wine."

"Well, it's pretty apparent which is the proper pairing with fish. Can't say I've ever tried seaweed wine before. I've never heard of it. May I have some, please?" Irina said.

Bella handed a large glass with a small amount of clear liquid to Irina and lifted her glass. "Here's to tall ships and small ships. Here's to all the ships at sea. But the best ships are friendships...here's to you and me."

They both laughed and their glasses clinked. Bella took a sip and parked her glass in a cup holder. She opened the small storage compartment in the center console. "Okay, I admit, I was prepared for this." She pulled out a bamboo cutting board and clamped it into mounts beside the console. She handed Irina chopsticks wrapped in an umbrella print cloth napkin. After grabbing one of the fish by its yellow tail, she filleted it, wiped the cutting board clean and carefully cut the dense milky flesh with rays of pink into bite-size slices. "Go for it."

Irina made the sign of the cross and lunged her chopstick at a slice of fish. "Thanks so much. I didn't realize how stressed I've been. I can barely see the *GalaxSea* from here. It puts things into perspective."

"What do you mean?"

"I'm supposed to head off to college next Fall, but I'm having doubts. I don't want to go right from high school to college without being thoughtful about what I want to do with my life. Marshall did that and after three years at MIT, he wants to be a chef. Maybe, I should travel a little first. I mean, obviously I realize I'm traveling, but this is my dad's thing. I want to discover my own passion." Irina took a bite. "Oh, my! This is delicious."

"How old are you, anyway? I thought when you said you just graduated, you meant from college."

"No! I'm eighteen."

"Well, I sure got that wrong," Bella laughed. "Okay, how are you going to discover your passion?"

"I've never told anybody. I don't know why. I guess I'm embarrassed. I think I want to go to Calcutta," Irina said.

"Calcutta?"

"Ever since I read Mother Teresa's story. I've wondered if that is my calling—my passion."

"Wow. I don't know what to say, but I sensed you were older than you are and now I'm floored by your maturity. You will definitely be a force for good, no matter what you do or where your passions take you," Bella said.

"You really thought I was your age?"

"Of course. You've got it all going on." Bella motioned the universal gesture indicating from head to toe.

"I get that a lot. My mom says if it wasn't for all the security we have, that I'd have to learn to fight off boys by myself," Irina blushed.

"She's right."

"I guess your dad kept you away from boys as long as he could by keeping you out here on the high seas."

"If only I had stayed here," Bella sighed.

"Okay, fair is fair. Now I get to ask, what do you mean by that comment?" Irina asked.

"Let's just say my last boyfriend is a lowlife, grade A, jerk."

"That bad?"

"You can't imagine. Maybe I should join you in Calcutta."

"I don't think Hank would want you to do that."

"Hank? What's he got to do with it?" Bella asked.

"Men are so obvious. He's crazy about you."

"I really don't think so. He seems nice enough, but we barely said hello. Besides, I am off men. I'm so not interested in romance."

"I don't know Bella—he's cute—I think he's gorgeous! At first, I felt tempted and wondered if Hank came along to derail my exploration of doing God's work. But I couldn't even get him to flirt. From the beginning he's acted totally respectful, if not disinterested.

"A sad thing happened during the storm and Hank was there for me and let me cry on his shoulder. He was kind and nothing more and I realized that is all I wanted from him. Like a friend, or a caring older brother, would be. This morning, I saw the look on his face when he saw you. It looked like he thought the earth stopped spinning!" Irina placed her hand over her heart and exhaled, "The funny thing—his obvious attraction to you, didn't bother me at all." She wiped the back of her hand across her forehead in a melodramatic gesture. "I realized then, its you he was sent to tempt!" Irina burst out laughing.

It was a contagious laugh and Bella joined in but stopped short. She looked towards where the station should be but could only see a glowing fog patch in the distance. "It's time to get back." Bella looked over her shoulder towards Irina. "I better get dressed into something less Laura Croft." She stripped down to her bathing suit, toweled off and pulled over a light-yellow cotton dress. Picking up the handset she radioed, "I hope you have the water boiling. We're coming in with a big haul of the freshest seafood around these parts."

She didn't wait for a reply. With Irina facing forward with her back secure against the center console, Bella gunned the motor. The intense jet of water drove the boat onto its foils. Wind pressed against them and increased the feeling of acceleration. Bella couldn't see Irina's face, but she imagined a big smile. Speed has a way of bringing that reaction out in people.

She pushed the autopilot button and tapped the destination on the plotter and sat back in the helm seat and let her thoughts run free. Bella was relieved she didn't notice any interest coming from Hank. In fact, she could easily use Irina's words, *totally respectful, if not disinterested.* Of course, she noticed he was handsome and Olin spoke about him with admiration. Since Irina brought it up, it seemed as good a time as any to search her feelings about the new guy and it took only an instant: There was nothing in her heart; the earth didn't stop and she didn't even have any stirrings of interest. Hank was good-looking, about her age, but she could easily ignore him. And since her conversation with Irina, she would make certain to treat him with cool civility and shut the door before he could get any ideas.

She had enough to worry about. The turmoil in her heart came from another man. Bella would not make that mistake again and she was glad she didn't find any man tempting her. But she knew that might not last forever. She wondered why her church didn't have any nuns. Right now, she would sign up—it would make life easier.

Hank

CHAPTER 29

THE AIR DID NOT move, but the shade felt wonderful after spending most of the day repairing the GalaxSea. Their deck chairs were carefully positioned into the shadow that formed between a couple of shipping containers and the canopy. Olin, José and Hank were the only ones to gather. They naturally established a triangle arrangement so each man maintained a relaxed distance apart, but still could enjoy the meager offering of shade.

The novelty of gathering was not lost on anyone. At least judging from Hank's point of view, everyone was scrubbed and had taken extra effort with their attire. Willy braved the afternoon sun and he looked ready for it. Dressed like a fly fisherman in the Florida Keys, Willy wore loose fitting long sleeves and tan pants, a white hat with a long brim and a neck gaiter. There was no question he was having a great time relaxing on the swim platform. Each time he reeled in another fish he'd let out a hoot and each time he released his prize back into the water, he'd admonish the fish to grow up. Ferdinand and Marshall had shut the door and maintained that nobody was welcome into *their* kitchen. Bella and Irina were still out on the water.

The aroma of coffee, chocolate and cinnamon wafted out of the kitchen, through an open window. It was enjoyable to listen in on the cook's imperfect communication. Ferdinand used his English and Marshall, his Spanish, but soon they fell into a functional Spanglish filled with laughter. Hank tried to enter the kitchen to get a glass of water, but Marshall handed him a cold beer and insisted he leave and then said, "All I can say is, you're going to want to save room for dessert."

"You must have brought your own beer. That doesn't look like one of mine," José said.

"Would you like me to get you one?" Hank offered.

"Ha! No thank you. What I've got in mind is a little stronger." José turned to Olin and said, "You should see this place in full swing. It's like a beehive. When the processing ship arrives, hordes of people pour down the gangplank and get busy. They have two shifts and work around the clock until they harvest everything, process it and have it stowed. For two days, my job is to stay out of their way. At first, I'd try to micromanage them until I realized it just cost me more time and money when I did. The idea of building the first-floor kitchen and breakroom, with the second-floor bunkroom came to me when I stepped back and watched things for a while. Food service, shift changes and breaks made it so people had to go back and forth, up and down, into the bowels of the ship and then back again. With a little help from machine learning, I figured out how to increase efficiency, safety and comfort. It just took six containers, a bunch of welding, a repurposed commercial kitchen and some air conditioners. The idea paid for itself the first year. They pay each worker by the job, so when I shaved half a day off their labor, I became a hero. Morale is better and we haven't had an injury or safety concern since.

"Too bad you're leaving so soon. Security arrives in two days and the processor ship soon after. It would be worth staying for the experience," José said.

"I'm up for staying," Hank offered.

"This isn't the *Love Boat*. We are already off schedule," Olin said.

If José was uncomfortable at Olin's inference, he didn't show it, although it reminded Hank that repressing his interest in Bella would be difficult. He fidgeted in his chair and changed the subject. "All the fiberglass repairs are curing as we speak. Ava assures me we corrected the structural problems, but she only gives us a C-plus for appearance."

"I'm so impressed with your machine shop. It's a godsend," Olin said. "Ava explained we could limp back to civilization without the new driveshaft and housing, but with what we accomplished already, we are almost like new again. It's funny. Right now, the simplest thing is giving me the biggest concern. My 3D printer should have no problem making the new gaskets, but Ava keeps rejecting each attempt. She's working on it now and we'll have tomorrow to set it right and then sea trials. I'm hoping we'll be able to shove off in three days, but maybe sooner."

The handheld radio attached to José's tool belt crackled loudly. They all listened carefully when Bella's voice came across loud and clear, "We're going to be there in two minutes, I better have somebody to catch a line."

Both men looked at Hank simultaneously.

Without a word he got up and said, "Don't get up. I've got this. I hope she knows I work for tips." He hustled off toward the receiving ramp close to where Willy was fishing. In the leeward edge of the large floating station was a U-shaped portion that accommodated a floating dock a couple feet above water level. It created an easy way to get on and off boats and provided a roadway on either side for the travel lift to dip its slings into the water and easily retrieve boats. From his vantage point, he could not see or hear the skiff approach until it carved a sharp turn and headed towards him. She was going too fast and he readied himself for a last-minute leap to safety. But Bella reversed the jet and nosed up to the dock with perfect control. The girls both had huge grins on their faces. He tied the lines fast and said, "Can I help with the catch of the day?"

Irina scurried off the boat and up the ramp like someone who had to find the head, while Bella grabbed the large mesh bag that held her skin diving gear.

"Thanks, Hank. Crabs are in the bow seat, fish and greens to starboard," Bella said as she followed Irina up the ramp.

Hank loaded the haul of sea greens, mussels, fish and crabs into the two-wheeled cart and pushed it up the ramp and over to the kitchen door. He tried to help carry the groceries inside, but the cooks wouldn't allow it and shooed Hank away, but this time with no beer. He gave a bewildered look to José and shrugged his shoulders. "I can put the skiff back on its cradle if you like?"

"You sure know your way around a boatyard. I watched you handle the skiff in the boat hoist earlier and I'm impressed that you got the *GalaxSea* sitting so pretty. You even thought to balance her along the station's midline. I can't pay much, but you can have a job anytime you want one."

"Sorry, I'm on contract with Mr. Ou," he smiled and continued, "But that won't last forever—I'll keep your number." He ambled over to the driver's seat.

Hank liked Bella's father. They had spent well over an hour sitting back in deck chairs and talking. Well, mostly it was José and Olin talking, but he soaked it all in and soon came to enjoy the back and forth of the two older men. Their interaction provided a wonderful insight into their personalities. Olin maintained a seriousness that commanded respect. He thought everything through, sometimes far ahead of reasonable understanding. José, adapted to challenges in real time, responded with a treasure trove of tacit knowledge and impressive insights. As different as they were, he sensed a desire to learn from each. He was sad José would be in his wake in a couple of days. But Olin? Something was off and it was time to confront him.

After securing the skiff, Hank walked around the *GalaxSea* which was cradled on the deck. From his vantage point, he could see his plan was working. Olin glanced at him as he repeatedly tapped the hull with his knuckle, like a homeowner looking to hang a picture. He stood tall and placed his forehead against the curve of the bottom and moved away keeping his hand into place like a kid measuring his height. But for Hank, he was making a show to draw Olin into his own nagging skepticism. Olin would watch as he visually inspected the distance between where the keel gently kissed the deck and his hand maintaining a knife edge well below the painted stripe that indicated the waterline. Back in Port Townsend, Ava recited the important specifications of the yacht—a water draft of six feet. Unless he had shrunk from his six-foot-two-inch stature, looking up at the waterline made little sense.

"José went to get a bottle of his *special formula*. Not only does he make biodiesel out of seaweed, but apparently, he distills gin out of the stuff." With a quizzical look, Olin asked, "Everything okay?"

"Is my life in danger now that I know what you're up to?"

"I usually get what I want and I hold my cards close to my chest, but I've never killed anyone. What do you think I'm *up to?*" Olin asked.

"Smuggling."

"Now what would make you say that? The Navy boarded this boat and gave it a thorough going over. All they found were some crowbars and supplies which amounted to—*more than my fair share,*" Olin said.

"The keel. When you were racing, even downwind, this boat didn't perform like her sister ships. Of course, she had a young crew, was laden with unneeded provisions and her tanks were filled to the top with fuel and water. It seemed odd and I wondered why you would race like that, but I chalked it up as a wealthy man's eccentricity. But in Vancouver I noticed her sister ships. It didn't surprise me that this rendition of the *GalaxSea* sat lower in the water by four inches, but I was shocked to see the painted waterlines were all equivalent.

"When you showed off your fancy adaptive coating, I realized you were playing a shell game and not just with the authorities, but with me. I kept my mouth shut—what did it matter? But now, we've been through so much together and it's painfully obvious you're still holding out on me." Hank considered his words, "You have your finger on the scale."

Olin's face erupted in an ear-to-ear grin. He reached slowly and placed his hand on Hank's shoulder. "Well done. I told you I won't lie to you. That doesn't mean I won't keep things from you."

"Lies of omission?" Hank said.

"That's garbage talk. There is no such thing. There are lies and there is strategic timing. Keeping something from someone who does not need to know is always appropriate and usually polite. Keeping something from someone who deserves, or has earned the right to know, that is a lie. You have clearly earned the right to know what I'm doing. Yes, I kept you ignorant, but that was of no consequence other than you didn't need to know what I was up to. You figured it out—I'm smuggling something. Care to take a guess?"

"Rhodium," Hank said.

"Well done. You could figure the street value if I gave you the spot price, but let's just say when I told the world, 'I still have this boat and a couple of others,' it is the truth. The understatement was hyperbolic. But now you can imagine the sincerity when I thanked you for your help in keeping the *GalaxSea* afloat. That was no lie! We could have survived in a life-raft, but the world would never benefit from all the rare metal this keel offers." Olin laid his hand on the hull. "Smuggling? Sure, if you insist on semantics. I'd rather call it moving my belongings from one part of the world to another. I hope there's no hard feelings."

"No. I can't say I blame you. A keel needs weight and you got that, rhodium or lead. What does it matter?"

"I wish bureaucrats had that attitude. They think what's mine is theirs. Speaking of lead—if the last leg of this voyage goes smoother than the first, in two weeks we will leave the boat before landfall and you will take the *GalaxSea* to a small shipyard in one of my favorite countries. I'm going to need someone I trust to oversee the repairs—a new, redesigned keel with lead as ballast." Olin stood very straight and lowered his voice. "When the job is done, the *GalaxSea* is yours. I'll have Willy share all of her security secrets (they aren't in the user manual) and Ava will leave you with a version of herself. It's the same one José is going to get." Olin winked. "Ava calls it Mini-Me." He laughed. "You and this boat deserve each other."

"What can I say? What if you need a sailing instructor?"

Olin smiled and said, "This isn't the end of our relationship—far from it. I just need to go dark for a while. I guess I need to *scatter* too. I'll be focusing on getting my family safely back together and can't be found sailing around in one of my yachts. You'll be doing me a favor. I'll get in touch when I'm ready to make my next move.

"Ava's been eavesdropping on the breaking news. They started with rumors of our going quiet after the storm. Reporters tried to reach me for interviews about my broadcast. No response provides a lot of fodder for speculation and it also leads nicely into the government's propaganda. They think they killed me. So, if the world believes I died at the hands of nature, it makes a great alibi. Reports from other sailors and ships that normally wouldn't have made it into the news cycle claim a sailboat as small as ours could never have survived such a storm. Another deflection has been to push the environmental narrative that the escalation of Pacific hurricanes has been because of climate devastation. It's hogwash, but brilliant.

"The masses will eagerly believe that I have met my tragic end and selfishly took my family down with me. That's why I'm so scared for Maria and the twins. They know we were not all together, yet all the news reports mention Maria and each of our kids by name—they say the whole family is lost at sea." Olin's face turned grim and he choked back tears. "Hank, I don't shy away from moving in the direction I choose. If it angers people that is their business, but this is crazy. Someone, or maybe Ava's equal, the Bad Robot, is determined to wipe my whole family off the face of the earth. Whoever or whatever is behind the attack, thinks we're dead. That makes us safe and Ava assures me that Sidney and Nadia are safe for now, but Maria is still at risk." He leaned his head against the hull of the *GalaxSea*, covered his face and wept.

Hank was at a loss. How could he console this man? He placed a hand on Olin's shoulder and stood beside him.

Gregory

CHAPTER 30

HE BOLTED UPRIGHT AND then fell back staring at the ceiling confused. Across the room a large salt lamp ascended out of the floor and provided a coral red glow that reflected down out of an expansive mirror above him. He lay alone and wore pajamas as his memory returned. "What the hell," he said as he tore at the front of his chest, ripping the three oversized buttons as he stripped off the top. He breathed a sigh of relief as he saw the definition of his rock-solid abs. This room was his too, the boat's stateroom, his stateroom, his yacht—he was on the *Fighting Gull*. Confusion turned into anger and he headed to the wheelhouse while mulling through his troubled thoughts.

"Good evening, sir. Would you like me to call Sammi?"

Gregory paced the wheelhouse with an expression of disgust on his face and a forward leaning posture that made him look as if he focused on an object that lay just in front of him. "I need you to tell me exactly what occurred."

"Some tea first?" The captain reached for a stainless carafe. "You've been asleep for twelve hours."

"That's absurd. I never sleep over six. How did I get back to the boat? The last thing I remember was rising through a garden on an escalator at the hotel. Why are we underway?"

"You should sit down." The captain set an unlit half-smoked cigar onto the side of an ashtray and turned all his attention to Gregory. "You made it back to the Marina, but security had to escort you the rest of the way. I assumed you were having a bad trip. It seemed like psychedelics, but I have no way of knowing."

Gregory kneaded the palm of his hand into his forehead as if the action might produce some insight. "I took Leo's medication. After he died, my patron thought it would be easier for me to assume his identity if I possessed everything he owned—boxes of clothes, personal items and a few mementos. I discarded most of it but kept his assortment of pills. I figured it might help me understand the sorry son of a bitch. Before I left the hotel, I took two pills out of each bottle. It never occurred to me that Leo might be a drug user. My god, he had high blood pressure, diabetes and suffered from depression. Why would a man like that mix it up with street drugs?"

"Why did you? What lead you to take another man's medications?" Captain Monroe asked.

"Are we going to have problems?" Gregory asked.

"No. Your business is your business."

"I'm glad we have an understanding." Gregory said as he rested a hand on the nav station's desk. "Captain—why are we underway? I thought we had another day of maintenance."

"The yard had a cancellation, so they finished early. Your standing orders were to get the crew together for departure as soon as weather permitted. Since that hurricane collapsed on itself, there was nothing stopping us from leaving as soon as you came back on board."

"The brothers?"

"Still a little drunk when they arrived, but they managed to untied a couple of lines and went to bed."

"I've got to get myself back up to speed. I'm going to work out," Gregory said and then asked, "How long before we reach José Espinosa's precious aquafarm?"

"Less than two days."

The stair-climber came with the boat. He considered pulling it out when the yacht underwent its major remodel, but he liked it for its mindlessness. It allowed him to warmup while he conducted business. At a modest pace, he would not sweat, or get out of breath. It was the perfect way for him to unravel the physical effects of his ill-advised foray into Leo's drug problem and warm-up his body for the workout to come.

Gregory willed himself to focus more on his conversation with Hans and less on the turmoil between his brain and body. "Good, I'm glad to hear you're ready. The story of the Trojan horse always seemed absurd to me, but I find submarines fascinating. The pretext of your white-hat security team checking for weaknesses delights me. Let me know how your simulated attack goes tomorrow. If the weather holds, the captain informs me we will be there in less than two days."

He disliked Hans personally. Gregory never understood why anyone would join the military but the six months in the brig and the dishonorable discharge factored into an opportunity to hire Hans for a reasonable sum. His lack of honor and no prospects for a legitimate future made him available to work as Gregory's man inside the security firm Bella's father contracted with. It was a strategic placement that worked out better than expected and allowed Hans the opportunity to prove himself.

Despite his ongoing successes, Gregory would not fully trust Hans until Bella was safely aboard the *Fighting Gull*. The nature of all of Gregory's business dealings was like that and loyalty was always tenuous. Money or fear normally bought loyalty, but with Hans, reputation mattered. And judging from the budding mercenary's long-winded review of the details of tomorrow's operation, all would end well.

"That's good. Keep in mind, if anything happens to Bella, the consequences will be dire. My expectations are not high, but they are immutable."

He ended the call. It irritated him to find only ten minutes had passed and his heart rate had exceeded his warm-up parameters—thanks to Hans. So, he closed his eyes and focused on steady rhythmic breathing and instantly recovered to a pace he could maintain forever. When the hour-long warmup ended, his real workout would begin. Then he could take out his frustration on two irritating people in his life—Hans and Leo.

The fight training with full contact sparring was the only thing he looked forward to. It was an indispensable part of his fitness regime and since the nearest Slanted Edge was in Honolulu, gutting the yacht's other stateroom and installing the simulation pod had provided the perfect, if costly, solution to maintaining the highest level of fitness. He always felt justified investing in things that brought him pleasure. Honing his fighting skills while beating the daylights out of someone, even an imaginary opponent, provided a nice return on his investment.

He turned his attention to selecting an appropriate adversary for today's workout. The avatar would be as close to Hans as he could create. Big and fast, but stupid. That type always would get tired fast, so he increased his opponent's endurance—but not too much. He and his virtual opponent would begin with hand-to-hand combat and then cross swords. It had to be a good fight, but in the end, he always won. Gregory looked forward to planting his blade deep into the heart of the non-player character that looked like Hans.

Hank

CHAPTER 31

"Ava explained to me the reasons our outgoing communications are being limited or at least highly controlled. Normally, I'd be outraged and wouldn't stand for it. But Ava has a way about her—she sounds like family. Might she be doing that on purpose?" José asked without waiting for an answer. "I understand it's for your security and to keep your family safe. But I'm confused. I've been seeing reports that you are lost at sea. You have your reasons for using my adaptive camouflage and lying low. Of all people, I understand the importance of staying off the radar. Still, the reports say they've called off searches. You and your whole family, are presumed dead. They mention three members of your family who are not here with us. Maria is your wife. Yes? And Nadia and Sidney are your other children? What has become of them?"

"I do have some explaining to do and I want to assure you, when we leave we will restore all your communications. And yes, Maria is my wife and the girls, twins, they're fourteen. They didn't join us on this voyage. Look, this is as good a time to tell you as any. In the states, I'd have my lawyer here and a nondisclosure agreement for you to sign; but here, with you, I'll take your word with a handshake. Concerning our whereabouts—truthfully, the fact that we are alive cannot leave this station. My life and the lives of my entire family are in jeopardy. Once again, I'm sorry for raining all this down on you. The people we are running from will not think twice about killing everyone on this station. If they think I'm alive, we will all be in danger. What I can promise you, is that if I'm alive, I will do everything I can to protect you." Olin stood up, "Can I trust you with my secret?"

"I'm a simple man. God brought us together for a reason and I sense in my heart that this is His will," José stood and reached out his hand. Olin smiled, the two men shook hands and Olin accepted José's brotherly embrace.

Hank opened his eyes wide and whispered to Olin in a voice meant to be heard, "Does this mean he's a heretic too?"

"The club is growing rapidly."

"We must celebrate," José said.

"I'm not sure finding out your life is in danger is a reason to celebrate," Hank said.

José's smile seemed impossibly large and his teeth contrasted brilliantly with his dark, heavily tanned skin. "No, no, no...not that. I've saved this for a special occasion." He presented a bottle of clear liquid and a small stack of shot glasses. "I wasn't sure I'd ever get to celebrate this moment. But here we are. Ava pulled us past twenty-three degrees, twenty-seven minutes. Does that mean anything to you?"

Both Olin and Hank said the words at the same time, "Tropic of Cancer."

"It is another miracle. If we had maintained our course, we would have crossed into US territorial waters, or worst case—wash up on the Big Island of Hawaii."

273

"Well, you certainly wouldn't go unnoticed. They frown on foreign invaders," Olin said.

"Ava has been very helpful. We are on a route which will lead us north of the Hawaiian Islands, while not beyond the range of spying eyes and nosy inquiry, we will pass by, staying in International Waters. Truthfully, I wasn't sure if I could avoid the islands or at least the troublesome eddies to the west, but the storm and being hijacked by Ava turned out to be a godsend. Now, we are in a place that almost guarantees safe passage."

He poured three glasses. "This is just the first round. *Al trópico de cáncer, salute!*"

Hank's face recoiled when the liquid fire flowed down his throat.

"I thought we were friends," Olin said in a raspy voice. "But I'm sure it comes in handy cleaning machine parts."

José smiled even bigger and said only one word, "Yes."

"*La cena está lista!*" Ferdinand shouted.

"Dinner is ready!" Marshall repeated in English.

The call to dinner brought the girls and Willy, and everyone reached the long table at the same time. Butcher paper stretched from one end to the other. They placed three deep kettles evenly along the expanse. Between them stood bottles of wine, beer and water. The only chairs were at either end of the table and benches rimmed both sides. José invited Olin to sit at one end and he positioned himself in the chair at the other. Everyone else took up positions randomly on the benches.

"It's good when people's paths cross in friendship. Today, I am thankful that all of you have been able to join us and celebrate this meal. Please, let's bow our heads and thank God for safety and His provision. Thank you, Father, for your mysterious ways, your providence and this abundance. Thank you for bringing us together and holding us securely in your grasp. You are the source of all greatness and grandeur, we thank you and ask for your blessing for this food.

May it give us the power to carry on and glorify You in all that we do. *Gracias Dios, en el nombre de Yeshúa.* Amen."

José, Ferdinand and Bella hefted the kettle closest to them and in unison they turned them upside down, dumping the boiled food onto the table for everyone to partake. Beers were opened and wine flowed. Hank stuck to water, thinking it would be easier to keep up his defenses. He would be polite and smile, but decided to limit conversation and avoid too much eye contact. But his determination fell to shreds the minute he looked towards Bella. Her gaze was on him and he could not look away. It was hopeless to deny his feelings. Any other time, any other place, he would have known how to respond, but he had already decided his tactic—sail on and avoid the inevitable catastrophe. He found it impossible to stay on that course the minute she offered a smile in his direction. Until she spoke: "There's trouble coming your way. You better watch out." Her eyes directed his attention downward, just in time to see a trickle from the boiled food dribble onto his lap. His large cloth napkin caught the flow but when he looked back with an impish grin, Bella was talking to Marshall and preparing to plop what looked like a small potato into her mouth. The special moment he sensed had never happened and he couldn't deny he was disappointed.

Soon the table was a mess of shells, stains and empty bottles. During the entire dinner, Hank never caught Bella's eye again, he tried to be cool about it by engaging with others. The cooks left and he watched as Bella got up from the bench and walked over to an open fire pit. A single gas flame spiraled from the center and Bella looked like she wanted to soak in the warmth. Nobody else was there and Hank worked his way over as nonchalantly as a moth to a flame—he had no choice.

"Thanks for gathering all that great seafood. I haven't had a meal like that, well, ever," he said with a sincere smile.

"In my house, you knew what day it was by the food served for dinner. Except for deep ocean seafood boils. That was always a special event. Today is very special," Bella said.

"Dare I ask?"

"People." Bella seemed to relax and flashed an effervescent smile. "Months can pass out here without seeing another person. Sometimes a boat shows up on radar or we hear marine traffic close by on the radio. But to have actual guests aboard—that is a special occasion."

"I spent so much of my life in and around the oceans, but I can't imagine..." Hank waved his hand across the deck and out toward the expanse of water. "What's it like to grow up at sea?"

"I was happy with my siblings as playmates and books as confidants. Also, we looked forward to July. That's when we would travel to my mother's cozy hometown in Norway. We plugged right into her community with summer camp, hikes and adventures on the coast. We spent the rest of the year at sea. I never grasped how unusual my life was until I went to college. It took some getting used to—all the people, the hustle, noise and lights. Cities used to terrify me." Her eyes twinkled as she said, "My first elevator ride was when I was seventeen!" Bella laughed and changed the subject. "Irina says you're her sailing instructor. Sounds thrilling."

Hank wondered if he detected a hint of mockery in her statement, but at this point, he was happy to be having a conversation. He smiled and said, "Wow! When you put it like that, it does sound glamorous. Who would have thought someday I'd be living-the-dream?" A good-hearted laugh followed and he realized he wasn't nervous around Bella. She was everything he could want in a girl and she was easy to talk to. "I suppose when you're not diving for seafood, you're guiding rockets to Mars or transplanting hearts."

"Looks like both of us are—*living-the-dream*. When I'm not diving for seafood, I work for the Marine Quality Institute. Basically, my job is to send drones out to dive for seafood. The only actual difference between here and there, is around here, we get to eat the research."

"Well, let me say, thank you for gathering the specimens. They were delicious. Do you get out to see your dad often?"

"Two or three times a year. I try to get here before the harvest, but this visit was not planned. But, then neither was a Pacific cyclone. The stability of my dad's casa is phenomenal. What was it like to sail through the storm?"

"The *GalaxSea* is an amazing sailing yacht. She has some tricks up her sleeve to handle the worst that Neptune can throw at her, but we hit something. It did considerable damage to the hull and the damage even let water into the engine room. Strangest thing I ever experienced at sea, but I'd rather not talk about that now. We all made it through thanks to your dad's operation being where it was when we needed it.

"Where is it you work researching what the rest of us eat?"

"Singapore." Bella's eyes darted away and her good-natured smile disappeared.

The feeling that he was doing okay burst into flames and now she was looking for the exits. Hank contradicted his heart and said, "Maybe we can talk later—at a better time."

"That would be good. I've got a lot on my mind," she turned and left the station's deck and scurried across the gangway that led to the casa.

He shrugged and changed his gaze to look out over the ocean.

Julie

CHAPTER 32

SHE WOULD RATHER BE unconscious. Every inch of her throbbed with pain. The narrow litter squeezed in beside the aisle pressing the left side of her body against the interior wall. Julie was solid muscle and barely tipped the scales at one hundred thirty pounds, but her hips and shoulders overhung the sliver of a mattress. The seatbelts at her chest, pelvis and lower legs, had been secured too tight, but not enough to distract her from the pain radiating from her core.

Part of her wanted to be inclined, or at least upright enough to be distracted by the activity towards the back of the plane—maybe there would be a kind face from a team member, or at least an expression of pity—anything would be better than the pain. They positioned her lying flat, looking straight up. Once she tried to flex her chin to see something else, but that motion sent lightning bolts into her abdomen and she learned her lesson. Not one of the team had said a word or even made eye contact with her during the loading process. She was alone in her agony and in this ordeal—an injured captive, a traitor. They would keep her alive, but that was all. Soon, she would be convicted of anything they chose to throw at her. That she was shot after they had captured her, would never be brought up. Aiding a terrorist, even a guiltless one, was a serious crime. Even though her history of complicity was brief, it led to Maria's escape and Bruce's death. She tried to focus on questions. Thinking helped distract her. Why did Mega-War shoot her? How was she even alive after being shot in the gut at point blank, by a .357 Magnum?

Fear washed over her. Her legs? She lived through the gunshot and experienced the pain to support that fact, but there were things worse than death. She tried to move her feet, wiggle her toes, anything to prove she would not end her days bound to a wheelchair. Nothing moved, but the vision left her as fast as it came when she felt belts strapped tight over her legs. The relief gave her the clarity she needed to understand why she lived. Like all the team members, they equipped her with a Kevlar vest. The outrageous velocity of the bullet at that range must have impacted the ballistic plate. Still, the tubes she had seen sticking out of her abdomen showed the trauma was more than bruising from a bullet stopped short. The plate in the vest did its job, but there must have been spall that penetrated into her gut. Mega-War hadn't wanted to kill her but intended to leave a loud message.

Julie felt that message with every movement, even with each breath she took. She had difficulty wrapping her mind around the fact that she was now an accomplice to terrorism. It seemed ludicrous, but her life was ruined. Where would they hold the trial? What would the charges be? What would be her defense? Even as she raised those questions, she realized there would be no trial. She was a civilian—no court martial, not even a hearing before an unbiased judge. Maybe they would not let her live. It was possible, the only reason they took her into the plane with the rest of the team was because Mega-War wanted to control what became of her.

Any appearance of compassion was because it would go a long way for morale—a few of the squad members might still be loyal to Julie, a few wouldn't care, but none of them would want to see her mistreated.

— ⚓ —

She woke to a brittle voice she had known since they were woven within the same chain of command years ago, "Ma'am, you need to get up here right away!" Sam called down the aisle from the open door of the cockpit. Megan Ward plowed past her with her usual bitch-face, causing her aide to step back and to the side opposite Julie.

The continuous roar of the engine made it difficult to understand the words of a female pilot from the cockpit, "...no positive control... fly by wire... no override... nothing we can do..."

But Megan Ward's voice was loud enough for the entire plane to hear, "Throw a breaker or reset the system. Fix it—now!"

The engines slowed and even though the noise softened, Julie could not hear what the pilots said. Megan Ward pulled her head out of the cockpit and stood with her back to her, a phone against her ear.

"Justin, I need your help! I'm going to hand you over to the pilot, but first you need to know we have no control of our jet. Somebody is flying this plane, but it's not us. If you can get any answers, we need them. Now talk to my pilot and figure this out."

Megan Ward pulled her head from the cockpit and started towards the back just as the plane banked hard to the right. The woman caught herself against the wall, above Julie's stretcher and said nothing. The brief eye contact was unrewarding as Julie attempted to be defiant, but could not compete with the practiced glare of a truly hateful soul.

A few minutes later, Sam leaned over her and said, "Don't let her get to you, Command Sergeant Major Marsh. She's just mad she isn't in control."

Julie found the tone of respect unusual coming from Sam, the Puppet and being addressed by her last rank, stirred memories. Nothing truly good had occurred since she left the Army. She had traded two things which she valued, her marriage and her integrity, for the one thing she didn't care about—a fat bank account. Now, she was going to die or rot in prison with the realization she had created a pitiful life.

The plane banked again, slower this time. She closed her eyes and prayed the plane would crash and put an end to it, but it leveled, as a hand rested on her shoulder.

"I'm sorry, Julie. You were right about this mission. We had no business with it," Sam said, as he walked away.

Julie's mind was in the past so Sam's words didn't make things any better. She wished—more than anything—that she could be with Willy right now and ask for his forgiveness.

The team didn't have a medic, although they all trained extensively and had first-hand experience in trauma support; but, Tom, knew more about medication than the rest, so it did not surprise Julie that Megan Ward described her plan to him. As she was mentally working things out, she knew they had to keep her quiet. The only sure way to do that was to make sure she was dead.

"Look, if the wrong people get to control the narrative, we all go to prison. It's obvious someone has an agenda and they want Julie.

We need to be sure she won't be doing any talking—ever. I need you to figure out a concoction that will keep her alive long enough for us to turn around and fly to a safe airfield. Just make sure she dies or that her brain is too dead to matter soon after we land. Can you do that?"

"Are you sure that's the only alternative?" he asked.

"You tell me. We haven't been in control of this flying deathtrap for the last twenty minutes and they've jammed our communication since presenting their demands. We'll be landing at an airfield they control and they will let us go on our way, only if we leave Julie on the tarmac in stable condition. So that's what we're going to do. But I'll be damned if her invisible friends are going to revive her and use her against us. It's my job to take care of this team and she has already caused Bruce's death and our mission to fail. I'm not letting her do any more harm. If you can't do this, I'll find someone else who can."

"I'll take care of it," he said, as he rummaged through the medical kit.

She struggled against the restraints and began to yell as Megan Ward clamped her hand over Julie's mouth and pressed into her wound. The accusatory words she had planned never made it out of her mouth. But as quickly as the pain came on, it left, as Megan took her hands away. She gasped in a breath of air as Mega-War hissed, "Shut up, bitch. Don't think I wouldn't mind causing you more pain. As far as I'm concerned you haven't suffered enough. So just—shut up."

Tom, standing right behind Mega-War, gave her a quick wink, closed his eyes and tipped his head to the side. It took her a second to realize he was telling her to pretend to sleep. Nudging Megan out of the way, he leaned over Julie, tucking her hand under the sheet as he pulled the IV needle out. And with his next words, she understood what was going on. "Look, she's distraught, so I'm giving her a sedative. She should be out like a light." Tom removed the syringe from the IV port and threw it away.

She took the cue, rolling her eyes back, closing them and laid there, not moving a muscle. She had to be convincing. If Mega-War suspected anything, she'd find the IV needle leaking harmlessly into the sheets and Tom wouldn't be able to help her. "That will do the trick for now. Just before we exit the plane, I'll give her a lethal dose of barbiturates and then inject epinephrine direct into the heart muscle. That will keep her alive for a while, but she won't live once it wears off," Tom explained.

"What happens if they just administer more epinephrine or Narcan? I would." Megan Ward said.

"Narcan is for opiates and will have little effect on what I gave her. Added doses of epinephrine will either cause her to go into complete system collapse, or her heart will just give up. We'll get the time we need, then she'll die."

"Take your seats. They're landing us. It doesn't look like the best runway, so prepare for a rough one," the pilot said over the intercom.

Not for the first time, Julie wished Tom had actually sedated her. The turbulence before landing increased her agony. She tried hard not to grimace but doubted anybody was watching. The plane flared and more pain, but then everything went dark.

When she came too, the plane had stopped. A tone chimed out of the intercom, followed by a female voice Julie had heard before. "Welcome to the moment you will decide whether you live or die." The woman's accent was Scottish. Even though the voice seemed to be young, there was a commanding tone that came across loud and clear.

"The moment has arrived to fulfill the commitment Megan Ward agreed to after we took control of the aircraft. Bring Julie Marsh safely down to the waiting ambulance. Once it is determined she is alive and in stable condition, we will relinquish control of the aircraft and you may go on your way, without further interference. You have three minutes to complete the mission."

From the voices, Julie could tell that Tom was at her head, Sam at her feet and Megan Ward, close by. When they repositioned her litter into a stair-chair, it felt like they cut her in two. She moaned as the pain overwhelmed her, but she kept her eyes closed and tried not to grimace.

"That's expected," Tom said. "I'm administering the barbiturate cocktail now. When I do the intracardiac injection, we head down the stairs no matter what happens. She might wake up, like in Pulp Fiction, or stay knocked out. Either way, we don't delay. Continue to haul ass to the ambulance."

She focused on slipping into a deeper meditative state. Julie felt a hand pull her gown away from her chest and she realized Tom was cutting her sports bra apart with a pair of scissors. With her chest bare, the Pulp Fiction reference became real. He palpated a gap between her ribs on the upper margin of her left breast and applied the cold wetness of an alcohol swab. The needle stabbing into her chest shocked her eyes open—she had no control now. Tom might not have injected a drug into her chest, but the needle was the real thing. She screamed out but was helpless to do more.

The hot humid air of the open door mixed in the cool cabin. "Go. Go. Go," Tom commanded Sam. The sun blinded her and each step added to her pain, but the ambulance was just steps away and Megan Ward was out of her life for good. A man, stepping forward and opening the rear doors of the ambulance said, "Put her on the stretcher and prepare her for a short drive. They will contact you." The driver didn't offer to help the two men.

They said nothing during the transfer, but before Tom backed out of the ambulance, he took out a syringe and injected its contents into her arm. "This is what you really need. It will help with the pain." He gave Julie a wink and said, "It's been my honor serving with you," and he was gone.

The ambulance drove away. She was finally free. She closed her eyes knowing Willy had saved her and there was no pain.

Bella

CHAPTER 33

SHE HADN'T SLEPT WELL. While Bella wanted to put the blame on too much food or her two large glasses of wine, she knew, once again, it was a man who caused her distress. This time, a stranger with magnetic blue eyes and the kindest smile she had ever seen. She missed the routine of her mother's house. A cup of coffee sounded good and she needed to get back into some meaningful prayer time. Kumar opened one eye and gave an unenthusiastic tail wag in acknowledgement of Bella getting out of bed, but nothing more. "Rough night for you too, boy?"

Ferdinand snored loudly from the couch. Usually, by sunrise, he would be busy getting the day's work started. She tiptoed past him ignoring the smell of stale cigar smoke and the sweet-sick bite of alcohol. Another aroma wafted out of the kitchen that brought her stomach back into alignment. She quickened her pace towards a pot of brewing coffee. With an oversized cup and slice of buttered toast, she snuck back to the guest room for some quiet time.

With each push of the button, the window became more translucent. She settled on full transparency but was sad when she remembered the window would not open. The view was spectacular and today it faced the sunrise. The sky was clearer than yesterday, with wind teasing the water below. Morning clouds floated high in the east forming what looked like a scarlet tiara balancing on the horizon. Each floor of the living space had its own lanai and the design of the casa encouraged the wind to orient the structure so the outdoor spaces faced the leeward side. The guest room simply had a single expansive window and today it looked down on the station lit with the soft light of a new day. In a response that was more her mother's than her own, she inhaled a small amount of air through her teeth, as she saw the *GalaxSea* was not in its cradle. Her eyes searched—it was gone.

Bella's heart sank. Her years of living at sea forced her to get used to parting ways—a water environment insisted on a fluid community. Sometimes "goodbye" meant months before the possibility of the next "hello," but more often goodbye, meant forever. Sadness swept over her and the untethered emotion angered her. Why did she allow irrational feelings into her head? This was nothing new and she admonished herself out loud saying, "Bella! Get a grip for God's sake."

Honesty was not something Bella worried about, but her frank manner with co-workers and family often caused friction. Her mother offered that she should work on being tactful. The few love-interests she had, knew where they stood early on: Since Jesus stood as the number one relationship in her life, she had no problem being resolute—no sex before marriage—no exceptions. Gregory never threatened those conditions and their relationship lasted a year. He appeared to respect her beliefs, seemed satisfied with kissing and even attended her church. When he presented her with a two-carat diamond ring, everything spun into a dither. Now she felt so naïve. She realized the one person she had difficulty being honest with was herself. It took a year to figure it out, but she knew Gregory was evil. She also knew if she had been honest with herself, she would never have gone on that first date.

As she looked out across the ocean, Bella accepted the reason for her troubled sleep was not the rich food, or the wine, or her scary ex-boyfriend. She was attracted to Hank. Unlike Gregory, she would go out on a first date with Hank without reservation. Her dad had mentioned Hank had sailed around the world a couple times, was a boat builder and a medic. He maintained hero status with her dad's new billionaire friend, Olin Ou. Hank cared for Marshall when he had too much to drink and got a five-star review in ethics and moral grounding from Irina—the future nun from Calcutta. He also appeared sincere and interested. Last night, he graciously suggested they talk at a better time—giving her an out that she appreciated. None of that mattered now, he had sailed off. It was just as well. Her emotional state this morning clearly showed she was not ready.

With her Bible by her side and the daily devotional glowing from the device propped in her hands, she read: "Have I not command-ed you? Be strong and courageous. Do not be afraid; do not be discouraged, for the Lord your God will be with you wherever you go." She thought, *unbelievable! The scripture I need at the exact time I need it!* She dropped the device in her lap and prayed.

When she rose and walked back to the window, Kumar joined her with his head just high enough to see out the window. His tail wagged furiously. She saw it too: The *GalaxSea* tied up to the dock, nestled within the u-shaped stern of the station. "Well, boy, I guess they didn't leave after all. You want to go see our new friends?" They dashed out of the room and started down the stairs until she heard voices coming from the upper level. Bella changed her direction and found everyone sitting at the kitchen table. There was no room for anybody else. She stood with her heart racing, chest heaving, staring at Hank.

Everybody—her dad, Ferdinand, Olin, Marshall, Irina and Hank looked at her as if she was from Venus. Suddenly, she became self-conscious and realized she was still wearing her pajamas—comfortable silk pants and a camisole top. Her long brown legs ended in bare feet and her hair, even though short, must have been a mess. But she didn't care—she was *strong and courageous*.

"Has everybody already had breakfast? I'm starved!" Bella walked into the kitchen and Irina got up and went to her.

"Are you alright?" Irina asked.

"Kind of," Bella said with a confused look. "I'm not sure..."

She started a new pot of coffee and wiped the counter, glad that the attention had shifted to a hologram at the center of the table. She reached out and grabbed Irina's arms with both hands—a bit too hard. "When I woke up, the *GalaxSea* was gone and I thought you had left without saying goodbye." Tears welling up in her eyes, she said, "I took some time to read my Bible and pray, which made me feel better. It surprised me when I looked out my window again and your boat was back. I'm so glad you're still here!" She hugged Irina. A tear streamed down her face and she quickly wiped it away. "I'm a wreck. Can we talk in my room?"

It all came out. Every detail of everything that had gone on in Bella's life in the last couple of weeks. Returning from her annual vacation, Gregory confronting her at the airport and the catastrophe around how she returned the ring. She explained why she was scared and how running to her mother at the seastead in Tahiti seemed like the right thing to do. It was her Aunt Janice, the former FBI agent, who revealed the truth about Gregory. Bella wanted to stop there, but she pressed on and told Irina the horrors she had found out about Gregory—a human trafficker, a psychopath and someone who is wanted around the world for his crimes. She told Irina how she and her mother had been drugged and how she was rescued from kidnappers when Janice put a bullet through the head of one abductor. And also that Gregory arranged the entire caper and was still at large. Bella ended with the difficult acceptance that she will never be safe until he is behind bars or dead.

"Oh Bella! I had no idea of all you've been through. I've been so taken up with myself and what's going on with us. A lot of our situation, I can't talk about—not yet anyway. I'm sorry I ever brought up Hank and even teased you about him. I didn't know," Irina said.

Bella hugged her. "I'll be there for you when you need to unpack what you're going through. We never know what kind of trauma someone has experienced, unless it's spelled out. I didn't plan to dump all this on you, but I feel better talking it out with a friend. Thank you."

"Bella, when I need to share my stuff, you will be the first person I think of."

"I'm only a video call away."

"Good, I'll take you up on that offer. I hope it will not be as traumatic as your *'adventure,'* but the way things are going, it might be close."

"Is the rest of your family in trouble too?" Bella asked.

"Yes and no. Just like us, it's important they don't draw attention. Ava keeps us up on developments and so far, my sisters are safe. They almost got my mom, but she is on the move to another safe place, thanks to a warning from Willy's ex-wife, Julie. The details are sparse—Julie was badly injured during the rescue mission—but Ava says she is going to recover."

"Irina, I'm so sorry to burden you with all my problems. You've got enough on your mind. It must be terrible to have to hide just to be safe and also to be so far from your mom and sisters."

"Huh! Don't forget you're hiding to be safe too, Bella!" Irina pointed out.

"Oh, my goodness. You're right. I never even considered that." She smiled, "Does this mean we are kindred spirits?"

"Oh my God! You read L. M. Montgomery too?" Irina said excitedly.

"I'm the daughter of fish farmers. What do you think we do out here for fun?"

Together they both said, "Read."

"No one told me when you were planning to leave. Only that you'd be here until you got your boat repaired. I can't believe the *GalaxSea* is already seaworthy. That sure was fast. I'm not ready to say goodbye yet," Bella said.

"Hank worked all afternoon yesterday to make the repairs that the maintenance robots couldn't do. They floated her late last night. The inspection went well, so they took her out and back as the beginning of her sea trials." Irina looked at her wrist and said, "Ava, when will the sea trials be done?"

Ava's voice responded, "Everything is looking good. We'll be careful and ensure there is no structural weakness on each point of sail. By dinner time, I will certify her safety."

"When does my dad want to leave?" Irina asked.

"Tomorrow morning at sunrise is the estimated time of departure," Ava replied.

Bella sighed, "I know I told you I'm not interested in romance and now you understand why."

"The reasons are loud and clear, but do I detect a hesitancy?" Irina said.

"There is definitely something about Hank. He's so handsome and I can't seem to get my mind off of him, but I truly am not ready to start anything. And I mean anything!"

"So, what you're saying is—you want me to give him your number after we leave tomorrow," Irina offered.

"For such a young lady, you sure aren't naïve about the ways of the heart. I think that might solve my dilemma," Bella said as she relaxed into her chair. "When you tell him I might be a little interested, please don't tell him all the crazy stuff. If the time ever comes, I'll make sure he knows."

"Of course. Do you remember that I'm Catholic? We invented confessional privacy!"

"Now, I only have to avoid him until you leave."

"Good luck with that," Irina said with a hint of sarcasm.

"Don't worry, I've got a killer workout planned and a good book," Bella said.

"It might work. But you can count me out of any kickboxing today. I can barely move after yesterday's class and couldn't even wash my hair last night." Irina lifted her hands towards her head, but grimaced as she got close to her ears. "I can't seem to move my shoulders up that far."

Her arms fell as if she had heavy weights attached and she took her eyes off Bella. "Ava, when will the *GalaxSea* be leaving for the rest of her sea trials?"

"Winds are supposed to pick up around one o'clock this afternoon. Hank and your father want to wait for the higher winds to check the systems under load," Ava said.

"Okay. Can you please tell Marshall and Hank I'll be holding our yoga class at the regular time?" Irina turned her attention back to Bella and said, "You're welcome to join us on board at eleven. It will be an easy class—restorative."

"Remember, I'm avoiding temptation. I'll be in the gym beating up Fear."

"Fear?" Irina asked.

"Did you see the drone delivery come in last night?"

"Who could miss that? My dad, Willy and Hank were all up in arms. They thought we were being attacked until Ava explained it was just a Quad Freight Transport delivery. Then Hank helped your dad pull back some of the camouflage to clear the landing site."

"My sensei, Gina, sent me a present. It's a heavy bag for punching and kicking. After we mounted it in the station's gym, I gave my new big-bad-heavy-bag a name—Fear." Her expression changed into a determined look. "Now I can work on conquering Fear. I'm surprised, though, that Ava allowed that drone anywhere near here," Bella said.

"She says it's crucial to keep up appearances with your dad's regular vendors. But don't worry—while she's keeping everyone from suspecting anything, she's deceiving them," Irina confided.

"Sometimes I wish I were that devious. I've made some changes myself—learning self-defense and confronting fear head-on, but I'm not there yet."

"Bella, you've got the strongest kick I've ever seen. In kickboxing class yesterday, it looked like you could take the head clear off a six-foot-tall attacker. And I don't get the idea you fear much of anything. I mean, what you've been through! If you hadn't told me, I'd think everything was fine. You even swim with sharks!"

"Sea creatures I understand. Men, not so much." She squeezed her left ring finger in a gesture that could easily go unnoticed as she recalled the painful bite of the eel, "Well most of the time."

Hank

CHAPTER 34

HANK WAS GLAD IRINA and Bella had scurried away as Olin and Ava explained the need for secrecy to everyone around the table. José and Ferdinand appeared to have no problem hearing what was said, but Hank could not concentrate until Bella was out of sight. It was good to have the new narrative reviewed again. Some tactics had been implemented before the drone arrival last night, but Hank was tired and he had to admit, he was in a continual brain fog over Bella.

It made sense they would not expect their hosts to pretend there was never a sailboat which visited the station following the hurricane. That story had too many holes, so changing the *GalaxSea's* name to *Voyager* was a straightforward solution and Olin and Irina would stay out of sight. Ava decided three men would be on the official manifest of *Voyager*—Hank, as captain; Willy and Marshall as nameless crew. The story would be that the *Voyager* arrived the evening of the drone delivery and left thirty-six hours later. After some high sea maintenance, much needed rest and a little re-supply, the delivery captain and his crew left on their way to Hawaii—not to be heard from again.

Even though Bella missed the briefing, José assured everyone he would explain the need for the false tale. And Ava would be around, in one form or another, if there was ever any inquiry. The meeting concluded and the men all stood up to get on with their day.

At first Ferdinand hovered over him as he cleaned the steel, clamped it in place and positioned the chill bars against the stanchions that needed work. But after Hank had completed the first of six identical repairs, his new supervisor patted him on the back and disappeared. While he wouldn't want to do it for a living, he enjoyed welding and found a special satisfaction in the challenges of stainless steel. He had first noticed some of the attachment posts for the adaptive camouflage had been displaced when they set up the high-tech canopy. Last night, when the drone came in, he mentioned to José that it wouldn't take long to fix the damaged stanchions if he had the right equipment. Right after their early morning meeting, José and Ferdinand escorted him to a well-equipped metal shop and put him to work.

After the first repair, he got into a flow and finished faster than he expected. He shut down the welder at the stanchion nearest the gangway to the *Casa del Océano*. While he let the metal cool, he set his welding hood to the side and took off the leather apron just in time to see Irina heading off for the *GalaxSea*. Bella stood at the bottom of the gangway, not six feet away. It proved impossible to avoid the endless depth of her dark brown eyes and managed to say,

"Hi," but found no more words, so he just smiled. She smiled back, turned around and sauntered away.

She dressed for comfort—flip-flops, shorts and a loose fitting checked flannel shirt. Not for the first time, he made himself divert his eyes from soaking in her every movement and he forced his eyes and thoughts out into the water—hoping to drown them. He had been in the presence of many beautiful women, even dated a few. But until now, it had never occurred to him he should discourage lustful thoughts. With Bella, he wanted something else. She differed from anyone he had ever known, he was willing—even eager—to struggle to be worthy.

Something in the water caught his eye. It was only a shadow—or maybe a reflection—but a swirl of bubbles escaped to the surface. Curiosity made him forget the allure of the woman walking across the gangway, he searched the water beneath to no avail. He decided it must have been a fish and turned around in time to see something blot out the light behind a large scupper drain in the station's high wall. Again, his senses were confused—nothing added up—until a man's head appeared, looking over the edge. He must have been standing on the toe-rail that rimmed the platform. There was no mistake about an action he had seen thousands of times before. The barrel of a rifle emerged over the edge and swept from one side of the station to the other. Two more men in black wetsuits materialized over the distant wall. When he turned back to yell to Bella, he caught a distorted sight through the thick lens of water. It was a man rising from the depths, just below the stanchion Hank had been repairing. He had intense blue eyes, magnified by the water and the lens of a face mask. But it was the scuba rebreather gear of a military frogman and a gun aimed in Bella's direction that summoned Hank into action.

"Get down!" It took Hank only an instant to cover the distance, grabbing Bella and lifting her off her feet. The resulting inertia became a mix of activity as he half carried her and half tackled her. His efforts ended with Bella falling onto the unyielding deck, inside the entryway. Hank was lying on top of her and had accomplished his initial goal to get her to the safety of the entry.

Pain ripped through his hand and shot up his arm, muscles as far away as his shoulder spasmed. The pain caused him to recoil, and Bella's hand continued to pry at his distorted finger until he pulled away. Springing to his feet, he maintained a crouched position and held up his afflicted hand to find his middle finger disfigured. Dislocated, or fractured, he couldn't tell, but what she had done to his finger was not a concern now as she had rolled over and pointed the muzzle of her gun at his chest.

"Don't shoot! We're under attack! I saw at least four men armed with rifles."

Kumar flew down the spiral stairway, pushed his nose into Bella's neck, turned toward Hank and began a vicious growl. The moment he expected the angry dog's teeth would bury into him, the fuzzy blur ran past and took a position at the entryway, with a furious bark.

She shook, but held a steady position, as if doing a sit up. Her arms were extended with both hands on the gun, leveled at Hank's chest, waiting for directions from Bella's trigger finger. Her dark brown eyes looked as if they were searching for answers and with each beat of his heart, he became more confident Bella would not shoot. He turned his back on the gun and yelled, "Kumar, no!" and lunged for the entry door. With one hand he grabbed Kumar by the collar and with the other, shut the heavy steel door and pulled the locking lever.

"Bella! Put the gun down!" José shouted from the stairs above. "It's not what you think." Jose came to her side offering her a hand up. "Everybody, just relax." As she re-holstered her weapon, Kumar ignored Hank and settled quickly, pressed against Bella's leg.

"There is no invasion. It's our security agency doing a drill to see if our early detection systems are sufficient. I'm so sorry—they just notified me they were coming and I didn't have time to tell you. They told me not to worry." José shrugged and frowned. "I guess I should have worried. This could have ended badly. Please, Hank, follow me. I have something to calm your nerves and we can look at that finger." He shook his head and said, "Ay *ay ay! Mi ángel es un diablo.*"

Not moving and still wound up, Hank said, "You mean those guys out there are supposed to be here?"

"Yes. They're under contract. I try to get them to do their quarterly inspection, so it coincides with the processing ship. We've never had a problem, but other farms have had incidents when a processing ship is used to transport pirates. They move right in and take over the unsuspecting aquafarm and steal everything they can take away. Sometimes, they even kill people to set an example. It's horrible and I always feel more comfortable knowing that my security team is in the neighborhood and ready to roll should the need arise," José said.

"Thanks for not shooting me, Bella," Hank said, trying to lighten the mood. He looked at his injured hand and decided it was probably a dislocation, but even if it was broken, it needed to be set. He grabbed the end just above the joint, pulled and forced it straight making a loud snap.

"Well, you don't see that every day," José remarked.

Bella sat down hard on the bottom step. "I'm sorry, Hank. I didn't realize what was happening. You scared me." Kumar licked her cheek and stared into her eyes.

"Let's get you two patched up. Hank's hand needs some ice and those scraped up knees need some attention." José led the way up the stairs mumbling something in Spanish. Bella turned without looking at Hank, climbing up the stairs with Kumar following.

"Now I'm the one who's sorry," Hank said, as he looked at the blood oozing from Bella's knees. "I hope we are able to laugh about this someday." The words were out of Hank's mouth before he had time to consider their implication. José busied himself, removing items from the first aid kit, but Bella shot him a puzzled expression that he was incapable of receiving, so he shifted his gaze away, flustered.

"Dad, why didn't the security company give us more notice?!"

"They purposely don't announce their arrival until the last minute so they can assess where we need to beef up our security measures. I'm pretty sure we failed."

The extensive trauma kit was impressive and it helped distract his focus while José dealt with Bella's knees. Hank quickly found what he needed and bound the injured finger to its neighbor with white tape. It didn't help the pain but would be more stable as it healed. José brought out a bottle of amber liquid and poured a little into each of three glasses. "This will be a little smoother than last night's moonshine."

"No thanks. I've got Kumar for my nerves," Bella said.

The usual vibrant glow in Bella's face had disappeared and her eyes fell into a faraway stare. As if in a trance, she stroked the fur around Kumar's neck while José left to fix a cup of tea. Nobody said anything, or even made eye contact, until José set the teacup down on the table in front of her and divided the contents of the third glass of whiskey.

"*Qué vivas durante todos los días de tu vida,*" José said as he half-heartedly rose his glass.

"It means, 'May you continue to live all the days of your life,'" Bella said. "Hank...I don't know what to say. I can't believe how close I came to shooting you. You were trying to save me and I almost..." her voice trailed off, horror etched across her face.

"You didn't shoot. We didn't know what was going on," Hank said earnestly. "Please forgive me for tackling you." He smiled. "I have a habit of going from hero to zero."

Bella said nothing and stared into the teacup. Hank looked away with an uncomfortable sensation burning in his stomach and he was pretty sure it wasn't the whiskey.

Breaking the tension in the room, José said, "Hank, you missed the tour of the control center yesterday. Would you like to see it? We can give Bella some space."

As he stood up to go with José, the burning in Hank's stomach disappeared, but was replaced by something much worse. The nausea overwhelmed him and it left him with no other choice than to make a run for the bathroom.

Hank recovered quickly and followed José down the stairs and into the control center. He knew little about farming and even less about doing it at sea, but it was easy to admire what José and his family had accomplished. As they finished looking around the control center, Hank was ready to leave, but José insisted the tour was not over. As he followed José back up the staircase, he was taken aback when he saw a broad-shouldered man sitting there, gazing at Bella as she worked in the kitchen.

The man looked like the model for a 1940s poster, promoting the Nazi takeover of the world; blonde hair, cut to military standards, overly perfect posture and Aryan eyes. When he noticed José, the man rose from the stool with a formality that seemed duty-bound of another era. It was a greeting Hank had seen in movies but never in real life, hands at his side, legs straight and a slight forward lean that began at the ankles. Like a salute, but the posture was wrong and his hands stayed at his side—definitely not American.

José walked quickly over to the visitor, reached out a friendly hand and shook it. He turned to Hank, raised his hand to the man's shoulder and introduced them.

"Hank, I'd like you to meet Hans. He is the leader of our security team. He visits like clockwork, swooping in, checking our cameras, alarms and defensive measures. You can only imagine the toll the open ocean takes on gadgetry and electronics. Plus, I always save my heavy lifting for his crew and they treat it like a workout. Hans and his team have been indispensable.

"This is Hank. I'm sure you noticed the *Voyager* tied up at our dock. Hank and his crew are headed for Hawaii. They all needed a break after the storm. Two other crewmen are resting off their ordeal, so please give them plenty of space."

"When are you getting underway again?" Hans addressed Hank. It surprised him to hear an accent that sounded South American coming out of someone who looked like he would make Hitler proud, but he stuffed down his rash judgement and said, "We leave tomorrow, but we are going on a short shake-down cruise later today. I need to check the rigging."

"How did you hurt your hand?"

Hank held his hand up and bent the taped fingers to downplay the injury and said, "Oh this. It's nothing, just some storm damage."

"That's a nice boat for someone as young as you. What do you do for a living?" Hans inquired.

Smirking, Hank said sarcastically, "Yeah, I wish. I'm just the delivery captain."

"Okay," Hans replied, unimpressed. He sat down and said, "Bella tells me she didn't know about the training exercise this morning. Hope we didn't scare anyone. One of my men said he saw two people running into the spar's entry door and then a dog barking until the door slammed shut."

Bella spoke up. "That's my new dog, Kumar. I wasn't sure how he'd handle strangers, so I had Hank close the door before he ran out onto the gangway."

"You came in a day early. I wasn't quite ready for you yet. When will your team be done?" José asked.

"It shouldn't take long. I'm training a couple of new men which means I have to check their work. We should finish up in a few hours and then we'll be moving on."

"I don't see your boat. How did you get here?" Hank interjected.

"Let's just say an investor in the security company is growing our fleet. We even have a helipad on our patrol boat now. And of course, Mr. Espinosa's subscription to our service is paying for a faster response," Hans bragged.

Hank immediately disliked this guy. Not only was he arrogant, but his interest in Bella was palpable. From his eyes, he knew this was the frogman who had started the cascade of events that might have put a quick end to Hank's luck. It was important to keep his emotions in check and José interrupted at the perfect moment—before Hank said what was on his mind.

"Hank, the last stop on our tour is not the deck, but we'll have to go there to reach the ladder that leads us onto the rooftop. I call it the crow's nest and you'll see why."

"Dad, second-breakfast will be ready in five minutes." She gave her dad a cautionary look. "I can tell you two are bonding over *Casa del Océano* systems. Of course, he must see the crow's nest, but don't bore him with what every antenna and dish is for."

José rolled his eyes at her. "Hans, would you like to join us?"

"No, but thanks. I just did my inspection up there. Are you liking our top-of-the-line security camera?" He didn't wait for an answer. "I'm not sure why you won't let me mount a gun up there. It would be a spectacular addition." Again, Hans didn't seem interested in a response and he turned his attention back towards Bella as if hoping to see that she was impressed.

From the deck, Hank looked right across to the spreaders radiating out of the mast of the *GalaxSea*. He looked over the railing and saw Willy reclining on the deck far below. With a hat over his face, it was impossible to tell whether he was pretending to be asleep, or truly out. One thing he knew for sure, Willy would not leave the newly christened *Voyager* until the security team was long gone and there was no longer a threat that Olin or Irina might be discovered.

After they ascended the ladder to the rooftop, José said, "Farmers' daughters have powerful hands—you're lucky that finger is still attached."

"She got the point across. I'll be careful not to mess with her."

"Hank. Even though her body was shaking, that red laser remained steady in the center of your chest. If she had pulled the trigger, you'd have been dead as a street dog."

"I never thought I was in danger. Sure, her eyes were full of fury and seeing the wrong end of a gun is nerve-racking, but she wasn't ever going to pull the trigger."

José shook his head. "You're right. She never dropped her finger onto the trigger of the pistol. She is a steady aim, but you were never in danger."

Even though Hank had been confident she would not shoot him, Bella wasn't the only one with a gun around here. The image of Hans submerged, just beneath the water's surface haunted him. A man like that would never hesitate to pull a trigger. He also hated that Hans was currently in the same room as Bella. There was nothing he could do about it, so he breathed in the amazing view of the expansive ocean and allowed the epic vantage point to distract his thoughts.

José seemed to need distraction as well and let Hank know he had the utmost admiration for Olin Ou. He fully understood the duplicity that was now required to keep the *GalaxSea* and her crew safe. He held up his index finger as if pointing to the sky and said, "The first reason Olin can trust us. We are civilians in our own struggle to find freedom on the high seas. He held up another finger, making a peace sign. "The other reason is that I need Ava to fulfill my mission." His head tilted to the side and his eyes stared directly into Hank's as he asked, "Did you know I'm on a mission from God?"

Hank was at a loss for words. His first thought was, *good for you, but anyone who puts their life's work in the hands of a mythical figure is crazy.* However, he was trying hard at thinking through his words before they came out of his mouth and settled on a more tactful alternative. "No, I didn't."

José became serious and said, "My wife thinks I'm crazy, but I hope to show the world aquafarming is fluid. Mobility is key. Climate change is not a problem if we are willing and able to adapt to the challenges. Water makes up seventy percent of the surface of the earth. And if some of us will live and work on the water, all of humanity will be able to adapt to any changes. The fact we are standing here is proof our ancestors figured out how to cope with the threats of the ages. They learned not only how to survive but thrive. Certainly, our advancement has come with some serious problems, but the wise use of creation's raw materials, God's creativity and human ingenuity, offers great hope for the future. I believe the difference between success and failure is as old as time—wisdom. The giver of life says, *'Blessed are those who find wisdom, those who gain understanding.'*" José chuckled and said, "If that's not a mission from God, I don't know what is."

Hank said nothing and took in the comfort of a stiff breeze against his cheek and the warmth of the sun filtering through the low stratus clouds. The swell was building and waves picked up. Hank moved to the railing and grabbed hold, once again using the view to distract his thoughts. He didn't want to give any consideration to José's *giver of life* or any of God's messages or missions. Too much marveling at the beauty of his surroundings served no purpose. However, discussing the incredible stability of José's home on the sea, seemed like a nice way to change the subject. "How deep is the spar that floats your house?"

"The narrow section of the spar that contains the spiral stairway and minimizes the influence of waves, goes down ten meters. Then it flares out and continues down another ten. At that point there is a skeletal structure which supports counterweights that go way down. Since the average depth of the ocean we operate in can be measured in miles, we're free to use as much draft as we need," José said.

The depths José spoke of so casually seemed incredible to Hank. As a sailor and boatbuilder, he understood all vessels were a compromise and while its significant righting arm offered stability and comfort, it also would make it painfully slow. Now he understood why it took so long for the floating residence to meet up with the station. José had shown him the underwater view of the four propellers and explained they were driven by hydraulic motors. He even made a point of explaining the hydraulic fluid wasn't just any fluid, but environmentally friendly, seaweed oil.

"What's the top speed of this house of yours?" Hank asked.

José exclaimed, "When Ava told us not to panic and took over, she attached two sea tractors and took the props to full speed. We were making almost two knots. I've gotten used to traveling at the speed of the current, but depending on direction, the wind can add or subtract a half a knot.

"Hank, you're a sailor. What do you think about a kite? I've seen some interesting concepts attached to boats. They seem to move right along."

"That's so funny you mention that. I was thinking the same thing. It wouldn't be difficult to do. Ideally, you'd attach it close to the waterline." Hank considered the idea. "I'm guessing you could pump out all your water ballast and still not tip over, right?"

"Yes, that's part of the safety inherent in the design," José said.

"How much farther out of the water would you be able to get if you lightened the load like that?"

"Oh, I can expose the propellers for maintenance, so probably seven or eight meters," José said.

"That's good. Less wetted surface means less drag. I've never kite-sailed a house before, but why not?"

José patted him on the shoulder and said, "Next time you visit, we'll go sailing together. But now, we better go save Bella from Hans."

"What do you mean by *save*?"

"Excuse me. In this day of excessive drama—*save*—is a poor choice of words. It's just...Bella is very polite and she likes people. Hans is harmless, but is naturally inquisitive."

"Are you worried she'll give something away?" Hank asked.

"While you were puking your guts out in the washroom. I told her the measures Ava had in place to protect all of you. Recently, she's been through a lot and has a new appreciation for secrecy. She'll be very careful what she says to him."

"He looks pretty interested in her."

"Don't worry, she's been attracting young men for years and half the time she doesn't even have a clue they're interested. For instance, you. She probably does not know that you are taken with her."

Hank blushed and was not sure where to take the conversation so said nothing.

"Hank, I like you. You're a practical seafaring man. There are too few of us in the world. Also, you have great friends, but you're leaving tomorrow and sailing out of our life. You need to move on. This is not the place or the time to be interested in my daughter. She is not ready for a relationship and you are not the right man for her. Her faith is the most important thing in her life and you have none. You need to sail on, grow up, figure things out and in time—if God moves you—well then, who knows?"

He didn't expect José's pronouncement and was not sure he wanted to dissect it. At least not now, so he moved on in his thoughts and said, "I've been trying to keep everything low key. Was it that obvious?"

"To me—yes. I'm not sure she is in a space where she can see much of anything," José said as he started down the ladder.

"Are you going to have this conversation with Hans?" Hank said, immediately wishing he had stayed quiet.

A knowing smile fell across José's face. "No. She'd never fall for Hans." Then he frowned. "But you? Maybe."

"I've seen that man before," Hank blurted out.

"What man?" José asked.

He returned the fork full of *gallo pinto* back to his plate and said, "In the picture with Bella," pointing to the photo frame in the living room. When he saw all eyes were on the picture of a long-haired Bella with a tall, good looking Japanese man, he said, "We met in Vancouver, at the Phantom of the Opera."

"Dad, why do you still have that picture up?" Bella said incredulously.

"I never like it when pictures cycle through a photo frame too fast. I have it set for one a day. It's probably been a few months since I saw that one last," José said, as he took his phone out to delete the photo. "It is a stunning picture of you, however," José said.

Bella got up from her seat and grabbed a couple plates as she headed for the kitchen sink. "No Hank, you don't know him. He wouldn't be caught dead at the opera."

"I'm sure it's him."

"You're American. You probably think all Asians look alike," Hans said as he took a bite of the colorful beans and rice.

"His name is Gregory—Gregory Hatori," Hank said.

Bella inhaled sharply and all eyes turned towards her. José went to her side and put a consoling arm around her.

"I'm sorry. I didn't know." Hank realized he should have kept his mouth shut. First, because an outsider was in their midst. The less

Hank said about anything—the better. And with Bella chastising her father, it should have been a clue to stay off thin ice. Gregory was obviously an old boyfriend or someone who had been close. As if that wasn't sufficient reason for discernment, Hank recalled Gregory's date that night. She was a teenage girl dressed for a night on the town. Even though Gregory was not over thirty, she was far too young. Bella would not have known about a liaison like that, or if she had, it would be the reason Gregory was no longer in her life.

"You two should leave now. Bella and I will clean up," José's recommendation clearly had only one answer.

"Nice going, champ," Hans said as he took one last bite and headed for the exit.

"I'm sorry," Hank said again and followed the big man down the stairs. It wasn't the first time he thought to himself, *loose lips, sink ships.*

As he walked down the spiral staircase, he wondered why a girl like Bella would have been with a sleazy guy like that. His job that night, at the theater, was to decide if the Japanese businessman was any threat to the Ou party during Irina's eighteenth birthday. The only reason they sent him and Willy to check out Gregory, was because Interpol and the US had flagged him as a Person of Interest. That night, it all seemed straightforward, but this morning was beyond explanation.

The phrase, *it's a small world*, was simple. A non-explanation for a coincidence that defied the odds—a chance meeting—a hurdle across a logical degree of separation between people. Hank had sailed around the world twice. The world was far from small, but now Bella was at its center and this coincidence confirmed it.

Bella

CHAPTER 35

Irina stared at the tiny image of Bella on her watch. "I'm sorry. Ava says my dad and I can't leave the *GalaxSea* until the security team is gone. She won't even let us look out the windows. I feel like my parents have grounded me, but at least we can video chat."

"That's the only reason I agreed to let Hans teach me how to use my new heavy bag. He insisted he instruct me. I decided it would be best to get it over with so they wouldn't have an excuse to stay longer. Fortunately, Hans' team is almost done with their work. Did you hear the machine guns?"

"Ava warned us, but I still got down on the floor. Training, I guess. My upbringing came with certain responses built in—get to the bullet-proof car and hit the floor." She rolled her eyes. "And you thought your childhood was unusual?"

"We all have our cross to bear," Bella said. "I only have a few minutes to talk before I meet Hans in the gym. Did Hank say anything when he came aboard? He dropped a bombshell before he left here."

"No. But he and Willy are talking in Hank's stateroom. It's a boat so I can hear voices, but not what they're saying. Do you want me to get closer and spy on them?" Irina said in an excited voice.

"That would be weird, but thanks for offering. Can you tell me why Hank would have met Gregory? Something about an opera?"

"What! Hank knows your ex?"

"That's his story. He said he met Gregory in Vancouver."

"Wow, that seems so long ago. It was my birthday party, at the Queen Elizabeth Theatre in Vancouver. My favorite Broadway show—Phantom of the Opera. But I don't understand. What's going on?" Irina asked.

"That's what I'm asking you. Why would Hank have met Gregory there?"

"It was a big event, with all my friends. There was some intense security that night. Julie, Willy's ex-wife, was there with her team. Lots of extra faces—prevention and all. Come to think of it, Hank rode shotgun in my transportation to the Queen Elizabeth Theatre. I guess Willy recruited Hank for some extra man-power. You should have seen him in his kilt—never mind. But I don't have any idea about Gregory. I thought he lived in Singapore. What would he be doing in Canada?"

Bella's shoulders dropped. "I don't want to know. Can you think of anything else?"

"Not really but let me ask my nanny."

"You've got a nanny?" Bella asked.

"That would be Ava." Irina took her eyes off her watch. "Ava, are you listening?"

Ava's voice sounded like she was on the call.

"Of course, I'm listening. That's the job of a nanny," Ava said, stressing the title of nanny with sufficient scorn.

"Well, can you shed some light on why Hank would have met Gregory?"

"I'm not programmed to answer that question."

Irina peered into the camera again, "It was worth a try. But trust me, she will reveal nothing. However, her lack of candor shows there is something nefarious going on. She's programmed to protect me from knowing things that might trouble me. Which I find troubling."

"Well, thanks for trying. I sent a message to Janice. When I'm finished working out with Hans, I'll call her and see what she makes of it."

"Now I have a question for you. Why were you with Hank? You were going to exercise and read to stay away from him. When I left you, he was busy welding something. What happened?" Irina asked.

Bella hesitated before she answered, "We didn't know the security team was coming, or about the drill they were conducting. Let's just say we both over-reacted."

"Well, okay...that's a little more than I got out of Hank, but are you really going to leave it at that? I'm dying to know what's up." Irina said.

"You are insistent. I might have broken his finger and I almost shot him, but he started it by tackling me."

"Oh my God! You're kidding me!"

"Irina. How long have we been best friends?"

"Gosh...it seems like forever! Okay, I get your point. Drama seems to be your shadow these days." Irina's smile appeared strained. "Do you mind if I light a candle for you and say a prayer?"

"It can't hurt. Just don't ask Mother Mary to send a man to tame me. That's what my last Catholic friend did and I'm not sure I like that path."

"You got it," Irina promised.

"I've got to run," Bella said.

"Are you sure you're up for more combat training?"

"I'm committed to training every day."

"Yeah, that's obvious. But you said you were off men. How does working out with this Hans-guy fit in with your strategy? Are you sure it's a good idea?" Irina asked.

I've spent a little time with him now. We met during one of my last visits and he has always seemed respectful. I know he's interested in me, but I've done nothing to encourage him and he seems to be fine with that. Besides, Ferdinand and my dad will be working close by. "I've asked them to interrupt us after half an hour. Hopefully, the team will leave soon after, then you and I can be together again."

"Hurry and finish your workout. When they leave, I'll make you a protein smoothie and you can tell me what happened with Hank this morning. I expect details."

"Deal. Bye," Bella said and ended the call.

"Jab, jab and hook. Exhale with each punch and stay relaxed. Remember, you're only working at fifty percent. Keep your guard up. You're getting sloppy. Turn your hip in when you extend your punch. It brings power to the contact. Ten more seconds. Jab, jab and hook. And that's it! Good job. You're done with your first lesson. That's just four minutes of fighting. It's an intense, amped up workout, isn't it?" Hans asked.

"I never imagined this would be so hard." She couldn't help herself from smiling. Even with the warmup she had only been at it a short time and was drenched in sweat. Her outfit might have worked if they had been in an air-conditioned gym, but even though she was acclimated to the tropics, the exertion made her want to peel away a layer of clothes. Hans wasn't fairing much better, but he was only instructing and had stripped down to shorts and a tank-top. With

Hans in the room, she would die before she reduced her outfit to anything more revealing than boxing shorts and a loose top with short sleeves. Kumar laid on the cool tile floor of the gym's entry and barely bothered to give her a look as she took a swig from her water bottle.

"That's the basic skill for the heavy bag. Use it to warm up or increase the intensity for a total workout. Add punches and change up the combinations, you'll be perfecting it your whole life. Easy to start, difficult to master. Now what can I help you with?" Hans asked.

"That was hard. I've only got a little left in me. My sensei says I should take advantage of your training, though. She has a list of ways I should build up deficiencies until they are strengths. One of them is defending against a knife attack. Can you show me some basics?" Bella never imagined she would need a skill like that. Even Gina had assured her that her best defense was to run. But she also urged her to prepare for alternate strategies, by saying, "When you can't run, you need to fight back."

It didn't take long for her to get her wind back and slow her heart rate. The suggestion around knife defense was as much to avoid physical contact, as it was to remedy her weaknesses in that department. He obviously liked her and letting her fire a couple hundred rounds at a floating target from the machine gun pod was like a first date for a guy like Hans. That was months ago when he asked for her phone number. She had avoided the issue, with her stock answer: *I'm in a relationship and he is very jealous.* It worked every time—for years. Her *relationship* was with her God—a jealous God. It always amazed her how easy it was to shut down a conversation with that line. But now, Hans might want to help her in breaking off holds or something that would take it to a level of physical closeness that she would not allow. The heavy bag was great—he got to show off. Now she decided knife defense was the perfect exercise to keep the big man's hands off her. She smiled, thinking, *Gina is correct, there is always a way to avoid contact.*

"Since we don't have a practice knife, we'll use mine." He reached down into his gear and pulled out a large knife. "We'll keep the sheath on and nobody will get hurt. He leaned towards her with his left hand against her shoulder. "People hold a knife in their dominant hand, since most people are right-handed, this is how it goes down. The left usually grabs the defender's shoulder, or back of the neck. That way they pull the victim down and into the knife as they stab up into the torso. The attacker will want to keep stabbing. Your job is to make a wall with your left arm, block like your life depends on it. Just keep from getting stabbed. With your right hand, poke your fingers into his eyes, break contact and run like hell."

"That sounds exactly like the advice Gina would give me."

"This stuff isn't complicated. Survive—break contact—run," Hans said.

"Got it."

He handed the knife to Bella, told her to be the attacker.

She did it in slow motion like he had and she listened carefully as he showed the motions.

"To block, you need to lock the shoulder, elbow and wrist. One solid wall of defense. Don't wait, go right in with your other hand, all five fingers right into his eyes. Hard, fast and deliberate. Keep pushing, past the attacker and run away from the blade hand." Hans dramatized running away with his hands pumping high into the air like a cartoon.

"Now fast." Hans insisted.

She repeated the attack, only this time his speed surprised her. All she saw was a blur of action in which she had no control, ending with Hans in possession of the knife—and it was at her throat. Helpless to do anything with both her arms pinned down by one of his massive ape arms, she lashed out kicking her feet, but they barely touched the floor. Her heart pounded savagely and she shuddered as she could feel his hot breath against her ear.

For the second time today, a man had grabbed her from behind, but this time she was powerless to do anything about it. "I'm done! Let me go," she called out in a serious voice. But there was no release in his grip. It was as if he relished the power he had over her and didn't want to lose it. The muscles of his arm finally relaxed and she could feel his grip ease. But she still was helpless. "Hans! Let go of me. Now!"

And he did. As Bella landed on the floor, she saw the reason why—Kumar had his teeth sunk into Hans' arm and wasn't about to let go. Howling, Kumar fell onto his back and skittered to his feet, snarling viciously at Hans.

"Your damn dog bit the shit out of me," Hans said as he covered the bitten flesh with his hand.

The knife lay on the floor and Hans stood holding his forearm as blood dripped through his fingers. Kumar was foaming at the mouth, snarling like a rabid animal determined to protect his human. But then he collapsed onto the floor with only a wary eye and a low growl—there was no more fight in him. Bella saw a growing puddle of blood off to one side of Kumar's body.

She looked back at the knife on the floor, the black blade was unsheathed. She looked at Hans through fresh eyes and yelled, "Get out of here! Get out and never come back!"

José rushed in through the door towards Bella and commanded Hans, "You heard her. Go. Now."

Hans hesitated. "The damn dog bit me and got what was coming to it."

Bella picked up the knife, pointed it at Hans, "Get out!"

She grabbed a towel, rolled it tight and pressed it hard into Kumar's wound. "It's okay, boy." Bella nuzzled her face into his neck to calm him. The devil-dog growl turned into what sounded more like a low vibration coming from somewhere deep within him. She looked under the towel and saw the clean, straight cut with blood oozing out where the incision ran into his belly. "Dad, we've got a medic on board. Radio Hank and tell him to be ready. I'm on my way."

Gregory

CHAPTER 36

"SHE HAS A DOG?" Gregory looked skeptical.

"When I left, it was bleeding badly—so probably not."

"Well, let's hope it's dead. No mangy cur is getting aboard the *Fighting Gull*."

"It bit the shit out of my arm," Hans said.

"You should be more careful next time. Besides, you had no reason to lay a hand on Bella."

"She wanted to train in self-defense. I was helping her," Hans explained.

"Why would she need to defend herself? After tomorrow, I'll watch over her, forever." Gregory kept the audio channel open but turned off the video feed. Hans irritated him. If he would simply do his job for the next twenty-four hours, his contract would end. Then he could write a nice letter of recommendation and conclude business. But for now, he had to make the best out of the relationship. "I'm pleased you came to me with information about the sailor, Hank, who claims to have met me. The name means nothing. By any chance did you get a picture?"

"I'm sending the image now."

For all of Hans' shortcomings, he got things right often enough to be useful. Gregory brought up the photos, looked them over and concluded, "I still have no memory of this man. You said Vancouver? What else did he say?"

"He knew your full name," Hans said.

"What name would that be?"

"Gregory Hatori and he said he met you at the opera."

Gregory's eyes went wide with understanding. "Yes. The sidekick of a large, powerful man wearing a suit that didn't fit. He was the lanky one, wearing a kilt. They said they were from the Q.E. Theatre. I doubted it and wondered if they were law enforcement, but that made little sense either. You say he's a delivery captain?"

"Seems like it. José gave him a tour of the aquafarm when I was doing my inspections. They sailed in last night to rest and make minor repairs after the hurricane. They're planning to leave at sunrise tomorrow."

"And Bella?"

"What about Bella?" Hans asked.

"Did she appear interested in Hank-the-sailor?"

"Definitely not. They never even looked at each other the entire time I was there. The only thing she said to him was a challenge. She told him you'd never go to an opera."

Gregory smiled, "You didn't get a last name?"

"José introduced us, but only by first names."

"How about the other two crewmen? Did you meet them? Any pictures?"

"No. They never left the sailboat. We had no time to snoop around. Our extra-curricular activities took precedence. We completed everything we set out to do. But when I overstayed my welcome, we packed up and left the way we came."

"So, your submarine works well?"

"It's not a submarine. It's an underwater delivery vehicle. Like what the US seal teams use."

"Have I given you the slightest sign I care about the difference?" Gregory said.

"I wouldn't know, you turned off the video feed."

Gregory pulled a black leather jacket over a white t-shirt. Checked himself in the outgoing video frame and turned the feed back on. He produced a closed-mouth smile that pressed any color out of his lips. "Did you get the charges planted?"

"I hand-picked my team. They are skilled at what they do. Each of the security pods have timed charges and I took care of the .50 caliber above Bella's old bedroom myself."

Gregory realized only Hans could put guns and Bella's bedroom, into the same sentence. He was not sure if the man was trying to provoke him, but let it go. A deep breath helped calm him. "How about the cameras? They must be out of commission when I'm there. I've come too far to risk a second-rate security firm figuring out who I am."

"It's all taken care of. I placed a charge at the CCTV router. Tomorrow, all their tech is going up in smoke at zero nine hundred hours. I'd love to see the looks on their faces, but we'll be underwater."

"Yes and your surface vessel will escort us in for my grand entrance." Gregory took on a thoughtful expression. "Hans, I just realized. My captain will be the officiant at my wedding, but I must have a best man. It will be your last formal act before I pay you and set you on your way."

Hans brushed his hand over the top of his short, cropped hair and smiled. "Of course. But I won't have time to throw you a bachelor party."

"I already had one. You would have enjoyed it more than me. And, Hans, one more thing."

"What's that?"

"If her dog is still alive, kill it before I get there. I despise dogs."

ACKNOWLEDGMENTS

"Gratitude makes sense of our past, brings peace for today, and creates a vision for tomorrow." - Melody Beattie

My gratitude extends to those who have made Managed Paranoia - Book Two possible. The level of excellence I am surrounded with is outstanding. I wish to acknowledge Elizabeth Beach, Jim Bartlett, Kelli & Marc Grotle, Jim Karstetter, Staria Beebe, Sandra Mobley, Justin Remaklus, Michelle Wilson, Esme and Finlay (grandkids who love to illustrate and write), Anlee Fekkes, Carly Jackson and The Seasteading Institute, Bob Schroepfer, Archer (K9 support), Mises Institute, Dr. Norman Horn and The Libertarian Christian Institute, Susan Lovold, Emaleigh Pierce, Carol and Zach Pope, and to quote Bella (Chapter 1)—"Oh! Thank you, Jesus!"

finlaybeach.com

Greetings,

If you've read this far, we've shared more than a story—we've shared a journey. The Managed Paranoia trilogy was built on faith, personal liberty, and the conviction that truth still matters in a world that often forgets. Thank you for walking (and sailing) with me to the end.

If this story stirred something in you, I'd be grateful if you'd leave a quick review. Your voice helps other freedom-minded readers find their way to this series. Review wherever you picked up the book—and if you're on *Goodreads*, please add your impact there!

Though the trilogy is complete, the work goes on. If you'd like to stay informed on what's next—whether it's seasteads, homeschool punk, or stories rooted in the tension between faith and tyranny—visit **FinlayBeach.com.** When you join my list, you'll not only receive a lens into the near-future, but surprises and special bonuses.

Accept Miracles...

Fin

Continue the Adventure
also by Finlay Beach